BLOOD MOON

THE HYBRID WOLF SERIES: BOOK TWO

CIARA DELAHUNT

DUBHLUNA
PUBLISHING

CHARACTERS

Eve O'Connor *(hybrid)*

CRESCENT PACK*
Luke Whelan – *surname pronounced 'wee-lan'*
Tom Whelan
Max Whelan (*human*)
Helena Whelan (*human*)
Alice Whelan (*hybrid*)
Darren
Paula
Dylan
Joshua
Liz
Sorcha
Maggie
Áine

FAOLCHÚNNA PACK*
Ryan McKenna – *surname pronounced 'mac-ken-ah'*
Damien McKenna – *pronounced 'day-me-en'*
Rebecca McKenna
~~Nick McKenna~~
Mary McKenna
Fiona – *pronounced 'fee-own-a'*
Nadine

** Werewolves unless otherwise indicated.*

OTHER

~~Kate~~

Craig

Treasa - *pronounced 'trah-suh'*

Agnes

Alison (*witch*)

Gabriella (*witch*)

Béibhinn (*witch*) - *pronounced* 'bae-vee-n'

Cadhla (*witch*) - *pronounced* 'kai-luh'

Lars (*vampire*)

Jonas (*vampire*)

Darius (*vampire*)

Alec (*vampire*)

Larissa (*witch*) – *pronounced 'la-ris-ah'*

Spencer (*hybrid*)

Harold (*vampire*)

BEFORE YOU READ

I write paranormal romance and as such, my books are aimed at adults. *The Hybrid Wolf Series* includes themes of an adult nature, and violent scenes typical of the paranormal romance and fantasy genres. This book contains certain subjects that some readers may be sensitive to.

Please stay safe and visit my website to check the content warnings for my books before reading:

www.ciaradelahunt.com/content-warnings

IRISH LESSON

Class is in session. By the end of this series, you're going to be fluent in Irish slang.

***Mam* is not a typo!** We don't say mom over here.

I know our names have too many vowels, but revert to this when you get stuck and enjoy the ride.

- **Boreen:** a narrow lane in the countryside
- **Cert:** certificate
- **Chips:** fries (we call chips 'crisps' here)
- **College/university:** interchangeable
- **Craic:** fun/entertaining
- **Faolchúnna:** wolves
- **Flash drive:** USB stick
- **"For fuck's sake!":** exclamation of frustration, similar to 'What the hell?'
- **Fresher:** student in their first year at college in Ireland *(approx. 18 years old)*
- **Garda:** police officer *(Bán Garda is a female police officer)*
- **Gardaí:** police plural
- **Garda station:** police station
- **In the nip:** in the nude
- **Keeping sketch:** view the area for approaching authority
- **Lie in:** to stay in bed later than usual in the morning
- **Lift:** elevator
- **Lose the plot:** lost their mind, to no longer be able to act normally or understand what is happening

- **Luas:** name of the tram service in Dublin
- **Mam:** mom/mother *(the Irish don't use mom)*
- **Path/footpath:** sidewalk
- **Piss:** to pee
- **Puke:** vomit
- **Punter:** your average paying customer
- **Runners:** trainers (shoes)
- **Snug:** a small room or area in a pub where only a few people can sit
- **Strop:** a bad mood
- **Tracksuit bottoms:** joggers
- **Twig:** to suddenly realise something
- **Wing mirror:** side-view mirror on a car
- **"You're taking the piss":** you're pushing it or you better be joking

It's highly possible I've missed something here. If you're ever confused, check my reader groups, or drop me a message on social media!

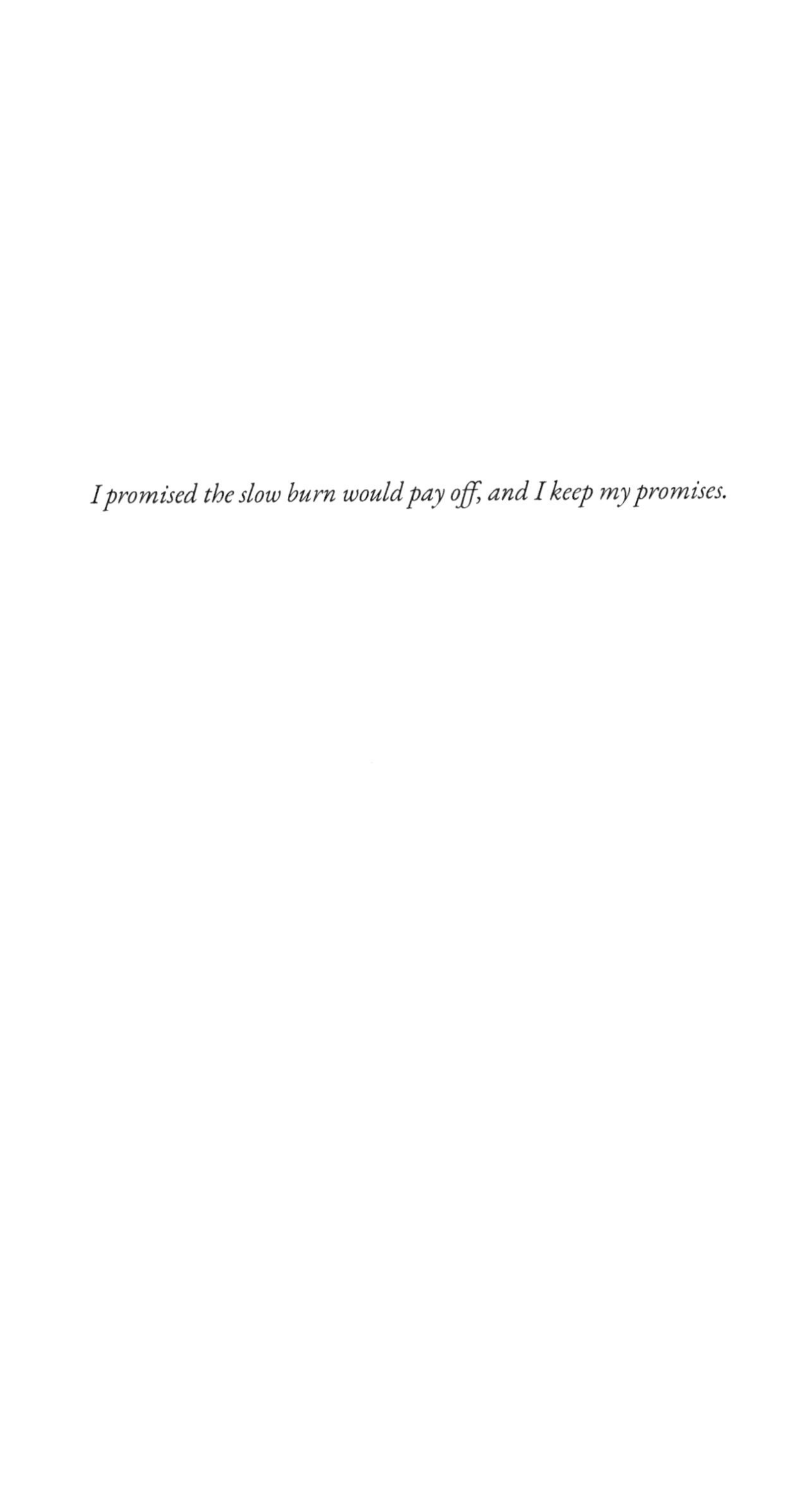

I promised the slow burn would pay off, and I keep my promises.

PROLOGUE

MARY

She'd never wished someone dead before, but with every rise and fall of his chest, she willed him to cease.

Damien's death would save them a world of pain. The alpha was beyond saving, born with an insatiable thirst for power and a penchant for violence. What began as an outcast with sick ideals and a vendetta had morphed into a powerful alpha with dangerous connections and a deep-rooted hatred of anyone who would dare stand in the way of him gaining power.

The loss of his father at a young age, coupled with his inability to connect with others, made him the perfect candidate for his mentor to lead astray. His first born dying at the hands of a hybrid werewolf was the alpha's breaking point.

Damien was never going to do good in the world. It took very little misguidance to mould him into the villain he was destined to be. The pack landing in his claws after Mary's father's passing was the beginning of the end. His rise to becoming alpha was steeped in her brother's blood, in lies, and betrayal. The Faolchúnna pack once stood for loyalty and strength. Now, one of the oldest packs in Europe was a shell of its former glory. All thanks to him.

Mary's fingers tightened around the handle of the blade pressed to the alpha's chest, the tip hovering over the spot his cold heart beat in spite of her.

Just one silver dagger to the heart, that's all it would take. He deserved it. She should have ended this years ago. It was a mistake to let Damien grow in strength. She remembered it clear as day. Something switched in his brain as he went from an angry young man out of his depth to a calculated monster.

All because she thought the pack could be saved.

Mary tightened her slick grip on the hilt of the dagger and exhaled a shuddering breath.

The intricate carvings in the bone-made handle dug into her skin, the small bite of pain centring her spiralling thoughts.

"You deserve this," she hissed, pure hatred lacing each word. "I never believed anyone was born evil until you came along. Everything you touch withers and dies. You're a poison to this world."

A lump formed in her throat as she pulled her arm back, ready to plunge the dagger into the depths of his heart, when the sound of footsteps pricked her enhanced hearing. She paused and cursed under her breath, quickly stuffing the dagger into the sheath, then the pocket of her apron as the footsteps grew louder.

When the door swung open, she was refilling the empty glass of water beside the alpha's bedside. Her hand didn't shake as she sat the water jug down, turning just in time to see Ryan rounding the corner, schooling her expression.

Ryan nodded in acknowledgement, his dishevelled ebony curls bobbing with the movement. His gaunt cheeks were only highlighted by the shadows of the dim room. The walls were a deep blue, almost black, with dull curtains to match. Panelled with gaudy gold finishes and antique furniture that were in pristine condition and appeared almost untouched.

"Is he awake?" Ryan eyed his father's sleeping form, fidgeting as he lingered by the door.

Nadine strode in behind him, her stilettos clanking on the

wooden floors with each step. She flung the curtains open. Despite the late autumn sunlight highlighting spores dancing in the air, Ryan's complexion stayed that of a ghost's. He looked worse off than his father.

A deep growl rumbled from the alpha's chest, and his eyes snapped open like a corpse waking on command. "Of course I am awake."

He attempted to sit up, grunting in discomfort and throwing out an arm to grab Nadine. A simple command for help which she all too graciously obeyed, an unnaturally wide smile fixed on her face as she fluffed his pillows.

"There." She handed the glass of water to the alpha, practically feeding it to him. The moment her gaze cut to Ryan, all pretences dropped, and she dipped her chin sharply, a silent order for him to step further into the room. An order for him to join her side, like a dog.

Mary drifted towards the door, unnoticed. It was as if she was a ghost, the last remaining family member of the bloodline which should have led the Faolchúnna pack.

No one paid her any heed as she shut the door behind her. People always underestimated her.

Although it was soundproofed by human standards, there was a gap in the wall panels that had never been filled. She grew up in the manor, after all. Mary moved down the corridor, leaning against the gaudy wallpaper with its gold floral design, and pressed her ear to the small hole.

There was a truth to the saying that behind every great man, there was a great woman, but the opposite also rings true.

Once the alpha was positioned half upright and he had slicked his tousled black hair back, back to his textbook emo-villain aesthetic, he turned his attention to his son and crooked his finger.

Ryan moved to his father's bedside, shooting Nadine a cold look as she huffed and stepped back at the silent dismissal.

The alpha lifted the glass to his lips again, taking a wearisome sip before clearing his throat. "Where is she?"

No hello, no checking in. Straight to the point. The alpha only had one question for his unloved son.

"Alice?" Ryan blanched, his left hand wrapping around his right and squeezing.

"No, you idiot child," the alpha scoffed, disgust etched into every inch of his face. "Alice was just another hybrid. Eve, the mutt you were playing with so much you lost track of your task."

"I wasn't—"

"She's with the Crescents now, sir. Where that kind of scum belongs." Nadine cut in, earning an eye roll from Mary.

The alpha's gaze cut to the redhead, anger blazing in his eyes. "That is not where she belongs. She was our leverage."

Nadine's brow furrowed in confusion, and she looked to Ryan for reassurance, but his expression mirrored hers.

"What do you mean, father?"

"She was our ticket out of that God's damned deal with Larissa." Spittle flew from his lips as the alpha snarled.

Ryan snatched his hand back and slammed the glass down on the bedside locker. "What do you mean?"

"You think I chose to risk taking another Irish hybrid after the heat we got for that Crescent pup?" The alpha sneered, somehow seeming to tower over his son even when propped up on cushions in the bed, beaten and bruised. "She wanted revenge against Tom. The rest are for the experiments, they are nobodies. But Eve—Eve is the key to keeping Larissa in line. That witch may be a royal outcast, but she is powerful."

"I don't understand, father—"

Nadine's upper lip curled. "She's not the only hybrid. We can get another one."

"She is the only hybrid that matters," Damien hissed and reared forwards, making her blanch. Dismissing her, his eyes narrowed on his son. "As always, you continue to disappoint me. Eve is not necessary for our plans and experiments, but she was the perfect leverage. Without her to even the playing field, our business arrangement with the witch is in jeopardy. That girl was the key to keeping the power in our hands."

"I'll get her back. She's just confused." Ryan wrung his hands.

The alpha grunted in disbelief. "She hates you. All you had to do was keep her under your thumb until she came here of her own volition. Then we had a nice little cover story to avoid raising suspicion. But you let feelings get in your way, pining over the mutt like she was your mate. You're a disgrace to our bloodline."

Mary swallowed the bile rising in her throat at the alpha's abuse. Unlike his father, Ryan was a sweet kid who had the potential to be a good man. But he was desperate to please a father who would never love him. Perhaps, if his brother hadn't passed away, Ryan would have been spared.

"Larissa has grown impatient. She still thinks I believe our goals are aligned, but we know the truth." The alpha narrowed his eyes at Nadine needling into his son's side. "The deal we had to strengthen the Faolchúnna pack and purify werewolf bloodlines has worked in our favour, yet the witch is growing frustrated that we have made no headway in her endeavour for power. I know the key, and it's our way out. She has served her uses, and I do not wish to be tangled up in her vendettas."

Ryan nodded, earning a cutting glare from Nadine who had her arms folded, her taloned hands curled into fists as she failed to follow their coded conversation. "I will get her back."

"Keep Eve under the radar. Do not draw attention to her." The alpha hissed in disdain as he shifted his weight to get more comfortable. "Play the game. I would gladly have you drag her back here by the hair as she bled out, but this drama with the Crescents is going to ruin everything, and we need her alive. If you can get her back here, do so without starting something you can't finish."

Ryan's lips thinned at that, but the alpha wasn't done twisting the knife.

"Your brother wouldn't have fucked this up." Spittle flew from Damien's lips as he sneered. "Keep her guarded until the time is right. I don't want our hand forced. We can extricate ourselves from this deal before a woman's temper lands us in too much trouble. And if we do it right, all wolves will bow to the Faolchúnna pack."

CHAPTER 1

LUKE

"I'm not the only hybrid they've taken."

My heartbeat throbbed in my ears, drowning out the silence as my brain stuttered at Alice's revelation. I opened my mouth to deny it, but my brain was short circuiting. Her words played on repeat in my head as I stared at my little sister, my body rigid with tension.

Shock settled over those of us gathered in the kitchen like a visible weight. Beside me, Eve covered her mouth and retreated as if she could run from the truth. Not a single word was uttered as we stared at the small girl standing before us, skin and bones, and gaunt with the stress she had endured while held captive.

Alice was alive. She was home. She was safe.

The nightmare was supposed to be over.

My sister sucked in a long breath before sagging back onto a kitchen chair, the fire that had been burning in her eyes snuffed out. She sat with her head bowed, twisting her hands in her lap until her haunted gaze lifted to meet mine.

Acid burned in my stomach at the thought of more wolves going through this. How many more had I let down? Various possibilities played out in my mind. Every time I came back to the same conclusion, that if I'd followed her that night, I could have stopped all of this.

Stunned silence stretched for what seemed like forever before something intangible cracked, and the pack descended into chaos all at once. Of course, Liz's shrill voice was among those fighting to be heard, with no one really listening to a word one another said. A mix of discussion and arguments sprang to life, fuelled by anything from fear to outrage that had Alice shrinking back against her father.

"They're just like me and you'd leave them?"

Tom growled, his jaw set. "Fear is never an excuse to leave someone suffering."

I stepped forwards, my mouth opening and closing as I fought for words that wouldn't come.

Alice burst into a fresh fit of tears as the noise levels soared and, before Tom could stop her, she sprang to her feet, clutching the back of her chair as she swayed. I thought her legs might give way until she pushed past the throng of pack members and bolted out of the kitchen.

The kitchen door slammed in my face as I followed, hot on her heels, but I tore it open, the door handle coming clean off as the door rattled on its hinges. I raced into the hall to find the front door swinging open and Alice striding away.

"Alice! Get back here!" I sprinted down the drive as she ignored me.

Each step of mine was worth two of hers, so I caught her before she could cross the road and continue across the park area of the neighbourhood. Telltale signs of curtain-twitches suggested the neighbours were trying to eavesdrop on our family drama. Humans who lived in the estate and had no idea what we were. I wasn't going to scream about our business in the street, but Alice was pushing it. I was trying to protect her; it was my natural instinct.

I reached out to grab her, but she ducked under my arm to

evade my grip. Cursing, I tried again, but she backed up towards the house and spun to glare at me. "Leave me alone."

Something in my heart cracked at the way she looked at me, but I kept myself between the house and her escape. I was not losing her again.

"Alice, we need to talk about this." I ground my jaw as I tried, and failed, to keep my tone level. Every word seeped with anger and the promise of revenge.

She didn't grace me with a response, her hands balled into fists as she strode back inside. Eve came out of the kitchen, flanked by both Dylan and Josh, but Alice rushed past them and stomped straight up the stairs. My shirt clung to my body, heat radiating off me.

I surged forwards to follow her, but Eve snagged my arm at the base of the stairs.

"Luke." Those big blue eyes of hers pleaded with me. "She needs some space."

I whirled towards Eve, anger clouding my vision. "She can't just drop a bomb like that and run." My voice cracked on the last word, the memory of losing her years ago on torturous repeat in my head. I wasn't angry at her. I was furious *for* her. For myself and every family that had to endure the pain of losing a loved one at the hands of the Faolchúnna's sick plans.

"Alice can do whatever she wants," Eve snapped, the authority ringing in her voice catching me off guard. She levelled me with a look to rival the daggers my sister had thrown my way and shoved my chest when I shook her off. "I get that you're angry. We all are. But she's home and safe, so cut the macho alpha act and back the fuck up before you say something you'll regret."

I got one foot on the steps before Dylan grabbed me around the waist and hauled me back against his chest. I might have been next in line for alpha, but Dylan gave me a run for my money. I struggled against his grip, but he wasn't moving.

"She's scared, Luke. She needs her big brother right now, not you acting out." He spun me to the side and braced his back against the wall lining the stairs as I fought against his hold.

Within seconds, Josh had my wrists in an ironclad grip as they forced me out the front and through the side gate, refusing to stop until I had been deposited in the back garden. Despite the force Josh had to exert to keep me still, he was as gentle as could be.

The crescent moon peeked through the clouds obscuring the starry sky, casting some light on the small suburban garden. I shrugged my friends off, tearing at the tie constricting my neck and flinging it to the ground, followed by my suit jacket, and proceeded to kick the rubbish bin until the plastic had splintered, along with one fence panel. Eve muttered something to the others, but I couldn't hear her over the pounding in my ears. I caught a glimpse of Helena watching from the kitchen window, her eyebrows drawn together in concern, but I couldn't stop the rampage.

"Breathe and we can talk about this properly," Eve ordered.

"I'll fucking kill him."

"That's not calm," Dylan said, only riling me up farther.

"How exactly is someone supposed to react when they hear about all the horrible things their little sister endured then? When they find out she wasn't the only one who is suffering?" I spat, raking my hand through my hair.

I stalked around the garden, kicking up piles of gathered autumn leaves and threw anything that was not rooted to the ground.

When I made a beeline for the wooden shed stuffed in the far corner of the garden, familiar arms wrapped around me. I spun to find Josh there, herding me into the corner surrounded by sturdier walls. Dylan flanked him.

I growled, the sound rippling from my chest and ripping from my lips as I fought my brothers until they wrangled me into submission.

Josh clasped me behind the neck and brought his forehead to mine, ignoring the snarl I released at the gesture. His deep brown irises bore into mine, sweat beading his bronze forehead from the exertion of keeping me from demolishing anything in my path. "I know how much you want to set things right and protect her, but this is not the way."

Dad had taken Dylan in after his mother passed away during childbirth, just like mine. Josh's parents joined the Crescents shortly after the pack was formed, and Josh was born soon after. We grew up together; they knew every part of my shitty personality and loved me nonetheless. I couldn't bear to look at them when I was falling apart, but they also watched Alice grow up. I knew that they mirrored the anger I felt and wanted revenge too. They just weren't so hot-headed. I needed to get my shit under control.

I locked eyes with Eve over his shoulder. She looked between us with uncertainty, chewing her lower lip as she came forwards to stand beside Josh.

"Deep breaths. In and out."

Josh slowly loosened his grip as Eve fought to pull me back from the darkness, just as I had done with her the night our paths first crossed.

I shook his relaxing grip off and scowled, my fingers curling around the garden lattice lining the wall as I braced my hands against it and hung my head, the red mist receding. I was far from calm, shirt was dripping with sweat and my fingertips itched to let my claws come out to play, but the object of my fury was nowhere to be seen. Eve was right. I squeezed my eyes shut. My sister needed me. I just wasn't good enough.

A hand rubbed soothing motions on my tacky shoulder.

When I opened my eyes, Eve stood over me, the source of my comfort. I hadn't noticed the guys retreating inside.

"I'm such a fucking mess." I growled the words, staring at my reflection in the glass of the living room sliding doors.

Blood dripped from my knuckles, the result of my tantrum. My shirt was ripped in parts, and my slacks were covered in mud.

"There's no right way, but this isn't helping." She rubbed her temples with a sigh. "Your sister is freaking out upstairs. Tom is with her, but she needs you too."

"I'm freaking out." I wondered how she could be so calm when Alice's truth should have been striking a painful chord for her too. "How are you so chill about this?"

Laughter bubbled from her throat, the kind of delirious cackle that showed how much she had been hiding. Keeping me in line must have somehow helped hold her together, but that wasn't right. I should be the steady one.

"We're all freaking out," she snapped, prodding me in the ribs with a clawed finger as she squared up to me, unperturbed by the fact that her head didn't crest the height of my shoulders. "I'm terrified. Do you think I wanted this? That I want to have anything to do with Ryan anymore?"

Something about her starting to unravel helped piece a part of me back together.

Eve glowered up at me as I fished for an answer.

"No, I wanted to forget all of that and try to move on. But now I know my bat-shit crazy ex has locked up a bunch of hybrids and is planning God knows what with them." Her eyes narrowed at the smallest spark of satisfaction I showed at her acknowledging that their relationship was dead in the water. At the same time, hearing her talk about what could have been her fate had my hackles rising again. "I can't walk away from this. You're the one going all macho and losing your temper when you're supposed to be an alpha in the making. You're the one with the power to fix this. You have the control, so get a grip and start bloody acting like it."

I stared at her, my mouth opening and closing. The fire burning in her eyes reminded me of Alice.

"I'm sorry." I wrapped my fingers around her clawed one still poking holes in my shirt.

She snatched her hand away, dropping her arms to her side. "I don't want an apology. I just want this to go away."

Eve failed to hide the waiver in her voice. I stepped forwards, pausing to give her the chance to refuse, before wrapping my arms around her slender frame. I tugged her against my chest, nestling my chin on the crown of her head.

She stiffened for a moment before melting into my embrace.

I wished for all the world that I could magic her problems away, but I couldn't.

"You're right." My lips brushed her hair. "I should react better. It's been a lot, getting Alice back. I need to get my head together. The thought of other hybrids going through that... and their families, it makes me so damn angry."

She mumbled, slowly wriggling out of my suffocating grip. "I'm always right."

I rolled my eyes at the 'I told you so' quirk of her lips, wiping the dried blood on my hands into my pants before leading her over to a wrought-iron bench that only survived because it was nailed down. Helena learned a lot during our teenage years, including how to salvage furniture. The wooden shed wasn't a mistake. Werewolves could still trash steel ones, and wooden sheds were cheaper to replace. She would be grateful this one had been spared.

We sat there for a long moment, staring up at the luminescent moon.

"This is a mess." I flopped back against the bench with an exasperated growl. "A giant fucking mess."

Eve nodded, picking up a stray, red-veined leaf in her hand and twirling it between her finger and thumb. "I thought once we got Alice back that this nightmare would be over."

"Something tells me it's just the beginning."

She snorted. "Well, that's ominous."

I sat back, tapping my knees as we both stared into space, all too aware that we were living a real-life nightmare. With a sigh, I slung my arm around Eve's shoulders and pulled her into my side, tracing the goosebumps on her forearm with my fingertips. A comfortable silence fell between us. Beyond the sound of her slow breaths and my heart still thundering, if I sank into my senses, I could hear my father's gentle voice promising Alice that everything would be alright. My sister seemed to believe his words more than I did. For all our sakes, I hoped he was right.

CHAPTER 2

EVE

The coffee maker nestled on the kitchen counter buzzed, the welcome scent of coffee wrapping around me like a warm hug as it emptied a capsule into my mug. Helena bustled around behind me, rashers and sausages sizzling on the pans while she multitasked and cooked breakfast for the family and then some.

"Morning!" Dylan beamed, the pep never leaving his step as he strode in, headed straight for the cupboard to grab a mug.

The house might as well have had a revolving door.

Dylan waited, tapping his Nike sneakers to the beat of the radio. His brown hair was ruffled to perfection, always walking the line between fluffy but also frozen in place. In his textbook style of a fitted T-shirt and jeans, with the small dusting of freckles across his nose and piercing blue eyes, he was a heartthrob with a heart of gold.

"Breakfast in five." The tired lines around Helena's eyes crinkled.

I gave Dylan a nod as I spun away from the coffee machine. "All yours."

"And where's mine?" His tone was playful, and his bushy eyebrows shot up into his hairline.

Helena cut in, whipping his arse with the tea towel so hard

there was a loud crack despite Dylan's attempt to dodge. "No woman in this house is here to wait on you."

A small smile curved my lips as I chuckled and moved to sink into one of the chairs lining the kitchen table. For a small moment, that all too familiar feeling of discomfort had taken hold. The one that made my shoulders hunch and my palms clammy. The urge to disappear because I didn't fit in. The rejection my brain waited for never came. Ever since I arrived on their doorstep like a lost puppy, Helena and Tom had welcomed me with open arms.

That included Luke's friends.

They were more like brothers, actually. From what I'd gleaned, after Dylan's mam had passed away, Luke's family had practically adopted the kid as a second son. He lived a few doors down now with a few other wolves the same age, including Josh.

As if summoned by my thoughts, Josh walked into the kitchen with a sleek black laptop tucked under his arm and planted a kiss on Helena's cheek in greeting. He was still in gym shorts and a T-shirt with the image of a wolf bench-pressing on it. A sheen of sweat on his bare arms was the only hint he'd been at the gym. He probably ran back home too. I rolled my eyes. He was a jack of all trades, and I was a potato.

"Morning." I nudged the chair beside me out from under the table with my foot, just in time for Josh to plop down onto it.

"You call this morning?"

Tom was next to join us. He wrapped his wife in a warm embrace and despite the weathered lines on his face, the way they hugged and joked, the way his face lit up at the sight of her in a dirty apron flipping eggs, they were like newlyweds. It warmed some cold icy space inside of me.

"Eve!"

I spun at the sound of my name. Luke stood in the doorway with Max perched on his hip.

Max squealed, bouncing in his older brother's arms in a wordless demand to be put down.

Luke's blonde hair was dishevelled, and he had purple shadows under his eyes to rival mine. Seeing him standing there in his red-checked pyjamas bottoms with his abs on show, and his cute little brother snuggled in his arms, did something to my ovaries.

I swallowed, crashing back into reality as Luke bent to let Max down. The kid wasted no time, speeding towards me in cute dinosaur pyjamas before launching into my lap.

"Ooft," I groaned as he knocked the air from my lungs, helping him twist so that he sat facing the table using me as a human high chair. "Hello to you too."

Max smiled, his cheeks dimpling as he stuck his tongue out at me, becoming distracted by the loose tooth he had and poking his tongue through the gap on repeat to dislodge it.

"You know, I can help get it out for you." Luke chuckled darkly, his thigh brushing mine as he took the remaining free seat beside me.

Little Max's lips formed an overdramatic 'o' as he blinked up at Luke. "How? I need the tooth fairy to come to me before Carol."

"Carl?" I leaned around Max to grab a fork off the table.

He swung his head to level me with a look ten times his age. "*Car-ol* sits beside me at school. Ms. Crampton gave her more gold stars."

When I didn't react to his satisfaction, he tutted and booped my nose with his little forefinger. I met Luke's eye; his lips curved in a wide grin as he watched the exchange. I sucked my lower lip between my teeth to hide my own smile.

"The tooth fairy will bring me gold. Then I'll be first on the star board."

Helena whipped past us, clipping Max around the ears with the force of a feather. "I don't know what Ms. Crampton is teaching you, but the tooth fairy isn't that rich. You only get a few coins, like pocket money."

"Jimmy got ten yo-yos," Max whined, making grabby hands

until Dylan passed him a slice of toast, which he handed to his father to butter.

I giggled, pulling a plate from the stack. "Euros."

"Jimmy's mam needs a slap," Helena muttered under her breath, shooting her husband a wry smile as she took the seat to his left and began filling her plate.

A look passed between Dylan and Josh, who were sitting opposite us, tittering laughter slipping from their lips. Both were already digging into their plates, which were stacked high with sausages, rashers, eggs, beans, and pudding. All the makings of a good Irish fry up. Unlike the Faolchúnna pack, there was no pecking order here. I smiled to myself as conversation buzzed around the table and I found myself exactly where I'd always longed to be.

Of course, Luke had to burst that bubble.

"So," Luke's tone was serious as he avoided direct eye contact with his father and focused on pushing the remains of his breakfast around his plate with his fork, "what's the plan?"

The atmosphere soured. I swallowed, busying myself hacking an innocent sausage apart for the kid on my knee. Helena glanced up from under her lashes, her expression sobering. Dylan eyed Luke with curiosity while Josh continued to eat, one eye on the conversation.

Tom was the last to react, finishing up the last of his meal before setting the cutlery down on his plate calmly. He looked up at his son, his bright blue eyes the opposite of Luke's hazel, but there was a likeness there nonetheless. "What plan?"

"It's been a fortnight, Dad, and we've done nothing." The muscle in Luke's jaw ticked as his little tell that he was *trying* to be calm.

"I have contacted the surrounding alphas to alert them about what happened to Alice, without giving out any... unnecessary details—at least, until we know where they stand. I have yet to hear back from a few." Tom dabbed his mouth with the back of his hand.

Luke didn't miss a beat. "So, no news. No investigation?"

"Have you forgotten what happened that night?" Tom challenged, keeping his voice level for the sake of his younger son in the room. "We came very close to losing someone, and they *did* lose someone. I will not provoke them or give Damien an excuse to come after us for what happened to Nick. I'm not ignoring the issue. I need to discuss this with the other packs and understand the bigger picture before we make any move. Rash decisions are not the answer; patience and educated action must be exercised."

When Tom was joking about with Max, or just chatting to me, he came across like any normal dad. But when he addressed the pack or spoke as our alpha, was no mistaking the authority in his voice. He was calm, reassuring, and kind.

Luke was all of those things, but with some added spice.

"We need to understand Damien's motives. Alice isn't ready to talk about her time there," Tom continued, knowing better than to give Luke a chance to counter. "I'm not ignoring the issue. We won't stand for someone harming hybrids, you know that. We just need hard facts, and then we can act."

Max munched away, oblivious to the conversation going on around him, but tension rolled off Luke. I reached out, his skin hot to the touch as I gave his arm a gentle squeeze. Josh shook his head as a myriad of expressions crossed Luke's face, Dylan placing down his fork with a clang.

Luke clenched his fists and then relaxed them, his fingernails digging into the surface of the wooden table and leaving crescent-shaped indents in their wake. "So we just sit and wait?"

Tom shook his head, a rueful smile curving his lips. "Sometimes knowledge is power."

CHAPTER 3

LUKE

A shrill scream pierced the night air, jolting me awake.

It had become the norm over the past few weeks. Every night, Alice woke from hellish nightmares, drenched in sweat and shaking. We never left her to suffer alone, forming an unofficial rota and taking the nights in turns. Tonight was Dad's shift, but no matter how much I tossed and turned on the lumpy couch, sleep wouldn't come to me. The sound of my sister's anguish was the lullaby from hell.

Quickly giving up on getting anymore sleep, I grappled around between the couch cushions until my hands closed around the cool metal of my phone. The screen flared to life, the brightness forcing me to squint as I checked the time. Four in the morning, possibly one of the best records so far. I'd take it.

There was no point in trying to sleep anymore. I threw the duvet bunched around my hips off and swung my legs off the edge of the couch. My back groaned in protest. Even super-fast werewolf healing couldn't account for the damage the very pronounced dip from my dad's favourite spot on the couch was doing after weeks on my makeshift bed.

I grabbed an empty glass off the coffee table and padded across the room to the adjoining door to the kitchen and eased it open. My dad's voice drifted from upstairs, no doubt comforting my sister. I shook my head as if I could banish the worry away and set about making a cup of coffee, my body running on zombie style autopilot.

Since sleep wasn't an option, caffeine was the answer.

"Fancy seeing you here."

I jumped as I closed the fridge door, my grip denting the milk carton for the split second as Eve lingered in the doorway.

"I couldn't get back to sleep." I sighed, setting another mug down beside mine for Eve.

She nodded in understanding. Every night Alice woke up, she brought the entire house with her.

Eve's fluffy-socked footsteps were silent as she drifted over to me, standing on her tiptoes to reach for the coffee pods. She was dressed in a pair of cream fleece pyjamas I recognised as Helena's, deep circles casting shadows under her eyes. Despite her sleep deprived appearance and bed hair, a playful grin turned up the corner of her lips.

The fact that I didn't hear her coming should have bothered me, but when a wolf got used to a fellow pack member's scent and our brains deemed them 'safe' we paid less attention to their scent in home settings. If we noticed every single noise or scent every moment of the day, we would go insane.

We set about making the coffees in comfortable silence, working perfectly in sync until we both reached for the metal frothing jug at the same time. My fingers brushed against the back of her hand and electricity sparked through my veins at her touch. I hadn't felt this schoolboy shit in years. She glanced up at me from under her lashes, smiling until her eyes narrowed to unimpressed cat-eye slits.

"What?" I frowned until I followed her eye line. My hand rested at the curve of her back. "I'm fine, I promise. I must have slept on the remote."

Eve opened her mouth to argue when another scream echoed from upstairs, followed by a howl of anguish that sent chills through my bones. We shared a tortured look, and I slid my hand across her wrist. Her heartbeat thrummed more erratically as the crying upstairs escalated.

I released a weighted sigh and knocked off the coffee machine. "Come on, let's get out of here for a while."

"I'vE something to tell you and you can't get mad."

Eve's eyes were wide and filled with worry as she peered at me over the latte she nursed between her gloved hands. The late autumn wind had an icy bite. Eve was wrapped up head to toe in an oversized coat of mine that swamped her, and knitwear I'd gifted her last week when I noticed her shivering on one of our walks. Although, I regretted it because I loved giving her mine to borrow. Her scent always lingered on it for days.

"Go on." I chuckled, pausing outside the small coffee shop at one of the picnic benches to right the lid on my takeaway cup. "Spit it out."

She pranced on the spot, fiddling with the cardboard sleeve on her cup.

"You know, you've a very nice furry coat that would keep you warm if it's the cold that has you dancing like that," I teased, knowing damn well it was nerves and not the cold. There was no way she was cold with that giant jacket on.

I was going around in a T-shirt, but I always ran hot. As a hybrid, that was one perk Eve missed out on.

She scoffed at me, flipping the scarf around her neck before flouncing away. I rushed after her, a grin tugging at the corner of my lips.

Taking her to Phoenix Park was a good call. The extensive parklands were nestled on the city outskirts and stretched for kilometres. The coffee wasn't the best, but the fresh air would do us good, even if the cold had her nose turning red. I resisted the urge to crack a Rudolph joke.

Eve rushed across the main road that dissected the park, choosing to follow a well-worn path under the trees and away from the more populated areas. I followed her lead, relishing the crunch of frosted grass under my feet. As a wolf, I was naturally drawn to nature. Yes, we lived in the modern day and had acclimatised to cities, but the earth would always call us home and centre us. A sense of feeling grounded was something we both desperately needed lately.

I could tell my plan was working by the spring in Eve's step and the way her face lit up as she set off in search of some deer. I didn't have the heart to tell her that they'd run a mile from us because we smell like predators.

"So, what were you trying to tell me back there?" I fell into step beside her.

She shrugged, buying some time by taking a long chug of her latte. The way Eve cradled her drinks was endearing, though I knew she'd smack me if I pointed it out. Last time I'd mentioned it, she kicked me under the table, and I'd choked on my drink.

"Anytime today," I teased, taking a sip of my own Americano and relished the burn as it washed down my throat. "Seriously, what is it?"

Her throat bobbed as she swallowed, her cheeks flushing in the way that they did when she was nervous. Just a slight rosy tinge colouring the freckles that dusted her cheeks. It was entirely different to when she blushed.

"I spoke to your dad about it last night…"

"Spit it out. I don't bite."

Unless you want me to. But I didn't add that part because I'm not cheesy.

Eve couldn't resist the smile curving her lips, her shoulders dropping as some tension lifted.

"I'm moving out," she blurted, the words beginning to tumble from her mouth before I could react, each sentence increasing in speed. "There's just not enough space now that Alice is home. Obviously, I'm so glad she's home, but you can't stay on the couch forever. And the nightmares... You've been getting no sleep. I spoke to your dad last night and he knows this guy. A friend. A work colleague—I think? He has this place on the north side, and it's gonna be empty while he's away doing some fancy work case study thing for months, and he needed someone to rent it, but he wanted someone he trusted. So, Tom checked if it would be okay if I used it and he said yes, so now it's a thing."

It took my sluggish brain a few moments to process her word vomit.

On one hand, I felt a slight sting of rejection at her choice to move out. Maybe it was the alpha side of me, or maybe it was me being a sap. At the same time, neither of us had slept properly since Alice came home, and I didn't blame her for wanting some independence. In some ways, it was a sign that Ryan hadn't broken her independent streak. We had several pack members in the city to look out for her, but they weren't me.

I'd really miss waking up to her every morning too.

"So, you're leaving me?" My tone teased, but the moment the words left my mouth, I cringed. That didn't come across the way I wanted it to. I meant leaving us, the pack.

Her eyebrows knitted together. "No, that's not what I meant."

She had been steadily building up speed the whole time. At this point, we were power walking.

"Eve," I cut in before she could spiral, placing a hand on her shoulder to force her to brake. "I'm joking. I get it."

"I just need some sleep." She reached out to give my hand a reassuring squeeze. "The house isn't big enough for all of us, and I need to start figuring out what my life is supposed to look like now. I can't stay there forever."

She could, I knew my dad wouldn't have a problem with it. But I wanted whatever was best for her, even if there was a possessive edge to the thoughts swirling in my mind. I tamped them down, I wasn't that guy. Okay, it was in my nature, but I believed in her right to make this decision. I'd take out my frustrations in the boxing ring later.

"Please stop overthinking this. It's okay, just so long as I get to visit."

Her smile returned, her cheeks dimpling. The dimple on the right side was always more pronounced. "Of course you can. Who else is going to carry all my shit?"

"So I'm a glorified donkey?" I deadpanned, pulling my hand away to flip her the bird before regretting the loss of contact.

She snorted. "You said it, not me."

"Smartass," I growled, and her smile only widened, and I couldn't steal my gaze from her face, the sun rising behind her head like an ethereal halo.

Eve's gaze slid past me, and she bounced on the balls of her toes, pointing over my shoulder excitedly.

"Deer!"

"No, an ass is a donkey—"

"No! *Deer*," Eve repeated, grabbing me by the shoulders and spinning me around. "Over there by the trees."

Sure enough, there was a small herd of deer with dappled winter coats gathered under a small grove of leafless trees. They were munching on some hay that must have been left out by the ranchers, oblivious to our presence.

We were about thirty feet away and downwind, their ignorance wouldn't last long.

Before I could warn Eve to stay back, she was already making a beeline towards the deer. I expected them to scatter the moment her scent reached them, but besides from the buck raising his head and appeasing her with narrowed eyes, as if he couldn't make sense of her. The rest of the herd remained unfazed.

She must have smelled human to them, despite her hybrid abilities. Did they even know what hybrids were? I doubted many hybrids hunted in the Phoenix Park since it was in the middle of the city. Typical werewolves had a distinct scent of wolf about them. Even so, Eve didn't go right up to the herd. Respecting the fact that they were wild animals and the males had their antlers as it was mating season, she stopped several feet away. Some of the deer wandered towards her. One doe with soft almond eyes even walked right up and started accosting Eve for the coffee cup.

I hung back, not wanting to ruin the moment for her. Eve stood there transfixed by the deer, her excitement like a kid on Christmas morning was tangible. She threw her head back and laughed as the doe head-butted her hand. It was so good to see her truly happy, and I would do whatever it took to be the reason she was smiling like that.

CHAPTER 4

EVE

It had been less than two hours since I'd been away from the Crescent pack, and I was already struggling. Luke dropped me off at the apartment with some boxes before heading back to pick up reinforcements. The place felt so empty compared to the buzz of his house.

It's not that I wanted to leave, but no matter how many times Luke and his family swore I wasn't imposing, I couldn't shake the feeling that I was overstaying my welcome. No amount of Helena's signature fry ups or kind words from Tom could stop me from worrying about it.

The apartment was gorgeous, a cosy, one-bedroom apartment in the finance sector of the city with large windows and an unobscured view of the River Liffey. It was completely different to my old apartment with Kate. That had been a converted Georgian building that had its fair share of quirks; a fireplace in the bedroom, creaking floorboards, and windows that rattled in the wind. This one had quartz countertops and a modern bathroom. Despite lacking character, it had no traumatic memories attached. This apartment was a fresh start. I needed that.

I also needed sleep. It had been three weeks, but Alice was still waking up screaming every night. If anything, time was making it worse.

There I was, with my new place, and I couldn't last an hour alone with my thoughts. So, I ran. I still didn't trust myself to shift alone, especially in the city centre, but the blare of music in my ears and the steady thump of my Converse hitting the pavement helped quiet my spiralling thoughts, if only for a little while.

It's funny, I used to hate running and avoided physical education at school like the plague. I guess being a hybrid did have some perks.

For the first time since the night we rescued Alice, I let myself tap into the well of magic coursing through my veins. It was always there, just lying dormant until it was called—not that I trusted it. Tom swore blind the silver bracelet was enchanted to block my transitions, but I wasn't so sure. It felt like the problem was me.

The noise of car exhausts, school kids messing about on their lunch break, businessmen haggling and ranting into their cell phones while waiting in hipster café queues flooded my ears. The smell of coffee beans and croissants lingered on the autumn breeze, and even the spicy chicken fillet rolls from three streets over wafted up my nose without overwhelming me. I could separate them all and tune them out at will, not like before.

I wound through the streets of Dublin, relishing being back in the city as I found myself having gravitated towards the south of the Liffey. Despite being a few streets away from Brady's pub, I decided to revise my old haunt on another day when I felt ready. If I ever felt ready. This was my new life now, a werewolf hybrid in the paranormal world, and I wasn't quite sure how people or places from my life beforehand fitted in now, if at all.

Cutting down Dame Street, I dodged tourists hogging the footpath by dancing in and out of the cycling lane much to the cyclists' chagrin. I was flashed the middle finger more than once even though my heightened speed meant I would avoid them. For some reason, I was more likely to stub my toe off the bed than run into a moving target.

I was distracted, caught debating between my favourite café on the north side and one that had the best hot chocolates in the city, when I rounded the corner and ran headfirst into someone's chest.

"Shit!" I yanked an earphone out with a grimace. "I'm so sor—"

My apology fell off a cliff when I looked up to see a familiar set of bright blue eyes and my best friend looking down at me, a wide grin stretching his lips.

"Eve!" Craig squealed, wrapping his long arms around my tiny frame, and hugging me with such force I was yanked straight off my feet as he twirled around, knocking the air clean out of my lungs. "I've missed you so much!"

I opened my mouth, waiting for the words to come, but the cogs in my brain were whirring aimlessly as shock set in. I was torn between latching onto my closest friend like a koala or bolting across the road like a skittish cat.

He planted me back on the ground and pressed an overzealous kiss to my cheek. "How have you been?"

"I... I—I'm good." I pressed my palm flush against my chest as I stared up at him. "What are you doing here?"

He grinned from ear to ear, while I struggled to stop a tsunami of tears from erupting.

"It's the city. Girl, what are you talking about? I was heading to Moore Street to get my nan some fresh cooking apples for her famous apple crumble." Craig chuckled, the twinkle in his eyes breaking my heart ten times over as guilt crashed over me. "Apparently it doesn't taste right if they're from the shop, or so she claims anyway. You should come over for dinner, she'd love to see you."

I'd thought about ringing him so many times. Tom had insisted on replacing my old phone, but I knew it was Luke's idea. I swore I'd pay them back. Even though I'd lost all my contacts, I knew Craig's number by heart. But every time I went to call him, I couldn't bring myself to go through with it.

Craig hadn't changed a bit since the last time I'd seen him, besides the frosted tips of his spiked hair being an ice blue to match the incoming winter season. A small nod to the friend we had lost. He was still living in his band merch and baggy jeans, along with a fitting scarf covered in skulls. It was like someone had frozen time, and he looked at me as if it had only been weeks apart, not months. As if I hadn't deserted him during the darkest time in his life or gone missing when our best friend died of what he thought was an overdose. I couldn't stop the tears from coming.

"Eve? I'm sorry!" Craig closed the gap between us and reached for my arms, his brow creasing with worry. "I didn't mean to pressure you, we can skip dinner. I'm just so happy to see you."

This time I fell into his arms and broke down sobbing. He looked around awkwardly and pulled me from the middle of the street to a bench on the corner, where I could cry with more privacy. But I didn't care who was looking. All of the pain, the regrets, and the hurt just came rushing back at once. Everything I kept bottled up bubbled to the surface and overflowed. Being there with Craig, crying on his shoulder, was like old times. Except it wasn't, and that broke my heart all over again.

"It's alright, whatever it is we can sort it out." Craig cooed, gently rubbing my back as I covered his band hoodie in snot and tears.

"It's not okay." I sobbed, burying my face in his chest as he held me. "You don't understand."

"Is this about that Luke guy?" Craig asked and my head snapped up.

I never told Craig about him. He might have seen him at his birthday party, but I never introduced them. Did Luke do this? I warned him not to ever wipe their memories.

He pushed a hair behind my ear. "It is, isn't it?"

"No, nothing to do with Luke. Who told you that?" I sat up and wiped my cheeks with the ends of my scarf. "How do you know about Luke?"

"Ryan told me what happened with you guys." Craig patted my hand with a sympathetic look. "The whole cheating thing with Luke."

I blanched at the mention of Ryan's name and unease settled in the pit of my stomach. Luke had offered to sort things out, call in a favour to make people forget that I vanished, make it like I was there for Kate's funeral. But I was sick of lies, I couldn't fake that. I wasn't ready to go back to my old life, but now it was staring right at me. This definitely wasn't something Luke would have asked a vampire to do. Only Ryan would wipe their memories and replace them with the kind of narrative that framed him as a victim. Only he would go against my wishes. Psychopath.

Craig wiped my cheek with his thumb, his expression brightening. "It's okay sweetie. We've all been there, you're not a monster."

If only he knew the half of it.

My blood boiled at the thought of Ryan toying with my friends. Did he send Craig here? Was this some kind of trap? They always say you'll run into someone you know anywhere in Ireland because it's so small. It's a running joke, but this wasn't funny.

"Craig, what do you remember about the funeral?" My stomach did anxious somersaults as I cast out my senses to see if there was any sign of Ryan, but the only scents I picked up were tourists and businessmen, strangers. At that, my shoulders relaxed an inch.

He linked his fingers with mine and pulled me into his side, his mood visibly sobering. "I remember it being horrible. You were too ill to go, but Kate would have understood."

"I don't think she would." I refused to meet his eyes.

I swallowed the lump rising in my throat and squeezed his

hand, desperately wishing that could have been the truth. At least Ryan covered for me in one way, but the thought of him being anywhere near the people I cared about made my skin crawl.

"Are you sure you don't want to pop over to my Nan's? It would be nice to spend some time together."

"What do you think I'm doing?" I blurted out the words, anxiety clawing at my insides.

"You've taken a year out to find your birth parents and figure stuff out?" Craig shot me a confused look, lifting my hand to his lips. "Has something happened with them? Is that it?"

I gritted my teeth and resisted the urge to cry and scream. *How fucking dare he use that!*

"Maybe I should give Ryan a call and ask him to check in on you?"

"No," I all but shouted, springing to my feet. "Do not call Ryan. Don't ever tell him where I am or that you've seen me. I need you to stay away from him."

Images of Kate's lifeless eyes flashed through my mind, and my stomach lurched. I needed to keep Craig out of this. He was safer without me. Losing him hurt, but it would kill me if anything happened to him too.

"I won't." Craig promised, his brow furrowed as he got to his feet. He raised his arms to placate me as I backed away like a startled deer. "I won't tell him a thing."

I exhaled, but my hands wouldn't stop shaking. Every noise in the distance made me jump, and my hair stood on end. I stared up at Craig, studying his silly spiked hair and those sapphire sparklers of his that made every guy he met swoon. I would never be his wing woman again, I couldn't be his best friend. It felt as if someone was using my heart as a pin cushion.

I knew what I should do.

But I'm a coward, so I threw myself back into his arms and nuzzled into his shoulder, inhaling the scent of familiarity and home. "I miss you."

"I missed you too." He rested his chin on the top of my head.

"So, are you going to explain why you're running around the city in Converse and acting so weird?"

I shook my head, blinking back tears and tightening my arms around his waist as if he might vanish on me if I looked away. I was being selfish, but even Luke had said I could still have my old life back. I'd just keep them as separate as possible. No werewolf stuff, just the only family I had left. I deserved that.

"No, but can we start over?"

CHAPTER 5

"**N**ext thing I know, Dylan is stumbling around the front garden half naked." Luke barked a laugh. "With his trousers around his ankles, screaming for Juliet like he was in a Shakespeare play."

Josh sprang to his feet and gave an overzealous stage bow, his deep brown eyes sparkling with mischief.

"Juliet, wherefore art thou—?"

Dylan groaned, covering his reddening face with his hand as he slumped deeper into the couch as if he could disappear. "That is not how it happened."

I couldn't breathe. Tears streamed down my face and I wheezed as I fought the fit of laughter overcoming me. Alice cracked a hint of a smile beside me, her drink completely untouched. She hadn't joined in the conversations, but she hadn't asked to leave either, and I could only hope that was a good sign.

"That is exactly how it happened, Lothario." Josh's grip on his beer bottle wobbled as he flopped back onto the couch beside Alice who had remained quiet for most of the evening.

"Juliet was his first love." Luke grinned widely at his friend.

"Too bad he was too drunk to remember where she lived and ended up serenading my parents instead."

I wiped my eyes, still chuckling as I grabbed my empty glass off the coffee table and walked in a not straight line to the kitchen in search of more alcohol.

"Refill anyone?"

A chorus of yeses came from the boys. Luke, ever the gentleman, was on his feet and striding into the kitchen to help within seconds. I wasn't going to complain about the company as I poured another vodka and coke while he helped cut up some limes.

He towered over me, his hard abs pressed flush against me as he picked up a lime and sliced it with more precision than I would have managed. I probably would have lost a finger, and I was pretty sure even hybrids couldn't regrow limbs.

"I saw Craig today." Ice cubes clinked against my glass as I emptied them in.

I wasn't sure why I blurted it out. Luke was the very one who said I didn't need to leave my past life behind, but Kate's funeral was less than a month ago, and my U-turn would give anyone whiplash.

The corners of his lips curved up in a warm smile, and my shoulders relaxed as he shot me a knowing look, as if saying 'I told you so'. "That's good, how is he?"

I'd forgotten Luke had gone to his house party at the start of the summer. Back when he was 'babysitting'. I wasn't sure if I bought that excuse anymore.

"He's good." I tugged my lip between my teeth as I debated telling him the rest. "He thought I was missing from the funeral because I was chasing info on my birth parents."

I glanced across at Luke from under my lashes. He kept his face neutral, but all of a sudden, the chopping board was taking a hammering.

"I think Ryan wiped his memories or altered them somehow." I tried to choose my words carefully until I decided that it was best to disarm him. I pried the knife from Luke's hands and set it down on the counter before continuing. "Ryan made him believe that I cheated with you."

Luke's jaw twitched, his eyes narrowing as they met mine. "Oh, did he now?"

He placed the knife down, his movements forced as he tipped the limes into a separate bowl.

I turned to face him, a bowl full of ice at the ready, knowing full well he'd slip into protective alpha mode, and I was so over alpha holes. "He did, and while I hate that he messed with my friend's mind, it was kind of nice that Craig didn't hate me."

At that admission, Luke's hazel eyes softened, and he reached out, delicately brushing a stray hair behind my ear. "He wouldn't hate you even if he knew the truth."

Goosebumps rose on my flesh in response to his touch.

"Well I can't exactly tell him that all the monsters that go bump in the night are real."

"No." Luke tapped my nose before picking back up the knife and finishing off the last limes with an unerring sense of calm. "But he knows you would never leave Kate if you had a choice. Are you going to see him again?"

"We went for coffee in Merrion Square, which was really nice." A wave of relief washed over me as I realised maybe I could make my old friendship and hold on to a relationship that tethered me to my old world. "He wants me to go out clubbing for Halloween. Getting tacky outfits and going out that night was our tradition."

Luke's smile widened into something mischievous as he dropped two lime slices into my coke, before spinning away to dump the knife in the sink. "I think traditions are very important."

I tried to hide my smile, pouring in an extra dash of vodka, and swaying as one of my favourite Taylor Swift songs began playing on the playlist booming from the small speaker in the living room area. Dylan cheered while Josh burst into song, knowing every lyric but he'd never admit to it in the morning.

Glass clinking sounded behind me as Luke transferred more beers from the freezer to the fridge.

"You know, there is a shot glass in the press. I'm not sure free pouring is in your skill set." He raised his voice to be heard over the music.

I poked out my tongue as I turned with my freshly poured lethal drink in hand. "Excuse me? I was a barmaid."

"A bad one, if I recall correctly." The corners of his eyes creased.

"Yet you kept coming back."

I couldn't help but think about the first time he swung by the old bar I worked at and knocked my world off kilter. I'd warned him off then, convinced he was trouble. When really, he was trying to open my eyes, and I was too damn stupid and stubborn to listen. Hindsight is a bitch.

He leaned against the kitchen island, one elbow propped on the counter. The position caused the buttons in his shirt to strain across his broad chest. Paired with black jeans, the blue shirt made his eyes pop even more under the bright kitchen spotlights.

"Eyes up here," Luke said, and when I listened, there was a cocky, knowing smirk on his face.

Blood rushed to my cheeks.

I'd had too much to drink. Yep, that was it.

I rolled my eyes, pulling a signature move Kate taught me when she tried to coach me into being a man-eater. Spoiler alert, she failed. But I did learn a thing or two. "You spilled some beer on your shirt."

Before my cheeks decided to ramp up to full scale beetroot, I snatched a can of beer off the island and slipped away before he could come up with a comeback. I didn't think any of us were sober enough for witty comebacks.

When the song switched to 'Love Story', Josh began reenacting the lyrics, dropping to one knee in front of Alice who was struggling to hide her smile.

"Juliettttt," Josh wailed, too busy laughing to manage half the words as he continued to rip into his friend—their favourite pastime was ribbing each other.

"Everybody makes mistakes." Dylan insisted, his lower lip sticking out in a pout. "It's been years. Will I never be allowed to live that one down?"

Alice arched her brow, and I swear she giggled. "Hannah Montana, are we?"

"Ohhhhh," Luke hollered, running back into the room at full speed. His socks slipped on the varnished floors, and he careered onto the couch, somehow twisting to save himself at the last minute. He plopped down between Alice and Dylan with the biggest shit-eating grin splitting his face. "Burn!"

I don't know how late we stayed up laughing, but it was the first night I didn't cry myself to sleep since Kate's death.

CHAPTER 6
LUKE

Nothing.

Hours of combing through old newspaper records and scouring the internet, and I had nothing. No leads, no clues, just a list of every missing person reported in Dublin for the last twenty years. The words were beginning to blur, I'd no sense of time anymore. My brain was straying into some very dark places after reading so many disturbing reports and autopsies. I couldn't stop though. Every time I thought of Alice sobbing her heart out after another nightmare, guilt swamped me. More hybrids were out there suffering and their families probably had no idea. I appreciated my father's point of view, but I couldn't stand by and wait.

As if sensing I needed a break, Jonas eased the laptop shut on my hand to pause my search. "I think that's enough for today."

The room we were in was always dark, but as I looked up, I noticed that the many CCTV monitors lining the wall in front of us had switched to black and white. A quick glance at my phone told me I'd sunk three hours into my fruitless search. Darius had offered me full use of all their records when he found out what Alice had revealed. The owner of the Dark Night wasn't an official elder, but his staff and vampires that he housed were those who refused to subscribe to the main coven in Leinster. The elder of that coven, Lars, was a sadistic man with a toe-curling reputation. Despite not being an elder, Darius had acquired quite a collection of ancient texts and had documented his family's rise in Ireland. Sadly, it had given more questions than answers.

I just wanted to help. I wanted to stop the Faolchúnna alpha's plans before he hurt more innocent people. Ever since Alice's revelation about the other hybrids, I had this sick feeling that Eve was a key part of their plans.

Jonas' amber eyes were sombre as we stared off, his will iron clad as he waited for me to relent. I did with a sigh, extracting my fingers from under the laptop screen and letting it snap fully shut.

"What do you know so far?"

I exhaled harshly. "He has taken other hybrids besides Alice. They were housed on the Faolchúnna pack lands with her, but in separate rooms. We don't know how long this has been going on for, or how many he's taken. We have no idea where they are and all we know about his plans is that he wants to *breed* some kind of elite wolf to bolster pure bloodlines."

His lips curled back in disgust to reveal two razor sharp fangs.

"I just need *something*. One clue to go on, and then I can dig up enough dirt to bury Damien and his twat of a son once and for all."

"We will stop him, but you've been at this for ages. The records aren't going anywhere." He nudged the untouched sandwich that he'd brought up towards me. "You're at work soon too, mutts like you can't run on fumes."

I bit back the urge to argue with him, my stomach grumbling in clear demand. Shoving the laptop aside, I reached out for the sandwich and took a bite, groaning as the taste of bacon and barbecue sauce exploded in my mouth. This place had the best food, drink, and people.

"Good, I thought you were going to put up more of a fight."

He sank back against the plush leather of the office chair, spinning in a slow circle.

I shot him a wry smile. "I'm a lover, not a fighter."

By the time he faced me again, Jonas' lips stretched in a wide grin. "Well that's a lie, you haven't gotten laid in forever. Unless you and Eve…"

He trailed off, eyes sparkling with mischief as he waited for me to finish the sentence.

"She's just a friend," I said firmly, planting my foot between his legs and pushing.

The chair drifted backwards, slamming into the edge of the desk with enough force to rattle a few monitors.

Jonas cursed, leaping to his feet so quickly he was a blur as he sped around, righting each of the screens before one could fall. He appeared back in the chair, his right leg folded over the other and not a single corkscrew curl out of place.

"Don't take your sexual frustration out on me." Jonas shrugged, musing with the lapels of his suit. They were a deep velvet burgundy, complimenting his rich complexion and the black fitted shirt. Darius didn't enforce uniforms, he encouraged style.

Did I fancy Eve? Yes, of course. She was drop dead gorgeous with a kind heart. What was there not to like? She'd grown into herself since we met, and she was the reason my sister was home safe. But Ryan is a fucking idiot and shattered her trust. I wanted to wring his neck for making that girl think she was anything less than amazing. I wasn't going to try to jump in her pants. Right now, she needed a friend, and that's what I would be without any expectation of more.

Not that I could imagine her with anyone else without wanting to punch a wall. But I'd torch that bridge when it came to it because she deserved to be happy.

I frowned, shoving the last piece of bread into my mouth, and slumped in my chair. "I'm not sexually frustrated, my family is just going through a lot of shit and there's a crazy alpha trying to create 'super wolves'. So excuse me if I don't have time for pointless hook-ups."

"At this rate it would only take ten seco—"

Before I could tell Jonas how wrong he was, Alec popped his head in the door, saving his fellow vamp from a tirade about how no woman would ever be subjected to ten measly seconds with me.

"We might have a problem, boss." Alec shut the reinforced steel door behind him with a clang.

Jonas sat to attention. "Problem?"

"Yeah, Catalina—you know, the young witch with the snowstorm issue? She said there was someone lurking around the alleyways on her way in. She said they felt human." He perched on the edge of the large mahogany desk spanning the expanse of the wall hosting the CCTV cameras. "But you know she's not got the best eye."

Jonas nodded, the chair swivelling so fast the hinges groaned. He hit a button on the desktop, and every single monitor flared into light.

Alec wasn't talking about her eyesight. Some witches had poor control of their powers and lacked the innate senses of their kid if their magic was diluted, often due to distant bloodlines. She'd gain control of her winter-based powers with practice, but some witches would never gain the ability to sense magic as acutely as first-generation ones.

I scooted closer, scanning the screens while his fingers glided over the keyboard, and he flicked through the different views.

The alleyway housing the entrance to the Dark Night was just like any other back street in Dublin City. Aged old brick work, cobblestones, poor lighting, and skips full of vermin and cats fighting for scraps. Darius made sure it was kept as clean as possible without drawing suspicion, even keeping the graffiti up to date so that the wall hiding the Dark Night entrance didn't stand out. Humans avoided the spot, subconsciously getting the urge to leave if they ever happened upon it thanks to intricate spells and some Fae magic.

"There." I pointed at a small figure obscured by the shadows standing beside one of the bins.

Jonas upped the brightness and zoomed the image in to reveal a slight woman, maybe five foot two, dressed in a long teddy coat complete with black stilettos that wobbled on the uneven cobblestones and a set of cat ears. When she turned her face towards the camera, my stomach somersaulted.

What was Eve doing here?

"Well, well, well, look what the cat dragged in," Jonas murmured, freezing the frame to highlight Eve's identity. "Your little pup looks like she's off out on a date."

Heat flared under my skin, but I took a deep breath as I remembered our conversation the other night. It was Halloween and Eve was going out with Craig, her best friend.

"She's just seeing a friend," I ground out, my gaze glued to the screen.

My eyes must have flashed silver because Jonas whistled, clucking his tongue. "Just friends, sure."

Alec chuckled behind me, and I resisted the urge to give him a friendly elbow to the balls, leaning forwards as I watched Eve pace in circles talking to herself before approaching the wall where the Dark Night entrance lay.

"Volo gallum Luci."

Eve's voice rang through the speakers as Jonas unmuted the footage. She stared at the wall, eyes narrowed into slits that told me this wasn't her first attempt at getting in. We were too caught up in research to pay much attention to the CCTV, it was more for crowd control in the club and catching dodgy dealings than keeping people out. The gargoyles and demons dealt with unwelcome guests.

She repeated the words as if they were a spell, tapping her foot in impatience.

"I want Luke's rooster?... His cock. I want Luke's cock,"

Jonas translated, barking a short laugh. "What the hell is she doing?"

"I believe she is trying to use a spell," Alec said.

Jonas snorted. "What kind of spell talks about dicks?"

"The kind that isn't real," I said, realisation dawning on me. I'd overheard Dylan and Eve having a conversation at the apartment warming about the Dark Night and it would not be unlike my friend to play a prank on her. In fact, it was practically a rite of passage. "I blame Dylan."

"Ah, that explains it," Jonas chuckled, hitting a series of buttons that caused a green light to flash.

I could tell what happened by the way Eve stumbled back, her eyes wide. She hesitated, looking up in the direction of the cloaked CCTV camera with a dubious look before disappearing from view. Seconds later, her image flashed up on the screen monitoring the inside hallway.

"Well, shall we go get your non-sexy friend then?" Jonas wiggled his eyebrows suggestively.

His words fell on deaf ears, my attention completely glued to the screen as she slid her coat off to reveal a slinky black dress that sparkled under the dim lighting of the sconces and highlighted the curve of her little ass.

When I didn't answer, Jonas gave me a cuff around the ear to jolt me out of my wandering thoughts. "You stay here, I'll go see what Eve wants. She's hardly meeting her human here."

Both vampires exited the room, leaving me to watch the CCTV feed like some kind of stalker. I wanted to stop, but the way she greeted the demonic bouncers with a nervous smile ignited the need in me to make sure she was okay. And when she wound her way up the spiral staircase towards the upper floor and her dress hitched with each step, I wasn't man enough to drag my eyes away from the screen.

I didn't touch my rock-hard cock that was throbbing, trapped in my jeans. No, I had a line.

Despite playing around with the keyboard, I couldn't figure

out how to unmute the right feed so I could only watch while Jonas spoke to Eve. When she spotted him, her shoulders relaxed and their conversation seemed to flow with ease. I tried to lip-read, but that was a fool's errand, especially when my brain wouldn't stop flashing with images of how her lips would look wrapped around my dick.

The sight of her in lace cat ears and a fitted dress that highlighted her little waist was doing all sorts of things that made me want to risk the friendship. But I wouldn't, I couldn't.

She threw her arms around Jonas, giving me a very nice view as she hugged him in some sort of... celebration? I swallowed hard, a low growl ripping from my throat.

If she was just a friend, then why did I want to rip his throat out?

As she walked out of view, her hips swayed, and I readjusted. I gave my dick a hard squeeze through my jeans and tried to level my breathing, just in time because Jonas was back outside the room in seconds thanks to his vampire speed.

He was already mid-sentence by the time the door was closing. "So, don't kill me, but I offered Eve a job at the bar part time."

"Is that it?" I surprised myself with how calm I felt about that proposition.

She needed her independence and bartending was something she had experience with. I wanted her to go back to college, but she wasn't ready for that conversation yet and it was her own decision to make. At least I knew she'd be safe here.

Or maybe it was because my monkey brain was too busy fantasising about those cat ears to think straight.

Jonas turned and took one look at me, shaking his head with the biggest shit-eating grin on his face. "You're fucked mate."

CHAPTER 7

"I did not cock-block you that night. I *saved* you."

I scoffed, arching an eyebrow despite the grin stretching my lips. "You didn't save me! He was cute, you cock-blocked me because you thought he was cute and wouldn't share."

Craig whirled on me, his eyes wide with feigned shock as he gestured widely while pleading his innocence. His vampire cape whipped around his outreached hands, battling with the wind. He wore a waistcoat and slacks, with a white shirt covered in fake blood. Claiming his hair wasn't historically accurate, he had used a shitty temporary black spray on it for the evening. His once-red velvet cloak was now covered in stains from people spilling drinks in the club, matching his half-melted face paint. He looked more like a zombie summoned to life for the evening than a vampire.

"Girl, I love you, but you're like a sister to me, and sharing was most definitely *not* on the table." Craig laughed as he took my hand in his and twirled me under his arm, before tucking me into his side.

I reached up to ruffle his hair, my hand coming away black.

"Dude." I groaned, wiping my hand on his shirt, and leaving dark blue marks all over it as I tried to get the dye off my hands. "You're shedding."

He rolled his eyes, swatting me away. "I am not a dog. What the hell is that?"

I took to using his cloak as a hand towel instead, refusing to let go when he spun in a full circle as if he might be able to see the culprit.

"It's your hair." I shot him a filthy glare. "That dye is shit."

There were patches of blue peeking through his hair and a trail of dye staining the back of his neck and ears.

"How are you feeling now?" He balanced on the edges of a curb as if he was walking the tightrope.

Despite everything that had changed over the summer, we had slipped back into our friendship with ease. We'd danced the night away in the club with bodies writhing around us, dressed or barely dressed in Halloween costumes. I'd long since lost the little cat ears Jonas had teased, my hair a tangled mess that stuck to the sheen of sweat on my back. My eye-liner cat nose was no doubt a smudged mess, but I didn't care. The music blasting, bass thumping in my ears had been heaven. As we'd danced, I'd been able to lose myself in the moment. I wasn't sure if it was the flaming sambuca he'd convinced me to knock back, but it was the first time I'd felt *normal* in a long time.

"Normal" had been followed with a wave of guilt, and the instant Craig noticed I was having a moment, he had whisked me out of there. I was busy sniffling while he argued with the cloakroom attendant when they couldn't find my coat, but the fresh air had helped sober me up a bit. It didn't cure me of the guilt or pain of missing Kate, but it did ground me. And Craig had used his sterling sense of humour to cheer me up, as always.

"I'm better. I just got a bit weird for a moment." I shoved my damp hair back out of my face.

He chewed his cheek for a moment before slinging an arm over my shoulder and pulling me close. "Feelings are not called 'moments'. I miss her too, you know, but she'd want this. Living life to the fullest was her wish for all of us."

My throat clogged at his words. He was right. I nodded, not trusting myself to speak.

"That doesn't mean I want you bottling up all your emotions though," he added, pressing a light kiss to my forehead. "Kate was a big advocate for venting. So, if you ever need to talk, I'm here."

It was everything I wanted to hear, but at the same time it broke my heart. Could we do this? Could I still be his best friend while keeping one half of my life a secret? I wasn't sure, but I sure as hell wanted to try. I made a silent promise to myself that I would guard him with my life. I wasn't losing another friend to this new world of mine.

We wound our way along the street, swaying back and forth. Craig propped me up with an arm around my waist to keep me stable each time my heels caught in the uneven pavement until we reached the end of a queue for one of his favourite kebab shops in the city. I was normally more of a burger and chips girl, but my growling stomach wasn't feeling picky.

"You're shivering." Craig's brows creased, crinkling the dried face paint.

I shrugged, wrapping my arms tight around my torso. Someone had stolen my coat at the club, or so the cloakroom attendant claimed. I ran hotter than a human, but sometimes I wished I was a furnace like Luke. "I'm grand."

"You're a shit liar." He chuckled, untying his cloak to drape it over the both of us. "Now, just call me your knight in shining armour."

We perched on a shop window ledge as we waited in line, my shoulders bunched with tension. I wanted to smile at that. I wanted to laugh and snuggle into his side, but his words rang in my mind. I was a good liar. Too good.

I stomped my heeled boots against the cobblestones in an attempt to knock some warmth into me. The autumn nights had a serious bite to them. Just as Craig stepped up to grab our order, my phone buzzed in my bag.

Slipping it out with half-numb fingers, a message from Luke

illuminated the screen. Nothing important, just him checking in to make sure I was having a good night. It didn't mean anything, but a smile tugged at the corner of my lips regardless.

"Right, I'm not buying it!" Craig's head popped up behind my shoulder with no warning.

Scrambling not to drop my phone when I jumped, I spun and mock-scowled at my friend in confusion.

"Not buying what?"

"The whole 'just friends' bullshit."

He snatched the phone from my grip and replaced it with a tray of chips and a chunk of battered cod topped with garlic mayonnaise that made my mouth water. I didn't give a shit about the phone anymore, but he did.

I unwrapped the foil on my kebab and took a messy bite of the corner to excuse myself from a response, that didn't stop him though.

"You're not gonna win him over with a mouth like that." He opened his mouth wide, taking an obnoxiously large bite of his own. Once he'd swallowed it down like an animal, he licked his lips clean with a knowing smirk. "I taught you the trick, remember? You fold your thumb inside your fist an—"

"I get it!" I groaned, feigning whacking him with my kebab.

He danced away laughing even though we both knew I wouldn't risk good food.

We crossed the road and made our way towards the quays, the frigid breeze making me pull my oversized coat tighter around my neck.

"So..." Craig interrupted my munching to wave the phone in my face, his mouth half full of fish. "Friends, yeah?"

"We are just friends," I insisted, despite those little butterflies that had been fluttering around more like bats after the meaningless message. "His family helped me out of things with Ryan when he turned out to be a dick, and he's been really good to me."

That was the short, human-friendly version that I'd given

Craig. He wasn't buying it. Not the bits I'd expected him to pick holes in, but the whole friendship between me and Luke. The moment I'd shown him a photo of Luke, Craig had insisted that it was not possible for the friendship to be platonic.

"You're doing it again." He shook his head with a knowing look. "That smile, I swear. If you're dating him, you can just tell me. I'm not gonna judge. Ryan was a dickhead, a rat, so I wouldn't even blame you if there was overla—"

"There was *no* overlap. There is nothing to overlap."

Heat crept into my cheeks as I thought about that night in the kitchen, the way Luke had looked at me. There was something there, but it was probably just an attraction. He was gorgeous after all, and we had been through so much. But I wasn't risking it, I couldn't go there. I'd just found my place, and I wasn't losing it because I couldn't keep it in my pants.

We dodged a drunk guy stumbling down the old brick tunnel marking the entrance to Temple Bar. Small shops with shuttered doors lined the walkway, closed for the night. One was actually a witch essentials store loosely hidden as a generic crystal shop.

"Eve." Craig sighed, shaking his head as he poked my flushed cheek with a chunky chip. "All I want to see is you happy, okay? I get that things with Ryan got complicated. And then Kate..."

I swallowed. Hard.

Silence hung between us as we crossed the road and made our way over the Halfpenny bridge. I paused in the middle, staring out at the sprawling city and the bright lights dancing on the water surface. Craig touched my arm and tugged me forwards, nudging the chip dangling from my fork towards my mouth.

"Luke seems cute, he has a kind face. And it looks like he probably has abs too." He offered me a cheeky grin before his expression turned serious again. "He's been there for you and that's more than he who shall not be named. I'm not saying rush into stuff, just don't close yourself off. You deserve happiness."

I was living a half-life with my best friend while the other one was six feet under, and a bunch of hybrids were being tortured, or

God knows what at the hands of my ex-boyfriend and his warped father. Did I deserve happiness when I didn't stop any of that? I wasn't so sure. Besides, everyone left me eventually, and I didn't want to risk that with Luke. Friendship was enough. It had to be.

As we stepped out onto the north side of the city, goosebumps erupted all over my arms and spread up the back of my neck, making my spine tingle. I tensed and reached out for Craig's hand out of reflex, my senses flaring and searching for the source of my unease. I'd gotten good at drowning out 'background noise' as Luke called it, but my wolf instincts had flagged something, and whatever it was had a warning sense of dread writing in the pit of my stomach.

Craig frowned, his lips parted as he looked at me. That's when a scream pierced the night, and my blood ran cold.

Another scream followed, close by to our right. I broke into a sprint. Craig yelled for me to come back, but I ignored him and ran towards the screams. I dodged a lone postbox, glancing over my shoulder to see Craig chasing after me. We raced around the corner and came to a stop in an alleyway to find a group of girls dressed as the Mean Girls cast standing around the remains of a girl. Her body was coated in blood, with limbs contorted at unnatural angles, and deep gauges covered her exposed skin. The girl's brunette curls fanned out, soaked in the blood pooled and flowing through the grooves in the cobbled ground. Her clothes were torn, and the remains of a black winter coat hung off her limp arms.

My coat.

CHAPTER 8

LUKE

T he moment I heard Eve's voicemail, I knew something was wrong. I bolted from soccer training, briefly apologising to one of the other football trainers for dumping her with my group and doubling her kid quota for the evening. It was volunteer work, but even if it was Christina, my grumpiest physio client, I'd have left in a heartbeat.

She was scared, said something about someone being murdered, but that she was safe. I held onto the last part.

Eve had been pretty incoherent when trying to explain her location, but the sirens and flashing lights were visible from the quays. I took a left two streets down, parking on the side of the road, and ran towards the chaos.

There was a crowd of drunken revellers in every kind of outfit imaginable filtering across the Ha'penny bridge to rubberneck, but I shoved through them onto Lower Liffey Street where the sea of people only swelled. Any other time of the year, I'd have looked ridiculous in the city on a Friday night dressed in my coaching kit. I fit right in with the Halloween costumes. There was no sign of Eve in the crowd near the parked ambulances lining the road, and as I moved further, elbowing people out of my way as my patience evaporated. Paramedics weren't in rescue or resuscitation mode, they were conversing with the police.

My gut twisted as I pushed forwards, dodging a Garda that was busy trying to control a bunch of girls hollering in panic by slipping between two vans that were parked up on the curb. As much as the vampire power to alter minds would come in handy, I didn't need Jonas' super speed to be stealthy. The Gardaí were too busy taking statements and managing drunken outbursts from the crowd gathering to notice as I snuck under the blue-and-white police tape marking the crime scene.

Eve was wrapped in the silver foil they give to patients, her hair that had been styled brown waves from earlier was now dishevelled and matching her smudged makeup. She'd lost her coat, braving the cold in her little black dress, and the cat ears were gone, along with her smile. Mascara-stained tears marred her cheeks as she stood propped up by the wall behind her. If I zoned out the sirens, I could hear her mumbling 'no' on repeat as her delicate hands bunched into fists, gripping the silver emergency blanket wrapped around her like it was a raft keeping her afloat. She didn't seem to notice me, her wide eyes fixed on the dead body sprawled at an awkward angle on the pavement. There was blood everywhere.

The Gardaí milling around the crime scene paid no heed to me as I rushed up to Eve, ready to crush her to my chest. Her vacant stare and the sheer terror contorting her features made me slow my pace as I approached as if she was a startled deer ready to bolt.

"Eve?" I kept my tone soft amidst the chaos, clasping her elbows as I turned and placed myself between her and the murder scene.

She blinked once as I obscured her view, looking up at me with a glazed expression that reminded me all too well of how Alice looked after one of her nightmares. Her lip trembled, every inch of her body shook, her chest rising and falling erratically with each ragged breath.

"It's okay." I kept myself positioned to block her view. "I'm here with you. You're safe."

I reached out, unfurling her rigid fingers to release their vice-like grip on the foil blanket that had slipped down. Unzipping my warm coaching sweatshirt, I shrugged it off and threaded Eve's arms through the sleeves. She moved like a zombie, her empty stare making my stomach churn. I pulled the zip right up to under her chin before tugging the foil back up around her shoulders and wrapping it around her properly. All the while, the movement served as a distraction which allowed me to gently walk her sideways and then back a few paces until we had turned a corner, and she could look around without seeing splatters of blood that would fuel her racing thoughts.

"Luke?" Eve looked up at me, her voice cracking as fresh tears streamed down her cheeks.

"I'm here." I offered her my open arms and wrapped them around her when she stepped into my embrace. Her heart was working overtime, and her shallow breaths left small puffs of vapour in the cool late autumn air. "You're safe, love. I'm not going anywhere. I know this is scary but keep breathing through it."

Eve's body was hot against mine, but the shaking still wouldn't subside. Her small hands gripped my T-shirt, clawing as if she was trying to tether herself to the present. I held her, stroking her hair with one hand while keeping the other pressed against her lower back, my thumb stroking the fleece material of my sweatshirt that swamped her tiny frame. I whispered soft words of encouragement and reassurance in her ear the whole time as I waited for her body to go through the motions.

Eventually, a choked sob escaped her lips. Wet pooled on my T-shirt as the tears fell in earnest.

The day Kate died, I had gone to the apartment. My heart had plummeted at the sight of crime scene tape covering the door, and I'd terrorised some poor beat-cop in my haste to ensure that Eve was alright. Being able to smell that the blood was Kate's had been the only thing stopping me from snapping. I could tell she'd been there though. I'd seen the puddle of blood in the kitchen area. I'd had Jonas coerce them into showing me the crime scene photos. While Kate's throat had been slit in a very human way, no doubt the scene before us reminded Eve of the moment she found her best friend murdered. Because it reminded me of that night, too.

"Talk to me." I ran my hands up and down the length of her arms in an attempt to get more heat into her body. "How many streetlights are on the street?"

Eve looked around, her movements still jerky as she counted under her breath.

"Six," she said finally, blowing out a harsh breath. "Six."

The knot that had taken up residence between my shoulders lessened as her heartbeat continued to settle. I didn't want to let her go.

Eve took a wobbly step back from me. The stiletto heel of one shoe caught in a crack on the uneven pavement, and her ankle snapped to one side in that way that should break a girl's ankle but never seemed to.

"Easy." I shot forwards, grabbing her waist to keep her upright, only releasing her once she was balanced, albeit jittery.

Her cheeks flushed and damn was it good to see some colour returning to her face.

"I'm okay," she mumbled, her shoulder hunched, and her arms folded across her stomach.

"You don't have to be. No one would see that and be okay."

"I'm fine." She ground out through gritted teeth, throwing some invisible wall up between us.

No way was I leaving it there.

"Eve." I reached out to grab her chin between my finger and thumb. She lifted her gaze to mine, her jaw tense under my touch. "What you saw was horrific. But I'd guess what's haunting you right now is the memory of Kate, and I need you to listen to me when I say this. Her death was not your fault. You are not responsible for the actions of Ryan or that psychopath he runs with. Being a part of the paranormal world is not a death sentence for human friends. You did not put them in danger by simply being who you are. None of this is your fault."

She stared at me for a long moment, those bright blue eyes of hers hollow and swimming with tears.

For a moment, I worried I'd gone too far. But then she opened her mouth to speak.

"She was wearing my coat."

My blood ran cold. It took every ounce of control I had not to storm back out onto the crime scene and scream bloody murder. Instead, only the tips of my claws extended as I took a long, deep breath.

"That doesn't change what I said." I stroked her cheek with my thumb and fought to keep my tone calm. She lowered her lashes, leaning into the touch. "I'm going to go talk to the guards and we'll figure this out, okay?"

Eve nodded mutely.

I watched her for a moment, subtly checking for injuries as I brushed my arms along her arms before deeming her safe enough for me to move away. Footsteps approached, the sound of sneakers squeaking on the damp cobblestones at a pitch that only heightened canine hearing would pick up.

I spun towards the source of the noise, placing myself between Eve and the man approaching. He was tall and lean, dressed head to toe in a very battered vampire costume, yet he walked with a sense of authority. A deep inhale flagged that her scent was all over him, which had my hackles raised. The blue patches peeking through what must have been temporary black dye on his hair made my testosterone stop surging. It was Eve's friend from the funeral.

"Craig?" I moved to one side and revealed Eve to him again.

"That's me." His shoulders were squared as he came to a stop in front of us. Even with red contacts in, the crease of his eyes suggested he was wary of me.

Good. I respected his want to protect his friend.

"Are you alright?" Craig crouched down, resting his forehead against Eve's as he pulled her into a hug. "I'm sorry I had to leave you when the team arrived, it was important that we secured the scene."

"I'm okay," she murmured, squeezing him back. "Is she…?"

"Dead?" The word rolled off his tongue with a sombre sigh as he straightened. "Yeah, she's gone. This is one of the worst crime scenes I've ever seen."

"You're in the force?" I held out my hand. "It's nice to finally meet, Eve has told me a lot about you."

"Nothing good, I expect." His expression became less guarded as he shook my hand. He noted the way Eve had embedded herself in my side. "I'm still a rookie and in training, but they need every officer they can at the moment with staff shortages."

I shot Eve a look, trying to communicate the truth behind what I planned to do. "Can you keep an eye on Eve for a moment? I need to ring my boss to explain why I ran off. Then I promise to take her home."

She frowned for a moment before nodding with a sigh, her shoulders slumping in defeat.

"Sure." Craig glanced back towards the crime scene. "I'm technically off the clock anyway. I just had to call it in."

"Great, thanks." I shot him a wide smile, raising my phone to my ear and pretending to have a loud conversation with my boss as I walked away from them and back in the direction of the body. A quick glance back told me Eve had understood my veiled message. She talked to Craig and had positioned herself so he was now facing the opposite end of the road with his back to me. I hated having to ask Eve to abuse her friend's trust, but I spotted one very easy opportunity for me to get a look at the crime scene without raising suspicion.

A mix of beat cops in their luminescent Garda uniforms swarmed the scene as I rounded the corner. Most of them were occupied with keeping the scene sealed off, speaking to witnesses. A few men in suits were gathered around the body, pointing to orange cones marking evidence on the ground. Camera lights flashed as someone dressed in a hazmat suit took photos of the body.

I hung back in the shadows, lurking behind police cars and an empty ambulance as I inched closer to the scene. Casting out my senses, I let my nose pick through the onslaught of scents. It was hard to blur out the background noise, the Gardaí and stench of alcohol from those gathered outside the barriers. I focused on the scent attached to the pool of blood trickling through the maze of grooves in the cobbled ground.

Female. Early twenties.

She must have died shortly before Eve and Craig stumbled across her. She was human, but there was a distinct scent of wolf that wasn't mine or Eve's. No, it wasn't one I recognised at all. Not a Crescent, but there was definitely a werewolf involved.

I peeked around the edge of the ambulance door, the contents of my stomach swirling at the sight. The poor girl had been ripped to shreds, deep claw marks marred every inch of her flesh. She was bloody, bruised, and broken. Her dress was completely shredded and she was sprawled face down. Bile rose in my throat as heat crashed through my veins, anger and disgust washing over me as the realisation hit. Between the hair and the black coat I recognised from the Dark Night CCTV earlier, she could easily be mistaken for Eve from behind.

And I didn't believe in coincidences.

CHAPTER 9

EVE

Why did it always feel like I was bringing bad news to their door?

I cursed under my breath as my shaking fingers fumbled with the seat belt buckle. A warm hand covered mine, unlocking it. I turned to find Luke watching me with concern shining in his eyes.

"I'm fine," I insisted before he could even ask, swallowing the lump that kept rising in my throat.

I was far from fine. The eerie silence of the apartment unsettled me. I could still smell the coppery scent of her blood, see that poor girl's mangled body. The night had been going so well, but there was clearly no escaping the dark nightmarish things that seemed to follow me. Maybe I was cursed.

"Care to tell me what's going on in that brain of yours?" He refused to let go of my hand as he unwound the seat belt from me.

I sucked a breath between my teeth. "Care to tell me what you found back at the crime scene?"

"Touché." His eyebrow quirked. When I refused to back down and answer his question first, he raked his hand through the gelled tips of his hair. "You know what I found. I know you smelled a wolf when you stumbled across her. That's probably what helped fuel your panic attack. You've seen enough blood and gore by now, but that one hit too close to home."

He was right. He was always right, and it drove me mad sometimes.

Tom was waiting in the doorway. Clearly Luke had made a call while I kept Craig busy. Or maybe he called on the way back, I had zoned out for the journey. The trip home was a black spot in my memory, along with half the night. I could only remember the pieces I wanted to forget.

The noise of Luke unlocking the passenger door and holding it open for me brought me back to the present. He helped me out of the car, and we walked up the driveway side by side, Luke's hand finding the small of my back as I slowed my pace.

On one hand, my heart warmed at the sight of his house. I'd missed the place in the brief time since I moved out, but I hated the circumstances of my return. I should have been coming back to have tea with Helena and Alice and talking about nice things. Not murder.

Yet here I was.

Tom was dressed in his pyjamas, his face drawn and his usually clean-shaven jawline had a fine shadow of stubble. His lips curved into a small smile that should have been somewhat reassuring, but I couldn't shake the feeling that I was like the grim reaper of this pack. The Crescents had accepted me with open arms, yet my presence was that of a banshee.

"Only Darren and Liz?" Luke eyed the cars in the driveway.

"It's late, and we don't know what we're dealing with." Tom nodded, clapping his son on the back as they embraced before pulling me into a hug when I hung back for too long.

Could alphas read their pack's minds? Tom had an innate sense of what people needed, and it was the most alpha thing I had seen. Nothing like Ryan's pack.

We were ushered inside and towards the heart of the home. I'd become numb to the cold, but the heat of the house made my skin tingle with a welcome burn. It was then that I remembered I was in a little black dress with smudged whiskers on my cheeks. My face warmed, and I wrapped Craig's cloak tighter around myself, silently thanking my best friend for covering my ass—*literally.*

"Oh good, you're home." Helena rushed over to us, her familiar scent calming my nerves as she pulled Luke and me into a warm hug that no doubt exposed my ass to the empty hallway. "Sit down and I'll make some tea."

We did as we were told, taking the two seats nearest that put Luke between me and Liz, with Tom to my other side at the head of the table and Darren flanking his left. Helena buzzed around the kitchen, helped by her husband as she set about making sure everyone had drinks and snacks, even at this hour. At a surface level, people would write off Helena as an Irish housewife who thought tea would save world hunger. That would be a mistake. She knew how to take care of her pack, keeping us fed and watered when we failed to take care of ourselves. She sat back, watched, and listened and would step in with a cutting comment to put someone in their place if needed. She knew when a soft word or a heavy hand was needed, and she spotted tempers rising or someone struggling from a mile off. So, while she was a fiery human woman with red hair whirling around the kitchen, she was also the glue that held the Crescent pack together.

Never underestimate an Irish housewife.

True enough, Dylan came charging through the door in black sports shorts and a tank top that needed more material, his pale cheeks flushed rose pink from the cold. Josh piled in after him in a T-shirt because he refused to be a "gym bro". Helena smiled at their arrival, the giveaway that they were her call. With Luke next in line to be alpha, they would be his closest confidants, so involving them was important. Luke might have been in denial about his future as alpha, but the rest of us weren't.

"Okay." Tom took his seat at the head of the table beside me, with Helena on his other side. "What happened tonight?"

All eyes were on us, and I looked to Luke in a silent plea for him to start.

I trusted the people at that table with my life, but my mind was still spinning and my mouth felt like cotton.

"I was at work when I got a call from Eve. She was panicked, but I could make out something about a dead body, so I jumped straight in the car," Luke explained, wetting his lips with the steaming cup of tea that had been placed in front of him. His eyes narrowed as he spotted the 'Baby Alpha' text on the mug Helena had chosen before he continued to recount his version of events up until he found me.

Then he nodded to me, his hand sneaking to my knee under the table to give a reassuring squeeze. His touch was always calming and distracting in equal measures.

"I was out with my friend, Craig. We were crossing onto the Northside when we heard screaming nearby." I forced my voice to stay stable as I recalled the events leading up to the scene that would surely haunt my dreams for months. "We found a group of girls standing around a body on the ground. The girl..."

Helena placed a mug in front of me, giving my shoulder an encouraging squeeze.

I struggled to find the words, nausea churning my stomach. "She was covered in cuts and there was blood everywhere. It looked like she had been thrown around the alleyway like a rag doll."

"Like a toy," Luke added pointedly, wincing in apology as I flinched.

His grip on my knee tightened as if he was trying to anchor me from the gruesome memories flashing through my mind's eye.

"I snuck back to the scene for a quick look before we left. It was definitely a werewolf kill." Luke dropped the final truth bomb of the story.

Liz cursed under her breath, slamming her fist on the table. Across from us, Dylan growled as his fist clenched around the dainty handle of his mug. Josh, the calmer of Luke's two best friends, shook his head in disbelief. Tom shared a tired look with his closest friend, rubbing his temple while he watched everyone absorb the news.

It was Darren who spoke up first. "Did you recognise the scent?"

"No, it's not one of ours or a Faolchúnna wolf that either of us recognise." Luke's teaspoon clinked against the side of his cup as he dropped more sugar into the tea, probably to sweeten the sour news.

Liz's lip curled back in disgust. "To kill like that, let alone in public."

"Maybe they were interrupted?" Josh offered, flipping a coaster in his hand as he mulled over the theory. "Leaving a body like that is either stupid or because they nearly got caught. The only other explanation is that it was a message."

Icy realisation flushed through my bloodstream, freezing me to the core.

"That's exactly what it was." Pure fury laced Luke's words.

Liz shook her head, leaning forwards as she drummed her bright red nails on the table. "You're saying it was Damien?"

"No, I think it was Ryan."

I shook my head. "He wouldn't—"

Luke's eyes flashed silver as he whirled on me. "The dead girl was wearing your coat. She looked just like you, that's not some bloody coincidence."

Dylan hissed in a breath, sharing a look with Josh and then both their gazes fell to me.

"You can't prove that. You even said it wasn't a scent you recognised." Tom's tone was firm but calm as he looked at each of us in turn. "We can't go throwing accusations around, especially not after—"

"Alice." Helena cut in, rushing across the kitchen towards the door that was now open a crack.

The door creaked as Alice pushed it open, dressed in a pair of purple pyjamas that matched the deep shadows under her wide eyes. She didn't speak for a moment. Helena fussed and tried to bundle her back into the hall, but Alice stood firm. Her eyes were glassy as she looked at her father.

"What's happened?" She demanded, wriggling out of her mother's grip.

Tom opened his mouth, but where he hesitated, Luke didn't.

"A werewolf has killed a human in the city." He braced his hands on the table as he met his father's smouldering stare. "It's not a scent I recognise, but we can't rule out the Faolchúnna's involvement."

Helena chewed her lip, sharing a look with her husband that made me nervous. Luke caught it too, his gaze snapping to the woman who raised him. "What?"

"It's not like Damien doesn't have blood on his hands." She sighed, moving to stand by her husband's side and placed a hand on his shoulder. "You know what he's like, love."

Tom looked up at his wife, his lips pursed in a thin line. Both Alice and Luke stared at their parents, wide-eyed. They weren't the only ones. Dylan and Josh were more serious than I'd ever seen them. Only Liz and Darren seemed to wear the same guilty expressions. They knew something we didn't.

"You're right," Tom admitted with a sigh, slumping in his chair. "They should know."

Helena moved as if to usher Alice back upstairs, but Tom reached out to stop her.

"No, everyone in this room needs to know the truth." He laced their fingers together as if she tethered him. "Including Alice. After everything, she deserves to know why she was targeted."

Luke snarled, retreating back to his seat beside me. "She was targeted because she was a hybrid. Damien and his fucked up kid have some master plan to create 'superior' werewolves. We've been through this."

Alice stared at them, dropping into one of the empty seats. I wasn't sure if it was good for her to hear this, but at the same time, she was a part of this pack, and it was important they made sure she was included. Plus, she withdrew enough as it was.

"Son, you once asked what happened when the packs split. It's something I didn't think you were ready to know, and I implore you to not act impulsively when you hear the truth." Tom's gaze was pleading. "You can't let anger fuel your decisions."

Luke nodded, his jaw ticking at the restraint. I wasn't sure if I believed in his ability to keep his cool, especially when Tom was amping up the anticipation of whatever he was going to reveal. The pack split because they disagreed on the direction they should take, or so we were told. Even Ryan insisted it was because one half wanted to move with the modern world and not keep with Damien's archaic traditions.

"You all know the pack split over twenty years ago around the same time Damien became alpha," Tom began, keeping a firm grip on his wife's hand as the words spilled from his mouth. "The reason I returned home from London was the passing of the Faolchúnna pack alpha. Luke was only a babe, and I was still in mourning. It seemed like the right thing to do. Normally, alpha succession is based on bloodline unless challenged. The previous alpha had passed away under suspicious circumstances, and his son was barely eighteen. He was a fantastic alpha, and his son was a kind man, with a good heart, but he wasn't ready to fill his father's shoes. Damien stepped up as alpha under the pretence that he was saving the pack, but he has only ever acted in his own interests."

Luke leaned forwards in his chair, watching his father with rapt attention. You could hear a pin drop in the room.

"I know I don't talk about my father much. We didn't get along. What I've never mentioned is that I also grew up alongside Damien," Tom explained, earning murmurs from everyone at the table that hadn't been around at the time. Both Liz and Darren, along with Helena, who listened with sombre expressions, clearly knew the story. "Damien was our alpha's nephew, and his father passed away when he was young. The man was an addict and got himself into debt, but Damien idolised his father and blamed our alpha for not stepping in to save his brother. He was always a strange child, it was as if he hated the world from birth. My father had a... thing with his mother for years, so we were sort of unofficial stepbrothers. Yet, we barely spent any time together because we had nothing in common, and he was always spouting toxic, negative ideals that I wanted nothing to do with. Unfortunately, he was the son my father always wanted. My father nurtured the darkness in him."

Darren snorted at that, mumbling about it being an understatement.

I frowned. The story sounded similar in parts to how Ryan was brought up. He was an asshole, but no one was born with darkness in them. Being brought up surrounded by messed up shit is bound to take its toll though.

"The alpha's death wasn't an accident, it was murder. Damien was responsible, heavily influenced and encouraged by my father." Guilt laced Tom's words as if his father's deeds were his fault. Though, his shoulders sagged as the story went on, as if the truth lifted a weight off him. "I worked with the alpha's daughter to uncover the truth. Darren and Helena helped too, but we weren't quick enough. Damien knew the pack would never accept him so long as the alpha's son lived on, so he murdered his competition and orchestrated the death to seem like suicide."

A deep growl rumbled from Luke's chest, the pressure grip on the table warping the wooden edges. "And you let him get away with it?"

Tom's gaze whipped to his son and slammed his fist on the table, anger flashing in his eyes at the accusation. "No, we gathered proof, and I almost died at Damien's hands when we exposed him. A witch intervened before one of us killed the other."

Alice jumped and swallowed hard, her jaw ticking as a

mixture of sadness and anger washed over her face. Luke bowed his head in submission, his lips thinning.

"What happened then?" My mind whirled with all the information.

Tom shrugged. "We gave them a choice."

"When they were fighting, Tom's magic recognised him as an alpha, so every wolf had a choice," Liz piped up, her ruby-red lips curled back in distaste. "Leave and form a new pack with Tom or stay with the Faolchúnna pack and be led by that psychopath. Not everyone chose right."

"More stayed than left," Darren spat, his brow creasing at the memory.

Luke scowled, a storm brewing in his eyes. "Why the fuck would anyone stay?"

"Fear." Helena held her chin high, still standing by her husband's side as her thumb brushed back and forth on his shoulder, a small sign of her unwavering support. Tom had told me before that she was part of the reason he left, because she helped him see a future outside of the old world. "Fear of the unknown. It was unheard of for a pack to break apart like that, or for a wolf to survive murdering their alpha. Not everyone wants to change. Not everyone can see the path to change. More left over the following years, but Damien held on to quite a few."

I shook my head, massaging my temples with my finger and thumb. "Why did no one mention this when I was there? Especially those who weren't around at the time. Surely Fiona would've thought to tell me?"

"The witch that interrupted wasn't exactly neutral in all of this. Between her powers and some of the elder vampires Damien was cosying up to, I've no doubt that he altered the memories of any family that was on the fence," Tom mused, taking a long sip of his cold coffee. "Anyone strongly opposed to Damien would have posed a threat, but you have to realise, not everyone did oppose him. There were many who hated change and refused to integrate with humans. They liked the old way and had archaic beliefs. Those who are unsure or weak in their morals are easily manipulated."

I thought back to how Ryan mentioned that the manor had once been packed with wolves. It did seem like the pack had been decimated over the years, though they were still at least double the Crescents. Then again, would half the younger generations be there if they knew the truth? I needed to tell Fiona.

"You can't tell anyone this."

The alpha's blue eyes were fixed on me, his mouth downturned, and his expression filled with sympathy.

"I know you want to warn the few who became your friends, but if they tried to leave now, it would only rile Damien up and give him an excuse to strike." Tom's gaze travelled over those of us at the table liable to spill the news. "We will uncover what has been happening with the hybrid disappearances, but until we are ready to make a move, this stays between us. The truth doesn't always set someone free, sometimes it costs them their life."

"Wait."

I leaned across the passenger seat, my fingers closing around Eve's wrist as she climbed out of the car in a desperate last attempt to convince her to come back to the house. Letting her out of my sight didn't feel right after tonight.

We were both still reeling from everything, especially my dad's revelations. Everything was much more complicated than I could have ever imagined. An intense anger burned in me that wanted to storm into the Faolchúnna pack territory and kill those responsible for kidnapping hybrids, along with Damien for his sick actions and bloodstained hands. At the same time, I understood my father's reluctance. I would never forgive myself if I endangered any innocents in all of this. No doubt, if we told half the pack members who hadn't been around for Damien's bloody past, they would renounce him immediately, and that wouldn't end well for anyone. But I couldn't shake the image of Eve's coat on the dead girl. She didn't believe she was being targeted, but I couldn't shake the feeling of unease.

"Luke," Eve sighed, pausing with one leg out the door and her free arm wrapped around the headrest to keep her balance.

Her cheeks were still stained with mascara from all the tears that she had shed. "It's been a long night, I just want my bed."

"And I want you to be safe."

I'd spent a lot of the car ride trying to convince Eve of my theory, but she was having none of it. Most of the time, she was spaced out and staring at the streetlights flickering past. I wasn't getting anywhere with her.

Eve perched on the edge of the seat and twisted to look at me, placing her hand over mine to lace our fingers together and give my hand a gentle squeeze, before removing my grip on her arm. "I will be safe *in my bed*."

A lesser man would have made a joke there. Not gonna lie, it crossed my mind. I'd sleep on the damn floor for a month straight if it meant she was safe.

I wasn't going to force her though, so I sank back against the driver's seat and watched as she walked along the sidewalk to the front door of her apartment complex. When she hovered outside for a few moments, I presumed she was fiddling with the ridiculous wolf teddy on the keyring I'd bought her as a move-in gift. But her body language was all wrong. When I cast my senses out to pick up what Eve was muttering, something I wouldn't normally do to respect her privacy, my stomach sank.

"No, no, no," she whispered, her voice cracking. "This can't be happening."

Within seconds, I was out of the car and striding towards her.

"Eve?" I reached out to grasp her shoulder as I caught up. "What's wrong?"

She stood in front of the door of the apartment complex, a modern door with frosted glass and a strong metal frame that now had a deep gauge across the lock, a large crack in the glass radiating from the point of damage.

She turned to look up at me, her eyelashes glistening with tears, and her warm breath creating white wisps of vapour in the cool night air. "The lock, it's broken and I—"

Every inch of my body was rigid as I wrapped an arm around Eve's chest and pulled her flush against me. "It's okay, I'm here."

I was acting on pure instinct, my vision sharp and my ears picking up everything from a siren in the distance to the rustle of an empty beer can rolling into the side of a trash can down the street. I reached out with my free hand to examine the damaged lock and door handle. The metal had warped and contorted on impact, the lock mechanism shattered.

The lock wasn't the only thing that had been vandalised. Even the keypad and buzzer for each apartment was trashed, as if someone had pulled the interface clean off. Exposed wires poking out of a black bracket in the top right of the door were the only remnants of the security camera that should have been there. A quick glance behind us confirmed that the cameras of the small café and newsagents across the road had also been destroyed.

Behind the heavy grade door there were voices and blurred shapes, two blue and one white. Eve clutched onto my forearm, her nails digging into my shirt. Her heart hammered in her chest as I brushed my fingers across the door handle and brought them to my nose, inhaling deeply.

Exactly what I'd feared.

The way Eve stiffened in my arms told me she smelled it too.

A mix of familiar scents from others living in the building, a handful of foreign ones, and one distinct scent that stood out. *Werewolf.*

Not just any werewolf, the one from the attack.

"Luke..." Eve cautioned, her grip on my arm tightening like a vice as I tucked her into my side rather than pushing her behind me. I'd rather my back be exposed than risk her in any of this. I wasn't leaving her outside either.

I placed my finger to my lips in a silent signal before planting my foot against the door frame and shoving hard, some of the loose cracked glass losing its fight and falling to the ground shattering as the door swung inwards to reveal two Gardaí, one of which I recognised from the murder scene earlier, arguing with a small old lady that was half their size and twice as loud.

"I'm telling you; he was tall with brown hair—looked like some kind of Edward Cullen fella."

The old woman I recognised as Eve's nosy neighbour stood across from two Gardaí who looked less than impressed. She brandished her walking stick like a weapon, her white hair that matched her deathly pale complexion wrapped in curlers completed the batty image. "He was in the hall when I came out."

"Agnes," Eve breathed, rushing forwards to the woman's side. "Are you alright?"

The old woman greeted Eve with a brief smile and a pat of recognition on the arm before continuing her tirade with the Gardaí. As if she could smell blood, she focused on the younger of the two who scribbled erratically in his notepad.

If there was one thing that got her out of fight-or-flight mode, it was saving someone else. I'd seen Eve do it with Alice, yet I had caught her many times since describing herself as a coward. I added this to the bank of counter arguments. The girl was blind to her own strength thanks to that gobshite making her feel like some wilting wallflower, nourishing her intrusive thoughts, and reinforcing her misbeliefs. She wasn't a flower, she was a wolf through and through.

"He had crazy eyes, you know?" Agnes continued, linking arms with Eve to hold her balance while whacking the poor beat cop around the shins with her cane. "Silver. And he was American."

The poor Garda nodded, his mouth set in a grim line as he added to his notes. Meanwhile, the other one disappeared upstairs for all of a minute before returning after a not so thorough search.

Glass cracked beneath my feet as I looked around the corridor for damage, and the nosy neighbour gave her own squeaky rendition of what I can only guess was supposed to be a wolf whistle.

"I see you've brought back some eye candy," Agnes purred, immediately lightening the tension in her own unique way. "And what about the other charmers that helped you move in?"

Eve bit her lip, hiding a smile as our eyes met.

Thankfully, Agnes was laying into the poor Garda again seconds later, saving us from an inquisition.

Still on high alert, I continued looking for clues, sniffing out anywhere the werewolf had touched. Aside from more deep claw marks gauging the metal of the elevator buttons and a smashed in security camera that was previously not working, something I'd complained to the maintenance company, there were no more signs of damage.

"I said *silver*." Agnes snapped her cane out once more and narrowly missed her target as the Garda leaped back. "I'm not fecking colour blind."

The second Garda, the one from the crime scene earlier, rolled his eyes. His notebook remained shut the entire time. "We'll have to corroborate your story with the security guard."

Eve blanched. "Someone was hurt?"

"Not at all, dear. He was out cold when I chased the intruder out of here. He came around after a slap, but he was mumbling all sorts of nonsense about dogs. He was clearly in shock, but he'll be fine." Agnes gave Eve's hand a reassuring pat before pointing a wrinkled finger at the two Gardaí. "It's my statement ye should listen to, not some security guard that was off his tits on God knows what."

The two officers shook their heads and shared a look of exasperation.

Eve blinked slowly, looking just as confused.

"So, there's no damage upstairs," the older Garda said, brandishing his camera. "We've taken pictures of the front entrance and the elevators. Is there anything else? We'll contact the security company later today, but I doubt they'll tell us much."

"Wasting your time not listening to me. Tall, American

accent, tanned like he came from the beaches. I told ye, he didn't make it far upstairs." Agnes scolded them, tapping her cane on the tiled floor in impatience, before shooting Eve a wry smile and adding, "The moment I came out, the bastard muttered something and then bolted. He knew it was a fool's errand trying to take me on."

The younger Garda snorted and then gulped hard when Agnes' narrowed gaze snapped back to him. "We've taken note of that, ma'am."

"Sure you have."

With that, Agnes turned her back on the two Gardaí in dismissal and hobbled towards the stairs. Eve glanced back at me with a 'What the fuck do I do?' expression, the old lady using her as a human crutch as they began their ascent.

Not wanting to leave her alone for long until I'd completely cleared the building, I hung back for a moment to nab a moment with the Gardaí.

"Sorry lads, I was just wondering, what actually happened?" I kept my voice low so as not to insure the wrath of Agnes and her trusty cane.

The officer that had also attended the murder scene shrugged, whipping out a cigarette and lighting it just as he walked out the door, leaving a trail of glass in his wake. He'd clearly seen enough for one night.

I stepped into the path of the younger guy, my expression a picture of genuine concern as I cornered the weaker of the two for information. "Please? I just want to make sure it's safe."

"There's nothing much to tell you. The old lady rang us saying someone had tried to break in." He glanced nervously towards the doorway after his colleague as the door swung shut. "She swore he had no weapons, but you saw the door yourself. Looks more like someone wanting payback for a deal that went wrong than a robbery. So long as your girlfriend has her nose clean, she'll be grand."

I didn't correct him, growing antsy as Eve and Agnes

rounded the corner onto the first floor. I was more concerned with scouting her apartment than arguing with the officer about why he should maybe have taken Agnes more seriously, even if she was crazy.

"You don't think it's related to the murder earlier?"

"How do you know about that?" His bushy eyebrows knitted together.

"Saw it online," I blurted, reaching out to shake his hand before nudging him towards the door. "Thanks man, you better get going. Sorry for keeping you."

He nodded, following his colleague out onto the street to begin discussing Agnes. She left a lasting impression on everyone she met. Not always in the best impression, but she was definitely unforgettable. I didn't wait around, turning and taking the stairs two at a time.

I could have told the Gardaí that Eve was the one who found the body, but sometimes it was better if humans were left in the dark. No doubt the wolf in question would maul any poor, unfortunate officer who happened to solve a mystery that extended beyond their part of the world.

I sprinted past them with a brief wave, not stopping until I reached Eve's floor. The door to Agnes' room was open, but the stranger's scent stopped a few feet away from the door to Eve's apartment, which was untouched. I used my spare key to go inside and quickly scout the apartment, but everything was fine. Once I was content, I started back down the stairs.

By the time I bumped into them, Eve was helping her neighbour onto the third floor.

"How on earth is the milk man going to get to me now?" Agnes grumbled, digging the tip of her cane into the worn carpet as she hauled herself up another step. "That lazy sod would never use the stairs."

I chuckled despite myself, dropping to kneel before Agnes with my hand extended. "Would you care for a lift, m'lady?"

"I've always said, don't take a ride on anything that doesn't get your engine purring." Agnes looked me over with a critical eye, one drawn-on eyebrow in a shade ten times too dark, quirked up into her hairline.

Eve shook her head, blood rushing to her cheeks as she fought back laughter. Despite the darkness of the evening, Agnes had helped Eve back out of her shell.

It took every ounce of self-control to school my expression as I hoisted Agnes' frail body into my arms bridal style. She practically tossed her cane at Eve and wasted no time in snaking her thin arms around my neck, taking liberties with my hair. When she murmured something about the smell of my sweat, I had to zone out the utter filth and madness coming out of her mouth as we continued up the winding stairs, focusing instead on the sweet sound of Eve's giggles all the way to the ninth floor.

More because I was afraid of her wrath than a gentleman, I only put Agnes down once I'd carried her over the threshold. A move I regretted as she planted a wet kiss on the corner of my lips. Eve was smarter and lingered by the doorway to her apartment, not so subtly examining it for damage.

"Thank you for the lift." Agnes cackled to herself as she stepped back further into a room that looked more like a bachelor pad than an old woman's home.

I saluted her, retreating back into the safety of the corridor. "No problem at all."

Before I could leave, her bony fingers latched onto my wrist. The playful glint in her eyes had been replaced with a cold, harsh seriousness to match her tone. "Make sure you don't let her out of your sight."

"I won't." I swallowed hard at the intensity of her stare, gently prying her fingers from my arm one digit at a time. "She's safe with me."

Eve was still lingering outside her apartment door, toying with the keychain, only looking up as I approached.

"You know I'm sleeping here tonight, right?"

"Luke—"

"Either you let me stay over to make sure you're safe, or I will throw you over my shoulder and drag you back to mine. Or worse, I'll tell Agnes." I cut her off before she could argue.

I was all for her independence, but not if it involved her being in danger.

The corners of her lips twitched, and I swear, the look she gave me made me wonder if she would have actually preferred the first option, before clicking the lock open with a sigh.

"Fine, but you're on the couch."

CHAPTER 11

It was weird. This whole thing should have felt weird.

Seeing him snoozing on the couch, *my* couch, should have felt strange. He was still fast asleep when I snuck into the kitchen for a glass of water. The way he sprawled out with one muscular arm thrown over his eyes to block the early morning sunlight filtering through the curtains should have looked out of place. He should have been at home with his family and his sister. Not here, minding me. But no matter what I tried, my brain couldn't get the image of how good he looked in my apartment out of my head.

There was only one shower in the apartment, so I went into the living room to offer him the first shower, but he was nowhere to be seen. A small torn piece of a takeaway menu lay on top of a carefully folded pile of blankets. It was a note from him saying he'd popped out for coffee. Complete with a smiley face that had me grinning like a lovesick teenager.

I shook my head, willing my thoughts to stop spiralling about the hot werewolf that had slept over, and flicked on the shower in my ensuite. Cool water made me snatch my hand back and hiss, perching my bare ass against the water basin while I waited for the water to heat.

When he knew there was a break in, the way he'd pulled me against his chest like something precious that should be protected. Then the shared looks and smiles as we tried not to laugh at Agnes' crazy behaviour with the police. He even sped upstairs to check it was safe before carrying the crazy old lady upstairs—no doubt fulfilling some lifelong fantasy there. And then telling me he was staying with no room for argument.

I mean, I would have argued on principle. I would be lying if I said having him around didn't make me feel safe, but it was more than that. Luke's presence didn't just make me feel safe, he made me happy. Somehow, even after one of the darkest, most messed up nights, he had made me feel okay.

Agnes had been a distraction, but he knew when we got into the apartment, the whole night came flooding back. And that's the image I couldn't get out of my head, the one of him holding me on the couch and wrapping me in a blanket. Luke was an idiot for thinking he wouldn't cut it as an alpha.

I stepped under the warm spray of the shower, relishing the sensation as it hit my tense shoulders and undid just a small piece of the damage caused by yesterday's events. If it wasn't for Luke's presence in the apartment, I wouldn't have slept at all.

Adrenaline pumped through my veins still, my mind spinning. Damien was a psychopath. His son, no doubt, was on the same path after that upbringing. Was he a murderer too? Luke seemed to think he had a hand in that girl's death. Did it freak me out that she was wearing my coat? Yes. Yes. But that didn't mean I was the target, despite Luke's insistence.

Luke insisted that I was the target, but he just wanted to presume the worst. I didn't exactly shop in posh boutiques. His broody act was endearing until he predicted some murderous lunatic had it out for me.

I was safe. I was home and safe. How could I not be safe with Luke as my personal guard dog?

The shower couldn't wash away the memories of last night, but at least it would go some way to reduce the tension in my body. This much stress couldn't be good for me, hybrid werewolf or not. As if my subconscious was on the same train of thought, my mind wandered back to Luke. He knew when to quit warning me about the stress of my life and focus on keeping me in the present instead. Part of me cringed at how I'd snotted all over him while crying, but the way he looked at me and wiped away my tears made the embarrassment fade to something else.

There was something between us—that was undeniable. But I couldn't act on it.

My core tightened, and I rubbed my thighs together for friction.

The Crescents were my new pack, my home. I couldn't risk it all over a guy. Even if he did have chocolate-brown eyes that I wanted to get lost in, and a small glimpse of his abs this morning had been a nice reminder of that night at the beach...

I tried to focus on cleaning myself and the way the warm water rushed over me. My brain was sabotaging me, thinking back to when Luke had taught me to fight, and I cursed myself for not dropping my gaze lower that time we'd shifted together.

No Eve. Now is not the time for that.

Or was it? I'd gone without sex for a while. That one time at the Faolchúnna manor was months ago—not that I got off. And before that, well, it had been sporadic. Plus, my vibrator had always hit the spot better than Ryan anyway. Kate had always joked that they would put men out of business someday. I'd lost everything when I left Ryan, and I could hardly spend the Crescent alpha's money on a vibrator. Especially when I would be fantasising over his son while using it. That was fifty shades of wrong.

"Oh for fuck's sake, fine," I muttered to myself, gliding my hand down my stomach and trailing my fingers lower.

I couldn't deny that the wetness between my thighs had little to do with my shower and everything to do with the image of Luke shirtless walking around the house every morning. One of the biggest things I'd missed since moving out, though I'd tried to deny it. I leaned back against the shower wall and spread my legs, a small gasp slipping from my lips at the cold tiles against my skin. Tracing slow circles around my clit, I increased the pressure until I bit back a moan. I told myself it was harmless as I imagined it was Luke, teasing that sensitive spot until I was panting.

Giving myself fully to the fantasy, I closed my eyes and slid one finger inside my pussy. God, I wished it was him in the shower. The thought of him pinning me there as the water washed over us only added to the pleasure as I pumped my finger in and out.

I added another finger and then curled them, my fingertips pressing against that sweet spot inside each time I slid them deeper inside. In my mind, it was Luke's hand between my leg and his piercing eyes staring down at me as he fucked my pussy with his hand while I was at his mercy. But I couldn't stop there, I wanted to feel what it was like to have him take charge of my body completely. I wanted him to make me come all over his hand, then pin me against the shower wall as he filled me up with his dick and fucked me until we were both shaking.

My free hand had found my breasts, cupping and kneading the sensitive flesh as I moaned and ground my hips against my hand as the pressure built. I let my head fall back with a moan and pinched my nipple between my finger and thumb, immersed in the fantasy of it being Luke's mouth torturing me as I rode my hand wishing it was his dick making my pussy pulse. I was lost to the dirty picture my mind was painting, breathless and my legs trembling as the waves of ecstasy built. I bucked my hips, fucking my hand, pressing my thumb against my throbbing clit as I reached the peak and tumbled into pure bliss with the image of Luke slamming his hard dick into me painted in my mind.

My chest heaved as I came down from the high and opened my eyes, exhaling a long breath as all of the tension seeped from my body.

Fuck, okay. I needed that.

I waited until my legs steadied, enjoying the warmth of the

shower as I soaped down. The fluffy towel I wrapped myself in once I finally decided to step out of the hot water and brave the cold air was the perfect icing on an enjoyable morning. The guy who owned the apartment had very fancy taste. Yes, last night might have been a thing of nightmares, but at least I felt ready to face the world.

Feeling too lazy or high on endorphins, I towel dried my hair and would deal with it after breakfast. My stomach rumbled in agreement as I towelled off.

My phone buzzed where it was balanced on the wash basin counter. The shot of happiness I got from seeing Craig's name flash up on the screen was short-lived, quickly followed by a wave of guilt. That werewolf murder had put things in perspective. *Was it safe for him to be around me?*

"One day at a time." I made a silent vow to keep him out of this side of things and to distance myself in a safe way if it came to it.

It took a few tries to unlock the phone with my wet fingerprint before the screen flared to life. Craig was just checking in to see that I was okay. Nothing bad, just normal friend stuff. I breathed out a sigh of relief and shot a quick reply promising to call him later that day. The time in the top corner of the screen told me I'd been in the shower for about twenty minutes.

Shit. What if Luke heard me?

There was a coffee shop across the road. Yes, it was popular and had queues, but how long did it take someone to get a coffee? Besides, the shower was on. That would have hidden any noise, right? I bolted out of the ensuite into my bedroom and threw on underwear, a pair of grey tracksuit bottoms, and a plain black T-shirt, casting my senses out to see if Luke was back.

The apartment was silent except for my hammering heart.

Ok, it's fine. He might have gone to get a breakfast roll or something.

"It's all good," I told myself, grabbing a pair of socks from the drawers and putting them on while trying to calm myself down.

It took a mini pep talk for me to brave leaving my bedroom. I opened the door a crack just as the sound of a cupboard closing came from the kitchen.

"Breakfast?"

I froze.

Luke's voice carried down the hall, and I swear, the breath left my lungs. "It's like one pm though. So, brunch?"

"Sure." The word came out as a squeak an octave higher than my normal voice. I coughed, only making myself sound weirder. "Breakfast is good."

I stood outside my bedroom in full scale panic mode, my heartbeat thundering in my ears. How had I not heard the door? How did he even get back in without ringing the buzzer? Unless he sweet-talked Agnes. Damn that woman. Any dopamine I'd earned from my little shower session had well and truly evaporated.

Put your big girl pants on. You had the shower running, he didn't hear. Everything is fine.

Luke popped his head around the corner, and I full on squealed like a mouse.

He chuckled, dressed in his navy tracksuit bottoms from the night before and shirtless. Because werewolves were hot. Ran hot. *Ran* hot.

Pull your shit together woman.

"Are you coming, or do you want breakfast in bed?" He asked with a smirk, amusement dancing in his eyes. He had a strawberry in his hand, and the way he bit into the fruit was pornographic. "I'm starving."

He knows. Fuck. He knows.

As if reading my thoughts, he gave me the last hint I needed.

"These pancakes smell pretty fucking good." He licked his fingers clean at a torturous pace before throwing me a wink, the final nail in my coffin, and sauntering back into the kitchen.

Heat flooded my body, and my cheeks burned red. All I could do was wonder how much he had heard and thank the stars that I hadn't moaned his name at any point, so he would never know that it was him I imagined the whole time.

I followed him into the kitchen, forcing one foot in front of the next while I tried to calm my racing heart. There was no hiding my red cheeks, but I took some deep breaths, tried to channel my old friend's man-eater ways, and held my chin high. This was my apartment. He was a guest. I had every right to get off in my shower.

I am a strong independent woman who doesn't need a m—

Luke was bent over the kitchen counter, his chin perched on his hands while he watched me with a mischievous grin. There were two plates in front of him stacked high with pancakes from the café nearby, along with two coffee cups. Mine had a winky face on it.

I looked between him and the pancakes before my gaze snagged on the can of whipped cream beside him, which only made his grin widen.

My cheeks heated.

"Sit down and get some food into you." His tone was playful, but there was an undercurrent of alpha in it that made me want to do what I was told. "Last night was a lot. You need something to keep you going."

I grabbed my coffee cup and a plate, taking them over to the couch in some small act of defiance as I tried to get some sense of control back. Still flustered as hell, I almost dropped my fork as I sat down and perched the plate on my knee. I shot Luke a dirty look, refusing to acknowledge the game he was playing. Despite my embarrassment, my stomach rumbled like crazy, so I set about stuffing my face with pancakes to avoid having to talk about the elephant in the room.

I wasn't going to admit to it. Who was to say that I wasn't just watching some random tv show in the shower? Unlikely, but I was holding onto any theory I could find that would leave me with a shred of dignity.

The tension in the room only thickened as Luke sat opposite

me and scarfed his pancakes down in record time, watching me with every bite.

I was busy staring at my plate, wondering how I was going to talk my way out of this one, when Luke jumped to his feet.

"I'm gonna grab a shower, if that's okay?" He kept his expression neutral but the hunger in his eyes gave him away.

Before I could answer, he flounced off down the hall.

I leaped to my feet, ready to run after him screaming for him to stop, but then I realised that would make me look.

Then the door to my bedroom shut and all I could do was wonder what he was doing in the shower, and if he was thinking of me too.

CHAPTER 12
LUKE

"Why was it so imperative that we came here this evening?"

I followed Eve up the winding staircase to the second level of the Dark Night. One of my steps was equal to two of hers, so I slowed my pace to enjoy the view.

She shrugged, flashing me a grin over her shoulder. "I just thought you'd like to spend the evening sitting on something that didn't double as your bed."

"You're a shit liar." I shook my head as a smile tugged at my own lips.

"Eve!" Jonas popped up from behind the bar, appearing beside us in the blink of an eye with not hair out of place.

She gave him a hug, something that had me doing a double take as he returned the warm gesture. Jonas was an old friend with an eccentric personality and tongue that could cut like a knife, or make him your biggest hype man, depending on the day and situation.

"Do I get one?" I opened my arms and looked at Jonas expectantly.

Eve giggled, and Jonas threw his arms around me with a dramatic sigh.

"You know, if you missed me, all you had to do was say," he purred, grazing his fangs along my neck, and then danced away with his damn vampire speed before I could grab hold of him.

Eve's laughter stopped, her cheeks flushed as she cleared her throat.

"Dick." I laughed, scratching my neck where his fangs had left it all tingly.

Plenty of paranormals rolled with vampires because of their venom. Apparently, it was one of the most potent aphrodisiacs and made sex amazing. However, it was lethal to werewolves. Fortunately, the thing that got my blood pumping lately wasn't undead.

The door behind the bar swung back and forth as Jonas disappeared out into one of their back rooms, before re-emerging as a blur and appearing in front of Eve with an apron in his hand and a silver name badge that said 'Little Pup'.

Her mouth dropped open, and I burst into a fit of laughter. Jonas was equally amused with his little joke.

Eve's gaze whipped to me as she glared daggers my way. "It's not funny."

I picked up the name tag, turning it over in my hand to where it was engraved with her name in calligraphy like the rest of the staff. The pin was on the same side as the fake name, but it was a cute touch all the same.

She growled something in the most wolf-like way, taking the apron off Jonas with a scowl. "Besides this, I presume I don't have to dress all fancy?"

Behind him, other staff milled about in black jeans and matching T-shirts. Only Jonas and his boss swanned around in fancy suits, along with a few other fashion-conscious baristas.

"I mean, I think Luke would appreciate you in–"

The words died on his tongue as he met my scorching gaze.

"Black clothes will do." Jonas took a pointed step out of my reach. "So, are you guys hanging around for a drink or...?"

Eve answered before I could. "Yeah, we'll stay for one or two."

Jonas motioned us over to a table by the large bay windows spanning the far wall of the café. "What can I get you?"

He flipped out his notepad even though it wasn't needed. He had a sharp brain and flawless recall thanks to his vampire gifts. I'd a theory that it was his very own Gossip Girl bible. There was no need for the ruse, no humans could set foot in the Dark Night. The exterior was warded, and the entrance hidden. Even if someone decided to bring a human friend along, an alarm would alert the owners immediately. It was for their safety, not ours.

Eve glanced at me from under her lashes, toying with a bear mat in her hand. "Maybe a vodka and coke?"

"Sérieusement?" Jonas looked like he'd been stabbed, his ebony curls falling forwards as he clutched his chest.

She rolled her eyes, not the least bit perturbed when a fang peeked out between his lips, or his eyes shifted from swirling gold to red. Eve had come a long way in a short time.

He looked at me with wide eyes, and I just shrugged, taking the seat opposite Eve. "The lady gets what she wants."

Jonas snorted, as did Eve, and we all broke a smile.

He was a food and drink snob thanks to growing up in France. Snob is the wrong word. He was a well-travelled man with great tastes, but us Irish liked the basics and weren't adventurous. Hence why we didn't go around building empires, we just sat tight and did our own thing.

He dismissed Eve with a sigh. "Whiskey?"

"With ginger, please." I smiled sweetly and fluttered my eyelashes in a way that had Eve laughing and Jonas looking like he wanted to smack me with his notepad.

He spun away with a flourish towards the counters lining the adjacent wall where Alec, a younger vampire, was cleaning out one of the coffee machines.

I sat back in my chair and surveyed the room. There were enough patrons to test out her senses.

"We're going to play a game."

Eve followed my gaze, her brow furrowing in confusion.

I gestured to the café seating area. "I want you to try to scent the different paranormal species around us."

A small group of young, rowdy vampires had taken up residence in the far corner. They looked like they'd partied the daylight hours away and intended to continue into the night. A mix of Fae and sirens weaved their way to and from the counter, and a harpy had positioned himself in an armchair beside the bay window to glean the last rays of the setting sun while getting his caffeine fix.

She cocked her head to one side, clearly already trying to figure them out despite the coy smile playing on her lips. "What do I get if I win?"

I shrugged. "A favour?"

"What kind of favour?"

"One you can use whenever you want for whatever you want."

Before she could fixate on the terms of the deal again, Alec came over with our drinks on a tray. He was new, younger than Jonas by a handful of years, but definitely more in terms of his vampire lifespan. The giveaway was in his movements. He was smooth, but older vampires had a certain air about them. Where he was unnaturally still, they had an ethereal grace.

Jonas hadn't given me the full story—he liked to gossip, but a vampire's origin story was always personal—just that Alec was a new vampire still adjusting that Darius had taken in. He was tall and broad, with cropped jet-black hair. Unlike Jonas' deep brown skin, Alec was deathly pale. He was the stereotypical vampire complete with the textbook golden eyes. Of course, he looked like he stepped out of the pages of some rock magazine. No doubt he'd have had tattoos if the vampire transition process hadn't destroyed them.

He held up Eve's drink first. "Vodka and coke?"

"Me, please," she said with a sheepish smile as she dropped the disintegrated pieces of beer mat onto the table.

Eve didn't seem to notice his looks, but the wolf side of me was feeling like having a pissing match with the poor guy.

"Whiskey for you, sir." Alec placed the glass of pale amber liquid down in front of me, eyeing me nervously.

He could sense my heart rate increasing, so I willed my temper to cool down and flashed him what I hoped was a friendly smile. Though by the way his fangs peeked out as he nodded and turned away, I must have let my canines slip.

"Weird." Eve took a sip of her drink as she watched a gorgeous blonde dressed in a light blue dress with a plunging neckline that sparkled under the lights. "I thought they'd smell like fish."

I snorted, choking on my drink and slammed the glass down on the table.

"What? I think she's a siren. It would make sense." She dropped her voice, sinking into the chair, probably for fear that the girl would have overheard her.

I grabbed a napkin to mop up the whiskey I'd spilled, chuckling as the siren glanced our way. "You are correct, but no, they do not smell like fish."

"Well I know that *now*," she growled, knocking back a mouthful of her drink as if it might wash away her embarrassment. "She smells like salt and... fresh air. I don't know, like the beach really."

She went around the room then, amusing and impressing me in equal measure with her guesses. Behind Eve, glimpses of the sun's receding rays warmed the pink skies with their glow as it set over the skyline of Dublin City, enjoying the way the light bounced off her brunette waves.

My gut instinct set off alarm bells as something caught the corner of my eye. My attention shifted to the top of the stairs just as the conversations around us died, though the steady beat of the music continued like a warning drum. Around us, everyone froze like statues as a woman stepped into view. She was tall with long blonde hair that fell in waves to her waist, dressed in leather pants and a tight tank top, complete with a cropped jacket which exposed a dagger hanging in her belt, the unsheathed gap glinting silver. She had pixie-like features and the face of a woman in her mid-twenties, but those cold, hard eyes belonged to a witch proficient in glamour spells. The overwhelming stench of magic made bile rise in my throat.

Larissa. She was technically a Royal, a descendent of one of the prestigious Irish bloodlines. But rumour had it, her family had shunned her. Though they would never risk doing so publicly. She had a nasty reputation, notorious for her psychotic behaviour and a penchant for torture.

She walked towards the bar and Alec practically danced on the spot. Jonas stepped out in front of her, his shoulders squared. Her lips twisted into a nasty smirk. "Get out of my way Jonas, I have business to attend to."

"You have no business here."

Between the adrenaline charging the room and the hearts hammering, the magic levels were rising, and everyone was coiled and ready to fight.

The witch tilted her head to the side, tracing Jonas' cheek with her finger and licking her lips. "I'll deal with you later, sweetie." She prodded him sharply in the chest. Her hand moving to the hilt of her dagger in warning as she stepped around Alec's hulking figure.

The witches were at the top of the food chain, in our world anyway. The Fae had their own realms, so they stayed out of it. Vampires and werewolves couldn't band together enough to overthrow them, with similar issues preventing any other factions forming between the different races. They had a monopoly, but they kept the peace. They kept our world hidden from humans and enforced the biggest rule of all, do not expose our kind to humans.

It was allowed on a smaller scale, where people like my father fell in love. But in cases of mass exposure, or the common case where humans went mad when they found out, the witches cleaned up. They doled out punishments and basically did whatever the fuck they wanted. Last I'd heard Larissa had been sent to America to stay out of trouble, what was she doing back in Ireland?

With each step she took, her heels clicked against the floor. The music had dimmed in the background, the club level having fallen unnaturally silent.

"Get everyone out, now." Larissa's bright amethyst eyes were fixed firmly on me and Eve as she gestured to the rest of the room as if the crowd gathered were contagious. "Only the wolves stay."

The hair on the back of my neck rose as my mind raced through all possible scenarios of why she wanted to talk to us. She could have cornered us anywhere, but making a show of emptying the Dark Night did not bode well. Only Jonas and Alec lingered in the doorway, glancing nervously in our direction. Jonas caught my eye and gave me a subtle nod that he was ready if needed.

Eve's eyes flashed silver, her wolf side sensing the danger. Unfortunately, mind links didn't work when we weren't in our wolf form, and the last thing I wanted her to do was shift, so I took her hand and squeezed, trying to communicate for her to stay quiet and not draw attention to us. Being able to shift outside of a full moon as a hybrid had its perks, but doing so would be seen as an act of aggression towards Larissa, and it would end in a blood bath because I'd kill the old hag if she dared lay a finger on Eve.

"We'll be just outside," Jonas promised, stepping outside the door with Alec.

The witch didn't even bother to check the room was empty. She stopped in front of us, one hand on her waist as she jutted her hip out.

"Do you mind if I join you?" She gestured to the empty chair at our table. With no intention of waiting for an answer, she pulled the chair out and perched herself on the edge. "Thanks."

A low growl ripped from my throat, my grip on the table putting dents in the wood. "What do you want, Larissa?"

"I have a message." Larissa flicked her wrist and pointed in my direction with black manicured talons as a superior smirk played on her lips. "For the mutt."

"The name is Eve, actually," she snapped, sitting up and straightening her shoulders as she looked Larissa dead in the eye.

I couldn't stop the swell of pride at the way she stood up to the witch. At the same time, a ripple of magic ran through muscles in my back as my wolf side stirred. I couldn't shift outside of the full moon, but I still wanted to cut the bitch for speaking about Eve like that.

"Eve, right." She repeated the name like it tasted dirty on her tongue, crossing her legs and reaching into her jacket pocket. "I have something for you."

We both tensed as she rummaged around and produced a small, folded piece of paper. She slid it across the table to Eve.

On instinct, I reached for it, but Larissa lashed out first and delivered a stinging slap to my hand. I jerked back with a snarl.

"It's not for you." Larissa seemed completely unperturbed by the murderous look on my face as she pushed the note closer to Eve.

Eve waited for the witch to retract her hand before cautiously picking up the note, holding it at arm's length as if it might explode in her face. Larissa watched with rapt amusement sparkling in her lilac eyes, like a cat eyeing their prey.

When the note didn't self-combust, Eve slowly unfolded it and read aloud as she scanned the contents. All blood drained from her face.

Before I could lunge across the table and see the message for myself, Larissa snapped her fingers and the paper went up in flames. Eve yelped and dropped it, the note turning to ash as it flowed onto the table surface.

"What did it say?" I balled my hands into fists so tight my

nails bit into my palm as Larissa laughed, a high-pitched cackle that set my nerves on edge.

Her throat bobbed as she swallowed.

"Eve, what did the note say?"

Though everyone had left the room, none of this conversation was in private, and the witch was loving every minute of her little performance. Where I was ready to strangle Larissa, she was eyeing us up like her own personal show.

Eve shook her head, her eyes brimming with tears when she finally met mine. "You'll always be mine. Love... Ryan."

Larissa cackled again, the shrill noise sending me over the edge. I leaped to my feet, knocking into the table and sending the drinks flying in the process. But I didn't care that the psycho witch had whiskey all over her clothes. I didn't care when Jonas and Alec burst back into the room. I couldn't have given two fucks about whatever vitriol Larissa spewed as she stormed out.

All I cared about was that bastard's message and the girl standing in front of me with tears in her eyes.

I'd fucking kill him.

CHAPTER 13

EVE

I used to think witches were cool growing up, but if I never saw one again, it would be too soon. I'm sure they weren't all psychopaths, but Luke had told me enough about witches and the Royals, and to steer clear of the powerful ones. This witch didn't have warts, she was gorgeous. But I got the distinct impression that the pretty mask hid a rotten core. I was surprised Jonas still wanted me to start there. I didn't want to be the reason the Dark Night emptied in seconds.

At least Luke hadn't trashed the place. I'd gotten him outside, and we'd taken a long cold walk towards my apartment to help him simmer down. Except he was still boiling. *Literally.* There was steam rising off his skin and evaporating into the winter air.

"It's just a note." My words lacked conviction. "You need to calm down."

"I'll calm down when you admit Ryan was behind that girl's murder," he spat, kicking an empty beer can out of his way. It ricocheted off the window on the other side of the road, setting off the security alarm of a charity shop.

The venom in his words caught me off guard. He was worried, but I wasn't going to base a murder's motive off a note from a jealous ex-boyfriend.

A couple ahead of us crossed the road, both girls eyeing Luke warily. I couldn't blame them, he was looking for a fight, and I was glad everyone avoided him. He met any dirty look, especially from guys, with a cold, hard stare that dared them to make one move on him.

I mean, I got it. I wanted to punch something too. I wanted to scream the place down and slap the universe for kicking me when I was down. I didn't feel safe in the city I called home all because of one man who believed I was his property.

"If it was Ryan, why wasn't his scent at the crime scene?" I tried to recite facts to force Luke to calm down and be reasonable about everything.

"It wouldn't be unlike him to expect someone else to do his dirty work."

There were unspoken words there. The accusation I had forgiven or forgotten Ryan for staging that wolf attack so he could be some kind of fucked up knight in shining armour.

"I haven't forgotten." I stayed on Luke's right as I shepherded him along the road and away from O'Connell Street where there would be less people for him to square up to.

He shook his head, pressing his lips into a thin line as he kept walking at a pace that had me struggling to keep up. Despite his temper and the tension between us, his gaze still slid to me every few seconds, and his hand lingered near my lower back, often pulling me out of the way of anyone who was brave enough to not cross the road.

I scented any new figure that appeared on the streets, jumping any time I spotted a redhead. It reminded me of the day I'd spent in the city, wandering aimlessly in the hopes Ryan wouldn't find me.

"I'm not happy about the note or his bullshit claims that I'm his." I gritted my teeth. "I'm no one's. There's no way for us to guess if Ryan is behind those killings. But his scent wasn't at the scene. You said it yourself, it was a wolf you didn't recognise. And why would he want me dead?"

"Men do stupid things when they're angry."

"No shit." I pulled down the zip on my duffle coat despite the cold. Speed walking with Luke and trying to knock some sense into his testosterone filled man brain was heating me up just fine.

We walked in tense silence for a while, Luke shadowing me as we passed the tall skyscraper offices of the IFSC and followed the Luas line towards my apartment. All the office spaces were closed, a few with security and the lights off where they had night shifts, but for the most part it was quiet. The grocery shops and some cafés dotted along the way were open, but Luke was on a mission to get me home safe. If he wasn't already on the couch, I would have put him there.

"Are you going to be like this all night?" I folded my arms under my chest as I glowered at him. "Alphahole attitude, taking out your anger on me when you're really mad at Ryan. I get that you're a werewolf, and I'm pissed too."

He stopped and turned to me, a muscle ticking in his jaw. "I'm not mad at you."

"Then tell your face that," I snapped, stepping into his space to prod him in the chest with a clawed fingertip.

"I'm not angry with you." His hand swamped mine as he wrapped it around the offending finger and stared down at me with an intensity that left me breathless. "I am only ever angry with Ryan and his fucked up pack. Though I do wish you would take the threat more seriously when it's your life on the line."

After what had happened to Kate, I was far more concerned about the safety of my friends and those closest to me than my own. I was the reason they were in danger, and why? Because I was born a hybrid. I didn't ask for any of this. I just wanted a peaceful life, but the universe clearly had other plans.

"I'm not important compared to everything else going on," I said quietly, slipping my hand out of his grip. Goosebumps rose on my skin in the absence of his touch as I stuffed my hands in my pocket, ignoring the way his eyes darkened and his jaw ticked, and started walking towards my apartment before he could dissect what I'd just said.

I didn't need eyes at the back of my head to know he was striding after me, the slap of his shoes against the pavement echoing with each step he took to catch up with me. Relief washed through me as we turned the corner onto my street and the apartment door remained undamaged. I kept my eyes on the ground in the elevator up to my floor, conscious of Luke's eyes on me at all times.

I planned on heading straight for my room once inside, but Luke finally spoke up, his words stopping me in my tracks.

"Why do you defend him and try to believe the best when you don't even value your life?"

Biding my time, I clicked the door shut and sucked in a deep breath as I turned to face him. He stared down at me, the chocolate brown of his irises engulfed by silver.

"I..."

"Every single sign points to Ryan's involvement. Yet, even after receiving a fucked up message from him delivered by a witch with a notoriously sick reputation, you still think he's incapable of murder?" Luke took a step towards me, his hulking frame towering over mine.

"I'm just saying we don't know all the facts," I snapped, slamming the keys down on the narrow console table beside the door.

"You're being naïve. That's the man who took my sister."

"I was the one who found her. I don't need the reminder."

He recoiled as if I'd slapped him. Then he advanced on me.

"Stop acting like he didn't practically admit to targeting you tonight."

"We still don't know if that girl was killed because of me." I retreated until my back hit the wooden door behind me.

A low growl rumbled from Luke's chest as he trapped me there, his face inches from mine. "He kidnapped Alice and other hybrids, held them against their will and has been trying to *breed* elite werewolves. What makes you think that he's not capable of murder?"

I swallowed hard, a small whimper leaving my lips as he cupped my chin between his forefinger and thumb and forced me to meet his gaze.

"Because I loved him." The admission fell from my lips, the truth causing my voice to crack. Tears pricked the corners of my eyes. "If I loved someone capable of murder, on top of everything else he's done... I can't be responsible for another person dying. If I can love a monster like him, what does that make me?"

Luke shook his head, our noses brushing as he dipped his head and pressed his forehead to mine.

"You could never be a monster," he whispered.

I bit my lower lip as it trembled, silent tears rolling down my cheeks.

"How could you think that your life being in danger isn't a worthy concern? You are just as important as any single hybrid they have taken." He refused to let me turn away from the burning intensity in his eyes as he pinned me in there, slamming his palm against the door above my head in a way that made my breathing uneven as he boxed me in. "In this world, the stakes are higher and murder isn't the worst offence. You might be okay with someone laying a hand on you, but don't think for a second I wouldn't kill anyone who hurt you."

Any response I had died on my tongue as his gaze dropped to my lips.

"You are not responsible for his actions."

I met his gaze, conscious my hands were now pressed against his chest where I could feel his heart hammering at the same pace as mine.

"It's not your fault." He nudged my nose with his as the silver faded from his eyes.

A lump rose in my throat when I tried to deny him, caught in his snare as he pinned me against the door with my vulnerabilities laid bare.

"Kate, that girl, Alice. None of it was your fault."

I gave the slightest of nods, my breathing shallow as I fought back tears while my body remained hyper-aware of his body pressed against mine.

"Say it," Luke ordered, that alpha tone seeping into his words which made me squeeze my thighs together.

He was so close his breath tickled my lips, I could taste the order on my tongue.

"It's not my fault," I whispered.

Those words hung in the air between us for a heavy moment before he closed the minuscule distance between us, capturing my lips in a kiss. His mouth crashed into mine. My lips parted as I gasped. He took the invitation, his tongue exploring my mouth with a feverish urgency bringing all my fantasies about him to life. I fisted his shirt, completely off kilter as he kissed me like he had hungered for it ever since we first laid eyes on each other.

Luke kept me pinned against the door, one hand cupping my jaw as he devoured my mouth. His other hand trailed down my throat and over my breasts, making me shudder under his touch, before he wound his arm around my lower back. I arched against him, pushing my body flush against his.

Moaning against his lips as the kiss deepened, I lost myself to the moment.

His hand slipped to grab my ass and squeeze as he growled in approval against my lips.

And *fuck* did that do something to me.

He froze as I sucked his bottom lip between my teeth, frowning as he stopped kissing me entirely, his body going stiff against mine in all the wrong ways.

"Lu—?"

Before I could finish his name, he pressed his lips to mine again, not to resume the kiss that had left my chest heaving and a puddle between my legs, but to silence me.

I wriggled against him, but he trapped me against the door,

pinning my wrists above my head. Then I smelled it. Witch. Footsteps I had been too lost in the moment to notice.

A bad odour lingered, like an undercurrent of magic laced with death. Whoever it was, they paced back and forth, waiting.

After a moment of silence, they knocked three times.

Luke released my lips, probably satisfied I now realised why he had been trying to silence me. It did something to ease the sting of rejection I'd felt when he'd stopped the kiss so abruptly.

We waited in silence, my heart beating erratically from both the high of the kiss and the fear now snaking its way up my spine.

I lost count of how many minutes passed, the stranger knocking several times until they dropped something. We waited until their footsteps faded and the elevator doors pinged shut, and then a few moments longer until we were sure they had left. Luke stepped away from me and loosened his grip on my wrists.

"Who was that?" I pressed my hand to my chest, willing my breathing to slow as I turned and peeked through the spyhole on the door. The hallway was empty.

I grabbed my keys, but before I could unlock the door completely, Luke shoved past me with a growl. "What did I say about being careful?"

With a dirty look that was more protective than angry, he eased the door open to reveal an empty corridor and a black box about the size of a shoebox in front of my door. There was a crimson ribbon tied in a bow on top and a small black paper envelope attached.

I stepped forwards, ready to pick it up, but Luke threw his arm out to stop me pushing past.

"Don't touch it." He dropped his arm to block my path as I tried to duck under it.

Luke crouched down, reaching out to feel the air around the box as if searching for some kind of booby trap. *How stupid am I?* If Larissa was involved, of course there could be booby traps. I didn't even have a clue about what kind of spells she could do. He treated it like a bomb, but its potential was far more devastating. A strange gift on the doorstep of my apartment less than a week after someone had tried to break into the place. With magic involved, it could be anything from instant death to a curse, and my stupid ass would have touched it straight away.

"Ok, no wards." Luke's eyes narrowed further in suspicion as he brushed his fingertips across my name stamped on the envelope.

"Wait, what if it's laced with poison?"

He looked up at me, raising an eyebrow so high it almost hit his hairline. "Since when do you think before touching things?"

I clicked my tongue, looking for a response, but I turned up nothing.

Luke opened the envelope, the colour draining from his face as he read the contents. His hand shook as he held the note up to me.

I took it from him, expecting something personalised to me. But the note had just one word. Another name.

"Alice."

"Why would they...?" I couldn't finish the sentence, afraid of what the box would contain. Ryan's message earlier was both a promise and a threat, but did this mean they would come for Alice again, too?

Luke's lips thinned. Were they planning on breaking in again? If I had been alone, would they have come for me? Ryan said I was his, but he never specified if he wanted me alive or dead.

"Can wolves mask their scent?" My voice trembled as fear washed over me.

"A witch could do it for them, but there is a scent here. It's just not his."

The black box was staring at us, an unwanted gift that had God only knows what in it. "Don't open it. What if it's something dangerous?"

"Well, there's only one way to find out." He slowly untied the ribbon. "Who knows? Maybe he carved out someone's heart."

I thumped him on the shoulder with a growl. "That's not funny. We should wait and bring this to your dad. Oh god, what if Agnes had found it?"

He shook his head, ignoring my panicked babbling as he threw the ribbon to one side and carefully opened the lid of the cardboard box. I peered over his shoulder, one hand grabbing the back of his shirt as if I could haul him to safety if this went wrong.

Inside the box was a bunch of newspaper cuttings and some old pictures, one or two polaroids and what looked like the type of photo you got for your passport. In the middle was another note written in red. My upper lip curled back in disgust, the shaky writing was actually inked in blood. Two simple words that led to a million questions.

Help me.

CHAPTER 14

EVE

Every full moon, the Crescents descended on their pack house in Kildare for the weekend. His dad had renovated the old farmhouse, maintaining the rustic façade while replacing the interiors to form one large family home with ten bedrooms, a spacious living room, and a kitchen, which had Helena written all over it. The stables had also been repurposed to form a kind of extension winding around the rear of the house and cordon off the garden.

The house was surrounded by acres of land backing into a public forest. That's where we would run. Unlike my previous experiences, Crescent wolves didn't begin their run in a secluded location in the woodland. Luke had warned me it was chaos, but to me it felt like one giant dysfunctional family.

There was no definitive start time, no real formalities. I found this out the hard way when I came downstairs to find two young wolves brawling in the living room while Liz screeched at them to behave. Around them, a few of the kids were lounging on the couches while the younger ones played with Lego on a table in the corner. The older ones were egging the pups on despite Liz shooting them death glares.

"Sorcha, if you break one more thing Helena is going to tan your hide." She cradled an antique-looking bronze lamp in her arms that had cracks in the glass lampshade while clipping a tan-coloured wolf around the ear. "This is your first run, so behave and act your age."

The wolf in question yipped, nipping at Liz's hand before diving on her playmate again.

She was one of the teenagers I'd met earlier. Luke had mentioned she'd had her first shift last night. Apparently, some boy had broken her heart, and she was in the middle of blasting music when her parents heard howling and realised it was coming from upstairs. Sorcha had shifted in her bedroom by accident. Most werewolves had their first shift around puberty, and it usually happened when the pack gathered to run under the full moon, the gathering call of magic triggering the change. However, strong emotions close to the moon could trigger it too. Luke was surprised, but there was nothing quite like feminine rage.

Max was playing with the Lego and beckoned me over, but being around the young wolves playing had set my nerves on edge, so I waved at him and ducked out into the kitchen instead.

Where I was met by more wolves.

Apparently, the Crescent pack shifted whenever they wanted. And while the fluidity of that was lovely, it ramped up my anxiety because I wasn't sure if I'd be able to shift. The night we rescued Alice was the first time I'd managed to shift without a struggle, and I still didn't understand why. But me and Alice had made a pact. We'd shift together. She was out of practice and I... I wasn't a very good werewolf.

"Eve?"

I turned to find Darren in the doorway leading outside, dressed in jeans and a loose shirt that was unbuttoned, as if he felt too old to walk around shirtless like most of the younger male wolves.

"Can I get your help for a second?" He disappeared out into the garden before I could answer.

I followed him, the evening chill causing goosebumps to multiply on my bare arms as I crossed the garden towards the back of the converted stables where a ladder was placed against the whitewashed wall. Darren stood at the base of the ladder, a hammer in one hand.

"I need to fix a loose slate, but I need someone to hold the ladder. I said it would be grand, but Paula insisted that I needed supervision," he explained, a smile playing on his lips as he spoke about his wife.

He was the alpha's right-hand man, but I'd met Paula, and it was very clear who wore the pants in that marriage.

"Sure," I said, happy for the distraction.

I held the ladder while Darren scaled it like a spider-monkey, moving gracefully for someone with bulging muscles rocking a dad bod. He was done in minutes, and I was beginning to find the noise of the hammer soothing when he decided to leap from the edge of the roof.

"What the hell?" I clutched the ladder as I waited for something to snap.

Darren landed in a crouch, the gravel grinding beneath his feet at the beginning. He straightened with a smirk, swinging the hammer in his hand. "All done."

"You nearly gave me a heart attack."

"You already looked like death warmed up." He dusted down his jeans, his expression sobering as he looked me over. "I'm serious though, are you alright?"

"I'm fine."

We walked back around the corner, Darren dropping to sit on one of the benches lining the stables. A few wolves paced in and out of the house, but no one seemed to have filtered out into the garden yet. I was about to keep walking, but he patted the seat. The way the corners of his eyes creased with worry guilted me into slumping down beside him.

"Look, I know it's been a bit intense lately, but you're safe here." He kept his voice low.

"It's not that." I sighed, shaking my head. "I mean, some of it is, but it's mostly…"

"You're scared to shift, aren't you?"

I didn't need to answer, shame setting my cheeks alight.

"Tom mentioned you had been struggling. Not to gossip," he clarified, raising his hands. "But you don't need to worry, the Crescents are different. I promise, no one will judge you. Lots of the younger ones struggle quite a bit at the start."

"I'm not some teenager though, am I?"

He reached out to lay a gentle hand on my knee to stop it bouncing. "You're new to all of this. We all had to start somewhere. You are a werewolf through and through, the magic is in you, even if you aren't always at one with it."

"I'm a hybrid though."

"A hybrid *werewolf*," he corrected, a gentle smile playing on his lips. "Besides, Luke asked me to look into what might have been causing you issues, and I think I may have cracked it."

I frowned. "What did Luke say?"

"He said you were able to change once before, the time you ran with him."

"Yeah, I guess, but I changed that night at the manor too."

"Only after destroying this." He pulled a piece of folded tissue from his pocket, unfolding it to reveal a blackened bracelet chain; its once-silver moon phases now charred. "Silver really does hurt werewolves, it usually sears our skin. But I have also heard of it being charmed to do all sorts of things, like bind or obstruct a werewolf's ability to shift."

The bracelet Ryan had given me. Could it really have caused all those problems?

My mind drifted back to the time Kate had convinced me to get a belly button piercing and how I'd screamed bloody murder when they tried to insert the silver stud. That was less than a month before the first time I shifted, but I was 'sleepwalking'. My inability to tolerate the precious metal must have kicked in then. I'd thought we'd just chosen a bad tattoo shop.

I said as much to Darren, and he nodded, crumpling the tissue back up and offering it to me.

"It was spelled to limit your access to your wolf magic. It was never your fault." He smiled, curling my fingers around the napkin as he pressed it into my hand. It was clear why Tom trusted Darren. They were one and the same. "You have nothing to fear from the full moon. Trust your gut instinct, connect to the power that's always been inside you, and let your wolf side run free."

I stared at the bracelet in stunned silence for a moment.

"You didn't need help to fix that tile, did you?" I narrowed my eyes, but a smile played on my lips.

Darren got to his feet, grabbing the hammer off the ground and swinging it over his shoulder like it was a mini pickaxe as he shot me a cheeky grin. "Nope, but don't tell anyone. Wouldn't want them thinking I was going soft."

With that, he sauntered off towards a shed marking the end of the extended stables, whistling out of tune.

I lost track of time, examining the remains of something so delicate that was gifted as an act of love, with such cruel intentions. Luke was right, Ryan would hurt me. He already had, and when he tried again, I wanted to be ready. The sound of the kitchen door opening brought me back to the present.

Luke walked out into the garden, my thoughts spiralling in a different direction as he stopped in front of me, shirtless and in a pair of grey sweatpants that left nothing to the imagination. I'd be seeing him naked before he shifted. But everyone else seemed to do it in their own time in private, so maybe I could avoid that. All of a sudden, my heart was fluttering.

He cleared his throat. "We'll be heading out soon."

"Right." Heat rose to my cheeks as he watched me with an unreadable expression. "What?"

"Can we talk?"

I swallowed. No girl ever wants to hear that.

"If it's about the other night, don't worry about it." I hoped my voice sounded surer than I felt.

He recoiled at my words, closing the distance between us so he was towering over me, and my eye-level was exactly where my addled thoughts didn't need it to be. Then he dropped down onto his haunches, his irises silver rings that danced in the moonlight.

"That's the thing, Eve, I am worried. Ever since the other night, you've been avoiding me."

My tongue felt thick in my mouth as I tried to look away, but he lifted my chin and electricity sparked in every nerve that he touched.

"You've been avoiding me too," I mumbled, cringing at my pathetic response.

"Only because I wanted to leave the ball in your park."

"There's no ball. There's no park."

"I met you in a fucking park, and from that moment I think I've been pretty clear about the fact that I liked you." Each word stole the breath from my lungs.

I blinked slowly, my heart pounding in my ears drowning out everything as

Luke stared at me with a burning intensity, his gaze unwavering as he waited for an answer.

Before I could answer, wolves spilled out from the kitchen and all around the property, congregating in the garden. Our conversation was no longer private, if it had ever been. Tom strode out onto the grass and barked his son's name. Sorcha danced around his legs, making Tom trip in the most un-alpha way, but he simply laughed and reached down to scratch her ear.

Luke's head swung towards his father for a moment before he turned to me again, holding out his hand. "It's time for the pack run. Come shift with me."

Over his shoulder I spotted Alice. Her arms were folded, and a giant hoodie swamped her tiny frame as she lingered in the kitchen doorway.

"I can't." I raced to explain myself at the wounded expression on his face. "I promised I'd shift with Alice, just so we can both get through it together."

He glanced across the garden at his sister, nodding as he took my hand and pulled me to my feet. We lingered there for a moment, our chests almost touching as the full moon watched us navigate whatever was brewing between us like she knew the outcome. He tilted his head down, silver eyes searching mine for a long moment before he stepped away.

"Luke." I clasped my hand around his wrist to pull him back.

He frowned, looking between me and his father who was waiting with the young pup.

I held out the charred bracelet remains, shuffling from one foot to another as I tried to find the right words.

"Thank you for helping Darren figure out the truth so I could understand."

"You deserve to enjoy your wolf side and not live in fear of something that's a part of you."

A smile that made my heart skip graced his face, some brown seeping back into his eyes as he nodded before heading over to his father who watched us with a curious expression. He clapped Luke on the shoulder and they both went back into the house, Helena stopping Tom to place a kiss on his cheek before they disappeared inside.

Watching him walk away, it felt like something might have shifted in the right direction.

I made a beeline for Alice who was in the process of shredding the cuff of her left sleeve. She looked up as I approached, her sombre expression brightening a tad.

"Ready?" I glanced around at the wolves gathering in the garden.

Alice shrugged, tucking her hands into her pockets. "As I'll ever be."

Some wolves sat on the dewy grass, some commandeered the picnic benches, others loped around chasing the younger wolves, and more were still filtering outside. The full moon hung high in the sky, its luminescent glow adding to the solar lamps in the flower beds and the fairy lights wound around the gazebo legs. In the centre of the garden, one of Sorcha's mothers, Maggie, was already coaxing the embers to life while her daughter played with the other pups now that she had no alpha to pester.

Everything felt so calm... except me.

Darren's revelation had gone a long way to reduce my fears and give me an ounce of confidence, but his theory was unproven. Plus, I could bottle it based on sheer anxiety, so there was no guarantee I'd be able to shift smoothly.

"Wanna do it inside?" A small smile played on Alice's lips. She probably saw her own anxiety mirrored in my face.

"Abso-fucking-lutely."

Her smile became fully fledged, and I followed her back into the house. I could hear Tom and Luke in the distance as she led me into a room off from the living room that Luke had never shown me. Alice flicked the light on to reveal a large oak table with eight chairs, all with backs that were intricately carved to depict wolves in different poses with detailed forest backgrounds. I ran my fingertips across the closest design. Everything right down to the veins on each leaf was so beautifully carved.

"This is where all the important decisions are made. Other than the ones done in our kitchen."

We both laughed, and the tension ballooned in the room.

Thanks to our shared experience with the Faolchúnna pack and Ryan in particular—thankfully Alice hadn't slept with him, then shit would have been *really* weird—we had a sisterhood bond between us. A trauma bond, but a bond nonetheless.

"So, we should probably get going before they leave without us..." She toyed with the zip on her hoodie.

I tugged my knitted jumper over my head with a sigh. "We've got this."

She shot me a look that disagreed wholeheartedly, gingerly dropping her hoodie to the ground, leaving her in a sports bra and leggings. Keeping my eyes to myself, we got changed, but I couldn't help noticing a nasty scar shaped in some kind of ruin on her shoulder. There were needle marks in the crease of her elbow too, but I didn't let my gaze linger or point them out.

Wearing a red thong on the night of a pack run was possibly not one of my best ideas, but I hid it in my jumper and stacked my pair of black leggings on top, stuffing them between a chair and the table. I prayed Helena didn't decide to do some cleaning while we were out running. Though she was in charge of minding the kids who were too young to shift, or the ones that were only human, so she had her hands full and my thong could stay a secret.

Alice caught me studying the pile of clothes and shot me a weird look.

I wasn't sure how to do this with company. When Ryan had barked orders at me as I was in agony, I'd run off to hide behind a tree with Luke.

But Alice had more experience than me, so she grabbed my hand and linked our fingers.

"Close your eyes."

I followed her instruction, self-conscious that we were both standing naked, but as I focused on my breathing, the familiar well of magic stirred deep within me. I focused on drawing on the energy within me as a shiver crept down my spine, and my fingertips tingled where my claws were extending. Remembering Darren's advice and Luke's last words to me, I gave into the pull of the magic, and my wolf took over.

The magic took hold of my body, its fire washing over me as the shift took hold.

Carpet felt strange under my paws, but I couldn't stop my little wolf-grin as I blinked my eyes open to find another wolf facing me.

We'd done it.

She was a rusty cream, her coat a reddish-brown along her back that faded into a similar wheat shade to that of her brother. Her shoulders were level with mine, but her frame was slight, and you could tell her ribs would be felt easily under that coat. No doubt, Helena would pile Alice's plate high that night.

She took a tentative step, as if testing her balance, and I whined as I realised just how long it must have been since her last change.

Leaning down like a cat, she dropped her chest to the ground while keeping her butt in the air, doing the downward-facing dog pose before righting herself and pacing in a small circle. Satisfied, she yipped and stepped forwards to nudge my side and gestured towards the door with her head, practically pushing me out ahead of her. Then she took off, loping through the house.

Alice went straight for her father, nipping the alpha's hind leg to get his attention. He whirled on her, both of them tumbling in the wet grass until they came to a stop with her pinning our fearsome alpha down and licking his face. I trotted over to Helena who was perched on one of the picnic benches, subtly dabbing her eyes as she watched the exchange.

"I never thought I'd see it," she murmured softly, her eyes glassy as she reached out to scratch the sweet spot behind my right ear.

Luke joined me, gently butting Helena's thigh with his wet nose in acknowledgement.

"Thank you," Helena added, leaning down to pat my head. "For making this possible."

Tom's howl pierced the night and all wolves jumped to their feet, the younger ones barking with excitement. He rubbed against Helena as he passed his wife, and she ran a hand through his fur as he continued past down the garden, to the head of the pack.

Luke followed at his heels with Alice by his side, and when I lingered behind him, he turned and grabbed me gently by the scruff of the neck and pulled me up until I was level with him. I wasn't sure what it meant, but I had no time to dwell on it when Tom threw his head back, his light coat shining under the silver moonlight as he howled again. The alpha of The Crescent pack launched into a sprint and disappeared into the forest, and every single wolf in the pack followed his call with open hearts. Including me.

CHAPTER 15

LUKE

I'd almost given up hope when two wolves had come racing out of the house at full speed. The way Eve had come straight over and Alice greeting Dad had my heart fit to burst with pride. But nothing beat running alongside them. Our paws pounded the ground as we raced through the forest, the welcome spray of water as we tore through a shallow break in the river and ran freely under the full moon and a cloudless night sky.

Each time I'd caught Eve looking at me, her blue eyes a contrast to the silver of a normal werewolf, the sight of pure joy on her face made me happier than I'd been in a long time. The howls of our pack filled the night, and I grinned as she added her own to the mix.

I opened up my mind, relishing in the feeling of her running as part of my pack.

It's good to see you like this.

Eve stumbled, ripping over a gnarled root sticking out of the forest floor. I swerved right, bumping into her shoulder to help keep her upright as she recovered. Her eyes were wide as she looked at me, her ears flattened against her skull.

We were nearing the edge of the forest to finish up the run

Eve trotted alongside Alice as they playfully nipped at one another when I decided to try again.

It's me.

Eve skidded to a halt and whirled to look at me, causing Alice to bump into her. Alice growled and shook herself off, picking up her pace to run alongside my dad instead as we left the cover of the forest canopy. From a distance, Helena's silhouette stood by the fire pit which was now roaring with flames. I nudged Eve with my nose, earning a whack of her tail as she surged forwards again.

We made our way back towards the house, different pack members splitting off to return to their rooms. The younger wolves preferred staying shifted for longer, so they gathered in the garden and commandeered one of the picnic benches. I nipped Eve's shoulder to try to get her attention again, but she headed straight into the house to join up with Alice again.

Maybe revealing pack members could communicate mentally if they had a close bond by just hopping into her mind was a bad idea.

It's not like I could read her thoughts, but I guess she didn't know that. And sometimes I did wish I could read her thoughts because I hadn't a clue what went on in that head of hers.

Sorcha was one of the wolves who chose not to shift back yet, and Maggie and Áine gathered around their daughter, showering the young pup with cuddles. The way both parents embraced her and were so vocal in praising her change made me smile. That girl would be just fine. Whatever stupid boy had broken her heart would rue the day.

By the time Eve re-emerged, dressed in a pair of jeans and a black T-shirt that cropped around her tiny waist, still on her high from shifting and warmer than normal, especially with the fire blazing. She seemed to have calmed down and was beaming. My sister looked equally pleased with herself, bouncing over to my mother to give her a bear hug before taking a seat on one of the benches surrounding the log fire. The fact that she was eyeing up the plate in front of Helena, displaying interest in food for the first time since being home, showed just how important and healing her wolf side was in this process. I made the mental note to bring her over more often until she learned to drive herself.

"Penny for your thoughts?" Josh dropped down beside me with his plate stacked high.

He wasted no time, taking a big bite of his burger, happily munching away as he took a swipe at me when I tried to steal a sausage.

"I'm just really happy that they're both here," I said, barely having touched my own food. I was too busy watching Eve queue up to the barbecue. The way she laughed so freely with Darren as he flipped some patties made unease crawl up my spine. She was settling in so well, things had gone perfectly until I went and opened my big mouth. I shouldn't have said anything. I went and took that unsaid tension between us and put a label on it. I wanted to be able to go over and wrap my arm around her shoulder, laughing with them as she waited. Better yet, I wanted her perched on my lap in one of my hoodies while we watched the fire pit and laughed the night away. Honestly, I wanted her in my lap in the other sense too, but I would settle for that flirty friendship we had if I had to.

Josh studied my face, a knowing smile tipping his lips up as he followed my eye-line to Eve. "Ah, I get it."

I didn't have the energy to deny it, focusing on stealing a chip from his plate instead, which he let me.

Eve took a seat beside me, offering me the smallest of smiles that did nothing to help the shitty rejection playlist my brain had on repeat.

"I hear you're in need of more training." Josh leaned forwards to talk around me.

She glanced at me, uncertainty in her eyes. "I guess?"

"Well, if you ever need a sparring partner, I'm always around the boxing club most nights." Josh shot me a smug smirk letting me know exactly what he was doing.

Pressing my damn buttons.

Eve shrugged, wiping some ketchup off the side of her mouth while she stalled. "Eh, sure. I mean… if that's okay?"

"Whatever works for you. The most important thing is that you can protect yourself."

The moment the words left my mouth I wanted to punch myself. I could have said no. I could have offered to pick back up our training. I should have done all those things, and the eye roll from Josh just solidified how shit I was doing with this whole thing.

Silence fell around the fire pit and the telltale noise of my dad clearing his throat saved me from digging my own grave further.

"I know it's story time and you pups are getting close to your bedtime." He threw a playful look in the direction of the youngster bench as he rose to his feet. "But I wanted to mention something before we start. First, I want to formally welcome Eve into our pack although she has been one of us for a little while, possibly longer than she realised."

Eve's cheeks flushed red, and she shrank back against me. Never one for attention, she probably would have hidden completely if she could, but the way the corner of her lips twitched, and her eyes sparkled told me his words meant a lot. Even if she did hate all the eyes now on her.

My dad chuckled at her reaction, raising his drink to the group. "And we have another hybrid home with us. I'd missed running with my daughter, and I know all of you did too. So, welcome home Alice."

Alice reached out to squeeze his hand with tears glistening in her eyes, while Helena looped an arm around her and snuggled close.

"Given that we have our two favourite hybrids with us, I thought it would be a good night to tell the story of our beginnings. The theory behind werewolf origins is sketchy, it's practically a myth, but it's a crowd favourite."

A whoop came from one of the younger kids, followed by a

hiss to shut up. A few others mumbled in confusion. No doubt they'd heard it before but were too young to remember.

Eve leaned in to whisper in my ear. "I thought only the witches knew of the true werewolf origins."

"Technically, yes." I was hyper aware that she had closed the space between us. "There are a few myths, but this is the most well-known one. The witches won't confirm or deny it, so no one knows for sure. At the end of the day, they're all just stories that have been passed down over the years. But the kid's love it."

"Get a room," Josh teased, throwing his eyes to heaven as he shushed us.

Tom kissed the top of Alice's head before moving towards the fire pit so more wolves could see him, the flames climbing high behind him in an ominous backdrop that would lend to the atmosphere.

"Mother Nature believes in one thing above all others, balance." My dad's alpha-tone commanded the attention of the entire pack. "Long ago, witches were once revered and recognised by mortals. They lived alongside humans, with villages deeming anyone possessing magic as blessed. They were healers, doulas, oracles. There's no such thing as complete harmony. Witches are bound by the same emotions and flaws as humans, but for the most part, there was balance."

Eve's blue eyes were fixed on our alpha, listening with rapt attention.

"No one really knows when the terms witch and warlock began, but it was known that magic passed through the maternal line. Women possessing magic were well respected and never short of suitors. But alas, despite being spoiled for choice, there were two sisters in one village who set their sights on the same man."

Liz mumbled something not child appropriate, nursing a glass of bourbon in her hand. The comment earned her a slap on the knee from Josh's mam who fought a laugh. Dad paid no heed, well used to the antics of his pack members. Especially Liz.

"Béibhinn and Cadhla grew up in a large village called Cruachan. They were two of the strongest witches of their generation. Béibhinn had the gift of water and air, Cadhla possessed power over fire and earth. They were two sides of a coin. Twins born from the same beginning, but they were not identical and different in about every facet you could imagine. Cadhla was a healer, working tirelessly to help those less fortunate in her village."

I rested my elbows on my knees and propped my chin on my hands, watching the red embers floating into the inky night sky as the familiar story unfolded.

"Béibhinn preferred to rely on status. She had her eyes set on a human boy called Ultán from an early age. He came from a wealthy family and the marriage was arranged from the time they were thirteen. But her eighteenth birthday passed, and they were still unwed. Then her nineteenth, her twentieth, and she grew frustrated with waiting."

Instead of focusing on my dad, I found myself watching the reflection of the fire dancing in Eve's eyes.

"His family were farmers, and he insisted he must learn the trade, claiming he was busy with the work and getting ready to take over from his ailing father whenever Béibhinn asked about marriage. She was still without a ring, and at that time, it was expected that they should already be building a family."

He skipped over that part.

"One night after the summer solstice celebrations, Béibhinn went in search of her sister, only to find her hiding in the barn with Ultán. Béibhinn was heartbroken, all of those years waiting. Ultán had her heart for years, all she could see was the perfect future she had planned going up in flames. She was blinded by fury and jealousy, and as we all well know, a woman scorned is a tempest storm. In exchange for her heart, she took the life of the man she loved in a fit of rage."

A log in the fire pit snapped, causing the front row of the kid's bench to jump comically. Eve squeaked beside me, her hand flying to her mouth. I chuckled, only earning myself an elbow in the ribs which I gladly took if it meant the icy confusion between us was thawing.

"They had been seeing each other in secret before her sister found out. She knew it was wrong, but they had grown up together and fallen in love in their teenage years. Despite his hand being promised to Béibhinn, he loved Cadhla. So, they stole moments of happiness where they could while he tried to find a way out of the marriage. But then he was taken, and her heart cleaved in two, never to be mended again. Her true love had been murdered at the hands of her sister." Our alpha paced around the fire in a slow circle, his voice carrying with ease around the garden area thanks to the walls flanking three of the sides. "When the red mist receded, Béibhinn couldn't believe what she had done. She turned to magic to save the man she claimed to love, taking his body, and fled to a secluded lake in the mountain. Calling on the ancient powers there, she sliced her palm open with a silver dagger and performed a dark ritual, begging the spirits under the full moon to give him life once more. The spirits and Mother Nature can be fickle and cruel. During the ritual, a drop of blood from the silver blade fell into Ultán's mouth. They returned him to her, but not as he once was. And so, the first vampire was born."

A few of the younger wolves gasped, but most remained silent, spellbound by their alpha's storytelling.

"Ultán woke up in her arms, lunging for her jugular. Béibhinn was strong enough to fight him off and he fled. Out of control with bloodlust, he tore through the nearest village, leaving bloody carnage in his path. He attacked villagers and witches alike, with no care for anything but his need for blood. Even as he neared her home village, Béibhinn could not bear to kill him. She travelled alongside him, stealing what moments she could with him, romanticising her love for a monster as some great selfless act. Each time his bloodlust receded, Ultán realised what he had become, but Béibhinn had complete control over the actions of him and any vampires he created. Her selfishness and thirst for revenge drove her to insanity."

I snuck another glance at Eve, finding her nose wrinkled her nose in disgust.

"News spread of an evil monster terrorising and decimating surrounding villages, where the dead were rising. Some said they were demons, all teeth and claws. Others swore they saw dead loved ones rise again, but soulless with red eyes and a thirst for blood. Since it was claimed they could be killed with fire, Cadhla was chosen to travel to the nearest village to investigate. It was there she found a monster looking just like her lost love tearing into the throat of the now deceased town bard, his ladle snapped in two beneath his mangled body."

A series of "ew"s rang out from the younger wolves, and I grinned as Max turned green.

"Béibhinn admitted to what she had done, claiming Ultán was hers in death as he was in death. Cadhla begged her sister to stop, but she refused to listen to reason. Desperate to restore balance and end her lover's suffering, Cadhla gathered Ultán's brothers and went to the same place the first vampire was born and called upon the moon again to give her the power and strength needed to save her village. Her wish was granted, but again, magic always has a price." Dad paused, amping up the tension before finishing the old tale. His deep voice and the fire crackling behind him only added to the drama. "Cadhla shifted into a wolf, but she was bigger and stronger than the average lupine. Along with their increased strength, they were fast and had the ability to see in the dark. Most of all, the stars whispered that they had venom on their canine fangs that was deadly to vampires. In the interest of balance, the reverse was also true. Vampire venom was lethal to wolves. But they returned to defend their village and fought bravely. Only two of the brothers survived, and they were able to drive the vampires back and Cadhla hunted Ultán down and trapped him in a cave, where she finally ended his suffering. His dying words in her arms were to thank her for loving him until the end."

"Aw." Liz chuckled, taking another swig of her bourbon.

"In her fury, Béibhinn cursed her sister and the remaining brothers to be bound forever to the moon, before killing herself with the very dagger she used to resurrect her unrequited love. In taking her life, Béibhinn severed her control over the vampires, and they were able to secure some level of control over their bloodlust. They still exist to this day, but all of their sires can be traced back to that first vampire. Cadhla eventually fell for one of Ultán's brothers and sired a child, thus beginning the first werewolf bloodline."

Dad took an elaborate bow to raucous applause, which woke up a few of the younger kids who had nodded off. Max bounced on his toes, jumping out of Helena's lap and running towards the fire, only to be scooped up by my dad who propped him on his hip before taking one last bow.

CHAPTER 16

EVE

My first full moon run with the Crescent pack had been perfect. I had bonded with Alice and really felt like part of the family. But my feelings for him could risk that. I would be an idiot to claim there was no tension between us, though I struggled to understand what someone next in line for alpha with good looks and abs of steel saw in me. Trouble followed me everywhere I went, and I had Ryan-shaped baggage that was bloody and would put any sane guy off.

Except Luke.

I'd avoided being alone with him the rest of the weekend. I didn't want to freeze him out, but thinking I *heard* him in my head during the hunt was a sign that I needed a time out. I had to get my head straight, and that wasn't going to happen when he was milling around the place in grey sweatpants. He'd gone around topless all weekend like most of the guys did. But he was the only one that made my head turn.

So, before we got back, I'd arranged to meet Craig after his shift to avoid a cosy night in with the sexy shifter I was desperately trying to keep my paws off. We also needed more details on what was going on with the murders, so this was technically a wolf business visit. A hunt for info, but also a way for me to try to shield Craig's involvement in the paranormal and keep him safe.

Of course, he had to be on rotation with Pearse Street Garda station, which brought back some bad memories. Instead of waiting inside and out of the dreary November rain, I grabbed a coffee in a small café around the corner while I waited for him. I was wrestling with my umbrella against the wind when a skinny guy in a blue uniform came out the front doors of the station, with blue hair to match.

Craig waved at me with a wide smile, taking the steps two at a time and diving under my umbrella for cover from the elements.

"Well, the weather is shit, and I'm knackered." He shuffled his backpack from one shoulder to the other like a schoolboy. "Fancy visiting my nan? She's only down the road, and you know she'll have some food going."

My stomach rumbled at that suggestion. His nan's baking was legendary.

"Sure." I linked arms with Craig.

He took the umbrella from me so I wasn't hitting him in the face with it so much, holding it over both of us as we headed deeper into the south of the city, arms linked together. He chatted about work along the way, not mentioning the case I was interested in, and I struggled to find a way to bring it up without it being suspicious or sounding morbid.

We stopped in front of the apartments in Temple Court, hitting the buzzer on one of the duplexes. When no one answered, Craig took out a set of keys and let us in. It was one of the older areas in the city where the interior hadn't been updated, so the red carpet with small yellow dots that lined the hallway had probably been there since the fifties. His nan wasn't one to keep up with changing trends. Most of the furniture in the place would have been deemed antique.

I ran my fingers along the yellowed wallpaper, different photos hung along the walls, my favourite a black-and-white photo of a young boy with no front teeth, grinning and having the time of his life on a swing. Craig had his arms out in the picture as if he was flying, as a younger version of his nan, with dark hair back then, pushed him and laughed. It captured him and their relationship perfectly.

"Spud!" Treasa came bustling into the hall, waving a tea-towel in the air.

Behind her, the air was smoky, and an oven timer bleeped. She was an excellent baker, but the odd time an experiment went wrong. Especially since she was too old to hear the timer sometimes. I worried she would burn the place down over a batch of cupcakes someday.

"Hi, nan." He cringed at the pet name she insisted on using, even though he was twice her height and all grown up.

The old woman was almost ninety, but she was slight and 'sharp as a tack', as she would say. Her white hair was swept up in multicoloured rollers, and she was always dressed in knee-length skirts with a sweatshirt in one of three pastel colours, complete with brogues that did nothing to dispel the American theory that we did indeed have leprechauns. Between her floral apron, button nose, and kind eyes behind wide rimmed glasses, she was the cutest thing ever.

She squinted, pulling her glasses off and wiping them on her apron before trying them on again. Her face lit up once she could see without the steam fogging them up. "Eve, oh it's been so long since I saw you!"

I was bundled into a hug from the small woman before she hurried away, mumbling about her bad hip.

Craig left my umbrella by the door to dry off, and we hung our coats up. He shook his hair like a wet dog before we followed her into the kitchen. I set about opening the windows to help the smoke clear while Treasa salvaged what she could from the oven.

The kitchen was small, with a retro look that was less to do with style and more to do with his nan's unwillingness to change the place. She had lived there ever since she married Craig's grandfather. She hadn't changed a thing since he passed.

Surprisingly, the apple pie responsible for the fire risk was perfectly fine. Better than fine, it made my mouth water, but when she caught me drooling over it, I got a whip of the tea towel across my ass for my troubles.

I yelped, backing away from the counter, and she chuckled, pointing to a plate in the centre of a small round table by the wall, stacked full of an assortment of cakes. "You two sit down and dig into those. That pie won't be cool enough for a while yet."

Despite Craig insisting that we should make our own tea, the moment he tried to use the kettle instead of a teapot, he was demoted to cake eating alongside me.

"Terrible business with that girl at Halloween," Treasa muttered as she set down two large mugs in front of us and one for herself.

I grabbed the opportunity, trying to keep my tone level as I poured some tea from the rose polka-dot teapot into each of our mugs. "That was horrible. Did they figure out who she was?"

Luke and I had scoured the news site, her identity hadn't been released publicly. That didn't mean the guards didn't know though.

"Her name was Alison Richards. She was from Cork but attending DCU to study genetics." He stared at his cup as he swirled the teaspoon to mix in the milk. "She had celebrated her eighteenth birthday only a week beforehand. Her parents asked us to keep her identity private, they didn't want to deal with the press on top of everything."

Treasa shook her head, muttering about the world today as she left the room.

"It was yours, by the way," Craig added, as if reading my thoughts. "They found black hairspray on it during forensics and both of our DNA, but I cleared things up with the investigator. I didn't think you'd want to deal with all of that after what happened with Kate."

Guilt crashed into me. The poor girl had such a bright future ahead of her and now her life had been snuffed out because what? Because she had been handed the wrong coat that night?

I swallowed the lump rising in my throat. "Thanks for that."

"I'm glad it wasn't you." He reached out to give my hand a gentle squeeze.

"How is the investigation going? I mean, are you allowed to work on it given you were at the scene?" I felt bad that my genuine interest in how his career was going was also a veiled attempt at details. "Do they let beat cops work on these kinds of things?"

"Sometimes they do, yeah. My supervisor was impressed with how I handled everything and maintained the crime scene until they could cordon it off, so he's been giving me tidbits and letting me read the case files."

"That sounds cool, very CSI." I took a sip of my tea and gagged when I realised his nan had slipped in what must have been a tablespoon's worth of sugar.

Craig passed me a napkin, along with a slice of Victoria sponge, chuckling as I wiped down the T-shirt I'd spluttered all over.

"It's cool, but the crime scene photos and stuff are gory. I'm not a huge fan of that bit."

"Considering you can barely sit through most horror movies, I'm surprised you even managed to look at them, let alone not puke on the night." I closed my eyes as I bit into that little slice of heaven, which felt sacrilegious given the discussion we were having.

He shrugged. "I was more interested in the profiling they were doing. The witness statements from those girls were useless. One said it was a wolf—she was clearly taking her witch costume too seriously."

I blanched at that description, but Craig didn't seem to notice, too busy talking about how that kind of thing wasn't real and how astrology girls were dangerous.

"My supervisor said they might let me go on a stakeout once

they identify the suspect." Craig's face lit up like a kid on Christmas morning.

Mine did the opposite.

"You can't." My hand shook as I lowered my mug onto the table, the liquid sloshing from side to side.

"What? Of course I can. I want to get more involved. The investigation side is what I want to get into."

I took a deep breath, but it did nothing to stop my voice from wavering as I struggled to warn him, knowing I wasn't making any sense because he didn't know he'd be facing off with something that could rip his face off. "You need to be careful. That kind of thing isn't safe."

"I'll be fine." He promised, giving my arm a gentle pat as he dismissed my concerns.

He rattled on about stakeouts and how they catch perpetrators like this one, but it was going in one ear and out the other. I was too busy having an internal meltdown and trying to figure out a way to keep Craig away from all of this without tanking the career he was so excited about building.

"But it was the bloodwork that was really crazy." Craig wrinkled his nose as he took a sip of his tea that been poisoned with sweetness too. "One of the guys keeps joking that the whole thing seems like some kind of Halloween prank."

Treasa appeared in the doorway, light on her feet for an oldie with a bad hip, clipping her grandson around the ear with a newspaper. "That is no way to talk about that kind of thing."

As much as I felt sorry for him, I was grateful for Treasa's intervention. Her antics managed to stop my spiralling thoughts in their tracks—or at least pause them until they decided to haunt me all night.

He rubbed the back of his head, cursing when his hand came away with a blue tinge. "That's it, I'm going back to black or red! This blue dye bleeds like a bitch."

Cursing earned him another thwack.

"That fucking hurt!"

"Do. Not. Curse. In. My. House." Craig's nan punctuated each word with a hefty whack until she was seemingly satisfied that his potty mouth was under control. "Handling this murder with respect and decorum is important for the sake of the family. They deserve answers, and I do not want to hear that details have been leaked to the press because you are a gossip."

"I'm not gossiping, this is Eve we're talking about. And you're hardly going to tell the women at bridge, are you?"

She scrunched her nose at that suggestion, the wrinkles around her eyes creasing. "I wouldn't tell those old bats anything important."

"Then there won't be a problem." He smiled sweetly.

Treasa surveyed him with narrowed eyes before harrumphing and dumping her weapon into the recycling bin. "Just so long as you don't use the story as something to make yourself sound cool to those boys on twinge."

"Twinge?" I asked, confused as hell by her babbling.

"Twinge, fringe... Whatever that app yoke is called these days, for the boys and what not." She waved a dismissive hand as she sat down beside us and heaped two *spoons* of sugar into her empty cup.

Craig stared at his grandmother, his mouth hanging open in disbelief. "*Hinge?*"

"Yeah, that one for the hooky ups." She seemed more interested in grabbing some cake than the bomb she had just dropped.

Both Craig and I burst into a fit of laughter. I had tears running down my cheeks, and my belly hurt, but I couldn't stop laughing enough to catch my breath. Each time we looked at one another, we set ourselves off again. His nan just rolled her eyes at us, blissfully unaware.

A message popped up on his phone screen as it buzzed on the tabletop. Craig tapped the screen and his face fell.

"You okay?" I asked, wiping tears of laughter from my cheeks.

"The bloodwork broke the haematology analyser." He shook

his head, staring at the phone as if it might give him the answer. "Something similar happened when forensics scraped her nails for DNA. How's that even possible?"

Treasa muttered something about mercury being in retrograde, but I knew the truth.

Unease bubbled in my gut, the familiar sensation of dread dragging its icy claws down my spine. My world was responsible. The supernatural creatures that lurk in the night with claws or fangs, and I was one of them.

CHAPTER 17

LUKE

My eyes were ready to fall out of my head.

I had read so many old news articles that the black ink was just a blur on the yellowed pages, and the blue light from the handful of laptops at our disposal made my head pound. I didn't think werewolves got screen fatigue, but then again, I never did study much.

"We're getting nowhere." Eve threw the article she was holding aside and flopped back onto the bed beneath her.

The mattress jiggled under me at the movement. I sat cross-legged at the head of the bed, with my back against the headboard, while everyone else was scattered around the room.

We had gathered in Josh's bedroom at the house he shared with Dylan. He had brought us in here to look at something he'd found in relation to the murders, and we'd never left. Yes, we could have all sat comfortably in the living room, but we didn't want one of the others walking in on us. Despite two more bodies turning up dead, Dad had given me an explicit order to drop this and wait until he knew more. But his sources knew nothing. Both Alice and Eve had been threatened, and the pint-sized portion of patience I possessed had run out.

It had been hours of looking and coming up empty. Darkness

had fallen, and we read under the glare of the LED lights lining the ceiling, but no one seemed ready to give up. A large black desk lined one of the walls, complete with three screens, and several different gaming consoles. The walls were decorated with posters of different gaming and fantasy characters, and the entire place felt a bit trippy after a while.

"Where did you get these again?" Dylan spun around in the gaming chair he had called dibs on.

Beside him, there was a stack of old papers we had printed from online repositories. Josh had run some fancy algorithm I would never understand to flag anything with suspicious deaths or injuries we might associate with werewolf kills. Unfortunately, humans didn't plaster 'Werewolf Kill' across those articles, so it was hit and miss, and we had to manually trawl through them.

"The box was dropped outside the apartment by some kind lovely stranger that wanted to eat me." Eve smiled sweetly as she sorted through the piles she had split out into articles, photos, and a few random hand-written notes.

Alice snorted, grabbing another article from the box. She kneeled on the floor beside Eve, helping sort through the information and look for links. I hadn't wanted to involve her. She'd been at therapy for a few weeks now and was slowly coming out of her shell again, but I was conscious something like this could trigger a setback. My dad would kill me for going against his orders, and Helena would skin me alive for undoing Alice's progress. Never mind how bad I'd feel for causing my sister more pain. But once Eve asked Alice, my sister insisted that she wanted to help. They both had me wrapped around their little fingers.

"How far did you go back with these articles?" I rubbed my temple, willing my eyes to focus on the text instead of skipping over it and forcing me to reread.

Josh looked up from the laptop balanced on his lap, having snagged the second-best spot on the small two-seater couch. "From the year Damien stepped up as alpha. Although, who knows when his kill-y-tendencies kicked in."

"He'd have killed animals first." Alice's tone was so matter of fact everyone's head swivelled towards her. She rolled her eyes with a shrug. "What? I've watched a lot of serial killer documentaries."

Dylan laughed, almost choking on the slice of pizza he was chewing. Karma for the fact that he had snatched one pizza all for himself. There was another pizza box on the bed between Eve and I, one on the floor beside us that Josh could also reach. Josh's mother had dropped them into us when she heard we were having a little sleepover to celebrate Eve's new job. That was the cover story anyway, and I felt like shit for lying because Beth was one of the sweetest people alive.

"Does killing people to create some super race count as a serial killer?" Eve sat up again to take a sip of coke from her plastic cup.

I gave her a strange look. "I don't know. I don't think they cover werewolf murderers in Netflix documentaries. Thinking of following Craig into a detective career?"

"Smart ass." She growled, leaning over to grab a slice of pepperoni pizza from my side.

The action gave me the perfect view of her tits. I wasn't sure if she meant it until the corners of her lips twitched as she sat back with her pizza slice and proceeded to wrap her lips around the straw in her drink.

Damn right she knows exactly what she's doing.

Now I was confused, horny, and surrounded by family and friends while digging through murder articles. Fan-fucking-tastic.

I watched as her expression turned from one of playfulness to concern, her eyebrows drawing together as she clutched one of the yellowed newspaper clippings close to her face.

"Wait, this looks familiar..." She studied the page for a moment before rummaging through the handful of photos from the mysterious box and sighed in frustration.

"What is it?" I took the piece of paper as she held it out and skimmed over the contents. It was one from about two years ago about a young woman who was snatched from the city while out running at night and never seen again. "She was a student?"

Eve nodded, flicking through the polaroids. "An international student, which fits the bill of them trying to take people that wouldn't be missed. She was from London, apparently."

"What's familiar about it?" Dylan contorted himself in the chair to catch a piece of ham that was sliding off his pizza. Josh would destroy him if he harmed the blessed gaming chair.

"I can't find her picture in any of the ones here, but I swear, I recognise her. I think she was one of the ones I saw that night I left the manor." Eve frowned as she dropped the stack of photos back into the box. "I should have taken more of them."

It was Josh who cut off her spiralling. "No, if you had taken more than Alice's photo, Ryan would know we were onto him. For now, he and his screwed-up pack think we just wanted Alice back, and we're done digging into things."

"I dunno, Damien was always really paranoid." Alice plucked the article from my hand to read over it herself. "I should recognise her from when they socialised the wolves, but her face doesn't ring a bell."

Any little spark of hope died, and we fell silent, returning to our hunt for answers and digging through so many pages I had lost count.

"Hybrids, kidnappings, murder... and for what? Super-charged werewolf powers?" Dylan still munched away on his pizza as he worked.

Josh shrugged. "I get that they hate hybrids, but if they hate us, why do they want to be able to change at will? Surely that's anti-werewolf."

"They want all of the perks while maintaining their 'superior' bloodlines." Alice's strawberry blonde hair pooled around her like a halo as she let her head fall back onto the mattress beside Eve. "That's not all, they wanted to boost their strength beyond that of a normal werewolf and make them immune to vampire venom."

I frowned, pausing my search for a moment. "That's weird, my contact in the labs said that the blood from the first victim literally *fried* the machine. It doesn't make any sense."

"Wait, if a werewolf bit someone who had vampire venom in their veins—would that not kill them?" Eve's nose scrunched in confusion.

Dylan swivelled his chair around to face us, kicking his legs up onto the corner of the small couch. "It depends on how long the venom has been there, how much it has spread. There's no way to know for sure, especially when those test results would have been done hours or even days later."

"Are we sure a wolf attacked her?" Alice tapped her chin with her fingertips.

Eve shrugged. "That's what the witnesses claimed, and there were claw marks, right?"

I nodded in agreement as she looked at me.

"Vampires have claws." Josh's fingers glided over the keys on his laptop the entire time.

"Not like ours." I squeezed my eyes shut as the crime scene popped back into my mind. The way her clothes had been shredded, and the deep gouges were textbook werewolf inflicted injuries. "There were even claw marks in the pavement. Her body... I've never seen a vampire leave damage like that. They wouldn't waste the blood."

Dylan muttered his agreement. "They are greedy fuckers."

His last fling, a pretty, friends-with-benefits siren had a penchant for vamps, and it was something Dylan was still sore over. The mere thought of Eve going back to Ryan every time we met drove me crazy even though I'd no claim there. I still didn't. I shook off the murderous image my brain threw up when I considered I might have to get used to Eve being with someone else.

Not the time. But at least anger had killed off the product of her teasing.

Small mercies.

Dylan finally passed the article to Josh, pulling another fresh pile of printed stories from the one of the stacks lining his desk.

"Can you not maul everything you touch?" Josh held the page up between his fingers with a groan, pointing out the fact it was smeared with pizza sauce.

"What?" Dylan frowned and then glanced down at his hands, holding up his sauce covered fingers with a wide grin. "Oh come on, it's impossible to eat pizza and not make a mess."

Josh shot him a dirty look, kicking Dylan's legs off the couch. "There's mess and then there's you eating like a caveman."

The girls giggled, and I couldn't help but smile too as I watched them bicker like an old couple.

Dylan snatched a piece of paper towel, making obnoxious sounds that made Josh's eye twitch in annoyance as he licked his fingers clean. Josh was a neat freak, and Dylan was the opposite, it was part of the reason Josh went home so often. I was surprised he showed enough restraint not to strangle his friend then and there.

"Ezra." Josh bolted upright in his seat so fast he made Alice jump and almost drop the drink she had halfway to her mouth.

"What the fuck, man?" Dylan looked our friend up and down like he was losing his mind.

Josh repeated the name, his brown eyes wide as he stared at the sauce-stained article before zoning out, hammering the laptop keys as he typed. "Ezra."

The rest of us watched him with matching expressions of bewilderment. Josh's super-brain abilities were unquestionable, but at that moment, I questioned if we had plied him with too much caffeine throughout the day, and he was short-circuiting.

"That's it!" He tapped the paper in excitement. "I recognise the same girl as Eve."

"Really?" Eve sat up straighter, suddenly wide awake.

"I couldn't figure out the connection at first, but I recognised the name. One of Mam's friends got married years ago to a guy called Ezra. They lived in London." Josh spun the laptop to face us. He pointed at the screen which was opened on his mother's social media page. There was a photo of his mam standing with her arm around another plump woman with long black hair. Between them was a younger girl in her mid-teens with braces, but the same features as the older woman, down to her tanned skin and the way her nose had a tiny bump. There was no doubt the two were related. He pointed to the older woman and then to the younger girl. "That's the friend, Valeria, and there's her daughter."

Eve jumped to her feet, sending papers flying as she moved to get a closer look. Alice followed, along with me, and even Dylan dragged himself to his feet to look closer as Josh held up the article alongside the image of the three women. The likeness was uncanny. There was every chance that the girl in the photo and the one murdered five years ago were the same.

Josh handed Eve the article and spun the laptop to face him again, his deft fingers thumping the keys until he stopped and inhaled sharply.

"Gabriella?" Those big blue eyes of hers swam with tears as she looked over the news report.

He nodded, turning the laptop to us once more. "Gabi. Gabi was a witch."

"Why would they kidnap a witch?" Dylan's voice was unusually quiet. "And why is there vampire venom in the latest victim?"

Unease grew in the pit of my stomach. "I have no fucking idea."

Our investigation had left us with more questions than answers. I couldn't get Gabriella out of my head, and it showed. I was having the worst shift imaginable. If I kept this up, my first night working at the Dark Night would be my last. Two broken glasses in one night was a record for me, and it was especially embarrassing when it's your first shift in a paranormal bar where most of the staff are graceful with super speed.

Yeah, I was a bit faster than a human, but speed was useless when your fingers felt like clubs and your brain was in the middle of having a nervous breakdown.

"Remind me how many years you worked at the other place?" The skin surrounding Jonas' eyes creased as he grinned up at me.

He was on his hands and knees for all of two seconds, brushing the broken glass into a dustpan and dumped it into the bin under the bar counter, appearing back in front of me without a single shred of lint on the velvet lapel of his black suit.

"I swear, I have a year's experience as a barmaid, and that is the fourth glass I've broken in my entire career."

Jonas chuckled, the rich sound bringing a smile to my lips.

despite the embarrassment heating my cheeks. No one in the bar seemed to even notice my mistake, too busy chatting to others on bar stools, hiding out in the snugs, or getting hot and heavy on the dance floor.

None of the staff judged me, everyone was lovely and eager to help me settle in. Probably because most of them were young— anything from twenty to a hundred years old—vampires that the owner Darius had taken in. They all respected Jonas, and because I was in his good books, they were happy to help me out.

Although, from the way Alec chose to serve a handsy cyclops with a roving eye down the other end of the bar over helping clean up my latest mess, he might have been over my shenanigans for the night.

When I wasn't breaking stuff, I was asking questions. Or fucking up orders, but how was it my fault that a Bloody Mary meant something different if the person ordering had fangs?

I had thought starting on a weekday would be a good way to get into the swing of things, but I had seriously underestimated the ability of paranormals to knock back their liquor. I'd also made the very human mistake of presuming they drank normal alcohol. Some did, but there was a book of specialty cocktails including everything from Fae wine all the way to type O negative blood, I needed to know off by heart or else these were going to be night shifts from hell.

The dance floor was a sea of bodies, everything from Fae that had glamoured themselves to appear human, to centaurs strutting their stuff. I was still wrapping my head around the extent of the paranormal side of the world and working here was introducing me to the extensive Dublin scene, whether my brain could keep up or not.

Each wall was lined by bars, encircling the club dance floor and breaking only for the stage, exit, or the winding staircase leading to the café-turned-bar and toilets. Bright LED lights wound around the top of the bar and around the pillars spaced along it, lighting up the black quartz countertops and mirrored walls that were lined with glass shelves filled with every alcohol and mixer imaginable, and then some. The setup was pretty damn cool.

Music pulsed through the speakers, the amplification spells making the volume stay the same whether you were right beside the half-circle stage the resident DJ was mixing from, or at the opposite end of the club floor. It was a small touch, but given I worked the end nearest the stage and behind the bar was spelled to have a volume low enough for the bartenders to be able to communicate, I was grateful. Going home at the end of a night shift with my voice still intact would be a welcome novelty.

"Oi! Focus." Jonas snapped his fingers in front of my face to draw my attention back. "Fae can be fickle. Piss off the wrong one by fucking up their drink, and you'll find your family cursed for generations."

The laugh bubbling up died in my throat as I thought back to all the old wives' tales I'd heard growing up.

I paid close attention as he added some pink gin to tonic water, swirling the mixture with a metal straw as he picked up a steel spice shaker and tapped the base of it. The powder that came out was definitely not human. Multicoloured sprinkles swirled in the gin mixture, causing the liquid to glow iridescent as it settled. Jonas stirred until it bubbled for a second and wisps of vapour rose from the surface. The tiniest tingle of magic passed through me as the glass cleared, now containing what looked like rainbow gin.

Jonas held his concoction up to the light, his fangs peeking out as he beamed with pride. "See? It's easy."

I leaned in to sniff the mixture as he held it out to me, my brow furrowing as I tried to pin down the scent.

"It smells like... cotton candy."

He nodded, his smile vanishing as he snatched it away from me when I attempted to take a sip. "Non et non! Not for you, little wolf. Definitely not while you're on the clock."

I rolled my eyes. "It's one sip."

"This is elderbloom. It comes from the spores of enchanted mushrooms in the *Fae* realm." Jonas placed the glass back down on the counter and slid it towards a pixie with purple hair that shimmered like the night sky under the flashing lights of the club. "They need some extra kick in their gin. You do not. One mouthful of that, and you'd be dancing on tables half naked."

I blanched, grateful that he had stopped me. The lopsided quirk of his lips in a half-smirk told me he thought about letting that scene play out.

"Don't worry, Luke would have my head if I let you near the stuff."

"He doesn't—"

Before I could proclaim that Luke wouldn't care. Or *shouldn't* at least, Jonas cut in.

"Oh great, here comes the boss man." He pointed towards the base of the stairs at the far end of the dance floor where the crowd parted like a wave.

I followed his gaze, fidgeting with the pocket of the apron tied around my waist as a broad man who must have been nearly two feet taller than me descending the stairs with unnatural grace. He had jet-black hair, chiselled cheekbones, and moved with an unnerving air of confidence. Striking golden eyes that accentuated his brown skin, roaming over the crowd as he stepped out on the dance floor and prowled towards us. Beneath the flashing lights, he looked every bit the part of the ferocious creatures myths painted vampires to be. Darius, the infamous owner of the Dark Night.

But as he paused in front of us with a disarming smile, only kindness shining in the depth of his striking golden eyes.

"Well look what the cat dragged in." Jonas whistled, his eyes dancing with mischief as he stood on his tiptoes, leaned across the bar, and pulled the hulking man across from us into a hug. "Nice to see you actually show your face."

Darius returned the hug, his hand lingering at the nape of

Jonas' neck for a long moment and squeezing gently. "Business in America took longer than we expected."

"All sorted though, right?"

"For now, I hope." He opened his mouth, as if ready to say something else before. He turned to me then, greeting me with the same warmth he showed his old friend, a French lilt to his baritone. "You must be Eve, I'm Darius."

He held his hand out, and I took it, a shiver rolling down my spine as the cool of his flesh met the warmth of mine.

"It's nice to meet you," I said, both surprised and not by the casual way he engaged with Jonas.

I had heard plenty of good things about Darius and how he helped out young vampires that were struggling, but he also had a reputation for being defensive of the little coven he had built in Dublin. Luke had told me about how Darius had defied Lars, one of the ancient Irish vampires, many years ago. Apparently, he was a cold, calculated businessman when needed, too. It was hard to equate some of the things I'd heard with the man standing in front of me.

"What happened in America?" I asked, curiosity getting the better of me.

Keeping my ear to the ground was important with all of the investigating we had been doing.

"It's important that we... take accountability for the actions of our community members when they lose control." Darius shared a private look with Jonas as he chose his words carefully. "The partner of a good friend was being accused of something, so I took a trip across the pond to help clear his name."

"You're a lawyer?"

Jonas barked a laugh at that, covering his mouth sheepishly as Darius glowered at him.

"No, I'm not a lawyer. Sometimes all you need is someone unafraid to speak the truth and call out inconsistencies to prove that claims are unfounded."

I cocked my head to one side, my brow furrowing. "Isn't that what a lawyer does?"

Jonas made a strangled noise, turning it into a poorly faked cough as he turned away and fussed with the coffee machine. Not that the man needed caffeine, he always had a pep in his undead step.

"I suppose," Darius admitted with a defeated sigh. His expensive looking cufflinks, with the letters 'D&J' inscribed on their silver surface clanged against the bar as he seated himself on one of the stools. "How are you finding your first night? Jonas tells me all of this is new to you."

My gaze flicked to the bin housing all the broken glass I'd caused. "It's been a bit of a learning curve alright."

"That's an understatement." Jonas appeared beside us with a perfect espresso martini in his hand.

He flicked a napkin in the air and it fluttered to land on the bar surface, just as he placed the martini glass down and popped two coffee beans on top with a flourish.

Darius brought the drink to his lips, his eyelids falling closed as he took a long sip. He set it back down, his thumb tracing up and down the stem of the glass as he opened his eyes and smiled at Jonas, their gazes locked in something unspoken. "*Savoureux.*"

I cleared my throat, moving a few feet away to serve a very sweaty, shirtless demon.

Jonas leaned in, dropping his voice as he spoke to Darius. "Did you find him?"

"No." He swirled his glass, staring into the depths of the brown liquid. "We managed to prove that he wasn't responsible for that human's death, but he hasn't been sighted since. I thought he would return home once we cleared his name, but no one has seen him in four months now."

Jonas hissed and cursed under his breath. I tried my best to focus on the weird mix of sambuca and tequila the demon had requested, watching the two vampires from under a curtain of hair.

"I can only presume the worst." Darius tilted his head so his nose brushed Jonas' cheek. "He must have passed beyond the veil. I don't know who would wish him dead."

"Surely no one wanted him dead, the only one that had a vendetta was his sister. And you've proven they were lying about everything now." Jonas growled, his eyes flashing ruby red.

"Perhaps he took his own life. The guilt of being accused of killing an innocent."

"No." Jonas pulled away and tossed the crushed napkin onto the bar. "Harold was a good man."

Darius ran his palm down his face. "Which is exactly why he might—"

"I won't hear it."

I slid the nasty shot-mixer the demon had requested across the bar, barely paying attention as he handed me a twenty euro note and told me to keep the tip. They were still arguing when I finished putting the cash through the register. But their discussion had grown heated enough for me to admit to hearing something without having been eavesdropping, so I took the chance.

"Did you say someone is missing?" I wrung my hands as the two vampires whirled on me.

Both of their eyes were now blood red, their black pupils morphing into cat-eye slits.

Darius went to deny it but Jonas lifted his chin, his fangs fully visible. "Yes. A good friend of ours has been missing for some time."

"A vampire?"

"Yes. He visited us some months ago and never returned home." Darius dropped back down onto the stool with a heavy sigh. "There were some false claims made against him back in America. I thought he was on the run because of it and went over to help, but I dispelled the rumours, and he is still nowhere to be found."

"And he disappeared here?"

Jonas popped open a fresh bottle of whiskey and poured himself a double, downing the glass without even flinching before pouring a second.

"Yes. Harold disappeared in the city. He went out for a walk and never returned."

CHAPTER 19

When Dad had asked me to help with pack business, I had expected something boring like finances or purchasing more real estate for the pack, or at best maybe a session in the boxing ring so I could take out some frustrations. But after a long quiet car ride, because he'd asked how Eve was doing and I'd gotten prickly, we left the winding countryside roads and pulled up outside a set of towering wrought-iron gates. They weren't painted a normal black, they seemed almost metallic and iridescent despite the lack of floodlights. It was nightfall, and if it weren't for the well-kept drive and shrubbery beyond the gate, I would have assumed the place was abandoned.

I had never been there before, but the crest at the centre of the ominous gates told me exactly why my instincts were screaming at me: to run.

Two blood-red serpents stood out against the black outline of the crest, their bodies wound around the moon and sun with silver bared fangs glinting the headlights. The crest of the oldest vampire coven, second only to one other European coven. The Abhartach.

I swivelled in the passenger seat, the belt catching on my shoulder as my father sat with a pensive expression. Every time his finger tapped on the steering wheel as we waited with the engine running, made my skin itch.

"What the fuck are we doing here?"

He let out an exasperated sigh, keeping his gaze fixed on the gate before us. "There's no need for the language."

As if he doesn't curse like a sailor.

"Why are we here, Dad? We don't deal with them. I could have gone to Darius if we needed—"

Before I could finish my point, the edges of the crest flared a deep red as magic sparked in the air. No doubt the estate was protected with all kinds of wards. The light travelled around the outline of the crest before vanishing, followed by a loud click of the lock, and the gates groaning as they parted for us.

"I guess we're going in then," I muttered to myself. Dad smirked in the corner of my eye as I slumped back in my seat.

We remained silent as he navigated the winding driveway. It seemed normal, surrounded by acres of parkland and old chestnut trees void of their leaves swaying in the wind, but something about the place gave me the heebie-jeebies. Unease crawled under my skin as a sprawling mansion came into view, a patchwork of ivy covering the grey brick exterior.

It would have been beautiful if I didn't know what awaited us inside.

My father pulled up alongside a blood-red Tesla outside the front of the property. The car was a perfect reflection of the creature we were about to confront. I waited until he killed the engine to ask the same question again.

"Why are we here?"

He sighed, finally turning to me with a resigned sigh. "Don't make me regret trusting you with this. No losing your cool."

"Why would I lose it?" I was immediately on guard.

"Because they found vampire venom in the bloodstream of the girl who was killed, the one in Eve's jacket." His blue eyes were haunted as he scratched his stumble. "I will tell Darius myself after this visit, but I didn't want Lars to get wind of this before I had the chance to gauge his reaction for myself."

Keeping my cool wasn't my forte. "Darius despises Lars and would never leak anything he was told in confidence."

"I know."

"Then your logic is flawed."

He clucked his tongue, but that was the only chink in my dad's irritably calm exterior. "Sometimes the walls have ears. I got this information late last night from a trusted source, and I needed to get to Lars before anyone else."

"Before Damien or Ryan." My tone soured at the taste of his name.

"Exactly." Dad nodded, undoing his seatbelt and motioning for me to do the same. "I know none of Darius' vampires would be responsible. Lars and his coven play by old rules, and we need to find out if this is a problem with them or if you are right about it being the Faolchúnna pack."

I stepped out of the car just as he did, bracing my hand against the roof as I swung the door shut with more force than necessary. It's not like the vampires wouldn't hear us coming. The place was guaranteed to have a bunch of hidden cameras, and the gates wouldn't have just opened for us if my dad hadn't arranged some sort of meeting. Plus, I didn't feel like being polite. If I woke a few asshole vampires up early, so be it.

"I swear, I smelled a wolf at the scene." I fell into step with my dad as he walked towards the two large doors marking the entrance. "And I know what I saw, a vampire wouldn't have wasted so much blood. Especially one of these."

Dad paused, placing a hand on my shoulder as he turned to face me. "I believe you, but we need to understand who or what is at play. So, let's see what Lars has to say on the matter. I need you to rein your emotions in, and act like the alpha I know you can be, no matter what your feelings are about them."

My *feelings* were that the Abhartach were a bunch of bloodthirsty savages with no respect for human life. They flouted the laws, keeping humans like walking blood bags, and that was only the tip of the iceberg. But they were old and had good connections, laying low and cleaning up their own messes just enough to be less trouble than it was worth to punish. They were the vampires myths and horror stories spoke of, the dangers that lurk in the dark. A complete contrast to vampires like Jonas who only took what they needed when it was offered willingly and kept their bloodlust under control.

He took my silence as agreement, giving my shoulder a squeeze before pressing his index finger to the doorbell—which was embedded in a human skull's eye socket. The other empty eye was fitted with a ruby encased eyeball surrounded with wisps of shadow. When the doorbell chimed, the shadows swirled, and the eye within it swivelled to focus on us.

Was it a victim's eye? The thought made me nauseous, and I dispelled it just as the left door opened with a creak to reveal a large foyer, lit only by a large, round iron chandelier with ever-burning blood-red flames fuelled by magic and the sconces lining the walls. In each of the far corners, two spiral staircases led both upstairs and also to the floor below.

"Welcome, please enter." A hoarse voice caught me off guard as we stepped inside, my shoes squeaking on the black marble.

A tall, lean man stood to one side, his bony hands clasped in front of him as he bowed in greeting. His willowy figure was swamped in a black cloak that swept the floor as he moved, tied at the waist with a single red piece of cord. He was deathly pale with blonde curls and no wrinkles, barely in his late teens. Then again, he was dead, so he could have been hundreds of years old for all I knew. It was common knowledge that Lars forced his new recruits to serve him for years before being allowed to enjoy the perks of his lifestyle.

The way his lips curled back to reveal prominent fangs, and the molten hue of his irises confirmed that. This vampire was starving, and I had no intention of being his next snack. Thankfully, my dad was on the same page.

"We are here to see Lars." Dad shrugged off his jacket and folded it over his arm. "He should be expecting us."

The butler eyed Dad up like he was a nice chunk of meat, his lips stretching into a thin line as he started towards the right-hand staircase and motioned for us to follow. I paused to peer at the pictures lining the red-and-black flocked wallpaper. They were a mix of portraits of Lars or paintings depicting ancient infamous vampires, each complete with a gaudy gold frame that was probably an antique.

My natural survival instinct screamed at me as we began our descent. A lone muffled scream coming from the floor above did nothing to dissuade my unease. I clenched my jaw and focused on my father's back, resisting the urge to run upstairs and stop whatever evil those monsters were up to. Lars' idea of incense was the light scent of human blood throughout the building. It wasn't easy to tune out, and ignoring it felt unnatural and wrong, and I really, really wanted to light this cesspit on fire.

Our footsteps echoed as we descended the spiral staircase, the vampire butler leading us down a wide corridor with dark tiled floors and walls painted a deep crimson. He came to a stop outside a black door, turning the serpent-shaped handle and motioning for us to enter with one sweeping, elegant flourish of his hand.

"Master, your visitors." The butler's breath on my neck set the hairs on end as he ushered us inside.

I shuddered at the sensation, almost bumping into Dad in my haste to get away from him. We appeared to be in a meeting room of sorts, with the same dim lighting and silver sconces. Black velvet drapes matching the windowless matte walls on either side broke to give way to a large bookcase that scaled all the way to the ceiling, lined with ancient texts with decaying spines. Between two bookshelves, there was a small doorway that led God only knows where. There were stories about the dungeons the Abhartach had, and I didn't want to find out if they were real.

The dungeons were the least of my worries as my gaze landed

on the large table in the centre of the room. It was surrounded by eight chairs, with the ancient vampire made of nightmares sitting at the head of the table. There was no tea party, only a single silver goblet styled with his crest, and no doubt filled with blood. But I couldn't smell it over the stench of the body laid out on the table before him like a meal.

My stomach lurched, and it took every ounce of control I had not to puke or let the red mist descend. Neither option would end well.

It was a male, probably in his thirties, but it was impossible to know for sure because his muscle mass had rotted away to leave nothing but skin and bones in its wake. His ashen skin was peppered with puncture marks from head to toe, a mix of purple and older yellowed bruising the only colour besides the blood still slowly seeping from some fresher wounds. A pool of silk around his waist gave him a shred of dignity.

The scene before me was abhorrent, but the vampire seated near the victim's head simply lifted a napkin to dab a single drop of blood from his lips. A sharp intake of breath from my father was the only giveaway that he too was in shock.

While we knew what Lars and his cretins got up to, and the world turned a blind eye to their behaviour, it was unheard of for Lars to flout his depravity like this. It didn't bode well.

"Tom, it's good to see you." Lars rose to his full intimidating height.

Despite his broad shoulders, he moved with the practised elegance of the ancient predator that he was. He was at least a thousand years old, but he didn't look a day over thirty. His pale complexion contrasted with the well-groomed ebony curls that were cut short to frame his chiselled jaw. He looked like a model from a Hollywood movie, dressed in an expensive black suit with deep burgundy velvet lapels and a tie to match. The crisp white shirt beneath showed no signs of his last meal.

A handsome face did nothing to hide the monster lurking behind those golden eyes, devoid of a shred of humanity.

"Thank you for agreeing to meet at such short notice." Dad's tone walked the line between politeness and respect, but leaving no room to doubt that he was here on alpha business. "I know you have a lot on your plate."

My mouth dropped open, but I schooled my expression.

Damn.

Dad wasn't here to play. Everyone knew 'nice' Tom, the guy who would go out of his way to help anyone, but I had seen this side of him before. The Crescent alpha didn't play nicely when his pack was in danger.

"Well, one must respect the summons when an alpha deems the nature of the call urgent." The vampire's top lip curled back in distaste at the challenge to reveal his fangs in a not-so-subtle threat.

My dad didn't take the bait. Lars shrugged, the casual motion at odds with his Dracula act, and gracefully dropped back into his chair. He took a languid sip from his blood chalice before waving his hand in a silent command to join him.

I didn't want to sit at the feast of a human, but when my father moved to take the chair at the opposite end to Lars, I forced myself to take the seat to his left by the corpse's feet. It was impossible to tear my eyes away from the carnage before me. Did it move? Was that the tiniest movement of the human's chest? The barest hint of a rise and fall? It was.

They were alive.

That sick motherfucker.

"So, what is so important that it requires my immediate response?" Lars circled his index finger around the rim of his glass to create a ringing sound.

If he set me any more on edge, I'd be free falling off a cliff.

"I presume you're aware, given your status and connections." Dad was not subtle in his purposeful massage of the vampire's ego. "There has been a spate of murders in Dublin over the past few weeks, and we are trying to get to the bottom of it."

The ringing stopped, and Lars lifted his drink to his lips once more before commenting. "Surely, that's for the witches to deal with."

"Not when it appears that one of my wolves was the intended target."

Lars quirked a perfectly plucked eyebrow. "And you have proof of this?"

"I have enough information to know that she was the intended target in at least one case."

"Well, she could hardly be the intended target when the most recent one was a male." Lars scoffed, peering over his glass at my dad. Luke, a predator waiting for his reaction.

Dad simply smiled, the expression so at odds with this entire charade. "Ah, so you are aware of the details."

"I have access to both the internet and newspapers." Lars waved a dismissive hand, sinking back into the plush cushions of his chair. Although they were all velvet chairs with ornate designs etched into the wooden frames, his was fashioned more like a throne. "And I do have 'connections', as you put it."

The veiled digs and slow back and forth grated on my nerves. Dad said I was like a bulldozer sometimes, but I couldn't understand the point in playing cat and mouse with someone like Lars. There was vampire venom in two murder victims, was he or his coven involved? Simple. In and out. No need to sit here at some kind of fucked up human buffet.

"Yes, well, in that case you are aware that the first victim had an uncanny resemblance to a pack member of my pack."

Lars cocked his head to one side. "Ah yes, the hybrid mutt that has caused such a fuss."

I leaped to my feet ready to launch myself at Lars, consequences be damned. But my father's hand was around my wrist in milliseconds, forcing me back down with an ironclad grip. He shot me a murderous look of warning. My hands shook, white knuckles clenched around a bunched corner of the white tablecloth that was splattered with blood in places. This monster deserved to die.

"You will speak of my pack with respect." Dad was every inch the alpha as he straightened in his chair. "I am here because two of the victims were found with vampire venom in their bloodstream."

The slightest flicker of amusement and annoyance in Lars' golden irises was all the confirmation I needed.

"I am not sure what you are insinuating, Tom, but I am not responsible for every single vampire on this island. There is many a rogue that hunts the streets. They are not my responsibility."

My dad didn't waver, placing his hands palm down on the table and leaning forwards in his chair. "Rogues that are turned by your coven's carelessness are still your—"

We were interrupted by another vampire coming through the door carrying a tray with two wine glasses and a bottle of what I hoped was normal wine. She was young, with blonde hair that hung to her waist which only highlighted her sharp features, gaunt from malnourishment. Like the butler, she wore a long black robe, but the cord around her waist was a royal purple. I didn't know what the different colours meant and quickly lost interest in wondering as she hovered by my side, inhaling too deeply for my liking as she placed a glass down for each of us.

"No, thank you, this won't take long." Dad placed his hand over his glass in a polite signal to the young vampire not to fill it.

The girl glanced at Lars, uncertain. "Master?"

Not for the first time that evening, bile rose in my throat.

"That won't be necessary, Mona," Lars snapped, his wrinkle-free brow furrowed.

She nodded, her hand shaking as she placed the wine bottle back onto the tray.

"Do you get some kind of kick out of terrorising your coven members?" I spat, losing the battle to keep my tongue in check.

Lars looked at me for the first time since I'd entered the room, seemingly not deeming me worthy of his time until then.

"Respect is earned *boy*, you would do well to learn that." Lars' tone was ice cold and filled with an intense hatred that was impressive given he'd just met me, and he was the one with a dead body on the table and no morals. "Mona here joined us last year and has been working her way up the ranks at an admirable speed. You see, many humans choose to join us. They seek the freedom and beauty of immortality, and in return for that, they give me their loyalty. But my trust is earned."

I wrinkled my nose in distaste. No doubt he preyed on struggling humans, I couldn't imagine anyone choosing this fate —especially when Lars didn't help vampires through their change. He didn't teach them to control their bloodlust. He let them sink or swim, and the few that wanted to change or escape, and some he had presumed dead, had graced Darius' doorstep at The Dark Night over the years seeking sanctuary.

Lars appeared to read all of this on my face, turning to the new vampire and then patting his lap. "Mona, dear, tell the two gentlemen your story."

She didn't bat an eyelid this time, not that vampires blinked much, crossing the room and perching on her master's lap. I resisted the shudder crawling its way up my spine at this performance, and a quick glance at my dad told me he was equally uncomfortable.

"I found out about vampires when I had a one-night stand with one, and he forgot to wipe my memory."

There was a posh lilt to her accent as she spoke for the first time.

Lars chuckled, the sound unnatural. "Some of the younger ones are careless."

I opened my mouth to interject, but a sharp kick to my shin under the table stopped me.

"I did my research and waited until I found one of the vampire lairs in the city. My parents have money, and I was raised to spend my life climbing the corporate ladder, but my older brother would inherit everything." She seemed content to sit on Lars' lap while a human bled out in front of her despite her having been one only a year prior. "No matter how hard I worked, I was never good enough, and I was sick of living in his shadow. I wanted power, and I knew that if I was a vampire, I could be my family's legacy for generations."

She was talking about some of the underground clubs where vampires fed 'consensually' on humans, but the consent part was questionable. Vampire venom was an addictive aphrodisiac, so they lured humans in and got them hooked on the high. Yet Mona didn't fit that bill. Sometimes humans turned to the paranormal for all the wrong reasons.

"Mona wasn't interested in partaking, she knew in her heart that she wanted to be a vampire." Lars offered Mona a sip from his goblet which she drained in seconds with a smug smile. Her eyes remained deep red, the small amount doing nothing to calm her bloodthirst. "One of my confidants vetted her, and we came to an agreement. She has been settling in so well and is very happy with her decision, isn't that right darling?"

She nodded, her smiling lips stained red. "I have no regrets."

The way she batted her eyelashes at a guy that was at least ten times her age was just another nail in the coffin for me. My self-control was rapidly slipping.

"That's all for now, I'll fetch you later." Lars lifted Mona to her feet and dismissed her with a satisfied smirk before turning his attention back to me. "Does that satisfy your curiosity?"

I had no doubt about what they would be getting up to later, and it was an image I wanted burned from my brain.

"Sure." I clenched my jaw as I ground the single word out.

"There's no need for the show, Lars." Dad broke his silence as the door swung shut behind Mona, his words clipped as his patience waned. "I did not come here as an enemy, simply an alpha concerned for his pack. I thought you would appreciate the warning that the murders may be implicated with your coven."

The coven leader levelled my father with a cold glare. "I would believe that if this were more of a warning and less an interrogation."

"I only ever act in the interest of my pack. An attack on one of my wolves is an act of war, and you know this." My alpha rose to his feet, his eyes flashing silver in warning, and there was little left to the imagination with his tone. "As you said, you are a *very* busy man, so I'll get straight to the point. Were any of your vampires involved in those murders? I don't believe in coincidences."

Lars looked up at my father with a mixture of boredom and irritation. "No, my coven was not involved, and I am not aware of any vendetta against any of the mongrels in your pack. It must have been a rogue, or maybe you should talk to that barman about the little coven he's building."

My dad didn't rise to the bait, simply giving Lars a curt nod that the bastard didn't deserve. "Then I have all the answers I need, and we will leave you to enjoy your evening."

He didn't wait for a response or dismissal, striding towards the door without looking back. The human on the table's heartbeat slowed, and their shallow breaths were barely visible now. Serving as a human blood bag was no way to die.

"Luke." Dad glared over his shoulder at me with a thunderous expression.

The alpha in me, the protector, screamed at me to savage that monster and put the poor human out of their misery. But I couldn't, not without risking my back, and that was one thing my dad had always drilled into me. Protect the pack. I stood and shot Lars one final look of disgust before forcing one foot in front of the other. I wasn't sure how I felt about turning my back on an ancient vampire or navigating the halls of this mansion when their venom was lethal to us, but I was more than ready to get out of that room.

Just as we opened the door to leave, a whimper came from the head of the table. It was cut short as Lars' hand shot out in a blur, followed by a loud crack as he snapped the human's neck in one smooth motion.

My dad flinched, his jaw ticking as we continued down the

corridor. Being alpha wasn't about making the right choices, it was about making the hard ones.

CHAPTER 20

Blood red was not my colour.

I stared at the material of the dress poking out of the paper bag on the leather seat beside me. Alice had picked it out for me, and while I appreciated that my wardrobe could do with a dash of colour that wasn't black, white, or some shade of grey, I wasn't sure that kind of dress was for me. But she'd sworn blind I looked amazing, and when Craig had turned up because I was late to meet him, he'd agreed, and they'd brought it to the cashier before I'd had the chance to squeeze back into my skinny jeans. I'd made it out just in time to pay myself.

Luke had offered to pay for whatever outfit I needed for Dylan's birthday, but I'd flat out refused to let him. I think my refusal wounded his ego a bit. Not in a narcissistic way, he shared his father's generosity and wanted to take care of people. But this was the first purchase with money from my new job at The Dark Night, and I liked the autonomy. I hadn't noticed how much Ryan had been controlling what I wore under the guise of 'gifts'. But that was the past, and this was my present.

"Eve?" Alice broke my little spiral, her chin propped on her hand as she gave me a knowing look. "Where did you go?"

"Somewhere I shouldn't have." I unfurled the napkin I'd bunched in my hand.

Craig arched an eyebrow at me in question but didn't push it.

Nor did Alice. Instead, she stuffed a French fry in my mouth with that bubbly laugh of hers ringing. "Good, now finish up because if I'm home late Mam and Luke will send out a search party."

Craig chuckled. This was the girl who was barely able to speak after she came home. Her knee still bounced under the table, and her eyes widened at any bang. She had been on edge all day, but she hadn't bolted. Not even when we made our way through the busy streets, brimming with weekend shoppers taking advantage of the early December sales.

"It's a joke." A genuine smile lit up her pixie-like features as she nudged me with her elbow. "You're allowed to laugh."

I swallowed down my shock and returned the smile. It was good to see her like this. Therapy was doing Alice a world of good.

Craig launched into an embarrassing story about me at college, something about me, Kate, and the reason I don't drink tequila anymore. I'd been worried Alice would be nervous around him, but he had an infectious personality. He was both a positive ray of sunshine and a ball of sour sarcasm all rolled into the perfect friend.

"It was a costume party band, and we had gone as the ghostbusters. Eve had been knocking back these cocktails all night, her tongue was bright green. But then her face was green to match, and I got there just in time for her to projectile vomit all over me. When Kate walked into the bathroom and saw me covered in Eve's cocktail puke, she just started screaming the Ghostbusters theme tune."

Craig followed up with his own rendition that had me cringing and covering my face with my hands.

"If you hadn't made me do that last shot of tequila, I'd have been fine." I pointed an accusatory chicken strip at him. "It was your own fault."

Alice laughed, her strawberry blonde hair that I'd curled earlier that morning bobbing with the movement. "I think I've gone off my food."

Out the windows of the restaurant, the daylight had faded, and freshly hung Christmas lights sparkled overhead, lining the length of Grafton Street. Add some snow, and it would be truly magical. I snorted at that thought now that I knew magic existed and found myself wishing that a certain someone was occupying the fourth chair at our table.

"Room for dessert?" Craig wiggled his eyebrows playfully.

He wanted to raid the gelato shop down the street. Despite being stuffed, I always had room for ice cream. But our bill never came to the table, which meant Craig had sorted on his not so inconspicuous trip to the bathroom.

"Sure, so long as I'm paying for it."

Despite my best efforts to wrestle it into submission, I tried and failed to stuff the paper bag containing the sexy dress into my small leather backpack while the others got their coats on, so I waved them on.

The backpack won.

Their laughter drifted up the stairs as I made my way down the stairs to them, tugging on my parka before the bite of the winter chill could get to me. Yes, hybrids ran hot. But Irish winters were bitter.

"So, do I get to know what the heart attack dress is for?" Craig asked, as we stepped outside onto the streets that were still bustling with people out shopping, and now the evening crowd out partying.

"Heart attack?"

A wide grin stretched his lips, and he nudged Alice with his elbow as if they were in on a secret together. But she was tiny, and he was well over six feet, so his elbow was practically at shoulder height. They made a comical duo.

"As in, it'll give whatever guy you're targeting a heart attack. A certain blonde-haired 'friend' with nice muscles?" Craig chuckled, and my cheeks flushed hot.

Alice rolled her eyes. "What, you think I haven't noticed something is going on there?"

"*Nothing* is going on there." I swung the paper bag my dress was in at Craig, thumping him in the arm, but it did nothing to stop his teasing laughter.

She didn't seem convinced, but her eyes glazed over as if she was looking right through me. Except she wasn't. Alice's mouth tightened, and she stood frozen in place. I turned to figure out what had caught her eye, reaching out to place a hand on her shoulder to calm Alice regardless of whatever was triggering what appeared to be a flashback. But my hand met air as Alice burst into action, shoving past Craig with superhuman strength that sent him on his ass, before sprinting down Grafton Street and disappearing into the crowd.

"Alice!" I roared, trying to keep track of her grey woollen hat bobbing in the crowd, but it was futile.

Craig scrambled onto his knees as I rushed over, grabbing my friend's hand and helping to haul him to his feet. He towered over me, his blue eyes wide with concern as he searched the crowd for Alice. "What's going on with her?"

"She's..." I paused, struggling to find the right lie because I couldn't explain a hybrid werewolf kidnapping to my human friend. "She has PTSD from a bad relationship."

It wasn't the truth. There was no relationship, Alice had confided that all her and Ryan had done was kiss, and it was sweet teenager romance until the asshole lured her to a date and kidnapped her for two years as part of his pack's fucked up experiments and research. But the truth would have sent Craig into a nervous breakdown that we didn't have time for. I needed to find Alice.

He didn't question the lie, nodding and following as I jogged towards where Alice had disappeared. It wasn't easy, winding our way through the crowd was more like a lot of shoving, disgruntled remarks, and my knees becoming increasingly battered from swinging shopping bags of those who refused to move out of the way.

I couldn't see her, but thanks to the fact that the black chunky knit scarf around my neck was hers, I was able to track her movements. Despite the general smells of the city coupled with the overwhelming clouds of perfume around some women we bumped into, Alice's scent filled my senses from the scarf, and I was able to zero in on it. Craig stayed by my side, his hulking frame helping the sea of shoppers and tourists to part. I followed Alice's trail down Nassau Street and then through the entrance to Trinity College.

Once we stepped back out into the open, she was easier to scent. But it wasn't just Alice that I was picking up. There was another constant she seemed to be following, but everything about it was wrong. Similar to the visitor to my apartment, but with a twist I didn't have the nose or time to pick apart.

The campus was pretty empty except for a few students crossing Library Square now that the daylight was gone. My sneakers slapped the damp cobblestones, echoed by Craig's beside me. As we passed the bell tower, a shrill scream pierced the night that sent a shiver rolling down my spine.

Craig skidded to a stop, his head swivelling as he surveyed the area, and one hand reached into his pocket, as if to grab his phone. "What was that?"

The howl that followed had my hand snapping out to wrap around his wrist before he could lift the phone to his ear. "Don't."

"Eve, I don't know what is going on here, but that didn't sound good."

I swallowed hard, unused to the authoritative edge to his voice. But too used to lying. "I'm sure it was just teenagers."

"Then why have you gone as white as a sheet?" He asked, his jaw set as his finger hovered over the phone screen ready to hit dial. "What is really going on? There's a Garda station around the corner. Let me call them."

Another scream sounded, and my grip on his wrist tightened.

"I promise that I will explain," I lied, peering through the darkness towards the buildings towering in the distance. "I need you to trust me. We need to call Luke, not the guards."

He frowned, his eyebrows knitting together as he lowered the phone from his ear and stared at the solid grip I had on his arm.

I stepped back, straining to pick up more muffled sounds of a scuffle and trying to convince myself that the very female scream I had heard wasn't Alice.

"Stay here until I message you that it's okay." I took another step backwards.

He shook his head, one of his steps eating up two of mine. "No way am I letting you go alone."

"Craig, it's too dangerous for you."

His expression darkened with concern. "If it's dangerous, I'm definitely coming."

Another scream had me hiss with frustration.

"Please, it's not safe for you."

A wave of guilt washed over me as I saw mistrust in his eyes. And hurt. "Either I call this in right now, or you let me come with you and we face whatever Alice has gotten herself into together."

My resolve slipped as Alice's panicked voice drifted from the distance, too low for Craig's human hearing to pick up. "Fine, but you stay behind me."

Another scream had me cursing and sprinting towards the noise. How was a human Garda in training and my weak hybrid ass was going to do anything? I fished my phone out of my jean pocket while running, the crumpled dress shopping bag slapping my thigh as I raced towards Alice.

Hey, I can't get to the phone right now, but if you want to leave a message—

"For fuck's sake." I resisted the urge to throw my phone at

the wall as Luke's voicemail played out. The moment the beep sounded, I launched into my message, scanning the area and on high alert while I fought back the tears pricking the corner of my eyes. "Luke, it's Eve. Alice took off, and she's in danger. I don't know what's going on, but she's somewhere on the Trinity college grounds. I need you."

My voice cracked on the last sentence, and I killed the call. Both Tom and Helena rang out too. Alice shrieked in the distance and I cursed, shoving the phone back in my pocket as I sped up. All I could do was hope Luke got the message. Of course technology was no use against whatever paranormal craziness I was about to run headfirst into.

I didn't have time to get nostalgic about being back on campus when the scuffle I'd heard was cut off by someone shouting, and what sounded like a door slamming.

We passed the closed food court, this part of the college campus was like a ghost town and the tennis courts were silent, the nets swaying in the breeze. Leafless cherry blossom trees rustled as I slowed my pace, and Craig stayed by my side, both of us stalking along the perimeter of the courts. My head snapped up as a muffled yell sounded in the night, but my friend just cocked his head and arched an eyebrow at my sharp intake of breath. As if he knew I was hearing things he wasn't.

I took the next right, and he followed on my heels. My body was tense and coiled, ready to pounce as we made our way down the path, and I focused on following Alice's scent until it stopped in front of one of the grey buildings. The glass panel of the wooden door was frosted, but I could make out the shadows of a silhouette crouching and peering through one of the ground-floor windows to the right of the entrance.

A glimpse of blonde hair in the pale light of one of the lamps lining the tennis court confirmed it was Alice. My shoulders sagged, but the relief was short-lived as the now recognisable tinge of magic swelled in the air and a strange light flashed inside the room she was spying on. There were muffled screams, as if muted by a spell, and Alice flinched, ducking down out of view of whoever was inside.

I crouched behind a small Mini Cooper parked there, and because we were downwind, I purposefully let myself step on a twig to catch Alice's attention. Her head shot up, but when I beckoned her to join us, she shook her head with her lips pressed in a fine line and leaned up from her couched position under the window ledge to sneak another peek inside.

I had no idea what had caught her attention on the street or why she had taken off, but whatever it was, it wasn't good. And that's when I caught sight of a figure I never wanted to see again passing the window.

A figure backed up against the door with a thud, and the sound of Alice pleading reached my ears, full of fear and a pang of sadness.

"Please don't do this."

I didn't stop to think before grabbing the brass handle. The moment my fingers brushed the dull metal, a blinding purple light flashed as large fissures cracked across the old wood. A heavy weight slammed into me, sending me flying back as the door exploded outwards.

A whip of blonde hair, and her scream told me it was Alice.

Shards of wood splintered towards us as the air sizzled as we were blasted back. On instinct, I wrapped my arms tight around Alice's torso as I broke her fall and landed shoulder first on the pavement. Pain radiated down my arms and stole the breath from my lungs.

"Eve!"

CHAPTER 21

LUKE

"**Y**ou need to calm the fuck down."

Josh growled from where he was lying on the gym bench, his muscles straining against the sleeves of his T-shirt as he repacked the barbell above his head with a loud clang. He sat up once Dylan gave him the nod that it was in place, tipping his head back as he downed a gulp of water before tossing the bottle back on the ground.

I ignored him, focusing my energy behind every single blow I landed on the punchbag in front of me. The chain attaching it to the ceiling rattled with each hit I landed, the bag swinging and smacking into the wall so hard a white spider's web of cracks began to form in the black paintwork as the plasterboard underneath took a battering. We were in the extension of the house the two guys shared where Dad had funded a mini gym area complete with a bench press, squat rack, and the punch bag that I was annihilating.

In the corner of my eye, Josh shook his head before starting another set, but I was beyond talking to. Seeing red, all of the pent-up anger and frustration needing a release.

Unfortunately for the punch bag, it was in my line of fire. The seams of the material groaned and stretched under the assault of my fists, but I kept on swinging punches, stopping now and then to throw in a lead kick that sent it flying into the wall with a loud bang.

"Enough."

In the time it took me to blink, Dylan appeared between me and the punch bag, catching my fist in his hand with a grunt of effort.

I hadn't noticed his approach, too lost in my thoughts. Sweat streamed down my face, and my knuckles were red raw, but I was numb.

"Who pissed in your cereal?" Josh swiped a towel over his face as he sat on the edge of the bench, a puddle of sweat on the leather surface from his last set.

"I didn't eat cereal."

Dylan rolled his eyes, lowering my fist before releasing my hand from his grip. "Oh, sure, I forgot your body is a temple."

"Not all of us can live on a diet of sugar and carbs." I snatched my water bottle off the shelf beside me that housed a few skipping ropes and resistance bands.

"Ah yes, I forgot whiskey counts as one of your five a day." Dylan smirked, checking the chain attached to the punch bag for damage. "Unless your dad fancies funding a refurb, you're done for today."

"Excuse me?"

He levelled me with a look, his usual humour replaced by a seriousness that didn't suit him. "You're about to put a hole in this wall, and I'm not losing our workout space to your rage."

"What he means is, we think you need to take a beat," Josh cut in, his brows drawn together as he watched the two of us.

Dylan shot him a look, but Josh stood up and grabbed me by the shoulders, pushing me backwards and away from Dylan before I could deck my friend. He snatched up two focus pads off the shelf and put them on, turning to face me with his hands up in a defensive pose. He set his feet, knees bent so he was balanced and ready to take whatever I threw at him, before nodding and beckoning me forwards.

"You punch, we'll talk."

I wasn't going to say no to that, adrenaline and the mixture of feelings I didn't know how to process were still pumping through me. I pulled my hand back and slammed it into the pad on his left hand, knocking Josh back a step with the force of the blow. He was strong, but I was stronger. Werewolf magic was weird, I trained the same amount as the guys, but it was like Mother Nature knew I had the blood of an alpha running through me and gave me a little boost for it. Which was stupid. I didn't deserve perks I had never earned and would never live up to.

"So, is this about Eve or your dad blindsiding you?"

Dylan watched the inquisition, drinking his water down in big gulps. The noise made my skin crawl, but I kept my fists focused on the pads.

I grunted, spinning around to land a kick to give my fists a brief break to heal. "Both."

Josh didn't miss a beat, lifting the pad higher to catch my foot with ease.

We hadn't told my father everything we had found because he'd be pissed off with me for going against his orders. Bringing me to that vampire lair with no warning and dropping the bombshell that vampire venom was found in the victim's bloodstream was fucked up. He had known for almost twenty-four hours before telling me. Apparently he hadn't even planned to bring me. He wanted to bring Darren, but Helena had insisted I go. If I was supposed to be alpha someday, why was he leaving me in the dark? More to the point, this concerned Eve and Alice. If he knew something that impacted Eve and me keeping her safe, I deserved to know. She deserved to know. I was hardly going to hunt down every vampire in the city and interrogate them, what was he worried about?

As if reading my mind, Dylan decided to chime in.

"Tom has as much information as us at the moment, the venom doesn't give us answers. Just more questions." He wrinkled his nose as he flopped down onto the gym bench. "Maybe he wanted to figure some of it out before he told us."

I flexed my fingers, the raw skin knitting back together and the redness dissipating. "Or maybe he's being an asshole."

Both of my friends stiffened at that remark, Josh batted my foot away with more force than necessary when I landed the next kick. A low growl of warning rattled from Dylan's chest. He might have been my father, but he was their alpha.

"Ok, let's move onto issue number two." Josh planted his feet to stay steady as I rained a series of hooks on him, alternating between right and left at random. "Eve's training went really well yesterday."

I slammed my fist into the pad in his left hand with a snarl, Josh's brown eyes widening as I forced him back a step.

"What? Don't tell me your little pissy party is about me training Eve?"

"Of course not." I shrugged, but the tips of my claws extended at the thought of him training Eve. Him being in close quarters with her, his hands on her, seeing her panting.... No, I didn't like the thought of that at all.

"You're an idiot sometimes, you know that?" Josh grunted as I landed another punch as Dylan chimed in.

"Eve likes you. She wouldn't have kissed you if she didn't." He poured some of the water over his head and shook it out like a dog as he watched us spar.

"Ah yes, the kiss that ended with me shoving my tongue down her throat to avoid being attacked while someone left a suspicious box outside that looks like a threat to both my sister and Eve."

Josh stepped forwards, refusing to yield as he continued to take every blow I gave. "That box doesn't seem like it was a threat, I think it was a gift. A clue. It helped us realise they're not just kidnapping hybrids."

"It did leave us with more questions than answers though." Dylan earned a scorching glare from Josh.

"I don't give a fuck about the box."

Dylan clapped his hands on his knees, whooping sarcastically. "Ok, we're getting somewhere. So you admit this is about the kiss?"

I glowered, and Josh snorted with laughter.

A few sarcastic retorts ran through my mind, but I dropped my hands with a sigh of defeat and voiced the thought that had been haunting me. "Our first kiss wasn't supposed to be like that. We were both angry and after all that shit with Ryan, I wanted things with me to be different. I wanted to be different."

"You aren't anything like him." Josh slipped the pads off his hands before grabbing two bottles of water off the shelf nearby and tossing one to me. "This isn't some romance movie, first kisses don't have to be a fancy affair."

Dylan rummaged in his rucksack, producing a protein bar that he wolfed down in one go, mumbling with his mouth full. "It actually sounded pretty hot."

"Well, she's avoided being alone with me ever since the moon run so maybe it wasn't that hot for her."

Those words made me sound like a moody teenager, but I couldn't help how I was feeling.

"What if she's worried about the same thing?" Josh took a swig of his water and dropped to sit on the mats with his legs crossed beneath him.

"What do you mean?"

He shook his head, sharing a look with Dylan. "I mean, what if she's worried you didn't enjoy it? That girl has been through hell and back. Ryan might have had some fucked up feelings for her, but he treated her like shit, and then she caught him with Nadine. She's gonna have trust issues after that."

"I haven't broken her trust though?"

Dylan—*Dylan*—of all people piped up with the most

insightful piece of advice on women I'd ever heard come out of his mouth, especially sober. "No, but Ryan did. She doesn't trust her own judgement anymore. She knows you're not an asshole, but she can't be sure this would work out or if your feelings are real. She's probably scared of losing the only real pack she's ever known. It's a big risk to take, especially when the kiss got interrupted."

Not for the first time, I realised I was being an idiot and too caught up in my man brain needs and not hers.

"Why don't you talk to her tonight?"

"She's busy," I muttered.

Eve was out shopping with Alice and the empty apartment was what had driven me to visit the guys. Alice wasn't very talkative after her therapy sessions. Although they were helping overall, she tended to hole-up in her room after spending an hour with the siren that had come highly recommended. So, Eve had offered to spend the rest of the afternoon with my sister in an attempt to cheer her up.

"Then talk to her tonight. Or go for a drink, food, anything. Just talk and lay your cards on the table." Josh held his hand up to silence me before I could interrupt. "I know you told her before that you have feelings, but our lives are kind of crazy at the moment, and you need to reassure her that whatever goes on between the two of you, this is her pack."

Dylan nodded in agreement, and I turned back to the punch bag. How exactly was I going to convince Eve to take a chance on me when I was likely going to be her alpha someday, whether I wanted it or not?

My phone buzzed on the floor by the bench press, and I turned just in time to see Dylan swipe it up, smirking as if ready to uncover some sordid message when it was probably just my dad.

"Give it here," I growled, stalking towards him.

But then all the colour drained from his face and he looked up, his eyes wide and irises flashing silver.

"What is it?" I grabbed the phone he held outstretched, my stomach dropping at the image that had flashed up.

There was a missed call and two messages from Eve, they looked like the automated ones that give your location and a photo attached. The one your phone sends when you hit the SOS button. I didn't know when or why I was set as her emergency contact, or if she knew I was. The first image was a blurry butt-dial or photo of the ground, but the second was a picture of Eve and a red line of blood on her cheek, sheer terror shining in her eyes.

CHAPTER 22
EVE

E ven with stars dancing in my vision I could hear Craig screaming my name.

I must have blacked out for a moment because I came to as someone or some*thing* latched onto my arm that was already on fire, biting deep into the bruised flesh and making me howl in pain.

I shook my head as my eyes readjusted to the darkness, wincing as it felt like my brain literally *rattled* in my skull at the gesture. A mop of black hair draped over my arm as the creature sank their teeth in far enough to graze bone.

"Eve!" Craig's voice cut through the chaos, dragging me back to the present.

He moved towards us, what must have been a small penknife clutched in his hand as he came at my attacker from behind.

"No!" I growled, panic surging through me as my friend waded into a magical fight with nothing but a knife and some basic self-defence training that wouldn't do shit if a paranormal set their sights on him.

I kicked out at my attacker, earning a grunt from them as I planted my heel firmly against their ribs and shoved with every ounce of strength I had.

Their teeth tore through my flesh as my attacker released me, searing pain making my vision swim. But I was running on adrenaline, keeping my eyes fixed on Craig who stared at us wide eyed with undiluted horror etched into his features as the creature stalked towards him.

The door to the building had been obliterated by the blast of magic, shattered glass crunching beneath my feet with each step I took. I kept waiting for a witch to appear behind one of the upturned tables inside the trashed tutorial room, but none did.

Fiery pain radiated down my arm, and my nerves screamed at me at the slightest movement, but my fear for Craig, and Alice's limp body against mine, overruled anything else. I rolled onto my stomach, gritting my teeth, and hissed in pain as I forced myself onto all fours despite my body's protests.

Alice lay beside me, unmoving and face down in an eerily familiar position. The last girl I'd seen lying like that had been ripped to shreds.

"Come on, wake up," I pleaded, keeping one eye on Craig as I moved Alice onto her back and breathing a small sigh of relief as I caught a pulse.

She wouldn't take much longer to wake up, which was good because I needed backup.

"Eve..." Craig jogged backwards, dodging between the different cars to keep some distance between himself and the attacker.

I scrambled to my feet, my left arm hanging uselessly by my side, the pain extending from my dislocated shoulder making me grimace.

"Oi!" I snatched a stone off the ground and flung it at the thing approaching Craig, catching it in the back of the head. "It's rude to play with your dinner. We're not done yet."

They swung to look at me, and I was caught completely off guard when a set of silver eyes and a normal human face stared back at me. Her blood-smeared lips curled back in a snarl. The eyes didn't make sense, she looked like a hybrid.

My nose told me she was a wolf, but the hairs standing on the back of my neck argued that there was something else, something wrong with the picture in front of me.

Craig took her distraction as an opportunity to double back towards us, picking up his pace when she leaped onto one of the cars, denting the roof of a fancy-looking Jeep and crawling her way towards us like she was demonically possessed.

"What the fuck is going on?"

I was way out of my depth here, we needed backup. I grabbed my phone from my pocket, tapping furiously at the cracked screen as I jogged backwards away from them, but it just blinked on and off. I bashed all the buttons, cursing under my breath as I threw another rock at our attacker to keep their focus on me. "I promise I'll explain, but you need to trust me right now."

"Trust?" Craig leaped back as the Irish version of *The Ring* jumped onto the bonnet of the Mini nearby with a metallic crunch.

The hairs on my neck stood on end as magic charged the air. Her eyes shone bright silver, but I didn't need my nose to tell me that this wasn't a wolf staring back at me.

The streetlamp above her acted like some sort of spotlight, highlighting the bloodthirst shining clear in their eyes as they monitored us like prey. She was dressed in a grey tracksuit, the top caked with blood and the bottoms stained with a mix of mud and crimson. Her sleeves were shredded in places to reveal claw marks lining her arms and neck, wounds Alice must have made that had already healed. A deeper gash on their stomach was exposed and still bleeding, but they barely seemed to notice it.

Alice stirred beside me, and my shoulders sagged. A deep purple bruise had bloomed on her cheek, and she had defensive wounds on her forearms, but she should be fine.

My relief was short-lived as a soft green glow emanated from the girl's hand as she placed it over the gaping wound. When she removed it, the skin had stitched itself together and all that remained was a thin line of blood.

Magic. She had magic.

It wasn't possible, but I didn't have time to decipher the puzzle pieces because the witchy bitch had grown tired of playing and stalked towards the three of us.

"What the fuck are you?"

She didn't answer, simply advancing on me with her brow furrowed and fury shining in her eyes, as if I was responsible for all the wrongs in the world.

Adrenaline surged through my veins as my wolf side woke up at the sense of danger, the urge to change and defend the people I cared about overwhelming me.

I knew what had to happen, there was no way I could take this thing on in human form. This wasn't how things were supposed to play out, but if I had to risk losing Craig as a friend to defend his life, I'd make the same choice every time.

My wolf side would heal most things, but injuries still hurt like a bitch. Craig's pale face turned green as I snapped the bone back into place with a grunt. "Keep her safe."

He didn't even ask about ringing the Gardaí this time. It was crystal clear that the demonic horror bitch was beyond their pay grade.

With that, I left him standing with a penknife and a shit tonne of questions, turning on my heel and running. The moment I gave it something to chase, our attacker would take the bait.

I was right.

Metal creaked as the girl demon thing sprang off a car bonnet and raced after me. I cast a quick glance over my shoulder and picked up my pace as she gained on me, skidding on broken shards of glass as I ran over the broken door and inside the empty building. I trampled up the stairs, trying each of the doors before an inhuman howl echoed from downstairs, and I put all my strength into kicking one of the doors until the lock snapped.

I closed the door behind me and shoved one of the shitty plastic chairs against it, along with a small bookcase. I'd never been in this building, but some of my tutorial rooms had two entrances. Sure enough, there was a thin partition wall lining the back of the classroom.

Thank fuck for weird old buildings.

My hands were clammy as the girl climbed the stairs. I ran a loop around the classroom and opened a window, rubbing myself against the window ledge like a cat in heat before walking on chairs and desks like I was a kid playing the floor is lava. I squeezed through the small gap I'd opened in the partition and cursed under my breath as my sweaty hands fumbled to get it closed.

Barely a second later, thunderous footsteps and a howl of frustration came from the corridor outside.

Out the window, Craig helped Alice to her feet. Plastic on wood screeching came from the other room as the magic wolf fought her way through my makeshift barricade. It was now or never.

I'm not sure what part of my brain thought leaping out a window as a wolf would scare Craig less than shifting in front of him, but it was too late for damage control.

I closed my eyes and let the innate magic wash over me, only the slightest hint of pain present as the change moved through me, contorting my limbs and forcing the shift. In seconds, I found myself standing on all fours in the middle of an empty classroom, staring at a chalkboard with illegible symbols all over it and an overturned desk beside me.

One I must have hit.

The single light bulb above me swayed back and forth before blinking out.

Shit.

Five claws spearing through the partition wall was my only warning before magic sizzled in the air, and a hole was blasted through it.

I spun to face the girl, sitting back on my haunches and ready to sprint around her rather than fight, but she was on me in an instant. She slammed into me with so much force that we snapped a desk in two and sent the surrounding chairs clattering across the classroom. The blackboard attached to the wall we hit snapped off the wall with a loud crack, showering us in a dusting of chalk.

We both managed to scramble out of the way just in time for it to smash into the desk which split in the middle and sagged to the floor under the weight of it. The girl clearly had no interest in self-preservation, not bothering to shift as she launched herself at me again. Had she only escaped being trapped under the blackboard because she was busy chasing me?

I circled around the room, jumping over destroyed desks and diving behind a chair as she launched a spell my way. All that was left in its wake was a charred plastic and the mangled metal of what were once the legs.

Another blast of magic came my way, and I had to dive across two desks, winding myself as the corner of one hit me square in the chest. The window shattered in a shower of glass as she hit it with what I swear was something like a fireball.

I backed up until the window ledge dug into my left hind, small shards of glass stinging under my paws.

The tutorial room was too small to play cat and mouse with another wolf, let alone one with magic that I couldn't wrap my brain around.

When she flicked her wrist and a flame sprang to life at her fingertips, I only had one choice. The door wasn't an option in my wolf form, so I turned and launched myself out the first-floor window, overshooting the jump slightly in my effort to avoid snagging on any glass caught in the window frame.

Craig's expression morphed from one of shock to horror as a large wolf catapulted itself out the window his friend had stood at minutes before.

Alice screamed my name, and damn was it good to hear her voice.

I landed on all fours, my legs screaming at the impact, and

somersaulted a few times until the momentum stopped, and I landed unceremoniously in a heap. I was sprawled on my side with bruising, some road rash on my hocks that would heal in minutes, and no broken bones.

"What the hell were you thinking?" Alice snapped, darting towards me but stopping short as her eyes widened.

I was barely on my feet again when a weight crashed down on me from above, followed by a sharp pain in my side from either teeth or claws sinking into the muscle there. On instinct, I dropped my shoulder and flipped onto my back, thrashing and kicking until I managed to dislodge the bitch.

She went straight from attacking me to the nearest target, throwing herself at Craig and slamming him into the side of the Mini. His ribs smacked against the metal door with a thud and his body went limp.

No.

All of the memories of the night I found Kate, the horror and pain, came crashing back down.

"Spencer, stop!" Alice screamed, grabbing a chunk of the girl's jumper with a clawed hand and flinging her away from my friend. The lamppost nearby blinked out as the hybrid crashed into it with a satisfying crunch.

I rushed over, nuzzling around his neck and chest until I heard a pulse and was satisfied that he was breathing unlaboured. Craig groaned and rolled onto his back, clutching his ribs.

Alice crouched beside me ready to shift, but I jumped in front and grabbed her sleeve, tugging her back over to Craig's side with a shake of my head.

"You don't understa—"

The hybrid girl scrambled to her feet like some alley cat, her gaze fixed on Alice who was kneeling by Craig's limp body.

Not on my watch.

A low growl ripped from my throat as the need to defend my pack kicked in, and I switched to the offensive. I kicked off my haunches, pouncing on the girl while she was distracted by Alice.

My open jaw clamped around the back of her neck, canines slicing into the flesh either side of her vitals as my larger body slammed into her human-sized one.

She twisted in my grip, kicking and clawing at me as she thrashed. A well-aimed clawed fist to my jaw forced me to release my grip, and I yelped as she sank her own teeth into the exposed flesh of my underbelly. I couldn't understand why she didn't just shift, but the canines that had extended from her gums were doing a fine job at tearing into me.

A scuffle sounded to my left, but I was busy latching onto the bitch's arm and flinging her off me to pay attention to anything else. I had her pinned beneath me when searing pain shot through my chest as her grip on me turned to an intense burning sensation.

She was *literally* playing with fire, and my furry ass was about to get burned.

Alice's desperate cry rang out again. "Spencer!"

I didn't have the time or ability to speak to figure out why Alice kept trying to throw herself into the fight, but at least Craig kept his promise and held her back.

The freaky magic hybrid was relentless, on her feet the moment she hit the ground. Teeth, claws, anything, she was super-fast and slipped through my grasp as I fought to get her under control.

But between dodging spells and the damage she inflicted every time I got my paws on her, I was quickly growing tired. Not to mention the way she managed to heal away every non-fatal wound I landed.

I dodged an ominous shadowy looking spell, weaving between cars to lure her away from my friends again. She followed like a good little pup—well, a murderous, demonic looking hellhound.

Wheeling around the corner, I found myself in a dark alleyway fenced in by a large brick wall with barbed wire lining the perimeter. I wasn't going to be scaling that.

I spun to face the attacker head on, preparing myself to shift, but she was on me immediately. She slammed into me with so much force one of my ribs cracked before we even hit the ground, rolling until my back hit the wall with a sickening thud.

Blood pooled in my mouth as I was pinned to the cold tarmac, grappling with the hybrid as she fought to wrestle me into submission. I howled in agony at the searing heat radiating from her hands, the pain so overwhelming I thought I might black out. This was it. And all I could think about were the two people I was supposed to be defending, but I was a weak hybrid.

"Stop!" Alice's voice pierced through the pain clouding my thoughts, and I turned my head to see her racing towards me, with Craig hot on her heels. "You don't want to do this!"

The girl paused for a moment, swivelling her head to look at Alice in a slow, sinister way that was straight out of a creepy horror movie. Blood dribbled down her chin. My blood.

That was my moment, she was distracted and her carotid artery was pulsing right there. I was inches from sinking my canines into her throat and ending this when Alice ran into view.

"Don't hurt her! That's Spencer." She spat out a mouthful of blood onto the concrete. "She's one of the hybrids the Faolchúnna pack kidnapped."

CHAPTER 23

LUKE

Whatever location Eve's phone had pinged was clearly wrong. We ran into the middle of Trinity college, staring around at the dimly lit historic courtyard that wasn't occupied by a single soul. Above us, the crescent moon glowed in the starry night sky, taunting me. I'd tried to call Eve several times, but it kept ringing out, and Alice wasn't picking up either. So, that left us with the dog tracker option.

It didn't take us long to track them, Josh caught Eve and Craig's scents by the bell tower and my sister's nearby. We had given my dad a call, and he'd asked us to tread carefully given the public place, but the moment Eve's howl of agony pierced the silence, all sense of control went out the window.

I'd fucking kill anyone who laid a hand on her.

Not being able to shift was a good thing because I was racing across the grounds, pure rage and fear pumping through me as I followed the noise. I could hear them, Alice's panicked voice and Craig's too. There was one other scent, wolf but then not, and the rising sense of magic charging the air made my stomach sink.

What the fuck has Alice gotten herself into?

My question was answered as we rounded the tennis courts

just in time to witness the unmistakable iridescent glow of magic ricocheting off one of the old stone buildings marking the entrance of a small alleyway.

"Wait." Dylan reached out to grab my arm, dropping it when I whirled on him with silver eyes. "If there's a witch there, we can't go barging in."

"You want me to leave my sister and Eve to fend for themselves against a *witch*?"

He flinched back at the venom in my voice, but level headedness wasn't in my repertoire while they were in danger.

Josh shook his head, his brow furrowing as a snarl echoed beyond us. "What about Larissa's threat?"

"No one threatens my pack. Witch, wolf, or otherwise." I growled, already striding towards the chaos and not bothering to check over my shoulder if they were following because they would.

I wasn't prepared for what I found. Eve was in her wolf form, cornered against a bunch of old crates stacked up against the far wall. Her coat was matted with blood, and she was unsteady on her right hind leg, but nothing obviously fatal. Her lips pulled back in a feral snarl as she faced off with a girl that smelled like a wolf, but had a ball of fire swirling in her outstretched hand. Alice stood a few feet away beside Craig who held some sort of tiny knife, her hands raised as if to placate, her brow creased with worry.

"Eve!" I pulled the attention of the witch to me.

But when she turned, her eyes were silver, and her claws glinted below the dancing flames she had conjured.

Josh skidded to a stop beside me, his mouth dropping open. "What the fuck is that?"

"That's not possible." Dylan breathed, his shocked expression mirroring my own.

"Luke." Relief washed over Alice's face as she caught sight of us. "Stay back."

I was not taking orders from my little sister.

"Like fuck am I staying out of this." I stopped short as the hybrid prowled towards us. "What the hell is going on here?"

We were forced into action before Alice could answer. Sparks flying from the hybrid's fingertips were the only warning before she launched a blast of power our way. I dived to the right, landing in a crouch beside Josh as the ground beneath my fingertips shook at the impact.

Dylan had split the other way, staring wide eyed at the hole left where we had been standing. "What *is* she?"

"She's a hybrid, just like me." Alice scraped her claws against the wall beside her, the shrill sound pulling the hybrid's attention back in her direction.

Craig jumped in surprise, wide eyed as he backed away from her until his heel hit the base of a chestnut tree that overshadowed the alley.

"Spencer." She kept her claws out, but her hands raised as if she was approaching a startled deer and not a rule-defying, magic wielding hybrid with a death wish. "I know you're in there. It's Alice, remember me?"

"Hybrids don't cast spells." A low growl ripped from my throat as the hybrid flung a spell my sister's way.

"Maybe we can debate her existence when we're not playing life or death dodgeball?" Josh's voice was strained as the hybrid snarled and threw a nasty bolt of magic our way.

The hybrid wielded spells with no finesse or control. In fact, with her long black hair whipping around her face and the way she staggered back after releasing the power told me she was struggling to contain her power.

She twisted out of the way, still approaching the hybrid despite the massive 'fuck off and die' vibes. "Spencer, I know you remember me. We were in that place for months together."

The hybrid paused, her irises shifting to olive for a brief moment before flooding silver once more.

"I was there with you. We talked about your parents. You have a brother, right? A little brother back home," Alice continued, the softness in her voice so at odds with the chaos around us. Broken glass, blood, charred remains of whatever Spencer had decided to cook. And yet, my sister looked at the hybrid like she was an injured kitten we needed to rescue.

The fire in the hybrid's palms paled to a yellow light swirling in the darkness, her vision seeming to clear for a moment as she finally spoke. "Alice?"

"It's me." Relief washed over her face.

"Please, make it stop. I can't fight this for much longer," Spencer said, an American accent slipping through as her voice wavered.

I sucked in a sharp breath as she inched closer.

"It's okay, we're going to get you somewhere safe and—"

Spencer shook her head, beginning to back up. "No, you need to get away from me. I tried to warn you, it's not safe."

Alice was a handful of steps away from the hybrid now, close enough that she could touch Spencer. And she did. No one spoke, no one breathed as she reached out tentatively with her hand as she took another step closer, emotion clogging her words. "What have they done to you?"

Her fingertips brushed the girl's cheek, then whatever connection was there severed.

Magic surged in the air, and with a flick of her wrists, Spencer released a blast of magic that sent Alice's tiny frame soaring through the air. Eve snarled, launching herself across the clearing just in time to cushion Alice's fall with her large body.

At the same time, the hybrid launched a barrage of magic our way. One misdirected spell hit a tree overhead, followed by a flash of light and a loud crack as a large branch broke off right above where Craig was sitting.

I sped across the alley, my arms outstretched and shoved him out of the way, but I wasn't quick enough.

Part of the branch still caught Craig's head. It hit the back of my shoulders too, but I took the blow with a grunt, falling to my knees with Craig in my arms. Eve's blue eyes met mine across the fight dividing us.

He's breathing.

She started at the sound of my voice in her head, but nodded, staring for a long moment at her friend before rejoining the fight.

I gave Craig a quick once over as I sprinted to the mouth of the alleyway to lay him down safely. He was out cold, but there was no blood oozing from the wound, and I'd done enough in med school before dropping out to know he was probably just concussed.

When I turned back to them, Josh and Dylan were forcing the hybrid back towards the base of the tree. She was so focused on them, she didn't see Eve coiled and ready to pounce.

Eve took her out from behind, her front paws slamming into Spencer's back. The magic conjured in her palm guttered out as she hit the ground face-first, howling in agony as Eve sank her canines into her upper arm. Alice ran into the fray, still in human form, but with her claws at the ready. Before she could reach them, Eve released the hybrid with a yelp and scampered back, nursing a fresh laceration to her thigh.

My claws shot out, and I closed in on the hybrid with the two guys flanking either side. The hybrid was cornered, her pretty features contorted into a mask of rage as she attacked us with magic. One on one, I don't think I'd have been able to outmatch her, but with the five of us, between attacking and dodging spells as we retreated, we were overwhelming her. That's why wolves travelled in packs.

"Give in, and we can try to figure something out." I ducked under another vicious spell launched my way.

But Spencer didn't answer. The girl who had appeared briefly was gone, and now she was moving as if possessed with a single order. Kill. Yet, she didn't seem interested in me or the guys. She would retaliate, almost as if we were an irritation. But each time, she swiftly refocused her efforts on both Eve and Alice.

The flame building in Spencer's palm flickered several times before winking out. She growled in frustration, mumbling under her breath and motioning with her hand to conjure another spell, but her well was tapped dry.

Josh looked to me for confirmation, and I gave him a curt nod, following through with the order I didn't want to make. "If that's what it comes to."

The hybrid seemed to understand what was being said and made a lunge at Eve, shifting into a black wolf mid-air before they both clattered to the ground in a mass of claws and snapping jaws.

"Luke, no!" Alice whirled on me, her bloodied state doing nothing to convince me to let the girl live.

"We can bring her back to the pack. Dad will know what to do, he'll save he—"

"Unfortunately, we can't allow her to leave." At the entrance to the alleyway, Nadine stood with one hand on her hip, her fiery curls swaying in the breeze. She was dressed head to toe in black with leather boots, looking like a cross between an assassin, a cat burglar, and a girl heading on a night out on the town.

"This is none of your business," I spat, not forgetting the hell that she had put Eve through.

"Wrong, again," Nadine purred, her hips swaying as she prowled past me. I took a step back and her lip curled back in displeasure. "This hybrid has exposed herself to the human world and therefore has broken our laws."

Eve wrestled with the hybrid, both of them fighting in wolf form now. They snapped and bit at each other, kicking and clawing their way to dominance. The tables kept turning, one pinning the other until they landed a nasty bite, and the roles reversed. Eve was holding back and trying to force Spencer into submission.

"You don't enforce our laws." I started towards Eve as the hybrid landed a nasty bite on her shoulder.

She was pinned beneath Spencer, both but her teeth were lodged in the hybrid's throat. I rushed at them, but before I could reach Eve, Ryan stepped out from the shadows and a loud gun shot rang out, echoing in the alleyway, followed by a high-pitched howl of agony.

It felt like time slowed, but in reality, it was seconds between me noticing the gun in Ryan's outstretched hands and watching helplessly as a silver bullet shot through the air headed straight towards Eve. Dread like I'd never felt turned my limbs to lead as I ran towards her, my throat raw as I screamed her name and watched the bullet speeding towards her and the hybrid as they fought.

Then everything went silent, and time came rushing back into play as the black wolf slumped and fell still.

I raced over to them, ignoring Alice screaming behind me as I hauled the hybrid off Eve. She was still in her wolf form, her coat ragged and clumped with blood, and she whined at me as I looked her over, finding only cuts and lacerations, no bullet wound. Eve nuzzled my arm, blinking up at me with those bright blue eyes of hers.

The air around us shimmered as Eve shifted back to her human form, naked and shaking in my arms, but she didn't move from there. Tears ran down my cheeks and she reached up, gently brushing them away wordlessly.

I'm okay Luke.

That wasn't possible. Being able to communicate with your pack was one thing if you were closely linked, but it didn't extend to human form.

Any shock was washed away with relief as I wrapped an arm around her neck and hugged her against my chest.

Alice ran over, screaming for her friend. Dylan and Josh were there in an instant, crouching beside my sister as she fell to her knees sobbing. They helped her cover Spencer with her jacket,

Alice whispering and clutching the hybrid's neck as she took a ragged breath. Blood spilled from the wound in the wolf's chest where a silver bullet was lodged with perfect aim in her heart. It was a fatal wound, and we all knew it.

All I could think is that could have so easily been Eve, and the thought of coming so close to losing her made my world come crashing down.

I heard Ryan approach, but not even my unadulterated hatred for that man could make me move from Eve's side in that moment.

"We are responsible for our packs," he said simply, shoving his hands in the pockets of his slacks. His casual demeanour only made me want to rip his throat out more. "Consider this taken care of."

"Kidnapping someone doesn't make them a part of your pack." I clutched Eve against me and wrapped her in the hoodie Josh handed me with a growl. "You think you'd have learned that lesson by now."

"At least I know how to protect what's mine."

There was something disturbing about the way Ryan's lips curved as the light went out in the hybrid's eyes, and the black wolf slumped to the ground. When she shifted back into her human form, he got to his feet, dusted his pants off, and stepped over her lifeless body without a hint of remorse.

"Well, isn't this quite the mess." A sickly-sweet voice came from behind. When I turned, Larissa walked into the clearing, wearing a floor-length black dress that matched the shadows and skimmed the ground as she sauntered into the aftermath of this bloodbath as if she were crashing a party.

Ryan straightened, his shoulder stiffening. "It's dealt with."

"Really? Because it looks like a dead hybrid is lying out in the open where a human could stumble across it." Her red lip peeled back in an ugly snarl as she threw her right arm out in the direction of the dead hybrid. "Is that a gun?"

Alice yelped and stumbled back as the body in front of her burst into flames. "No!"

I scooped Eve up, running back with them away from the growing fire as the guys grabbed Alice by an arm each and pulled her back. They held my sister in a firm hug as she tried to claw her way free and save Spencer. But it was too late. Eve remained still and silent in my arms, her fingers laced with mine as she clutched my hand against her chest.

Spencer wasn't the monster here.

CHAPTER 24

EVE

Luke was silent as he carried me bridal style into the apartment complex and entered the lift. He was topless, much like the night I'd met him. In fact, the circumstances were eerily similar. Except this time the blood on his T-shirt was mine, not his, and I wasn't naked. The moment we got back to his house, he'd bundled me into one of his giant hoodies, but I was soaked to the skin thanks to the lashing rain that had started when we left Kildare. Tom was furious about what happened, not at me, but at the Faolchúnna pack. I think Luke might have flipped out too, but he had spent the whole time holding his gym vest to the wound on my thigh despite my protests. It was healing, but slowly, because I was exhausted. Since confirming Alice was okay, he had refused to take his eyes off me. Even on the drive back to the apartment, he spent more time watching me in the mirror than the road. It was intense, even as he held me in the lift, any time I glanced over he was watching me with an unreadable expression.

An awkward silence hung in the air, and I couldn't find the words to break it. Time ticked by until a shrill ping told me we'd hit my floor.

I shifted as if to stand, causing him to tighten his grip on me in a silent command to stay. I did as I was told.

He took a tediously long time to get the key in the door. *Was his hand shaking?*

Once we were inside, he set me down on the black leather couch before stalking to the kitchen. Each step was purposeful, silent, and tension held his bare shoulders as he moved about, filling a bowl with water and searching through the drawers before producing a clean tea towel. My breath caught in my throat as he locked eyes with me, the intensity of his stare still my racing thoughts.

"Come here." His voice was rough as he broke the silence and gestured to the island separating the kitchen and living room. "The lighting is better in the kitchen."

I didn't know why we needed good lighting. I got to my feet with a grimace, clutching his bloodied vest that was more like a rag now to the wound. I didn't get to take a step before he was in front of me again, his hands gripping my forearm to steady me.

"I'm fine."

He ignored my grumbling, wrapping a gentle arm around my waist and ducking down so I could sling mine around his neck. "Kitchen island, now."

I rolled my eyes, telling myself it was just adrenaline as my body tingled with anticipation under his touch. "Yes, sir."

It came out as a joke, but I swear his eyes darkened, and I fell silent again as he helped me over to the counter. In the same bossy fashion, he didn't wait before grabbing my hips with a feather light touch and lifting me onto the island so I was perched on the edge of the countertop, the perfect white quartz now smudged with splotches of blood. My blood.

I found myself staring at him again as he brought the bowl and towel over, along with a small bottle filled with a silver liquid that looked like mercury. His hair was darker when wet, it looked tousled like when he was just awake. There was an innocence to that, a complete contrast to the dark promises in those hazel eyes.

"May I?" He gestured to the hoodie that was hitched up to just above the wound.

"That's the first time all night you've asked."

He arched an eyebrow, his lips quirking up in a lopsided smirk. "I was making sure you were safe."

"It's customary to ask if you can touch a lady's leg." I bit down hard on my lower lip as he peeled the gym top off the wound. The hoodie was riding up dangerously high now, and I had nothing underneath, but Luke had seen me naked twice now. Neither of them were planned. It's not like he hadn't seen me naked after the fight, he was the one who wrapped me in a blanket after. I needed to get used to being naked around people. But this wasn't anyone, it was *Luke.*

"You're not a lady."

I kicked out at him with my other leg. "Rude."

"A lady doesn't go around kicking the shit out of blood crazed hybrid monsters," he teased, clearly trying to distract me as he damped the towel and pressed it against the deep laceration on my inner thigh. "Or knock back vodka like it's water. Or call the man next in line to be your alpha an asshole."

"No, I called you an alphahole." I hissed in pain as he dabbed the cloth around the edges of the wound.

He kept his body pressed up against the island, pinning that leg with his hips while my other swung back and forth as I rode out the pain and tried to resist the urge to kick him. He gripped my thigh with his free hand as he cleaned it as gently as possible, but it still hurt like a bitch.

"Semantics."

I kicked out at him again, my nails digging into the countertop as I gripped the edges. "Well, I'm sorry I'm not a lady."

"Why? It's a good thing." He shook his head, his expression hidden from me as I lurched forwards in pain.

"If you say so."

"I do." Luke released his grip on my thigh briefly to dip the towel into the water, and I swear, despite the pain I mourned the loss of contact. He rinsed the towel and rung it out before beginning his torture once more. "I don't think you realise how badass you looked when you were fighting. Even if you did give me a heart attack."

I didn't fail to notice how his voice tightened on those last words.

"I was fine." I reached out to place my palm on his chest.

He turned his head, his lips brushing across my wrist as he fixed me with another intense stare that had my heartbeat racing. "What if you weren't? Do you know what would have happened? I'd have ripped Ryan to pieces along with that mouthy redhead. And then the witch."

I swallowed hard. "You'd have started a pack war. Larissa would have killed you."

"If I'd had to watch you die, I wouldn't have given a shit about my life or my pack."

"That's not true," I argued, my mouth going dry as I found myself squirming under his gaze.

Luke shook his head. "I've told you before, I'm not alpha material. I'm selfish."

"You care about your pack, they're like family." I clenched my jaw as he dabbed the deeper part of my wound with the bloodied cloth, breathless because of the pain, and my head spinning because of his words.

"They are, but I care about you more. I'd kill for you in a heartbeat."

He looked down, focusing on fiddling with the lid of the little bottle while my mouth opened and closed as I searched for the words.

"This is unicorn blood, it'll help the wound heal faster. I think that girl caught you with a spell as well as her claws, so it's just taking your body a while to figure it out. This will speed up the process."

My body might have been busy with figuring out how to

heal, but my brain was too busy reeling. The goosebumps left in the wake of his touch told me that all of me was a bit too concerned with what was happening to focus on healing. It was so low on the priority list that not even the mention of *unicorns* existing overrode Luke's revelation.

He poured about a thimble full of the unicorn blood onto the bloodied towel—that was definitely being tossed away after tonight—dipping his right index finger in it before swiping it across the wound. The silver liquid was mesmerising as it danced in the light before shimmering as it seemed to melt into the skin. It stung for a brief moment, and I tensed in response, accidentally digging my nails into his chest. Before I could apologise, the pain receded, and the wound began knitting itself together until the bleeding stopped, and the skin returned to its normal colour. Only a fine red line remained in its place that was already fading.

"Pretty cool, right?" His expression didn't give anything away as he looked up at me, his hand still pressed on my thigh while he braced the other by my side on the countertop, boxing me in.

Who goes from declaring that they would have murdered your ex in cold blood to 'pretty cool' when talking about unicorn blood magically healing your leg?

What the fuck is my life?

"Eve?"

I had reached out to catch a single droplet of water that had come from his hair and slid down his chiselled pecs, stopping where my palm was resting against his chest beneath the crescent-shaped nail marks I'd just left. And some carnal part of me really liked the sight of my marks on him.

"Yeah?" My voice shot up an octave, my body now very focused on the wrong things now that I was healed. I squeezed my thighs together in the hopes he wouldn't notice, one knee still pinned in by his hips while the other had at some point hooked itself around the back of his thigh.

This was dangerous. He was going to be my alpha someday. I had a shitty track record with men. Tom would never kick me out of the pack, but if this didn't work out, I'd never be able to face staying.

"What's going on in that brain of yours?" His heartbeat remained irritatingly calm under my hand despite the way I could feel his breath on my lips. His hand didn't move from my thigh, maddening in its stillness.

I shook my head, trying to put some distance between us, but if I leaned back any further that hoodie was going to ride up and betray me completely. "Nothing."

He released my thigh to reach up, his thumb brushing across my forehead and smoothing out the lines there. "You're worried."

"Sort of."

"About today? I promise, you're safe here now."

I tugged my lower lip between my teeth. "Not that."

"Eve." Luke chuckled, the soft timber of his laugh rumbling beneath my hand which seemed to be glued to his chest. "I'm going to need more than a few words to help, I'm not psychic."

"I thought you could do everything Mister Alphahole," I murmured, a small smile tugging at the corner of my lips.

He towered over me, tilting his head so his nose brushed against mine and my breathing hitched. "I'll show you exactly what I can do, just say the word."

"We can't," I whispered, my fingers curling against his chest.

"Why not?"

"The pack, you're going to be alpha." I dropped my head, my cheek resting against his as I finally voiced my fears out loud. "If we didn't work, I'd lose everything, and I'm only just finding my feet."

He surprised me by grabbing my chin between his finger and thumb and forcing me to look up at him, all gentleness in his gaze replaced by a burning desire that caught me off guard. "Eve, if we don't work out it won't be because I don't want this. If you decide I'm not for you and want to walk away, I would still want you in my pack. Seeing you with another man would drive me crazy, but your happiness means more to me than my pain. I'd rather have you in my life as a friend than lose you altogether."

I opened my mouth to respond, but he shifted his hand to press his thumb to my lips, his fingers brushing against my throat in the process and sending my heartbeat off the charts.

"I would never forgive myself if we didn't try this."

He went to continue, but I slid my hand up his chest to the back of his head, tangling my fingers in his hair.

"Shut up and kiss me."

And he did.

Those hazel eyes of his were molten as he grabbed me by hips and pulled me so that my ass was barely perched on the edge of the kitchen counter, my hand caught between us as his lips crashed into mine in a bruising kiss. He slid his tongue along my lower lip before biting down and forcing my lips to part for him. I didn't have time to catch my breath, his hands exploring my body while his tongue explored my mouth.

I was on fire, the pain in my thigh a dull ache in the back of my mind as I cupped the back of his neck and pulled him closer. Months of pining, miscommunication, and pent-up sexual attraction spilled over. And yet, there was something *more* to it.

Our first kiss had played on my mind on repeat, but it had nothing on this. Luke was different this time, he wasn't holding back, and every stroke of his fingertips or the way he let his hand fist my hair as he crushed his body against mine set my nerves alight. He tugged my head to the side, his uneven breaths making goosebumps rise on my neck before he dropped his lips to my collarbone, and a low moan escaped me.

He paused just long enough for me to glance down and meet his hooded eyes before he bit, scraping his teeth along my collarbone and eliciting another moan.

The corner of his mouth lifted in a smirk as he did it again, holding my gaze the whole time and making me squirm. "That's going to get addictive."

"What?" My eyes fluttered closed as he tortured me with his tongue.

"You."

If I'd been wearing underwear, that one word would have destroyed them.

He trailed his tongue lower, stepping back an inch so he could slide a hand down the leg he'd trapped there, applying the lightest pressure to the inside of my knee in a clear command. I didn't have time to think before his lips were back on mine, and I had spread my legs. He closed the space between us and I wrapped my legs around his waist as he deepened the kiss. The movement caused the slightest hint of pain as the unicorn blood worked the last bit of its magic on healing the wound on my leg. But I was pretty sure even if I was bleeding out, I'd have been content to go like this.

Luke confirmed this when he pressed his body against mine, his hands going to my ass and squeezing as he forced my body against his. I ground against the seam of his gym shorts as he hit just the right spot, and I moaned into his mouth. Maybe unicorn blood was an aphrodisiac, maybe it was adrenaline. But I'd fantasised about this for far too long, and I needed it. I needed him.

The sound of him groaning as he devoured another noise of mine was sinful. I wrapped both arms around his neck, leaning into the kiss as he slipped his hands under the hoodie that had bunched around my waist. He ran his fingertips along my side and across the exposed planes of my stomach, leaving goosebumps in his wake. I shuddered and let out a pathetic whine when his touch skimmed the crease of my thighs but didn't go lower.

He chuckled against my lips, breaking the kiss to nip my jaw as he slid his hands higher and brushed his thumbs across the underside of my breasts. "Tell me this isn't all you've thought about since I started staying over."

"W-what?" I swallowed, my breath coming in soft pants as one of his hands climbed higher and he pinched my nipple gently.

"You're not a very good listener." He tutted softly, pinching again and that signature smirk appeared as a moan slipped from my lips.

"I'm a little distracted."

"Well, it was a little distracting when you were moaning my name in the shower while you got yourself off." Luke leaned in, his lips brushing the shell of my ear as his gravelly tone had me grinding my hips in slow circles against his. "But you didn't hear me complaining."

Despite the fact I was half naked in the kitchen with the blinds open, and his sweatshirt barely covering my chest while I tried to get whatever friction I could, my legs locked around his waist, my cheeks were still burning at his confession.

"I knew you heard me," I grumbled, his familiar scent of burnt orange and pine filling my senses as I nuzzled into his neck.

He pinched my other nipple hard, and I gasped, jolting upright. "Don't you dare go shy on me."

"I-I..."

Before I could manage a response, he slipped his other hand down between us, trailing a torturous slow line down my stomach and continued lower. "I want the Eve that was grinding against me just now, the one that wasn't worried about what anyone would think. The Eve that's fearless, brave, and hot as fuck."

I'd never heard myself described like that, and I didn't feel it. But he looked at me like he wanted to devour every inch of my body. His hand dropped lower, his fingers brushing across my sensitive flesh had my head emptying of any thoughts but him.

I arched my back, digging my nails into his shoulders as he brushed his thumb across my clit before running a finger down my slick centre. This was a million times better than any time my mind had wandered to him in the shower.

"That's more like it," Luke purred, his irises flashing silver as he felt just how wet I was for him. But this time I didn't blush, I pushed my hips towards his hand needily, and he growled in approval. "Good girl."

I dug my heels into the back of his thighs as he slipped one finger into my pussy, my head falling back. He braced his free hand on the countertop behind me, caging me in. I dropped back onto my elbows, and he captured my lips in a hungry kiss that muffled my moans as he added another finger. I was trapped beneath him and at the mercy of his touch as he hooked his fingers to hit the right spot, leaving me breathless. I wanted to tangle my fingers in his hair, to rip off his clothes and fucking jump the man, but he had me trapped and bucking my hips as he brushed his thumb across my clit in torturous circles until he pressed down at the perfect moment. A wave of ecstasy washed over me, he broke the kiss to nip my lower lip and trail kisses down my neck as I came apart for him, riding the waves of pleasure as I came down from the high.

I expected him to stop, but as soon as I came down, he plunged his fingers deep and swiped his thumb across my sensitive clit, making me cry out. He wrapped his arm around my back, kissing me deeply, a low chuckle rumbling from his chest. I ran my hand down his taut abs to the drawstring on his shorts and tugged them down. His laugh cut off abruptly, morphing into a possessive growl as I dipped my hand under the material and wrapped my fingers around his hard dick.

And fuck did that have me clenching my thighs around his waist in anticipation.

He curled his fingers inside me to hit that sweet spot, rolling my hips in rhythm with his, stroking his hard length as I whined. His dick twitched under my touch, and when I kissed along his jaw, biting down on the nape of his neck as I worked my way down just at the same time as running my thumb across the tip of his dick that was wet with pre-cum, he snapped.

"Bed, now." Luke growled, withdrawing his fingers from me before grabbing my ass with one hand and scooping me off the counter while he wrestled the sweater off me and tossed it onto the floor as he carried me down the hall.

"We don't need a bed." I moved my hips against his to emphasise my point, forced to wrap my arms around his neck to keep myself upright.

He nipped at my earlobe, spinning us so that I was pressed against my bedroom door. The photo frame on the wall to our left rattled but I couldn't have cared less as he drove his hips into mine, his hard dick rubbing against my clit as he pinned me there.

"I'll happily fuck you on every surface in this apartment, but the blinds are open, and I want you all to myself tonight."

With that, he squeezed my ass and shoved the door open, his tongue tangling with mine as he carried me to the bed. He didn't even break our kiss as he dropped me down on my back and kicked off his shorts before climbing over me, nudging my legs open with his knee.

"Luke, please." I rolled my hips in rhythm with his as he deepened the kiss.

"My name sounds so good on your lips." He ran his hands over my breasts and stomach with a look of admiration that had me squirming as his touch moved lower.

A condom wrapper rustled and I whimpered with anticipation as he ripped it open with his teeth. It didn't take long before his attention was on me once more, trailing his thumbs along the crease of my thighs as he squeezed them and forced my legs further apart. I was completely exposed to him, and I swear, Luke looked at my pussy with a hunger I'd never seen before. His eyes flashed silver again as they met mine.

"I've said your name before."

"That was from another room while you touched yourself." He ran his hands along my sides, lacing his fingers with mine and pinning my hands either side of my head as he leaned over me. He lined up his hard dick with my entrance as he brushed his lips against mine. "It sounds different when you're breathless and moaning for me."

My only answer was his name in a long, drawn-out groan as he quite literally stole my breath away. His dick stretched me in the most satisfying way as he pushed until he was buried to the hilt. All gentleness went out the window when I moaned and rolled my hips in a clear command for him to move.

I'd never admit how many times I'd fantasised about Luke Whelan fucking me, but my imagination did not do him justice.

Luke trailed kisses down my throat and collarbone as he moved his hips against mine, quickly finding a rhythm that had me a panting, moaning mess. He read my reactions like a book, fucking me with hard, deep strokes. The scent of sex filled the air and sweat beaded his brow as he released my hands so he could brace his either side of my head, taking my commands to 'keep fucking going' very seriously.

I was lost to his touch, my fingers tugging on his hair as that delicious pressure built in my core. He was stretching me in the most delicious way and his touch was everywhere, but I needed more. I wanted him all over me, I wanted to drown in him. His eyes never left mine as dropped his hand between my legs, teasing my overly sensitive clit and that forced me over the edge into oblivion.

My back arched off the bed and I cried out his name as pleasure washed over me. Every muscle in my body spasmed as I climaxed, riding a wave of pure ecstasy. At the same time, he thrust deeper inside me and came with a possessive growl that had my pussy clenching around his dick as it pulsed.

"Fuck." Luke stilled against me, the huskiness in his voice fuel to my fire. He dropped his forehead down to mine, his biceps flexing as he held himself braced above me.

He swept his thumb over my clit just as I was coming down and my body jolted, my garbled protests muffled as he stole a kiss.

"Luke," I mumbled, my head falling back against the pillows. "Holy fuck."

Mischief danced in his eyes, just like it had every time he turned up in my bar all those months ago.

He smiled against my lips. "I'm nowhere near finished with you."

CHAPTER 26

LUKE

I wasn't lying when I told Eve I was a selfish alpha in the making. When Jonas had called asking to meet up at the very respectable hour of five in the morning, I'd told him to fuck off. Eve was fast asleep beside me, her brunette hair tousled and covering half her face. If it wasn't for his promise that it was an emergency, I wouldn't have woken her.

She looked like an angel in my arms, so tiny and breakable it made a lump bob in my throat. I would never forget that fleeting moment when I thought the silver bullet had hit her. Being a part of the paranormal world came with its own risks, especially when we weren't willing to let the Faolchúnna pack continue with their sick plans, but the thought of losing her was unbearable. I had never felt like this about a girl before. I'd dated, slept around a bit, but this girl. Fuck. Not only that, but she made me want to be more selfless. Which is the only reason that I agreed to meet Jonas at all.

The alpha wolf part of me would quite happily have kept Eve trapped in her bedroom all day and night.

That part of me was still well and truly awake when I watched her walk past the demons guarding the Dark Night, her hips swaying in the gym leggings she'd thrown on as she made her way down the dimly lit corridor.

I was dreaming. I had to be dreaming.

But I wasn't. Eve turned to me, her eyes still hooded as she shot me a sleepy smile.

Josh and Dylan were already perched at the coffee bar on the upper level of the Dark Night when we arrived. The place was pretty empty at this hour, morning for the nocturnals and evening for those still chilling in the café upstairs that was being readied while the club downstairs was being cleaned at vampire speed. Jonas waved as he passed the balcony, zipping around behind the counter, looking impeccable in a three-piece suit. Unlike us mere mortals, he didn't have bags under his eyes.

I hadn't told the guys. It was normal for me to stay at Eve's, but for some reason the moment we walked in, Josh threw me a grin—as if they knew. I hadn't told them anything, though Dylan had given me a look when I rushed over to help him talk down Craig in the early hours of the morning. I'd left Josh outside the apartment, making sure Eve was safe. Trying to salvage their friendship was the only thing that would override my overwhelming desire not to leave her side.

And as Eve waved as we reached the top of the winding staircase, I realised they would know.

My scent was all over her and not in the friend kind of way. Yes, we'd showered. But seeing her in the shower had led to more fun and now I felt really guilty for not warning her about how everyone would know we'd slept together. We hadn't planned to keep it a secret or anything, but I felt bad that she was left out.

"Eve, come here for a sec." I grabbed her by the elbow before she could skip over to our friends, my lips twitching at her bewildered expression as I led her away towards the toilets. I didn't stop until I'd pulled her into the women's bathroom area, deciding that this was not the conversation to have beside a urinal. The bathrooms were tastefully decorated, the women's one complete with black doors and walls, a floral ceiling, and gold-framed mirrors with matching taps and extravagant sinks. Along with a whole shelf area and a wide mirror for makeup touch ups, despite the fact that nearly half the patterns had magic or glamours.

"I think it's a bit early for a quickie," Eve quipped, fixing her bedhead in one of the mirrors.

A young female vampire came out of one of the cubicles with a mop in hand and scattered in a blur of motion when I gave them what Josh called the 'Alpha Stare', leaving the toilet door swaying behind her.

"I forgot to tell you something."

Eve arched an eyebrow, folding her arms as if she was afraid I was about to hurt her. This wasn't going the way I'd planned.

"So, eh, you know the way we had sex last night?" I said, rubbing the back of my neck like a nervous schoolboy as she eyed me up.

Eve kept her expression guarded. "I was there, yes."

"Well, eh." I glanced at the door as if someone might walk through it and put me out of my misery or else slap me for being in the wrong bathroom. "The guys are going to know what we did."

Her mouth popped open, her lips forming an 'o'. "How?"

"You smell."

She paused, and for a moment I thought she was going to deck me, but then her eyes wrinkled, and she burst into a fit of laughter. "Wolves and their fucking noses. This whole smell thing will never get normal for me. So what, I smell like sex?"

"Sort of. You smell like me." My shoulders relaxed at her amusement.

"Well, I guess there's worse things I could smell like."

My wolf side perked up at that. "You won't be smelling like anyone else."

But she was already striding out the door, waving her hand. "Whatever you say, alphahole."

I had a smug grin on my face as we walked back inside, and

she hopped onto the stool between Dylan and Josh. She flashed me a taunting smirk, and yes, my alpha side did go a little possessive but they were like my brothers.

"You look tired." Jonas turned to face me with two cups in hand, one black Americano for me and a latte which was probably ninety percent syrup and cream for Eve. The corners of his eyes creased as he fought back a knowing smile.

She was deep in conversation with Josh, so I slid hers down the counter before taking a sip of my own.

"It's the middle of the night. Not all of us can survive on a diet of O negative," I quipped, sighing with satisfaction as the warm coffee took the edge off being hauled out of bed so early.

Dylan sniggered, pulling his steaming cup of coffee out of my reach before leaning in and whispering. "Two guesses what your diet was this morning."

Unlike Jonas, Dylan was about as subtle as a human on Fae wine.

A low growl rumbled in my chest, but I tamped it down before he could draw Eve's attention. No doubt, my eyes were silver because Dylan held his hands up in surrender, glancing over at her with a half grin, half grimace. "I'll behave, I swear."

Werewolves could fuck around, sex was just sex. Unless there were feelings involved, then our true nature came into play. The whole alphahole thing wasn't a complete myth, but we had brains, and I liked to think I was a modern man in control of his emotions. But considering how *fresh* the whole thing was, I wasn't ready for jokes.

"As much as I'd like to stand here and say 'I told you so', there is a reason I asked you all here." Jonas sighed, wiping down the countertop before tossing the towel over his shoulder. "A young vampire has gone missing. She's a friend of Darius, one of his wards. She's new to this world and only turned three months ago. She disappeared on Wednesday morning and hasn't been seen since. We sent some of our best to trace her down, but there is no trail. No clues. Nothing."

Dylan paused with his coffee an inch from his lips.

"Shit."

Eve's brow furrowed with concern, and she knocked back a mouthful of her drink, her throat bobbing as she swallowed. I did the same.

"Darius is looking into it, but given what we know about the Faolchúnna pack and what happened yesterday—"

I shook my head and placed my empty cup down. "There's no point in Darius chasing shadows, this is no coincidence."

"My thoughts exactly." Jonas set about pouring a whiskey for himself, the golden liquid swirling in the glass matching his molten irises. "But we can't go up against them with no proof, and Darius won't be seen to do nothing. You know he'd do anything for those he's taken in."

Despite his reputation, I'd witnessed myself the softer side of Darius. Behind the cut-throat businessman and elder vampire façade, he was a softie. Not the cuddly type, but the kind that had strong morals and cared deeply for those who placed their trust in him. He hated the way the elders ran things and how they abused humans and new vampires alike, so he was known for taking in freshly turned vampires and anyone in need of sanctuary. That's what the Dark Night was, a sanctuary for the paranormal.

"How are we supposed to get proof when they cover their tracks?" Josh scrunched his nose, no doubt as the image of what they had done to that poor hybrid flashed through his mind. It wasn't something any of us would ever forget.

"By catching Damien and his fucking pawns in the act."

Hinges creaked as the door behind us swung open, and I glanced over my shoulder to find Alice striding across the empty dance floor. She wasn't in her scruffy tracksuit bottoms like I'd left her back at the house last night. Gone were the mascara-stained cheeks, replaced by a steely look of determination that reminded me of her mother.

Eve's face lit up as she pulled another seat over between herself and Josh and pride swelled in my chest. There was a tinge of fear and worry at the edges. I'd been convinced that seeing her friend die would have set Alice back. I was terrified she'd crawl back into her shell, no one would have blamed her. But Alice was here and finally ready to bite back.

"How are we supposed to catch them mid-kidnapping?" The legs of Dylan's bar stool squealed as he scooched across to make space so that we were sat in a kind of semicircle around the bar with Jonas behind it completing the arc.

Alice motioned to Jonas for her usual. "We can't. Vampire, hybrid werewolf, witch, we don't know who or what they are targeting. But we can catch them with someone they've already taken."

Eve cocked her head to one side, giving Alice the 'Are you serious?' look. "As in go back to the manor?"

"Well, they don't exactly bring them out for walks, so yeah."

"Not happening."

All eyes switched to me.

Josh sighed, rolling his shoulders as if readying for a fight. "Luke, it's probably the only option we have."

"Not fucking happening," I repeated, emphasising each syllable.

"We can't just run in there blindly. It sounds like they moved the hybrids just before we took Alice. We could be starting a pack war for no reason and your dad would kill us." Dylan shifted in his seat. How was he the voice of reason on my side? "I don't think they're with the Faolchúnna pack anymore, it's too risky. We need to pinpoint exactly where they are holding whatever supernaturals they've taken, and then we pounce."

"No, we do not—"

"Ryan would know." Eve cut in, staring at the bottom of her cup as she traced her index finger around the rim.

The loose tether I had on my temper snapped.

"What part of no are you all struggling with?"

"Inaction isn't an option here. I have an incredible amount of respect for your father, Luke, but this involves more than just wolves now. We need answers, and Ryan's ego and temper may give us them." Jonas, who had remained silent for most of the conversation, finally spoke up. He turned to Eve then, his expression softening. "So long as Eve feels up to it, she might be the only one who can get him to slip up."

I snatched the bottle of whiskey off the bar and poured myself a double, downing it in one go before slamming the glass down so hard it cracked.

"She is not meeting up with Ryan. I don't care if he has the answers, we will find another way."

"Excuse me?" Eve's eyes narrowed like a cat's. "*She* will do whatever she likes."

"I'm not telling you what to do, I just don't want you in danger." I sighed, wiping my hand down my face as I fought to find the right words. I wanted to tame fire in her eyes, not set a match to it. "He is dangerous, and I don't like using you as bait. You did this once before, and it almost went south."

Alice rolled her eyes. "It turned out fine. Eve can hold her own."

"It's just talking. We can meet in a public place."

"A conversation, man. It's not like she's fucking him." Dylan flinched, probably rethinking his choices when my eyes flashed silver in response. Alice smacked his arm, and he yelped, nursing the non-wound overdramatically.

"What he meant was, it's a controlled environment." Josh levelled our friend with a dirty look, reaching out to place his hand on my arm as I went to pour another double. "I can pick the spot, scout it out to make sure it's well populated with humans, so he can't try anything funny."

"I want to be there." I ignored them all, focusing on Eve. "I need to be there."

She shook her head, coffee sloshing in her cup as she balanced it on her lap. "He won't talk in front of you."

"I can call in a favour." Jonas swept the whiskey out of my reach and placed it back on the top shelf. "I'll get a witch to mask your scent so you can be close but hidden. Only if you promise to keep your temper in check and let Eve get the information she needs."

Eve chewed her lip for a moment before nodding. "Okay. It might work in our favour. If Ryan is being difficult, seeing me with Luke might goad him into spilling something. I'll send him a message saying that I want to meet, and we can figure out a plan. I think he'll take the bait, he's always been the jealous type."

"That's a wolf thing m'dear." Josh chuckled, raising his iced coffee in cheers to me before tipping it back.

She bit back a smile, her mood lightening as her bright blue eyes met mine. "I'm beginning to realise that."

"Drink up, pup," I muttered, shoving my empty glass towards Jonas who had moved down the bar to serve an old lady that was a well-known banshee and a gossip. "We have somewhere you need to be."

Luke lingered in his car after dropping me off outside Craig's house. He tried to be subtle by driving down the street a bit, pretending to hunt around in his dashboard for something. I could have called him out on it, but it was sweet, and I needed his unspoken support.

My heart thumped as I reached the gate blocking the driveway, black paint flaking off on my hand as it creaked open for me. The house was still the same as I remembered, weather worn pale yellow bricks and windows with those old net curtains that looked like doilies. It was a student house and hadn't been updated in years by the owners because they knew what college kids got up to. The pavement was cracked, the garden more like a muddy field, and the heating broke once a year, but it did the job. The rent was reasonable, and Craig loved to throw parties, so it worked. I'd so many good memories in this place, but that street corner Luke lingered on was where I'd attacked my best friend. Kate was dead because I was a part of this world, and now my only remaining friend was a part of it too, despite my plans to keep him away.

My hand shook as I reached up to rap the old brass knocker.

The bell didn't work. Neither did the alarm, but that's what neighbours were for.

Time ticked by, and I glanced at Luke's car. Maybe this was a mistake. I'd no idea if Craig even wanted to see me.

I was ready to bolt when the door opened to reveal Craig, dressed in a black hoodie and grey sweatpants that were more like pyjama bottoms. His hair was still blue, his limbs were intact, besides one bruise on his cheek, he was alive and safe, just like Luke had promised.

Tears sprang to my eyes as I looked him over, my gaze finally settling on his face. He had bags under his eyes, but that was nothing new. He was smiling. It was a nervous smile that had his lips twitching at the corners, but he was smiling.

"Are you going to keep staring at me like that, or would you like to come in?"

I nodded, struggling to find the words as emotion clogged my throat. I felt like a vampire being invited inside, but there was no fear in his eyes. A little nervousness, but no anger.

The story I'd prepped, the lies I'd planned, the truth I'd debated, all of the rehearsed conversations I'd prepared vanished. He looked at me like I was his friend. Eve, the normal girl. Not the wolf he'd seen with blood dripping from her canines.

Craig motioned me inside, closing the door behind us before leading me down the hallway into the living room. It was sparsely decorated with cream walls, a giant whiteboard with chores, timetables, and a bet scrawled on it, two couches that had seen better days, with a spare mattress stacked behind one against the wall. The coffee table was a mix of magazines, coursework, and two coffee cups, one of which needed to be dumped in a radioactive disposal bin. Netflix was playing *Friends* on the tv in the corner—Craig's favourite comfort show. It was a typical student house, down to the beer stains on the carpet by the kitchen door.

I perched on the edge of the couch nearest the doorway, while he sat on the one opposite. All I could focus on was the distance, reading into his every move. Was he scared to sit near me? Did me being a hybrid werewolf disgust him? Watching me ready to *kill* someone. I didn't know what he saw when he looked at me.

My knee wouldn't stop bouncing, and my brain was no closer to forming words when Craig broke the awkward silence that was in full bloom.

"Breathe," he said with a low chuckle, reaching out for the free Starbucks cup and taking a sip. "You look like you've seen a ghost."

"I... I just don't know how to do this. I never wanted you to find out."

He arched an eyebrow, his movements so casual that they were throwing me further over the edge into my anxiety spiral. "That you're a werewolf?"

"Actually, I'm a hybrid." I corrected him, frowning when his lips curved upwards in the corners.

"I know, he told me."

Memories of Ryan telling me Kate wouldn't remember a thing and the knowledge he had vampires wipe her mind without her consent had my stomach sinking. "What do you mean?"

"Luke explained."

"What?"

I shook my head. *When would he have had the chance?*

"He came to find me the night it happened, after one of his friends—Dylan, was it?—insisted on bringing me to A&E to get checked over." Craig rubbed his side, slurping as he tipped the Venti coffee cup up to get every last drag of caffeine.

"They're sure you're okay?" My gaze snagged on the bruise blooming below his cheekbone, and I shuddered at the memory of the hybrid attacking Craig.

He nodded, shrugging as if it was *nothing*. "Just bruised ribs and a lump the size of an egg on my head. Luke offered to get me some vampire blood to speed up the healing, but I decided that was one step too far into Buffy territory for me."

Craig cracked a smile at that, but I couldn't find the humour in it. I was confused, his chilled exterior was sending me off kilter. It wasn't normal to accept the batshit crazy reality like this. Denial was one thing, I'd tried that route until Luke had rocked up at my workplace days later. Days! Being so calm less than forty-eight hours after seeing your best friend turn into a wolf was not normal.

"What did Luke say?"

"He told me about you, hybrids, werewolves, vampires, witches... The whole shebang."

Luke had been with me all night. I mean, I'd passed out, but he was there in the morning. Surely I'd have noticed him sneaking out? Then again, shifting and then shagging until the early hours had left me exhausted. I just couldn't imagine Luke leaving me on our first night together, especially when he was in overprotective alpha mode.

"How are you so calm?" I blurted, my fingers digging into the scarred leather couch. "You shouldn't be this calm."

He shrugged, leaning forwards and resting his elbows on his knees. "I wasn't calm after it happened. I was in shock for a bit, ran the whole way down Grafton Street, jumping at my own shadow. Dylan took me somewhere quiet and eventually coaxed me on the Luas to St. James', and then when I realised the guy with me was also a werewolf, I had a bit of a meltdown in the hospital car park. I thought I was losing my mind."

I swallowed hard. "I'm so sorry."

"Dylan talked me down, and then Luke arrived. We went to Beschoffs, grabbed some fish and chips, and they explained everything."

"They decided to bring you to Beschoffs to explain that the paranormal world is real?"

"Well, I heard you were naked in a park when you found out, at least I kept my clothes on."

A hysterical laugh escaped my lips.

The thought of Luke sneaking out of my bed in the dead of

night to share curly fries with Craig and explain the paranormal world to him was something I wasn't sure I'd ever wrap my brain around.

He smiled at that. "I promise, I'm okay. I was angry that you had to hide it from me, but I took most of that out on Luke."

The thought of him having a go at a *werewolf* on the same day as he'd found out everything had me smiling too. Craig was crazy in the best way and so much braver than I'd ever given him credit for. Despite the fears I had about his safety, I couldn't deny that a steady sense of relief was beginning to unravel the stress contracting every muscle in my body.

"I wish I could have told you sooner." I scooted along the couch, reaching out to take his hand in mine as that familiar sensation of tears clogged my throat. "I was trying to keep you safe. What happened to Kate... it was my fault."

Craig squeezed my hand, his gaze softening. "Luke explained what really happened. The cover story never really sat right with me. Kate would have kicked the shit out of anyone who tried to break in."

"Remember that time we fell in the door drunk while she still had one exam left around Christmas and she came at you with a wooden spoon?"

"Of course, she nearly broke my arm."

He laughed, but I didn't, my mood darkening again as he ruffled his hair. Blue in memory of our best friend.

Grief was unrelenting. One minute I'd think I was beginning to find my feet again and then a memory of Kate would pop up. A small spark of happiness ignited at the good times we had, but then guilt came crashing down like an avalanche, burying me under a mountain of grief. It felt wrong to feel anything good, to be happy with Luke, to still get to have Craig as a friend when she was six feet under with no future. Did my chance at a future steal hers away?

"Kate would still be alive if I wasn't a part of this world." My voice was raspy as tears caught in my throat.

Craig shook his head, balancing on the edge of his chair as he leaned forwards and forced me to look at him, his big hand swamping mine as he held it between us. "You don't believe that."

"It's true."

"No," he said firmly, gently tapping my nose with our joint hands. "You are not responsible for the actions of your psycho ex-boyfriend. It could just as easily have been me that he went after. Him being a werewolf, and this whole fancy magic world has nothing to do with it. Humans kill people all the time."

"I miss her so fucking much." I wiped my eyes roughly with my sleeve.

"Yeah, well I missed you too when you disappeared, so you're not doing it again."

"But it's dangerous..."

Craig quirked an eyebrow, his voice dripping with sarcasm as he held up his bruised forearm. "Oh really? I hadn't noticed."

"I can't lose you too."

He leaned in so our foreheads were pressed together, giving my hand a gentle squeeze. "Then don't push me away."

I searched his gaze for any ounce of fear, hatred, or any of the many negative things he would be entitled to feel towards me, but all I found was love. He was my best friend, the only tether I had to my old life, and despite finding out I was a hybrid werewolf and had kept all these secrets from him, Craig still wanted to be in my life.

"But I have one rule." He wrapped his arm around my shoulder and moved so he was perched on the arm of the couch and could pull me into his side for a hug. "No more secrets."

I breathed a sigh of relief, tears pricking the corner of my eyes. "No more secrets."

And this time I meant it.

"Now, tell me what's going on with Luke." Craig slid off the arm of the couch and nudged me over to make room, grabbing his coffee cup off the table and taking a swig like it was whiskey.

My cheeks were burning as I shook my head. "There's nothing to tell…"

"Nu uh, I want the whole truth. You guys are not just *friends*. The way he rushed in all guns blazing—I mean, he is fit as fuck—to rescue you last night? I saw his face when he thought you were shot. It was like something out of a movie."

Craig's gushing only made my blush deepen.

"I mean, the tension between you guys is so freaking obvious. And Luke's been sleeping on your couch? He let that one slip, you cheeky little bitch. How can you have him all alone in the apartment and not jump the man?"

I glanced away for a millisecond, and that micro action was all it took for Craig's pupils to become saucers. He threw his head back, full on belly laughing crossed with a cackle as he read me like a book.

"I want every sordid detail."

"I'm not giving you a play-by-play on my sex life." I covered my face with my hands.

Craig nudged my shoulder with his. "Oh, come on. Ryan wasn't exactly rocking your world, and I know they say 'it's not the size of the boat, it's the motion of the ocean'."

"Ryan was more like a canoe without a paddle," I muttered, unable to resist smiling at how giddy my friend was getting. Craig's happiness was infectious, and I'd been so busy worrying about what could go wrong that getting excited about the possibility of there being a me and Luke was a first, and it felt good.

"I bet mister next in line to be alpha fucked like an animal," Craig teased, wiggling his eyebrows.

I fell back against the couch with a groan of defeat, biting my lip as I tried not to giggle. "You have no idea."

CHAPTER 28

LUKE

Helena's voice greeted me as soon as I arrived. "Your father is going to be furious!"

I was barely in the door when Max came sprinting down the hall, a blanket covered in cars whipping behind him as he put on his imaginary brakes and crashed into me with his arms wide. Thanks to my quick reflexes, I managed to catch him and scoop him up into my arms before he could clock his head off my hip.

Helena poked her head around the kitchen door, her frown smoothing out once she saw it was me.

"Your dad will be home in a few minutes." She rolled her eyes as my little brother clung to me like a well-behaved koala. "Max is just back from a birthday party, and it will be the last one he goes to if he keeps these antics up."

He was practically vibrating, hyped up on sugar and smirking despite the dressing down from his mam.

Helena ushered us into the kitchen with a weary sigh.

I followed her inside, ruffling Max's auburn hair that matched hers with a chuckle before flicking on the kettle and setting about emptying the dishwasher to save Helena another job. "I've missed you guys."

"We've missed you too." She sank onto one of the kitchen chairs, the edges of her eyes creasing as her expression softened.

I smiled, making her a well-deserved cup of tea along with one for myself while she watched Max zip back and forth like the kitchen like he was a rookie on his own Formula One street track. Home sweet home. Except home felt like somewhere different these days.

Helena didn't say a word about the extra teaspoon of sugar I snuck in that she'd never allow herself, sipping the steaming mug with a sigh.

"I'm glad you're both okay after what happened the other night."

I shrugged, but that fleeting moment where I thought Eve had been shot slammed into me like a ten-tonne truck. "I'm fine, it's Eve I worry about."

Her auburn curls bounced as she shook her head, a wry smile curving her lips. "Of course. How is she doing?"

"She's alright, considering everything. She was more concerned about her friend, the human that witnessed the fight… I couldn't wipe his memories, it wasn't right. That's why I need to speak with dad."

The teaspoon clanged against the edge of the mug as Helena stopped stirring.

"I know, it's what Dad decided. I'm disobeying direct orders, but I don't give a fuck. Eve would never forgive me fo—"

Helena held up her hand to stop me, glancing over at Max who watched us with wide eyes and a grin that threatened he would repeat every curse word to his teacher on Monday.

"Max, love. Can you go play in the living room for a moment?" She pointed to the fridge before he could argue. "You can take a chocolate bar in with you."

The momentary frown that had clouded his expression vanished as he sped over to the chocolate drawer in the fridge and snatched two bars. His little feet were a blur as he raced out of the room before his mother could argue, but Helena didn't seem too interested. Instead, her worried gaze was fixed on me.

"Luke, I understand why you want to do this for Eve, but not every human can handle this."

"You handled it just fine." The moment the words left my mouth, I wanted to snatch them back.

Helena had helped raise me and put up with far more shit than the average mother when I was being both a moody teenager and a cantankerous werewolf. She lost her daughter for years because of me.

She didn't bother scolding me, knowing full well I'd do enough of that myself. Instead, it was the way her brow furrowed and a look of disappointment flitted across her face that really shoved a dagger in my heart and twisted.

"I wasn't just a friend," she said softly, reaching out to place her delicate hand over mine. "And your father told me out of necessity. He regrets not being able to wait longer. Her friend just witnessed two wolves fighting in front of him, a witch turning up, and someone being murdered in front of his eyes. Not to mention one of those werewolves was his best friend. That's a lot to ask of anyone."

I chewed my lip, focusing on how my hand dwarfed hers. If Helena could handle this, surely Craig could? He had taken it better than expected when we had told him that night, but whether or not he could handle seeing Eve was the real test. Human brains could lock trauma away, denial was a strong emotion. Seeing Eve would force him to face the truth.

"Eve lost Kate to those bastards." A low growl rumbled in my chest at the memory of the phone call she'd left me that day. She had sounded so utterly broken. "I can't be responsible for her losing the only friend she has left. It's not fair, she doesn't deserve to lose everything from her previous life."

Helena fell silent for a long time, studying my face. "Okay, we'll try it your way."

My phone buzzed in my pocket. I withdrew my hand to pull

it out, my shoulders slumping with relief as a text message from Eve flashed up on the screen.

> EVE
>
> He's ok. Thank you for saving my friendship.

Helena leaned over to take a peek at the message, her expression warming. "Leave your father to me. As long as the friend copes with everything, there's no harm done. We can never have too many allies in our corner, human or otherwise."

"Thank you." I smiled, squeezing her hand as I slumped back in my chair and basked in the relief that I'd done the right thing.

Dad wouldn't be delighted, but he would understand. He may have been the alpha, but Helena's word was as good as his.

She watched me over the rim of the mug cupped between her hands for a moment, a smugness seeping in as her emerald eyes narrowed. "So, is there anything else you need to tell us?"

It was the same look she gave me when I lied about stealing sweets from the cupboard as a kid, or when I snuck in late as a teenager drunk. The "mother knows" look. I wasn't sure what kind of sixth sense allowed her to read us like a book, but Helena always knew everything that was going on. She was the one who had warned me to be careful about training Eve. I'd no idea how she'd found out, but Helena knew all. It was a terrifying skill, and I'd yet to learn how to hide anything from her.

"Like what?" I took a long sip of my tea, trying to smooth my expression as heat crept up my neck.

She arched an eyebrow, tilting her head to one side. "About Eve?"

The sound of a car beeping locked came from outside, and for a moment I thought it was Dad and was readying my speech in my head, but then a different scent filtered into the house as the front door burst open.

"Oi oi!" Darren nudged the kitchen door with his foot, carting two shopping bags in either hand that were filled to the brim with different meats and other goodies for the pack run coming up. "Anyone fancy helping me with these?"

I chuckled as one of the overfilled bags split and a dozen packets of burger buns spilled onto the floor. "I think it's a bit late for that, you seem to have the domestic goddess thing covered."

Ever the joker, he rolled his eyes, unpacking at record speed and putting things in the wrong place so often that Helena jumped up, cursing him as she fixed the mess he'd made of her fridge. I tried to help, but after I put the sauces in the wrong place, I got a smack of a tea towel and both Darren and I were herded over to the kitchen table with a fresh pot of tea.

"Useless, the both of you." She rearranged a pile of bread that looked like a very unstable Leaning Tower of Pisa. "You know this was on a podcast the other day? Weaponised incompetence must be on another level for werewolves."

Darren laughed, dodging another blow of the tea towel as he scooted into the chair beside me.

"So, what gossip session did I interrupt?" He poured himself a cup of milk with tea. Darren made a shit cup of tea.

I shook my head when he offered me some.

"It wasn't a gossip session. I just needed to explain that Eve's friend didn't need his memory wiped of the attack, he's able to handle the truth."

He pulled another chair out with his leg, using it as a footrest. "Are you really that boring? You're the young one, I need to live vicariously through you."

Helena made some comment about Darren never growing up, and I couldn't help but laugh as their bickering began. He was Dad's best friend. He and Helena got on like a house on fire, but their friendship was based on a foundation of good-hearted slagging, and it made for great entertainment.

"Luke was just telling me about Eve," Helena explained with a wide grin, kicking his feet off her chair before finally dropping back into her seat at the head of the table once she had reorganised the kitchen.

Darren's bushy eyebrows furrowed in confusion. "What about her? I thought she was okay after the attack?"

He looked to me for an explanation, and from the mischievous glint in Helena's eyes and the way she was pursed her lips in an effort not to laugh or spit out the truth, I was cornered.

Darren sniffed, and his face lit up, then I was well and truly falling off a cliff.

"Don't tell me the kid is finally settling down?" He teased, giving me a firm clap on the back that almost winded me.

I shook my head, burying my face in my hands to hide the fact that my cheeks were burning. "I am not having this conversation."

The front door clicked open, and this time it definitely was Dad.

Helena cracked a grin, but behind all of the teasing I could tell she was truly happy for me. I just needed to not fuck this up.

"So, do you want to tell him or will I?"

CHAPTER 29

EVE

It felt like an age since Alice had talked me into buying that red dress, and I'd no idea how it had survived the night without being shredded or covered in actual blood, but somehow it had and now I'd squeezed myself into it. It was a low-cut bodycon dress with thin straps that I had zero confidence in and ruched material that hugged my waist and skimmed my ass. Despite their protests, I'd refused the matching stilettos Alice and Craig had tried to talk me into, opting instead for thigh-high black boots to give me some protection against the bite of the winter wind that was destroying my perfectly styled curls. I'd burned my finger for nothing.

Luke had offered to book a taxi for me, and I'd regretted not taking him up on that offer the moment the apartment complex closed behind me. I ran hot thanks to the werewolf genes, but Irish winters were no joke. We rarely got snow, but you'd freeze your ass off, and I was pretty sure mine had frostbite.

"This is what you get for being a strong independent woman who wanted to take the Luas." I pulled the heavy teddy coat tighter around me as my numb fingers fumbled with my phone.

Dylan had decided to kick off the celebrations at a paranormal cocktail bar on the north side of the city. I thought it was overkill until I realised they wanted to be able to be themselves and some of the invitees might not fit in so easily in the human world. Human drunken antics were one thing, but a Fae dropping their glamour because they had one too many shots was entirely possible. Plus, I was excited to go somewhere different. The Dark Night was full of surprises, but it was time I widened my horizons. No doubt we'd end up there at some point during the night anyway.

I took a shortcut between two apartment blocks and headed towards the tram line. A group of guys fell out the door down the street in front of me. The loud noise would have once made me jump, but I'd heard them coming. It felt good not to fear the dark anymore, walking through dodgy streets and knowing that I could handle any trouble was an ego boost.

I smiled to myself, glancing up at the waning moon. By the weekend we'd be back in the pack house in Kildare, a place filled with laughter and good memories for me.

The tram dinged in the distance and I picked up my pace. Red-brick buildings towered above me, showered in darkness. The bottom floors of most were dedicated to offices, the glass panelled walls shining under the moonlight.

Before I could round the corner onto the main street, an arm shot out from the shadows and fingers locked around my throat from behind.

"Hello, Eve," an all too familiar voice purred as tears blurred my eyes.

Ryan spun me around, his fingertips digging into my windpipe as he shoved me up against one of the deserted office blocks, the rough brick scratching the exposed skin of the back of my thighs. His face was half cast in shadows, those chiselled cheekbones I'd once admired hollow as he stared down at me like I was prey that he was torn between fucking or killing. His piercing blue eyes were narrowed and shone with the promise of nothing good. It wasn't the first time I'd seen his distinct brand of unhinged, but it still caught me off guard.

Why the fuck didn't I leave sooner?

I gulped a deep breath, ready to scream bloody murder, but he released my throat in favour of clamping his hand over my mouth. Which was exactly what I wanted.

Luke's training kicked in, and I bit down hard, letting my canines extend just enough so that my teeth dug into the nerve sensitive area of his palm. I didn't need to be a fortune teller to know that pain was in his near future. At the same time, I wrapped my hand around his wrist, my claws snapping out on instinct and sinking into his wrist.

He growled, his grip holding firm, and I kept my lips pursed tight, fighting the urge to gag as his blood smeared over my face. The coppery scent of his blood made my nostrils flare, but I didn't need him to release me. I just needed him distracted.

Sure enough, he didn't expect me to fight like a human, and I drove the four-inch block heel of my right boot between his legs with perfect accuracy.

"Get the fuck off me," I spat, my words leaking with venom.

I twisted in Ryan's grip as he doubled over in pain, breaking his hold, and shot across the street and out of arm's reach. Never letting him out of my sight, I swiped the sleeve of my jacket across my face and spat out any trace of his blood. It took him a full minute to straighten to his full height, and a sick thrill of satisfaction ran down my spine at the sight of him hurting.

He finally looked at me, something akin to surprise in those wide eyes, and I found myself grateful I'd refused to settle into the damsel in distress role he'd planned for me. Learning to defend myself against a man, be it a human or a werewolf with a daddy complex and boundary issues, was one of the best decisions I'd ever made.

"Eve, I'm not here to play games." Ryan took a step towards me, a harsh breath of irritation misting in the winter air as I backed away and maintained the distance between us. "You are the one who requested to meet up."

I scoffed, pulling my coat tighter around me. "I messaged

asking to meet up in a public area during the day with plenty of witnesses. I asked to meet on *my* terms."

"You expected the next in line to the Faolchúnna pack to meet up with a known outcast, let alone a hybrid, in public?" His irritation was clear in the way tension bracketed his mouth and his eyebrows were climbing towards his hairline.

"How dare I ask such a thing of the chosen one," I muttered with a low chuckle.

I'd be lying if I said I wasn't scared of what he could do to me. Ryan was stronger if it came to a full-on fight, but something about having my ex-boyfriend who mistreated me, on the back foot, was giving me a dangerous ego boost.

Ryan scowled, his hands balling into fists by his side as he took another step towards me. "You said you wanted to talk about us."

My smile only widened at the storm that threatened to break his hanging-by-a thread composure.

"I said I wanted to *talk*. I never mentioned us." I stood my ground this time. "Did you seriously think I meant us as a couple? After everything you put me through? You're fucking delusional, Ryan. You let your pack hunt me."

"That was a misunderstand—"

"A misunderstanding?" My voice jumped an octave. This time it was me stalking forwards, the noise of my heels hitting the tarmac echoing off the walls lining the street around us. "So, you grooming me and kidnapping me for some fucked up hybrid power trip breeding plan was a mistake then? Daddy Dearest didn't send you to add me to his fucked up collection?"

He opened his mouth to spew more lies, his brow furrowed like he couldn't quite believe what I was saying. Just how much had his father brainwashed him? Did he really think I would fall at his feet just because I was a hybrid?

"Do you really think you were saving me?" I stopped a few feet away from him as the realisation hit.

"I was doing what was right for my pack. Hybrids are not natural."

He reached out his hand towards me, but I smacked it away, leaving three red claw marks in his skin for good measure.

"Your family's thirst for power is what's unnatural. You think you can find some cheat code to hybrids and boost yourselves to be stronger? Take the perks and then eradicate us?"

"This is bigger than just you and me." There was an edge of worry in his voice that made me curious.

"No shit. Hybrids aren't the only ones going missing."

His eyes widened a fraction as a fleeting hint of shock crossed his face before he schooled his expression. "You and that boyfriend of yours need to keep your nose out of things."

Luke and I hadn't defined our relationship yet, but I wasn't about to get into that with my ex.

"What's going on, Ryan?" I cocked my head to one side as I watched the muscle in his jaw tick. "What do vampires have to do with your plans? And witches? Why do you need them?"

He shook his head, his lips curving into his signature smirk as he regained his composure. "That's a very big accusation."

"Either you know something, or your alpha has been keeping you in the dark. Which is it?"

"Was that your plan? Even *if* I knew what was happening to them, I wouldn't tell you anything."

I wanted nothing more than to smack that smug look off his face. He was a lying, twisted, psychotic prick, and my anger was simmering on the edge of boiling over so much that I didn't need my heavy coat anymore. My temperature had skyrocketed, fuelled by every ounce of hatred I felt towards the rat in front of me.

My phone buzzed in my pocket and Ryan's eyes narrowed.

"You should run along, I'm sure lover boy is growing impatient," he said coldly.

I killed the call without even looking at the screen. Of course it was Luke. I was late and he was a worrier. But I wasn't leaving until I got something out of Ryan. My makeup was ruined thanks to him, and I'd need to stop off for breath mints to get the taste of him out of my mouth. I wasn't letting all of that be for nothing.

"I'm not going to stop looking into this." I kept my chin raised high as he glowered down at me. "These sordid plans of yours can't keep going. And if you thought I'd leave the other hybrids behind, you don't know me at all."

Ryan's expression soured. "Alice never could keep her mouth shut."

Pure anger took hold as I stepped forwards to close the distance between us. My hand connected with his cheek with perfect precision, the force of my slap knocking his head to one side.

Once I caught up with reality, I stared at my stinging palm and backed up out of reach. I'd wanted to do that for a very long time. That was for Kate, for the older version of me that fell for his lies, and every goddamn hybrid he'd ever tortured.

"Wow, too bad you never had this fire in the bedroom." Ryan growled, his fingers brushing across his lower lip where a steady trickle of blood dripped down his chin.

Thanks to his werewolf genes it would heal in minutes, but I took a savage satisfaction in drawing blood.

"You can't light a fire with damp wood." I rubbed my fingers together to stop them stinging. "I'm not going to stop looking for them, so you can either tell me the truth or I'll uncover it anyway."

"You're out of your depth, Eve." He pulled a tissue out of his suit pocket, dabbing at the wound already knitting back together. "You're new to this world and insist on flouting the rules. I came here because despite your stupid decisions, I still care about you."

I shook my head, waving my hand in dismissal. "Stop changing the subject."

"If you think I'm the only one you need to fear, then you're more stupid than I thought."

I was new, not stupid. And I could have been wholly more prepared if he hadn't lied to me for so long.

"You sound like Larissa."

Ryan blanched, dropping the bloody tissue to stare at me with wide eyes. "Do you have a fucking death wish? Stay away from the witches and stop digging into this."

My phone buzzed again, earning me another dirty look.

"He clearly doesn't give a shit about you if he's letting you—"

"*Letting* me?" I cut in, my canines slipping out a fraction. "No one is letting me do shit. And I don't care how much you or Larissa throw your weight around."

"You're playing with fire and might as well have doused yourself in accelerant. Stay away from the witch and stop drawing attention to yourself. Vampires disappearing is none of your concern, and if you value your life at all, you'll drop this. I know you think I'm a monster, but I promise there are worse, more ancient things that go bump in the night. You are a very small pawn in a much bigger game, and you are out of your depth."

"I'm not a pawn in anyone's game."

"Oh Evie, you don't even know what game you're playing." Ryan chuckled, that taunting smirk still frozen in place as he glanced down at the expensive gold watch that now had some dents from my teeth strapped to his wrist. "I have to go, there is much to do before the full moon. I presume the Crescents still leave to go to their pack land in the countryside?"

I didn't answer straight out, unsure as to how much he knew about Luke's pack. Not to mention the emotional whiplash of going from dramatic threats to him trying to make conversation as if he was remotely normal. As if anything about this, or us, was normal.

"How is Fiona? And Mary?" The all too familiar guilt climbed up my spine, winding knots into my shoulders.

"Dead for all you know." He shrugged, a sick gleam in his eyes as mine widened. "Maybe if you stayed out of trouble, you wouldn't need to worry about them. You chose to leave them and the pack behind. You've made your bed, Eve, now lie in it. And stay the fuck away from the witch."

Eve looking drop dead gorgeous in a red dress that hugged her figure in all the right places wasn't enough to stop my blood from boiling. If anything, it fuelled my anger more because his scent was on her when she looked like a fucking goddess. I stiffened when she went to give me a kiss on the cheek. It took every ounce of self-control I had to rein my rage in while she explained what happened. I don't remember a word. It was a blur because all I noticed his blood on her chin and hit the fucking roof.

I didn't relish the look in her eyes when I froze, his blood on my thumb as I cupped her face. Dylan and Josh were on me in an instant, trying to bundle me towards the bathroom without causing a scene.

So here I was, locked in a toilet cubicle like an unruly child.

I loved being a werewolf, but sometimes the wolf instincts sucked, and this was one of those times. I'd never had a true connection with any woman I'd ever dated, and although I'd seen my dad and a few friends like this, nothing prepared me for it. The thought of her being in danger or that dickhead near her sent me spiralling. Thanks to my human side, I was aware of my

Especially after a few cocktails.

"How are you doing bud?" Dylan asked, the cubicle door bouncing on its hinges as he leaned against it.

"You should be out there enjoying your party." I ran my hand through my hair with a sigh. "I'll be calm in a bit. I just freaked when I saw the blood."

"Relax, we get it. If I loved a girl and she came in saying her ex had grabbed her by the throat, I'd be pissed too. Eve just isn't used to the... wolfier side." Josh balanced on his toes, peeking over-the-top of the door with a wide grin. "Plus, I didn't want Dylan getting banned unless it was his own fault."

Dylan snorted, and the door rattled. "Oi! I haven't been banned from anywhere since I was like eighteen."

"Darius has banned you from the Dark Night at least twice in the last year."

Blaring music filtered in as the door to the main bathroom creaked and swung open, Eve's scent filling my senses. Her presence was calming, until I caught the small hint of Ryan left over, and I wrung my hands again. I'd already put a hole through the first bathroom stall they'd put me in.

Deep breaths. One, two, three...

"Darius loves me really." Dylan chuckled, his shadow retreating from under the door as he moved away.

"Can I talk to mister grumpy pants alone please?" Eve earned another laugh from the guys.

I never considered myself special because I was next in line to be alpha. They both knew I didn't want the title, but the way Eve was so blasé about it was still highly unusual. I'd no doubt that she'd happily call me baby names if I was losing it in front of anyone, be it my family, or even the witch Royals.

The guys made their way out, Josh promising me a shot while Dylan continued to protest his innocence. Their departure left the bathroom eerily silent but for the distant thump of the bass from the dance floor.

"Are you going to stay in there sulking all night? Craig is

going to be here soon." Worry seeped into her tone at the mention of her friend. We'd pulled some strings to let a human be allowed in. Despite his antics, Dylan knew one of the bouncers, and we'd booked out a VIP section so as long as he laid low, it would be fine. We'd just keep him away from the Fae wine.

I opened the door now that my brotherly barricade had left. Eve stood by the sink, one hand on her hip while she tapped her foot. My gaze wandered from the thigh-high black boots that cut off mid-thigh, scorching a path to her face and drinking in every inch of her. The bathroom was covered floor to ceiling with black glossy tiles, the sinks and urinals all gaudy gold, complete with a large mirror framed with a gothic border to match. With the red dress and the way her eyeliner was drawn on, she looked like a succubus, and I was here for it.

She looked up at me expectantly, her red-stained lips pursed in a thin line. But the impatience was a mask because her blue eyes shone with worry. We were so new, and no matter how many times I tried to tell Eve I wasn't angry with her, it never seemed to sink in. That bastard had taught her to blame herself, and I'd never forgive him for it.

"I'm sorry for losing my shit out there." I closed the distance between us, wrapping my arm around her waist, the other hand cupping her now clean cheek. "The thought of him cornering you like that freaked me out. I know it's a cop out to blame the wolf thing, but it really does drive me mad."

She scowled, prodding me square in the chest. "I am so sick of people telling me how I smell. I promise Ryan didn't hurt me. All of your training paid off, and I'm pretty sure he left with a bruised ego to go with his balls."

"His balls?"

"Yep." She nodded, popping the *p* and tugging her lower lip between her teeth as she fought a smile and kicked back her right leg to show off her heels. "I kicked him in the balls."

I'd taught Eve to fight to defend herself, but fuck. My sense of pride wasn't the only thing swelling at the thought of her protecting herself like that.

"Ahem." Eve cleared her throat as she no doubt felt my growing erection against her hip, but I only dropped my hand to cup her ass and pull her closer against me. The little hitch in her breath, the way her eyes widened and her pupils dilated as she looked up at me was more than enough for the anger I'd been feeling to be overridden by a more feral instinct. I ran my thumb along her jaw, tilting her head as I trailed kisses down her exposed throat. Now the last thing to touch her was my lips, not his hand.

She caught my hand as it slid down her chest, a breathy moan escaping her lips. "We're in the men's bathroom. You're not fucking me here."

"Darling, I would fuck you in the middle of that dance floor if I wasn't such a jealous asshole. Don't think I won't bend you over that sink."

Something buzzed against my thigh. The small black velvet purse Eve wore rattled as her phone continued to buzz, Taylor Swift blaring from the speaker as the phone rang.

"Don't answer that," I ordered, swirling my tongue over her collarbone and smirking against her skin as Eve shuddered under my touch.

Eve fumbled around in her bag, mischief dancing in her eyes as she lifted it to her ear and answered the call. "Hello?"

I couldn't hear the words coming down the line, but it was Craig's voice. My plans to fuck Eve against the wall had been derailed.

"Mhm." Eve nodded, biting back a moan as I groped her breast through the thin material of her dress. "I'm coming now."

I growled at her choice of words, and she bit back a groan as I pinched her nipple in payback.

"We're on our way now. Just wait outside, and we'll get you in. I promise, everyone is gonna love you." Eve's voice was strained as she killed the call and turned to glare at me with a mixture of murder and mischief dancing in her eyes.

I leaned down to brush my lips against hers in a gentle kiss, dropping my hands to squeeze her hips.

"Would you really have fucked me over the sink?" Heat coloured her cheeks.

When would this girl realise just how much of a hold she had over me?

"Play your cards right and you might find out later." I winked, reluctantly releasing her from my arms. "Now, let's get Craig before the guys can scare him off. Talk about baptism by fire."

)) ● ((

WHEN I'D SUGGESTED INVITING Craig to the party, I hadn't really thought it through. A human in a paranormal bar? Meeting a bunch of werewolves for the first time while they're drunk? It was a recipe for disaster. He had taken Eve's revelation well, but this was asking a lot of a human. So many of them needed their memories wiped, not just to hide our world, but because their brains simply couldn't process the truth. It broke them. Eve was dead set against wiping Craig's, but if we overloaded him, it wouldn't be optional.

Eve and her best friend danced up a storm in the middle of Fae, vampires, and anything else you could imagine. I'd suggested keeping him to the section we had booked to help him feel safer, but Craig seemed unbothered. And he was *sober*. I was baffled, but Helena had once told me that some humans were meant to be a part of this world. She'd never struggled with it, so maybe he was one of the special ones. As I watched him spin Eve around the dance floor, her hair whirling and her head thrown back as she laughed freely, I really hoped that was the case.

I was playing wingman for Dylan with a poor siren girl who kept scanning the crowd for her friends while he regaled her with the story of us rescuing Alice, when Craig plopped down on the bar stool beside me.

"She's gone to the toilet." He flashed me a knowing smile when I searched the room for Eve's whereabouts. "And probably a gossip session with your sister."

I nodded, wincing as I took a sip of the sickly-sweet cocktail Dylan had shoved my way. I wasn't sure what was in it, but it tasted like candy floss and turned my stomach.

"Thanks for coming. It meant a lot to her." I raised my hand to politely signal a waiter down the far end of the bar.

Craig shrugged, propping one arm on the bar. His biceps had grown since I'd seen him at the funeral. "Maintaining our friendship is important to me. Besides, werewolf or human, she's still the same girl."

"Not everyone understands that. Especially when they realise how much more dangerous our world is."

"Humans are dangerous in their own right. My line of work is dangerous. Besides, surely I'm safer now that my friend is a badass hybrid werewolf?"

His positivity was infectious, and I couldn't help but mirror his smile. "Very true. She's learning to own it."

"She's grown a lot," Craig agreed, emptying the dregs of his beer. "I've never seen her this confident or happy in herself. Thank you for helping her find that."

His expression was sincere as he held his hand out for me to shake. I swallowed the lump growing in my throat and returned the gesture, heat creeping up the back of my neck.

Before I could put my foot in my mouth and ruin the moment, Eve and Alice came running over.

"Shots!" My sister hollered, immediately ordering a bunch of shots from the waiter I'd called over, which she carried over to one of the tables on a large tray and beckoned us over.

Jonas and a few other wolves from the back, along with a few other trusted friends had arrived. Craig and I joined them just in time to hear Eve recount her little run-in with Ryan.

"You slapped him?" Dylan fell back on the leather couch, his hand clasped over his mouth dramatically as his half empty glass sloshed in his other hand. Josh dodged a drop of drink that spilled, scooting down so he was out of the danger zone.

I laughed, knowing she'd told him the story three times now, but the birthday boy was hammered. Thankfully, my anger had stopped flaring at every mention of the prick. Whatever was in the sparkling blue concoction Jonas had dared him to down earlier had shoved the poor guy over the edge. Dylan was a fun drunk though, a little messy, but harmless and hilarious.

"I wish we could've been there." Josh took a sip of his own drink. "But maybe it's for the best since Luke would go into grumpy alpha mode."

"He's ridiculous." Eve shot me a knowing look.

Dylan rolled his eyes, pitching forwards on his seat with a grin. "He's a wolf and in *luuurve*."

"Bottoms up everyone," Alice demanded, saving me from the conversation that had left me bright red. Eve had dropped her gaze to the table, her own cheeks heating.

Her shoulders rose as she tensed, her posture rounding as she stared down at the circle of shot glasses. We were surrounded by friends here, but it was too easy to forget how some things were new to Eve. Of course she was nervous about trying anything but human alcohol for the first time.

"Okay, but how strong is this?" She pinched the shot glass between her forefinger and thumb and examined the contents. The liquid was black with sparkles and an iridescent glow. "I don't want to end up dancing on the bar doing a strip rendition of *Coyote Ugly*?"

I wasn't wholly against that image, but I grinned and scooted closer to her on the leather couch, dropping my arm around her shoulders. "I promise, if you start stripping, I'll take you home."

"Don't worry about it, that drink isn't gonna hurt you. He'll sober up again in a few minutes. We process alcohol faster." Josh nodded to my untouched drink as Dylan turned a new shade of green, gesturing to Alice who had disappeared onto the dance floor with a dark-haired vampire I recognised as a regular from the Dark Night. "You'll just get a nice buzz. Alice drank it, and she's perfectly fine."

I glanced over at my sister, resisting the urge to go all big bro on the guy, and instead focused my attention on Eve. I leaned in, nipping her earlobe and dropping my voice so only she would hear me over the base. "If you get out of hand, maybe you'll need a timeout in the bathroom too."

She licked her lips, trying to keep her expression straight, but I caught her sharing a knowing glance with Craig and they both burst into a fit of giggles.

"Okay, but if I end up pissed, it's on you guys." Eve eyed the drink for another moment as the sparkling liquid swirled like the night sky before knocking back a mouthful to a round of applause.

Dylan joined her. The only person stripping was going to be him. I'd lost count of the number of times I'd bundled my best friend into a taxi, but he'd done the same for me. Either way, I wasn't getting laid that night.

CHAPTER 31

EVE

"Can everyone do that?"

I was high on adrenaline and the excitement of our run together. Being able to communicate with Luke in wolf form had felt so natural, but I couldn't wrap my head around it.

Luke shifted his weight, rolling onto his side with his arm propped under his head. I nuzzled closer, curled up beside him with my head resting in the crook of his arm while he traced lazy circles along my bare hip and thigh with his fingertips. Above us, stars danced in the night sky and the full moon peeked out from behind the blanket of winter clouds as if she was watching us.

"Not everyone. Anyone who claims they know exactly how magic works is a liar." His lips lifted at the corners. "Magic has its own nature and will, it often defies logic. But werewolves being able to communicate mentally is usually limited to close familial bonds, the bond to your alpha, or—"

"Tom can hear what we say to each other?" I cut in, worried that he had heard some of the filth that had come out of Luke's mouth when we were running.

We had arrived a day early to the pack house in Kildare to get some alone time. It was Luke's idea and a lovely surprise. We had alone time in the apartment but being here meant spending more time with my wolf side and this had been the first time we had run together properly. Then one thing led to another, and we ended up camping out under the moon, our clothes scattered all over the ground and snagged on the picnic benches that would be occupied tomorrow. But for one night, it was just us and the moon. And it had been perfect.

Until Luke had spoken in my mind and freaked the shit out of me again. It wasn't the first time, he'd done it the first time I ran with the Crescents, but I'd kind of... ignored it? I'd nearly tripped into one of the estuaries leading to the lake, and he'd found it so hilarious that he took it as a challenge to freak me out.

I was officially freaked out.

Luke laughed, his hazel eyes soft under the moonlight. "No, my dad can't hear us unless we want to speak to him. It's kind of natural based on our will, you're safe."

"But we're not family? And I'm a hybrid?"

"I can hear Alice when we're running as a pack, so it's definitely something hybrids can do." Luke reassured me, stroking my cheek with his thumb as he tucked a stray hair behind my ear. "It's not nearly as strong with her though. Maybe because we're only half-siblings?"

I frowned, shifting so my legs lay across his where they were better covered by the blanket. "That doesn't explain us."

Luke tugged the blanket over me completely, forfeiting his own feet to the elements. And they say chivalry is dead.

"It's known to happen between wolves that share strong bonds." He hesitated, as if choosing his words carefully. He looked down at me as if he was afraid I might spook and bolt like a shy horse, his eyebrows drawn together. "Strong emotions."

I swallowed hard, my hands growing clammy. "We could do it the night we rescued Alice though."

"Are you really that blind?"

My heart was hammering, and he could damn well hear it trying to erupt from my chest. "Maybe."

"I had feelings for you before you joined the Crescents.

Agreeing to train you went against my dad's command." Luke's tone softened, his hazel eyes swimming with emotion as the intensity of his gaze pinned me there. "I couldn't say no. I couldn't stay away even if I wanted to."

"I knew you were stalking me," I mumbled, tugging my lower lip between my teeth to hide the goofy smile that was forming at his confession. "You didn't know who I was before the park, right?"

"Nope, you were just some crazy naked chick in the park that smelled nice."

I groaned, burying my head in his chest. "Stop with the smell thing."

"What?" He grinned, placing his thumb under my chin and forcing me to look at him. "You smell like light rain on a spring morning."

"That's not a smell."

He laughed, booping me on the tip of my nose, and my heart did a somersault. "It is, you just need to continue refining that nose of yours."

"I had feelings too." My cheeks warmed as I admitted it out loud. It was obvious by now, but he deserved to know. "I just didn't know what to do with them. Even after Kate... I was scared of losing you, of losing the Crescents."

Luke shook his head, leaning down to nuzzle my cheek and brush the ghost off a kiss against my lips as he murmured softly. "You will always be a Crescent."

I kissed him back, my lips curving into the widest of smiles. "Yes, Mister Alpha."

"Don't you start." Luke groaned, his chest rumbling with laughter.

"Can any other couples in the pack do it? The mind thing?"

"Darren and his mate, and one other couple. My dad could do it with my mam before she passed away."

His throat bobbed at the mention of his mother, and I silently kicked myself for ruining a perfect moment.

Way to go Eve. Foot in mouth pro.

"And now us," Luke added, any shroud of sadness lifting. "The boys will be jealous when they find out."

All of the couples he'd listed had lasted long term, and that made my heart warm. Even if I didn't understand it, I was glad we had our own secret way of communicating.

I pulled him closer using my legs, reaching up to stroke my fingers through his short hair. "I'm glad we can do it."

"*Anamacha gealaí*," he murmured and leaned into my touch, his hooded eyes falling half closed.

"*Anamacha gealaí*?"

"It's what they call the mind communication thing. It means lunar souls."

"Pretty," I mused with a soft sigh of contentment, the moon disappearing behind the clouds above us.

"Like you."

I laughed, giving him a gentle tap behind his head. "You really have a way with words."

"I'm getting you a mug with 'World's Harshest Girlfriend' on it," Luke joked, his hand slipping to my ass and spanking.

"Oi!" I felt like a teenage girl again. I didn't just have butterflies in my stomach, I had a bunch of little wyverns bouncing around. At the same time, a nervousness crept in. "Is that what I am?"

"Harsh? Yeah, you've got quite the snake bite tongue when you feel like it."

I tried to glare, but instead a blush crept up my neck as I locked eyes with him.

"You're my girlfriend, if you want to be." He held my gaze, those hazel eyes of his swimming with emotion. With his stubbled jawline and tousled hair coupled with his broody act and chiselled abs, he was perfection. But that wasn't why I was having palpitations. He made me laugh. He cared about my welfare, was protective, but would never stop me doing what I wanted. And from our very first meeting, he had encouraged me to trust my gut and back myself.

His brow furrowed. He'd taken my pause as a bad sign.

"Your girlfriend? I like the sound of that." I arched my back to lean up and steal a kiss.

He smiled against my lips, running his hand down my side where the blanket had fallen away. "Good, because I like calling you mine."

Heat pooled in my core at the possessiveness ringing in his voice, and he damn well noticed, his eyes blazing a path down my body as he whipped the blanket off us and tossed it aside.

"Luke, you're going to kill me," I whined, a breathless moan slipping from my lips as his hands began roaming my body. He'd already fucked me senseless when we shifted back after our run under the moon, but the man was insatiable.

What a way to die.

CHAPTER 32

EVE

I was well on my way to unravelling under his touch when a knock came from the distance. We both froze, Luke's head snapping up in the direction of the sound. It was two-fold, coming through the house as a muffled noise, and a louder one from outside. Someone was knocking at the front door. But the pack house was in the middle of nowhere, situated on a winding back road and surrounded by fields and forestry. Plus, judging by the height of the moon, it was well after midnight.

Luke scowled, winding his arm around my waist as I went to stand. "No, last time it was a phone. I'm not being cock-blocked by someone lost looking for directions."

The knock came again, and Luke was on his feet in an instant, completely naked and unbothered while I reached for the blanket to wrap around myself.

"You said no one was arriving until tomorrow afternoon." I scrambled around for a pair of pants.

"It's not a Crescent."

Unease settled in my gut as I rummaged in my bag, conscious that whoever had rocked up at this hour could walk around the side of the house and find us like this.

"Here, put these on."

I snatched Luke's shorts off a bench nearby and tossed them at him, rolling my eyes as he had to stoop to catch them around his ankles, too caught up in trying to scent the intruder. Maybe my priorities were skewed, but I didn't want to be naked when confronting them.

I found my tracksuit bottoms, hopping on one foot as I tugged them on while also rooting around in the pocket until my fingers closed around my phone. It was ringing but on silent. I'd knocked it off earlier when a random number called twice in a row, and Luke had jokingly threatened to throw it in the lake. I'd presumed it was some mobile provider cold calling, but now there were forty plus missed calls, and I was doubting myself.

Another knock sounded, and a voice called out, carrying to us on the wind along with a scent I recognised.

Fiona.

I was dialling my voicemail at the same time I started running towards the back doors of the house. "It's Fiona. Something is wrong."

Luke followed, our wet footsteps hammering and slipping on the wooden floors as I raced through the living room and out into the corridor. I tugged Luke's T-shirt over my head, not stopping until the front door was in sight. The hallway was dimly lit, but someone's silhouette was clear through the frosted glass lining either side of the door.

"Are you sure?" Luke reverted to his calm alpha-in-training voice.

I understood his concern, but a sense of dread was brewing in my gut. "Yes."

The door swung open to reveal Fiona, wrapped up in a winter coat and a fluffy hat, but she looked anything but festive. Her long blonde hair was a mess, knotted and tangled from the wind as if she'd rushed straight here. Her eyes were puffy and red with dark circles beneath them, her cheeks gaunt. Gone was the bubbly, positive girl and I'd befriended.

"Eve!" Relief washed over Fiona's face at the sight of me, and she rushed forwards, throwing her arms around my neck.

I hugged her, noticing how her willowy frame seemed impossibly lighter. She pulled away first, but her touch lingered, and she clasped my wrists in her hands, her expression grave.

"I'm so happy to see you."

Her cheeks were stained with tears.

"Are you allowed to be here?"

She shook her head, her warm breath hanging as a puff of vapour in the cold winter's night. "No, but I had to come. I tried to call, Jonas said you were here."

"What's wrong?" Luke's chest pressed against my back as he braced his hand on the top of the door frame above me.

"Mary told me everything, she told me what they were doing to hybrids. She said I had to tell you straight away." Fiona tripped over her words as the story spilled from her lips. Her voice rose higher with every breath.

Mary knew? Had she known all along what Ryan had planned for me?

A stinging pang of betrayal hit me, but I forced it to the back of my mind. Something was wrong, Fiona shouldn't have been on Crescent land. Hell, she had been so fucking scared about me training with Luke, I couldn't imagine what would have made her risk coming here.

I frowned, squeezing her hands. "Tell me what Fiona?"

"They have your friend Craig."

My heart plummeted as my worst fear was confirmed. The nightmare I'd been trying to save him from. The very reason I wanted to leave my friend in the past no matter how much it hurt.

"Who took him?" Luke's hand dropped to my shoulder where he squeezed, and I swear he was the only reason I was still standing. "Where is he?"

Fiona's throat bobbed, tears springing from the corner of her eyes. "The witch took him."

CHAPTER 33

LUKE

Watching Eve reliving the nightmare she'd feared this whole time was torture. After Fiona's revelation, we'd grabbed whatever was to hand and jumped in the car. Dad would probably stumble across my boxers in one of Helena's flower beds once everyone arrived at the pack house later that day, but I didn't care. My gaze flitted between Eve's face and the road. She alternated between staring blankly out the window at the blurred countryside flashing by, nervous babbling, bursting into tears, and then vehemently damning Ryan and his fucked up pack. I rolled with it as she rode the rollercoaster of emotions, squeezing her hand and unfurling her fingers each time they balled into fists so tight her nails cut her palm.

Fiona's headlights followed us all the way to the city, and by the time we reached the apartment, Dylan and Josh were waiting for us in the kitchen. Alice was there too, rationing Chinese takeaway out for everyone along with a cup of tea. Just like her mother would.

"Why are we wasting time here?" Eve snapped, her eyes narrowing at the food being plated up. With each word, her voice grew higher and panicked. "We need to go to the manor and rescue Craig, not have a fucking spring roll."

I sighed, trying to squeeze her shoulder only to have my hand slapped away. "You heard Fiona earlier, he's not at the manor. Larissa has him, and until that Faolchúnna event starts in the city tonight, we won't know his location. We have to wait."

"I don't want to wait." Her voice cracked, a single tear falling down her cheek and Alice rushed forwards, pulling Eve into a tight hug.

Watching Eve in so much pain was agonising, but I wasn't going to risk her losing Craig by rushing in. I had encouraged her to keep contact, I had promised he'd be safe.

The boys had stayed frozen in the kitchen, at a loss for words. Fiona hung back behind us, an outsider. But she was someone Eve trusted, and she'd helped Eve sneak out to train with me.

"This is Fiona, a friend of Eve's." I stepped to the side and motioned for her to join us with what I hoped was a welcoming smile.

Dylan sped into action, grabbing a bag of chips off the counter and offering them to Fiona as she stepped inside, the door falling closed behind her with a click. "Any friend of Eve's is a friend of ours."

"Thank you." Fiona's freckled cheeks warmed as she politely declined a chip.

Josh walked over and clapped a hand on my back, a silent promise, before steering me over to the fast food spread Alice had laid out. I sat down on one of the leather bar stools and tugged my shorts down as a gust of air reminded me that I was half clothed. The girls joined us, and Eve was ushered into the chair beside me, Dylan politely offering Fiona the last stool and perching on the corner of the couch nearby instead.

"Bring us up to speed, captain." Josh stuffed a forkful of shredded chicken into his mouth.

Dylan dug into a mountainous plate of curry like we were about to discuss a football match. But that's what they did, they kept me grounded. I was broody enough for the three of us. They knew how serious this was and that we were likely going to end up fighting the other pack tonight. They knew I wouldn't stop at anything to get Eve's friend back and hated the Faolchúnna pack just as much as I did. They also valued human life. When it came to it, they'd follow me into battle without hesitation.

But they could see how on edge Eve was, and my heart swelled with pride at how they kept bringing her back to the present each time she spiralled. They were family and had accepted her as such too.

"Larissa and Ryan, or one of them, took Craig late last night. We're not sure about the motives. It could be Ryan being a jealous prick or else the witch could be up to something more sinister."

"Ryan warned that their plans were bigger than me, but what could they want with a human?" Eve wiped her tear-stained cheeks with a tissue that then joined the tissue graveyard accumulating on the table. "It feels personal, but something in my gut says this isn't a revenge plot."

"From what I heard, it was more the witches doing." Fiona spoke up, staring down at the half-eaten portion of curry on her plate. "He didn't sound too happy about it. It has something to do with this big event the pack is throwing in the city tonight."

Dylan frowned. "Throwing a party isn't unusual for them."

"It is when Lars has been spotted out and about," Josh chimed in, tapping away on his laptop before bringing up a fuzzy CCTV still image of the notorious vampire.

"What the fuck is he doing in the city?"

Alice shuddered, her nose wrinkled as she placed her chips down. "Nothing good."

Worry gnawed at my resolve and I thought about asking Dad for help. We were out of our depth. But I knew despite Craig being in danger, he would refuse to risk the pack by going in there. He'd say it was too risky. Maybe I didn't have what it took to become alpha, but I wasn't going to leave Eve's friend to the wolves.

"I've asked around a little and apparently a few alphas are in town too, according to Jonas' intel." Dylan started on his second burger. "Something is up."

Fiona nodded. "Damien has been on edge the last few weeks. Whatever this event is, it's something big. Mary roped herself into the catering to keep an eye on things under the guise of helping make sure everything was up to scratch."

Dylan scowled. "I didn't know she cooked humans."

Eve flinched, and he winced when I shot him a murderous glare, holding up his hands in apology.

"Sorry, this just sounds dodgy given how many fancy people are turning up. Those old-style vampires don't play nicely with the humans, so holding the event in the city is a weird choice."

"No, it makes perfect sense if Damien is trying to position himself as the stronghold of Irish werewolves. He has had dealings with Lars before. Between him and Larissa, they are clearly planning some power play. Taking Craig must have something to do with that."

Alice frowned, her hazel-green eyes round with worry as she looked at me. "You don't think it's a trap, do you?"

"Possibly, but I don't believe we have any choice if we want to save Craig."

"I don't want to endanger anyone else." Eve's tone softened, tears welling up in her eyes as she scanned the faces surrounding the table. "I can do this alone."

Dylan stopped mid-bite and shook his head. "Like fuck you can."

"He's right, there's no way I'm letting you go in there alone."

Fiona brushed her long blonde hair back, worry creasing her brow. "I can't go there with you, I have to keep my family safe."

"I don't expect you to." Eve squeezed her friend's hand. "You've already done more than enough."

"Once Mary calls, I'll head back to the manor to keep an eye on things from there."

My phone buzzed on the counter for the billionth time, but I ignored it. It was my dad. I'd texted him the bare details and explained that Eve and I would miss the run. He knew I'd go and rescue Eve's friend, but I'd made sure to leave out any information that would help my dad stop us. He had no idea where we were going, and I'd left out Larissa's involvement too. A little white lie. Regardless, he was gonna be pissed.

"Hello?" Josh strode out of the open living room and into the small hall leading towards the bedroom, holding his phone to his ear.

Fuck.

"Josh! Don't answer that!" I jumped up, striding across the room, but it was too late.

He turned to me, his eyebrows shooting up and his mouth curving into an apologetic half-smile, half-grimace as he answered the voice booming down the line. "I'm sorry Tom, he's not here."

Even without the phone being on speaker, I could hear my father yelling, his voice thick with the power of an alpha.

"I know damn well he is. Put him on the phone," Dad demanded, and Josh winced, holding the phone away from his ear.

I ran my hand down my face, my shoulders slumping in defeat as I held my hand out palm facing up. "Give it here."

Josh handed me his phone and mouthed 'sorry' before hightailing back down the hall towards the living room.

"Luke." My father's voice crackled from the speakers, thick with disappointment. "I know you're there."

I counted to ten before bringing the phone to my ear. "Yep?"

"I know you like to pretend that becoming alpha is some sort of punishment that you can run from, but you are my son. Getting Alice back was one thing, but if you trespass on their lands and fight Ryan, it can and *will* be deemed an act of war." His tone rang with authority that made my skin crawl. I was never good at being ordered around. "You need to lead with your head, not your heart. We can contact Damien and reason with the Faolchúnna pack to save Craig the proper way."

"The proper way? They *kidnapped* her friend. He's human,

they're going to kill him. Negotiating for his dead body isn't going to cut it."

"You need to do this the prop—"

"There is no proper way to negotiate this, *Alpha*." I kicked the baseboard in frustration, causing a crack to splinter through the wood where my foot connected. "They're breaking the rules by kidnapping a human under this circumstance, but no one cares. I will not let Eve lose another friend."

"We can notify The Royals of the breach." His tone soured. He hated it whenever I called him his official title, and I knew it.

"They're not going to care when it's Larissa." The moment the words left my lips, I cursed and began futile damage control. "The witches have a loose hold on Ireland, this is between us and the Faolchúnna pack."

Dad wasn't buying it. "Larissa is involved? Absolutely not, this is too dangerous."

"I have to go."

"Is your sister there?"

I paused. "Yes."

"We only just got her back." Dad knew full well he was manipulating me by using Alice. At the same time, concern bled into his pleas. "This is too dangerous. Your job is to keep your sister safe, not dive headfirst into danger without a second thought."

"I'll keep her safe," I promised, and I meant it.

Noise levels rose in the living room and Fiona called out. "Mary called. We have the location!"

My dad overheard and spewed more demands down the line, but I spoke over him.

"I have to go, dad. I'm sorry you think I'm a failure, but I won't watch Eve lose another person she loves. You say I need to protect my pack, but that includes Eve. No one is going to get hurt. I'll call you later."

I killed the call and hoped I was right.

CHAPTER 34

I *can't breathe.*

My heart hammered erratically in my chest like it wanted to burst through my ribs to free up the crushing pressure on my lungs. The black satin dress that Alice had stuffed me into was claustrophobic. I was sweating through the heavy material, the floor-length skirt pooling around my feet in the passenger side of the car. Luke was going over the plan for the hundredth time, but I wasn't listening. We parked around the corner from the fancy hotel the Faolchúnna pack was hosting their secret event at, and all I could think about was Craig. Was he in pain? Was he even alive?

"Eve?" Luke's voice broke through my panic, tugging me back to the present. He gave my hand a gentle squeeze and I returned it, but the furrow of concern in his brow remained. He glanced down and spotted my phone in my hand, another call going to Craig's number that just went dead. I'd lost count of how many times I'd tried him.

He pried the phone from my hand, and I fiddled with the black mask on my lap instead. Glitter smeared my hand as I fingered the delicate lace lining the edges and wound the ribbon around my hand. How fitting that Damien was hosting a masquerade ball, no doubt they were all monsters well used to hiding behind a mask.

I caught a glimpse of the guys stuffed into the back seat. Dylan and Josh sat either side of a squished Alice in the centre, all dressed up like we were out to celebrate and not crash the party. She'd fought with her brother before we left, refusing to be left behind. From the steely resignation reflecting in her eyes under the light of the dim streetlights, this was something she needed to do. I understood that, but Luke would always protect his little sister.

"Mary is going to let us in the back entrance. First up, we locate the main players, the alpha, Ryan, Lars, and the witch." Luke sounded more like his father with each sentence. He fidgeted with the black bow tie around his neck before levelling the others with a serious look. "Do not approach them under any circumstances. Eve and I will locate Craig, you are to watch their movements and do your best to keep them in the main room. The glamour masking our scents will only last for about two hours."

The moment we notified Jonas of our plans, he'd offered to help in any way he could. One of the barmaids at the Dark Night was half-Fae, so the glamour wouldn't hold up as long as if a stronger Fae cast it.

Alice pursed her deep burgundy lips, coupled with her black, Bardot neckline velvet dress and the way she'd styled her strawberry blonde hair half-up, she had a gothic badass look going. Jonas had dropped off the outfits courtesy of Darius' extensive collection, and Alice had done my hair. Luke scrubbed up like a supermodel, whereas not even her skills could mask the bags under my eyes, red from crying. I hadn't slept since Fiona turned up in the early hours of the morning. When everyone else napped before nightfall, I spent the time hiding in the bathroom crying until Luke found me and carried me to bed where I sobbed in his arms for hours on end. He stayed up the whole time, murmuring soft words of comfort in my ear and promises that did nothing to chase my fears away.

"Has Josh shown you how the earpieces work?" Luke looked between me and his sister as the rookies.

I nodded, touching the subtle earpiece in my left ear that was hidden by the way Alice swept my hair back and pinned it.

Luke's phone buzzed on the dash, and I stiffened as he put it on speaker.

"Luke? It's Mary. We're good to go. Take the last right before the corner, and I'll let you in the back."

All too soon her familiar voice was gone, and the line went dead.

My hands shook as we piled out of the car, running on pure adrenaline as we gathered on the sidewalk. All of the guys were suited and booted, looking uncomfortable in stiff black tuxedos. The hotel was in one of the more affluent areas of Dublin. We were surrounded by old Georgian buildings on all sides and above us, the full moon shone on a bright winter's night as if she was watching. Waiting.

I swallowed hard, my mouth dry as I slid my mask into place and tied the bow behind my head.

Luke tapped his earpiece, and his voice sounded both in my ear and beside me. "Ready?"

We all nodded dutifully. I set my shoulders, gathered up the skirt of my dress to expose the Converse I had on underneath and strode down the street. I wasn't going to be some damsel in distress stumbling around on stilettos. As much as I would enjoy stabbing Ryan in the chest, this was a rescue mission.

The hotel was huge for the city centre, spanning at least three old Georgian houses which had been renovated and merged to form one large hotel, while still holding an old worldly charm. With black wrought-iron balconies that stood out against white pillars, the original windows and red-orange brickwork, it screamed affluence. Damien was definitely intent on proving a point tonight.

We turned down an alleyway at the back where a door to our immediate left swung open to reveal Mary, dressed in black slacks and a white shirt. It was the first time I had seen her without her signature apron, and a small pang of sadness hit.

"Quickly, get inside," she ordered, ushering us in with a tea-towel in hand.

We stepped into a narrow hallway, the noise of dishes clanging ringing in the distance. Mary snapped the door shut and turned to us, her gaze softening as it landed on where Luke's hand was joined with mine.

"I'm so glad you're okay." She smiled warmly, but an iciness rose up in me that I didn't quite understand.

She had always warned me to be careful, but if she truly knew how evil her pack was, why didn't she tell me the truth outright?

Her smile faltered, and she sighed, wringing the towel in her hands. "Your father called me, Luke, and I couldn't lie to him. I didn't know you were going behind his back."

"I had no choice."

She nodded, glancing down the corridor as another bang sounded and someone cursed. It didn't sound like the kitchen was faring too well.

"You have maybe an hour before he gets here. They have rented out the main function room." Mary strode down the hallway, and we all followed suit. She walked alongside Luke, looking at him with a fond familiarity that confused me. "Both Lars and Larissa are here, along with the alpha from London and one of the other European packs. I didn't recognise the faces, but there are definitely a few high up vampires around too, and at least one Fae royalty."

Luke's frown deepened. "That's not good."

A wave of heat hit me as we passed the kitchens, but Mary forged ahead.

"No, it's not. So lie low and focus on getting your friend out or else your dad will never forgive me." She led us up a winding staircase towards the source of music in the distance. The noise of chatter rose as we emerged on a landing, the grey carpet giving way to a polished red-and-white checked marble. "Craig is here somewhere, but I haven't been able to pinpoint his exact location."

I swallowed the lump forming in my throat. "He's alive?"

"As far as I know, yes." Mary's eyes were full of sympathy.

My shoulders sagged with relief, but we were nowhere near out of the woods. Mary stopped abruptly behind a green marble pillar just before the corridor ended, Luke stopped just short of bumping into her. The foyer was bustling with people, and the different scents of many paranormals filled my senses. The hair on my arms stood up, and it had nothing to do with my decision to forgo a coat.

"This is as far as I can take you." She motioned for us to adjust our masks before leaning forwards and kissing a rather surprised Luke on the cheek. "The function room is to the left. Don't get caught."

With that, she hurried away, and we all looked to Luke for direction. Any sense of bravado I had mustered vanished at the sight of so many paranormal creatures walking through the foyer. The vampires were easy to spot from the way they moved gliding effortlessly, and the old money adorning the women. I'd never seen so many werewolves in one spot. Each one of them treated the hotel staff with disdain, practically throwing their coats at the poor cloakroom attendant manning the booth to the right of two large white doors. A suave looking wolf strode past us, the woman holding his arm dressed head to toe in pure opulence complete with a fur shawl. Bile rose in my throat as I clocked the very real fox head attached.

What the actual fuck?

These people were pure evil. I couldn't explain it, but I was certain in my gut.

Luke reached between us, his thumb brushing mine in a

silent gesture of understanding. His shoulders were tense but set with an air of confidence I wished I could emit.

Pull your shit together. Craig needs you.

If I walked in there showing a single shred of fear, I would be slaughtered like a lamb.

He looked at me, a silent question in his eyes. I rolled my shoulders, straightening to my full height that only came to Luke's chest, and nodded.

With that, Alice hooked an arm with both Dylan and Josh, and I followed suit with Luke as we led the way. We stepped out into the chaos in sync, hidden behind our masks with our chins held high as if we belonged here.

"Stick by my side." Luke placed a possessive hand over mine on his arm as another werewolf's masked eyes landed on me. He was smaller than Luke, but with broad shoulders that threatened to split his expensive tux at the seams. A low growl rumbled from Luke's chest, and the man dropped his gaze.

Wow. I wasn't sure if that made me wet or pissed off.

Deciding better of it, I didn't snatch my arm away and call Luke an alphahole. The white doors were opened for each guest individually, guarded by two extremely tall demons with sour expressions on their red faces. Black tattoos lined their cheeks in some intricate matching design, matching the black horns on their head. They stood with their legs spread shoulder width apart, their reptilian gold eyes scanning the foyer. Their clasped hands were empty, but with thick black claws that glint in the light bouncing off the massive gold chandelier hanging above us. They had no need for weapons.

I'd have chewed my lip off with nerves if it wasn't for the heavy layer of lipstick Alice had applied. Instead, I focused on Luke's hand on mine and used his touch to ground me and slow my racing heart as we approached.

"Josh spotted something and took them to see if we could kill the CCTV." Luke dipped his head so his lips were brushing against my ear with each word.

He smirked at the security guards as if he was whispering something dirty in my ear, and I plastered on a smile, glancing back just in time to see the short train of Alice's dress disappear around a corner.

Both the guy working the cloakroom and the woman manning the door barely looked at me. The demons inclined their heads, and the woman stepped forwards to open the door for us without hesitation.

I inhaled the scent of her perfume and... *human?*

My brow furrowed with concern as she stepped back beside the demons like they didn't look like something that spawned from nightmares.

"Glamours, they can be set to only trigger for humans." Luke placed his hand at the small of my back and guided me inside. "It takes an extremely talented Fae though. Damien is definitely out to make a statement."

We stepped into a large function room brimming with guests all dressed in black tie. Waiters wove through the crowds with platters of appetisers and champagne flutes. As far as I could tell, no humans were present within the room. But holding such an event in a human location and fooling the staff was a disturbing statement indeed.

I smoothed the skirt of my dress, making sure my Converse were covered as we moved deeper into the room. The plush sapphire carpets complimented white panelled walls and gold crown detailing on the ceiling. Real icicles hung from the ceiling, complemented by hanging lights and blue flowers I didn't recognise casting a glow over the entire room. Each table had an extravagant ice sculpture centrepiece surrounded by white roses. There were even trees dotted around frosted white.

Cold and lifeless, like them.

But it wasn't the beauty of the room that stole the breath from my lungs. As I meandered through the crowd, acting like we had a known destination while scanning the room for a sight of the familiar culprits, my gaze snagged on where a stage was set up at the far end of the room. There was a podium in the centre, with a banner displaying the Faolchúnna pack crest, a band playing a song that didn't even register with me because three wrought-iron cages hung from the ceilings. Fairy lights wound around the bars as if they were part of the decorations—part of the show. Each one was occupied by a different paranormal creature.

CHAPTER 35

LUKE

S ick. They were all fucking sick.

Above the lavish party hung three cages with a paranormal creature in each. A werewolf in their wolf form, a witch slumped against the bars of her cage staring out at us with dead eyes, and a thin vampire with bright crimson eyes lost to blood lust.

Eve rushed forwards, and I grabbed her arm, spinning her to face me and planting a kiss on her lips to stop her from causing a scene. It was the least romantic kiss we would ever share.

"Luke..." She breathed, her chest flushing pink as she warred with her emotions. Tears pricked her eyes, and her throat bobbed as she took in the sickening display above us. "I can't do this. We have to get them out."

I brushed my lips against hers again, hoping the display would put off anyone trying to eavesdrop. Thankfully, super strong hearing wasn't as much use in a room so packed unless someone knew what they were listening for. Otherwise, we would have been well on our way to joining those held captive above us.

"I know," I released my grip on her forearms before leading

her towards the refreshments situated underneath the vampire. "But we can't cause a scene."

She took a deep breath, smoothing her hands on her dress before nodding reluctantly.

Bile lingered in the back of my throat as I fought to keep control. I couldn't think about what Damien had done to the people in those cages without wanting to seek him out and smash his face in. It wasn't lost on me that every waiter was some form of creature that was deemed "lesser" and that the more elitist paranormals were the ones attending.

I focused on the crowd, trying to pick out the scheming rat Ryan and his father, but the room was overflowing with people, and everyone was masked.

The cage above us rattled and Eve flinched, her lips pursed into a thin line as she glanced up again. The vampire was practically drooling, gripping his cage so tightly the bars were bending under the pressure. His eyes were devoid of any gold flecks, his lips pulled back in a feral snarl as he followed the movement of people below him. He didn't look young enough to be behaving like a freshly turned vamp. He had definitely been starved.

Eve frowned at her phone, her thumb a blur as she scrolled until she froze.

I tapped my earpiece to see if something was up with Josh and the others. "Everything okay?"

"I think we might have found a way to kill their cameras for an hour," Dylan answered, and Josh argued in the background about timing and footage loops.

"Go for it. Nothing here yet."

Eve hadn't even looked up, her gaze snapping back and forth between her phone and the inhumane entertainment above us.

"What's wrong?" I tried to look busy by pouring myself a glass of Fae wine that I'd no intention of drinking.

"It's him."

"What?"

She shoved her phone in my face, nodding her head in the direction of the caged vampire salivating over the punch bowl of human blood beside us. "It's Harold."

I studied the photo. It looked like the same person, except the vampire's brown hair was longer and unkempt and his cheeks gaunt.

"How do you have this?"

She tucked her phone back into her purse just as a siren with silver hair down to her waist and a nasty case of resting bitch face shoved past us to get to the drink.

"My manager mentioned a missing colleague." Eve kept her explanation vague as the nosy woman lingered beside us, unwilling to implicate our friends. "I googled it out of curiosity, just in case I could help."

The missing vampire.

Jonas had told me about his old friend and how worried both him and Darius were. Harold slammed his fists against the bars. The siren now held up a glass filled with blood towards the vampire. She was stunning, with cat-like eyes, and a low-cut white dress that accentuated her curves. But it was the sick smirk on her pretty face, the look of unfathomable satisfaction as she watched the vampire snarl and stick his arm so far through the bars that the metal was biting into his underarm. In his blind desperation, he paid no heed to the laceration on his arm, his ruby eyes locked on the glass she taunted him with.

Sirens fed off others' emotions. The stronger the emotion, the more satisfying. It was a sickening, immoral display of her power.

Before I could act, Eve swept past me. The siren was so fixated on torturing her prey that she didn't notice Eve sticking her hip out and making sure she caught her side against the woman's elbow, knocking the glass out of her hand. It was like a scene from Carrie, her dress was splattered with blood and completely destroyed in seconds.

I snatched Eve's hand and whisked her towards me and onto

the crowded dance floor. Because of the clientele, it was less of a dance floor and more of a ballroom. Thankfully, Eve didn't fight me and fell into step as we spun across the room and away from the screeches of a siren that now sounded more like a banshee. Fortunately, the spillage had sent Harold into a frenzy so some of Damien's cronies were more focused on calming him down and avoiding a commotion than the woman throwing a hissy fit.

If Eve didn't know how to waltz, she sure knew how to fake it well.

"Nicely done." I couldn't resist a smile despite the sombre circumstances. "Since when can you dance?"

The intricate black mask hid most of her face, but I could tell I'd earned myself a dirty look. "I couldn't let her get away with that. And I might be clumsy, but one of my foster parents had a thing for Strictly Come Dancing. They even sent me to a few ballroom classes."

She fell silent, and I knew not to push it. Eve had told me about her bouncing between foster homes. Some stories were okay, some made me want to hunt people down and break their legs.

I brushed my thumb against the small of her back, wishing that the clock wasn't counting down on someone's life as we moved across the dance floor. She was my girlfriend, we should be going on dates. I wanted nights like this where I was showing her off, not hiding. Eve laced her fingers with mine. She was breathtaking in the black dress Jonas had dropped off, complete with a white gold necklace with a teardrop diamond that probably cost more than my car. Dragons weren't the only ones who hoarded treasure, Darius gave them a run for their money.

My favourite version of Eve was when we first woke up in the morning, her combination of a sleepy smile and bed hair was the cutest thing I'd ever seen. But all dressed up, her blue eyes piercing against the black mask, she was stunning, and I wanted to lose myself in the moment. I wanted to sweep her around the dance floor under the twinkling lights all night. I wanted to lose myself in her.

"Damien has arrived."

I followed her gaze to see the Faolchúnna alpha standing across the room. He wore a flashy tuxedo, and his black hair was slicked back like a Bond villain. No matter how hard he tried to polish up, he was still a prick. His mask was a wolf, of course, with a moon on the forehead complete with ears and everything.

Her gaze was fixed on the table beside Damien where more wine and blood were laid out, except this time it came from a live source. A young Satyr was slumped in the chair, rope that was clearly charmed wrapped around her waist and chest. Both of her arms were strapped to the table, blood flowing freely from her upturned wrist into a golden tray. A vampire sat to one side, a mop of black curls masking her face as she fed from the living buffet.

She stumbled, and I caught her under the arm, spinning her into my chest and swaying with my chin on her shoulder. "Breathe."

"How is this possible?" Eve took one laboured breath, and then another, but she was still deathly pale beneath her mask when I spun her back out. She wrapped her arms around my shoulder as the music slowed, her lower lip trembling. "How can they get away with this?"

"The Royals normally prevent things like this, but vampires like Lars have lived like this for many years. When they're too powerful to take on, sometimes they decide not to rock the boat."

"Cowards. They need to sink this like the fucking Titanic."

I nodded, turning us in a circle so I could watch Damien over her shoulder. "Agreed. Most of us aren't like this, it's a small minority, but that doesn't make it okay to ignore."

"There are some pretty messed up humans walking the earth, so it makes sense that this world has its own share of psychopaths." Eve exhaled a slow, shaky, breath as she searched the crowd. "Speaking of."

She pointed subtly to our right where Ryan stood in a corner where the lights were dimmer. A redhead in a skimpy emerald number clung to his arm, and I stiffened at the sight of the blonde he was in deep conversation with.

"Looks like it's the witching hour too," I muttered.

Larissa wore a deep purple dress that matched her eyes, her long blonde hair shimmering as it fell over her shoulder. She clutched Ryan's forearm, her jaw set as they engaged in a fight I couldn't pick out over the rest of the noise. The redhead didn't look too pleased with the discussion, a permanent scowl fixed on her face.

Movement by the door seemed to catch everyone's attention as all heads turned. The door opened to reveal the devil himself as Lars strode into the room. There was no mistaking him. It may have been a masquerade ball, but the slim gold mask that matched his eyes barely skimmed his cheekbones. He paused, his lips thinning as he surveyed the crowd.

Damien rushed over, receiving a limp handshake for his troubles.

"Thank you so much for joining us, Lars." He beamed, not the least bit perturbed by the vampire's frosty reception.

I didn't hear Lars' response because on a signal from the alpha, the band burst back into action, everyone spilling out onto the dance floor or busying themselves with a drink. It was ironic that the scum of the earth was here and even they were uncomfortable around Lars. His reputation really did precede him.

"Who is that?" Eve's voice was barely a whisper as she leaned up on her toes.

"Lars, the vampire my dad and I visited." I sighed, wishing I'd told Eve about my trip to Lars' lair properly before tonight. I'd thought sparing her the details was a kindness, I'd never once imagined Damien would have taken a leaf out of the vampire's warped handbook. I had, however, told her how he treated young vampires. Given the state of the poor satyr blood bag across the room, it didn't take a genius to know a human wasn't safe here.

Eve paled, tugging at the neckline of her dress and eyeing the exit. "We need to find Craig."

"Luke?"

Josh's voice buzzed in my ear, and Eve's head snapped up as she got the message too.

"How's it going?" I tried to sound like I was talking to Eve as we moved towards the end of the crowd, dancing our way through the busy dance floor.

"Cameras are down, but you need to get over here now. We found a room in the basement level that's locked off, Alice is convinced she can smell Craig."

Something banged, and Alice grumbled down her own line. "You can't kick it in Dylan, I'm very familiar with a locked door, and I *can* smell him."

"You need to get down here, now," Josh cut in. "Take a left down the corridor from the foyer, the same one we came through. Keep going until you hit the stairs, there's two flights, and it will feel like you're heading towards a dead end. I'll meet you halfway."

I nodded and Eve did the same, both of us stepping off the dance floor as we reached the edge.

"Let's go." I took her hand and led her through the crowd towards the exit that was now manned internally by another set of demonic security guards that looked grumpy as hell, but taking my girl to the toilets shouldn't be an issue.

My arm jolted as Eve stopped, our fingertips brushing as we lost contact and a figure stepped in front of her. A man in a suit far too fancy that he didn't have the shoulders to fill blocked my view.

"Oh, my apologies." Ryan turned to face me, wearing an over-the-top wolf mask to match his father's. His lips turned up in a smirk as he took Eve's hand from mine, holding it up as if we were at a royal ball and he was asking for her hand. "May I steal a dance with this beauty?"

Eve's expression darkened like a storm rolling in, and she snatched her hand away, her eyes narrowed into a murderous glare behind her mask. "You may not."

She made to grab my hand again, but Ryan caught her wrist, and a low growl rumbled in my chest.

"I don't believe you received an invitation. So, unless you want to be escorted off the premises immediately, you owe me a dance," he hissed, leaning in too close for my liking before adding. "It would be rude to deny a host."

"I don't owe you shit."

The red mist was descending when my sister's voice came down the line. "Hurry up, we need you here now."

Heads were starting to turn in our direction, and Ryan still held Eve's wrist in a vice-like grip, it didn't look good, and we couldn't have people talking. I didn't doubt the jealous asshole would blow our plan up and cause a scene if she didn't comply. But at the same time, I had a strong urge to snap his neck, fuck the consequences.

My wolf side agreed.

Eve must have noticed my eyes flashing silver because she nodded, snatching her arm away from Ryan. "Fine, one song. That's it."

I wanted to grab her, tell him that we had to go and drag her out of the room and as far away from this hellhole as possible, but I couldn't. She locked eyes with me as they walked back towards the dance floor, in a silent plea for me to behave. Craig was the priority. We had to save him. I couldn't paint this room with Ryan's blood *and* save her friend, but I was frozen in place watching him guide her onto the dance floor.

She kept her eyes trained on him as he wound an arm around her waist, and I twitched from the urge to tackle him to the ground.

"I'll be fine, get him," she said softly down my earpiece.

It took all my control to tear my eyes away from my girl and leave her in the arms of a monster.

CHAPTER 36

EVE

"Y ou'll be more than fine, I'm a great dancer," Ryan purred in my ear, and I jolted.

Of course the conceited dick presumed I was talking to myself. I wasn't an expert on this mind link thing, but I willed the thought into existence and hoped Luke heard me.

Get Craig, I'll follow as soon as I can.

Luke nodded but didn't look the least bit reassured.

My heart constricted in my chest as he turned away, shoving his way through in the direction of the exit until he disappeared into the crowd.

The music slowed. I arched my back so that the gap between us grew. It was bad dancing form, and I probably looked ridiculous, but I didn't care. My skin crawled under his touch. No doubt some onlookers thought it weird, but Ryan wasn't popular among his peers. Especially the women. Even if the ones here were soulless, we all had an innate sense of when a man was unhinged. Then again, Ryan had hidden his daddy issues and pathetic need to prove himself from me for a long time.

"You don't look like you're having fun." He sounded like a petulant toddler as his hand slid down to the curve of my waist and pulled me closer. "It's such a beautiful event, you should really try enjoying yourself."

I kept my gaze trained on the canopy of icicles and lights above us, clenching my jaw as his words sent a wave of nausea rolling over me. "It is very pretty."

We spun past the siren from earlier with a vampire getting to know one another intimately at one of the corner tables and Ryan chuckled, his laugh ringing hollow. "You went to all this effort to sneak in, might as well make the most of it."

"I didn't sneak in, I walked in the door. Maybe you should blame your security."

He spun me into a little dip, leering over me like the hungry vampire suspended in a cage above us. "This event was invitation only and kept under wraps. We weren't expecting any gate crashers."

I caught Nadine's eye as she stood at the edge of the dance floor. Her red hair was pulled back in an elegant half-up, half-down do at odds with a deep emerald silk gown that clung to her model figure. Stunning as always, but her black-and-silver mask, a toned-down version of Ryan's, couldn't hide the furious scowl twisting her features.

"How prestigious."

His lips thinned at my tone, and he righted us, roughly pulling me back into hold. "Is that what you're doing? Planning to ruin the event my father and I have worked so hard on?"

I didn't answer, counting the icicles on the ceiling as I tried to ride the song out.

"Look at me." Ryan dropped my hand to pinch my chin between his fingers. "What are you doing here?"

"Watch it or I'll storm out of here and leave you looking like the sad little reject you are." I ripped my head from his grip.

"You do that, and I'll make sure Luke doesn't leave this building." Ryan's eyes flashed silver. He meant it. I had no doubt Luke could take Ryan on in a fight, but there were so many werewolves here. Let alone the vampires, demons, and whatever else.

"The best of the best are here tonight, some of them even came all the way from America." His voice swelled with pride as he gestured to the crowd of paranormals. "Some of the most prestigious alphas and vampires have turned up. Even a Fae royal couldn't resist attending."

"What are you playing at Ryan?"

"Tell me your secrets, and I'll tell you mine," he quipped.

I fought the urge to puke. That was something he used to say during the early days when we dated. We would share stories and truths. Or at least, I thought we did. But looking back now, his stories were mostly twisted in his favour or outright lies. Though, is it a lie if he truly believed it?

The lights and fancy centrepieces became a blur as he led me around the dance floor, and I focused on faking it. My skin tingled under his touch in all the wrong ways, my instinct to recoil from the broad smile pasted on his weaselly face. He was putting on a show, but I didn't get it. No one here knew who I was.

I kept waiting for someone to speak in my ear, but the lines were all quiet. The only reason I could keep my feet moving around the dance floor while Ryan held me was the thought of them rescuing Craig. It was too risky to ask in my earpiece and despite reaching out mentally to Luke, he wasn't answering. He'd mentioned a distance limitation, but we hadn't gotten around to testing it out. If Alice thought Craig was in the room, I believed her. And I trusted them to get him out safely. Stomaching one dance with Ryan was worth it to free my friend.

Just as the song was coming to an end, Ryan signalled for them to repeat the chorus once more to prolong the torture. He spent the whole time staring at me with gooey eyes as if we were having a moment, the smile pasted on his face making him look insane. Which I guess he was, because he spun me by the Satyr being drained, and we were dancing under people he happily held captive.

Above us, the wolf howled. A sorrowful sound that made my heart feel like it was cleaving in two.

I shoved Ryan away from me, my resolve breaking just as the song came to an end.

"I believe your time with me is up," I ground the words out, bowing my head in a fake sign of respect that would only rile him up.

Barely holding my shit together, I gathered the skirt of my dress in one hand and made a beeline towards the exit. I kept my gaze on the ground, refusing to look at the satyr as I passed or what I realised were some body parts and other weird fucking delicacies plated up on a side table. Mumbling false apologies, I kept going and was barely six feet from the door when Ryan caught up.

"Eve, don't you—"

I stopped in front of a broad-shouldered demon with what was possibly a kind face. It was hard to tell with the horns and weird teeth.

"Excuse me. Could you point me towards the ladies' room?"

The demon's snake-like golden eyes morphed into a bottomless pit of black as they slid to Ryan who looked like he was about to burst a blood vessel. My ex's hands were balled into fists by his side, and an ugly vein popped in his temple.

"Of course, miss. It's just outside to the right." The demon gestured with his hand as he bowed and opened the door behind me.

I dashed through with a brief thanks and turned just in time to see them shutting the door in an outraged Ryan's face.

A delirious laugh slipped from my lips. I guessed his shitty treatment of people had finally bitten him in the ass. You can have someone on your payroll, but a bad attitude won't earn you loyalty. It made sense they had to hire security considering half the pack didn't seem to be aware of what they were up to. Fiona's family didn't know, God only knows how many of them were in the dark.

I took a deep breath to steady my racing heart and focused my senses, trying to channel the adrenaline coursing through my veins. A security camera panned my way. They were dotted around the ceiling, and I silently thanked Josh for being a tech whizz and making sure none of this could be traced back to us.

The foyer was empty but for a human working on the reception, but there were so many different scents and species lingering in the air that I struggled to pick out Luke's.

"Left, then stairs," I muttered to myself, my trainers squeaking against the spotless checked marble tiles as I started in that direction.

White doors lined the panelled walls of the corridor that seemed to go on forever. It was only when I reached the end and found a staircase to my right that I realised the far wall was a mirror. I'd always hated the house of mirrors in the circus.

I glanced over my shoulder to make sure I was alone before tapping the earpiece in my left ear. "Two stairs, yeah? I'm on my way."

No one answered. The marble floor gave way to a plush blue carpet that matched the one in the function room as I descended the winding staircase. I brushed my fingers against the wooden banister, the familiar scent of Luke, Alice, and my friends filling my senses among the noise of older scents.

I'm coming Craig, hold on.

At the bottom of the stairs, I stepped out onto another corridor that was narrower but stretched out like the first. A small spark of excitement fuelled me as I hurried along, knowing I was getting closer to rescuing my friend.

"You are becoming a peculiar thorn in my side." Larissa stepped into view, the short train of her dress trailing behind her. Her reflection was just as terrifying as the real deal, and I whipped around to find her standing in the corridor behind me. Her lips, painted a dark purple to match the dress, were pulled back in a smile that was more reminiscent of a snarl.

I scrambled for a lie, taking a step back towards the second staircase. "I'm sorry, I must have gotten lost on the way to the bathroom."

She closed the distance between us in a second. I barely blinked and she was in front of me, her blonde curls swaying as they settled from the movement. "You're a poor liar. Which is surprising given you fooled Ryan for so long."

How the fuck did she do that?

"My, my, you really are fresh to our world." Larissa purred, her high-pitched cackle bouncing off the panelled walls. "I don't blame you for leaving him, by the way. Your latest catch looks delicious."

The way she looked like she actually wanted to *eat* Luke like a dessert had me shifting from foot to foot, my instincts screaming at me to run. My wolf side begged to shift, but that would start a dangerous game I wasn't sure I could win.

"What's wrong? Cat got your tongue?" She pouted, tapping long manicured nails against her purse in annoyance.

I took another step back, my hand finding the wooden rail at the top of the stairs. "What do you want?"

"I'm not sure yet." She cocked her head to one side, eyeing me up like some sort of plaything and before closing the distance between us. Her talons tapped against the banister as she walked her fingers until our hands were touching. She flicked her wrist, sending my purse over the edge and teetering down the stairs out of reach. "But you keep popping up, and your jilted lover acted oddly the night the hybrid caused problems."

"Her name was Spencer." I lifted my chin.

Larissa's face lit up, the corners of her lips quirking in amusement. "Oh, you are fun. The way Ryan gets all wound up about you, it's made me wonder if there's something more."

She lifted her hand to my face, and I recoiled as her nail scraped my cheek as she pushed a stray curl behind my ear.

Just as I went to slap her hand away, she grabbed a fistful of my hair and forced my head back. Her strength surprised me, sharp nails digging into my scalp as she shoved me off balance. Tears pricked my eyes, and my Converse slid against the carpet as she dragged me towards the door, ripping it open with her free hand.

"This has to go." She snatched the tiny earpiece out of my ear and held it up to my face, sneering as it burst into flames between her fingers.

I screamed, but she simply threw her head back and laughed as she hauled me into the room. The door rattled on its hinges as she kicked it shut with a spiked stiletto.

She released my hair to dump me on the carpeted floor. We were in some kind of office, sparsely decorated with a desk in one corner and shelves full of files. There were no windows, we were below ground level. Panic constricted my chest. I was trapped downstairs with the witch.

"Scream all you want, sweetie." Larissa leaned over me, the diamonds adorning her neck dangling over her exposed cleavage as she smirked down at me with a wicked glint in her eyes. "No one can hear you."

CHAPTER 37

LUKE

"What do you mean she's gone?"

Josh paused too long for my liking. It had only been minutes since I'd left her behind at the function. The moment I'd met everyone outside the door holding Craig, I'd sent him straight back up to fetch Eve. How could she have gone?

"Eve?" Our mind link wasn't working at this distance, so I tapped my earpiece, my voice growing strained. "Where are you? Make a sound, anything to let us know you're ok."

Silence.

I'll fucking kill that bastard if he lays a hand on her.

Behind me Alice tried to pick the lock, bickering with Dylan over what method to try. Every couple of minutes he grew impatient and took a run at the door, throwing all of his weight behind it. Each time his muscular shoulder smashed into the ordinary wooden door and didn't even make a dent. Alice would then yell at him and go back to lock picking with her claws out.

"She's not here, but Ryan is. So is Daddy Dearest, even Lars is still skulking around."

Alice stopped her fiddling with the lock to glance over at me, worry lining her brow as Josh relayed the information over the open line.

"Find her," I ordered, unease stewing in the pit of my stomach. "And be careful."

Josh's side went quiet, and I turned my attention back to the door. We needed to get to Craig. My sister was right, someone had tried to mask it, but the faintest hint of his scent came from beneath the door. Despite knocking several times, we never heard an answer. But the familiar tingle of magic told me that there was some kind of silencing bubble there, and no doubt a protection spell or two which explained why the hulk of muscle charging at the door beside me wasn't making any headway.

Fucking witches.

"I can make a call, but I don't think any witch willing to go against the Faolchúnna pack would get here in time."

Just as I finished my sentence, the lock clicked audibly, and Alice turned to me with a wide grin. "Got it."

Dylan high-fived her, and they both shared a look of triumph. I hadn't told them the full extent of the evil upstairs, only that three others were being held captive. It had shaken Alice, so she was laser focused on our rescue mission and getting the hell out of this place as soon as possible. I was very much on board.

"Careful." I raised my hand in warning as Dylan went to bulldoze his way through the door. "It's spelled."

He paused, hand hovering over the old-fashioned brass doorknob. "I know that, but unless you've picked up some magic powers or telekinesis, we have to open it one way or another."

"Let me go first."

"Don't pull that alpha shit with me, mate," Dylan joked, arching his eyebrow as he turned to me and wrapped his hand around the doorknob and turned it. "Calm your tits. Josh is going to find Eve, we'll rescue Craig, and everything will be fine."

I waited for his hand to go on fire or something to blow up, but the corridor remained silent.

My best friend's superpower was being able to stay calm in the face of any crisis. His positive attitude was unshakeable, and I envied him for it, because the ball of dread in my gut was growing into a steady storm. My mind raced through the endless possibilities of what could be happening to Eve, throwing up fears of her being trapped in those cages. I wanted to throw up, murder someone, and cry all at once. But I couldn't, so I steeled myself and joined Alice by Dylan's side as he pushed the door open.

That's when magic sparked before our eyes.

A blinding light flared to life, followed by a loud bang, and the sound of wood splintering had me ducking and shielding my ears. An invisible force crashed into us, knocking me off my feet. Everything happened so fast. I flung my arm out on instinct to protect Alice. My back hit the wall panelling behind me with a disturbing crunch, and I slumped to the ground with a groan. My ears rang as I blinked my eyes furiously in an effort to get them to focus. I felt around beside me, finding a hand and squeezing.

"Alice? Dylan?"

Someone coughed to my right before Dylan answered. "I'm okay."

My vision slowly cleared, and Alice was on her knees, squeezing my hand in return. The corridor around us was destroyed, the floor covered with debris, and the walls charred and breaking apart. Dust hung in the air, illuminated by the lights further down that had survived.

"Sore, but I'm alright." Alice ran her hand through her blonde hair and winced as it came away red.

The shoulder of her dress was shredded, but it had held up better than Dylan's tuxedo. He dumped the shredded jacket on the ground and scowled at the burn marks on his chest that were already healing. Much like mine, his shirt was also stained with blood. His dicky bow was perfectly intact.

I shoved a lump of plaster from the ceiling off my leg, ignoring the ache and large gash below my knee as I fought to my feet. The panelling behind us was cracked and charred in places. As for the door, it hung on one hinge and cracked with a gaping hole in the middle.

"I really hate magic," Dylan muttered, and we both murmured our agreement.

A groan came from inside, and we quickly dusted ourselves off. This time no one argued with me as I stepped forwards and nudged the destroyed door open with my foot. It creaked open to reveal an empty room, with a bare cement floor and peeling walls revealing the original brickwork behind the plaster. Metal shelves lined the windowless walls, full of boxes spilling over with work tools. One of those large ride-on cleaning machines sat in the corner of the room gathering dust and, in the centre, a basic foldable chair lay on its side facing away from us.

"Craig." Alice rushed into the room towards the chair and bound legs sticking out from it.

I fumbled around on the wall beside the door until my fingers snagged on something plastic. I flicked the switch and a lonely light bulb flickered to life, highlighting the blue tipped hair of the figure lying prone on the ground. Craig's hands were bound with rope which stank of nightshade.

Alice dropped to her knees beside his still body, pressing her fingers to his throat. "He's out cold, but alive."

We breathed a collective sigh of relief.

"Untie him, we need to get out of here. Josh only killed the camera for an hour, and we need to find Eve."

"This was definitely Larissa's handy work." Dylan flicked out a penknife from his pocket and cursed when the blade rubbed against the spelled rope like a butter knife. "I fucking hate magic."

I took over slicing at the rope while Dylan rummaged around the room looking for something stronger.

"I've got this." Alice crawled around to the back of the chair, shoving me aside with an impatient scowl. "Wake him up."

My eyes widened as her claws extended, and she bent down towards the rope. "Don't you fucking dare."

"It won't kill me, and I'm not the best fighter anyway." Alice grabbed the rope, pulling it taut between her hands. "You know witches, there's always a loophole."

I watched in horror as she bit into the rope, ready for another fucked up booby trap to spring into life. But it frayed easily under the pressure of Alice's canines and fell slack.

She sat up with a smug look. "Told you so."

"That was too easy." I eyed the stinking rope with unease.

Only a hybrid would be able to break Craig free, and I highly doubted Alice was on Larissa's hit list, but she had taken a liking to Eve. Now all of this felt like a trap.

Craig stirred as Alice freed his arms. He opened his eyes with a groan, blinking several times as the harsh light bulb above assaulted him.

"Where am I?" His voice was dry and gravelly.

Alice helped him sit up, rubbing the dust off the shoulders of his navy Garda uniform.

"You're in a swanky hotel basement while the evil overlords live it up at their little gala." Dylan deadpanned, the door creaking as he eased it open a crack to peek outside. "And we need to get going."

Craig shook his head, leaning an arm each around me and Alice as he struggled to his feet. Nothing seemed broken, but he was pretty cut up. It looked like either Larissa liked kicking a man while he was down, or she had some cronies do it for her.

"What do you remember? A friend of Eve's turned up to warn us that you had been taken, so we came to rescue you."

"I... I was on my way to work a night shift." Craig's brow furrowed, as if the memories wouldn't come to him. "Someone grabbed me from behind. I didn't see them, they knocked me out cold and then I woke up here in this room. There was a woman and these c-creatures—"

"You're safe now." Alice cut in as his face paled at the memory.

Craig nodded and unhooked his arms from around us to stand on his own two feet. He rubbed at his wrists where they were raw from chaffing, flexing his fingers as the blood flowed back into them. "I'm okay. Where's Eve?"

He wasn't anywhere near okay, but that was to be expected. The fact he wasn't running a mile from us knowing we were from the same world as the bitch who kidnapped him said a lot about his trust in Eve and her word.

How do I tell him that I've lost track of her?

I tapped my earpiece. "We have Craig. Any sign of Eve?"

My heart sank as Josh's voice came in. I'd hoped she'd answer.

"Negative. But Ryan has just left and he looked stressed out, will I follow?"

A shadow passed by the door, and I spun just in time to see the door come crashing down completely. A cloud of dust rose and cleared to reveal Larissa standing in the hallway, not a hair out of place. The breath left my lungs as she pulled Eve into view, an ornate silver dagger held to her throat.

"Oh goody, we're all here. Just in time for the main event."

Larissa carefully picked her way over the door, the noise of her stilettos echoing on the cement floor. Dressed head to toe in an extravagant gown, with a mask that was crafted with diamonds and shrouded in shadows that moved, she looked like a box office villain.

She scowled, her lips twisting in disapproval as Eve wriggled in her grip. A single bead of blood travelled down her neck as Larissa pricked her skin with the blade and tutted like she was scolding a bold child. Eve's eyes widened with fear, her claws slicing into Larissa's wrist, but the witch simply dug the blade deeper.

"SOS. We found her."

The earpiece screeched in my ear, a burning sensation turning to intense pain. Alice screamed, and I pulled the tiny piece of tech out just in time to watch it self-combust. The others did the same, and I growled, turning on the witch.

"I don't understand why you'd want to fraternise with humans, let alone care for them." Larissa's voice dripped with disdain as she swiped a bead of blood from Eve's throat, her lilac eyes alight with excitement. "But they do make rather useful bait."

CHAPTER 38

I t burned. Not so much the blade itself, but the silver edge pressed against my throat seared my skin even when Larissa relieved the pressure a fraction. I dug my claws into her forearm as if she was my personal witchy stress ball and gritted my teeth, refusing to make a sound or any sign that she was inflicting pain on me because I knew she liked it. The psychotic bitch seemed to thrive on hurting others, and I wasn't about to let her win.

Luke stared at me in horror, his hands balling into fists as he stepped towards us.

I've got you, it's going to be okay.

"Ah ah." Larissa taunted, removing the dagger to wave it back and forth in warning. "Don't do anything stupid, pretty boy."

I hissed, and she cackled, throwing her head back laughing at her own joke.

Craig stepped out from behind Dylan, and my legs almost buckled as my body sagged with relief. I wanted to call out to him, but I bit my tongue and stayed silent. Showing affection towards my friend would only make him a bigger target.

He was in his work uniform, except the sweater was torn, and the epaulettes were hanging off. There were bruises on his cheeks, and his knuckles were bloody as if he had been defending himself. My throat clogged at the sight of him hurt, but he was alive. And that was what mattered. He gave me the smallest of smiles, and I swallowed hard in an effort to keep it together.

Tears swam in my eyes as I looked at Luke, communicating a silent thank you.

He was frozen to the spot, his beautiful face was twisted into a mask of fury.

"Okay, reunion time is over," Larissa snapped, carelessly pressing the dagger against my neck once more as she moved further into the room.

Alice took Craig's arm and pulled him against her side, and Dylan closed in on him too as Larissa advanced. Luke stood in front of them, ever the alpha in the making even if he was blind to it. Josh wasn't there, and I prayed he knew something was up from the loss of contact.

"Stop cowering." The witch pointed to my trio of friends backing away and trying to subtly edge towards the door. "I'm not interested in you. The human was a means to an end, but act up, and I'll snap his neck. And don't even think about running, you won't get very far."

Her gaze snagged on Dylan, and she paused, a sultry smile that made my blood boil curving her lips as she checked him out. "On second thoughts, you might be fun to chase."

Luke cut into her line of view, towering over her at his full height. "Leave him alone."

"You're no fun."

He didn't rise to it, standing his ground and protecting his pack. Except I was on the wrong side of things with my back pressed against Larissa's chest, and he wouldn't make a move if it risked my life. Even though I'd gladly trade mine for theirs.

"What do you want?" Luke gestured to the destruction surrounding her. "Why did you need Eve to come here?"

"I wanted to know what all the fuss was about."

She drew the dagger across my throat, enough to wound but

not sever anything too important. My werewolf powers kept working on healing the wound which she constantly reopened.

"Get your fucking hands off her." Luke seethed, his irises flashing silver.

"Okay." Larissa cocked her head to one side. I breathed a brief sigh of relief as she removed the dagger, only to bind me with magic and force me to my knees before her. She kept me trapped in place, her magic pressing in on me from all sides so I couldn't move my legs to stand, and my hands were glued to the ground in front of me. The concrete sprang to life, cement seeping between my fingers and spreading up my arms.

Luke lunged for her, his head snapping back as he slammed into an invisible wall.

He had told me that witches of the royal lines controlled multiple elements. I'd seen her use fire, air, and earth now, and I really didn't want to find out how many bingo squares she could cross off on that magical list.

"You see, I've been working with Damien and his little shit of a son for some years now," she revealed, walking in a slow arc around me while tossing the dagger back and forth between her hands. "But last year I noticed they were keeping secrets from me, and I don't like being left out."

Alice scoffed and Larissa's attention snapped to her, the shadows of her mask whipping back and forth like angry flames.

"I believe you're familiar with our research. Though I don't think I ever met you," Larissa sneered, waving her hand dismissively. "I never paid much attention to the low-powered hybrids. My aspirations were greater."

Panic surged as the cement spread over my knees, barely subsiding when it seemed to stop just below my elbow. I was trapped, but at least I wasn't being buried alive. My mind whirled. I could barely focus on Larissa's half-baked explanation.

"Damien was very young when he became alpha, so we struck up an alliance. We had mutual interests in maintaining purity in the magical bloodlines. Strengthening a werewolf line that was in allegiance with me would help levitate my status, and his research aligned with some higher goals of mine." She commanded the room like it was her own private show. "I kept these plans to myself and now, it appears, Ryan and his cowardly father were doing the same. Our plans are no longer aligned. Years of research, and I have only ever solved half of the puzzle."

I dropped my head, giving up on trying to tug my hands free. "Stop with the riddles."

Larissa's upper lip curled back in an ugly snarl, her lilac eyes glowing beneath her mask. "Stupid girl. There are no riddles here, only a prophecy."

A low growl rumbled in Luke's chest. He started forwards, but she grabbed a fistful of my hair and yanked my head back to expose my throat once more. She flipped the dagger, and I hissed as the precious metal bit into the skin there.

"We have nothing to do with your plans or bullshit prophecies, witch." Luke shrugged off Dylan as his friend tried to keep him calm. "Ryan wanted Eve because he was an obsessive prick. She *is* special, but none of us are part of some higher power or bullshit prophecy. They're not real."

"My dear, they are."

I squeezed my eyes shut as they argued back and forth, focusing on keeping my wolf side under control as the pain built. I was too scared to shift like this. It could break me free, but just as likely snap my legs, and I couldn't risk the latter.

"Unlike Damien, I'm not desperate for any sliver of power." Larissa's grin was manic as she watched me struggle. "I want the ultimate prize. If I lift the curse my ancestor placed, I can bind the creatures they created to me and wield the greatest power of all."

A piece of plaster scattered on the floor outside snapped like a twig and the witch spun, everyone's head snapping in that direction. I couldn't look over my shoulder, her grip of the dagger unyielding as blood continued to trickle down my neck and chest, starting to form a small pool on the ground beneath me.

The last voice I wanted to hear boomed behind me. "What on earth is going on here?"

Luke went rigid, and Larissa's grip on my hair tightened.

"Ryan, dear. Come join in the fun." Larissa's tone was clipped, his name rolling off her tongue like he was a thorn in her side. She tapped the dagger against my throat, a high-pitched giggle bubbling from her lips. "I was just telling Eve here about how special she is."

Polished, expensive, black shoes stepped into my peripheral as Ryan entered the room. Unlike the others, his tux wasn't clouded with dust and debris, but his face was as white as theirs as he spotted the steady trickle of blood rolling down my chest.

"Larissa, we never consented to any act of aggression towards the Crescents."

"Ah, yes. She *did* join their pack rather quickly." Larissa smirked, running her tongue over her teeth. "How long did you try to get her to join you?"

He shrugged, stuffing his hands in his pocket in what was supposed to be a casual gesture, but tension bracketed his mouth. "I told you yesterday, the girl means nothing to me now. She was a plaything. Nothing more."

Luke's jaw ticked. "She's a Crescent, and she's *mine*."

In any other circumstance, I'd have argued that I wasn't anyone's. I was my own woman. Except my heart *was* his.

"Good, well then you won't mind me finishing up. I've been informed that I should get to the point."

With a flick of her wrist, the magic binding me spread in a different way. Suddenly the pressure of anxiety on my chest was a suffocating tightness that I couldn't shift. My throat felt like it was closing up, and I tried to cry out, but all that came out was a hoarse groan.

Sweat beaded on my brow, and I winced as she removed the dagger, only to shove my head forwards and yank my hair to the side and expose my back.

"A long, long time ago, there were two women who fell for

the same man," Larissa began in a sing-song voice that grated on my ears, glancing between my ex and Luke with amusement. "Kind of like this!"

Ryan tried to snatch the dagger from her hand, only to be forced back by a blast of air. A warning. "Larissa, stop this immediately."

She glowered, pointing the dagger towards him. "Oh, shut up and call your daddy."

"As I was saying, the two sisters fell for the same guy. Béibhinn found out, and she was *pissed*, so she killed him in a fit of rage. You know, everyone says she was the bad guy, but I think she behaved appropriately. Anyone who lies deserves to die." Larissa continued with her story as if she was sharing a piece of girly gossip, shooting a pointed look at Ryan. All the while, pacing back and forth like an excited child while her magic filled my lungs. "Then she had regrets and rose him from the dead. A neat trick if I do say so myself."

She flashed us a wide smile, and I vaguely remembered Luke telling me something about witches having extra skill sets. Necromancy was one of them, and Larissa was the type to raise the dead. I doubted she had any friends that weren't decomposing.

"She wanted to bring her lover back in his entirety, but the spell backfired a bit, and his price was to feed on the human life force to survive. Again, a small price to pay in my eyes. Her sister decided she needed to play the hero. So, Cadhla asked the moon for help, and Mother Nature decided to create werewolves."

Larissa wrinkled her nose in distaste, but no one paid her any head. Luke looked between Alice and Dylan, clearly trying to come up with a plan. Craig watched her every move, while Ryan stood there like a limp dick. Fucking useless.

"We know the story." Luke's eyes were still silver.

"But you don't." Larissa drifted towards him, and I tensed as she placed her finger under his chin. "You only know the kiddie version."

A snarl ripped from his lips, his hand snapping out to slap hers away. "Don't touch me."

"You're right, I'll touch her instead." Her long legs carried her across the floor to me, and my head was forced down as she pressed the tip of the blade between my shoulders.

Ryan shuffled his feet as if he might come to rescue me, meanwhile Luke wrestled against Dylan and Craig, even Alice held him back.

"Don't interrupt," the witch warned them, accentuating every word. "Long story short. Those witches were blinded by love, and once Béibhinn's lover died, the subsequent vampires were no longer under her control. Due to Cadhla's bleeding heart and wolves being wolves, werewolves never obeyed her. They were idiots, but I can fix that."

I tugged at my hands bound by the cement, gasping like a fish for air as she continued to rob my lungs of it. My vision was beginning to blur around the edges, my werewolf genetics could only do so much.

"So, this is what you were hiding from me. *The true heart of a hound.*" Larissa gasped, dragging the dagger along my back as she traced some symbol spanning from my shoulder blade to my spine. "All along, you knew she was the key?"

Ryan shook his head, answering through grit teeth. "I have no idea what you mean, Larissa."

"Liar."

I cried out as she dug the blade deeper.

"Enough, this is madness!" Luke growled, struggling against his pack to get to me. "Eve, I need you to listen to me. Remember when we raced the other night? How you kicked my ass?"

My body shook with the pain. If not for her magic holding me in place, I'd be writhing around in agony, but I was trapped and unable to move, forced to endure every ounce of torture she inflicted.

This is it. This is how I die.

I thought back to the night we spent together, how we had

raced freely through the forest under the full moon. He'd joked that I'd cheated by going on the count of three instead of 'go'. I'd called him a sore loser.

Tears slid down my cheek as I looked up at him, his hazel eyes mirroring the panic in my own. "I remember."

My eyes were closing as I spotted Luke's hand by his side, tapping his leg. One finger then two, one finger then two. He counted to three, and all hell broke loose.

CHAPTER 39

LUKE

I'd never shifted so fast in my life, my wolf side bursting from my skin fuelled by pure rage and the urge to protect what was mine. Watching the pool of blood beneath Eve grow steadily was agony, but the image of her fear morphing into resigned acceptance was something I would never forget.

Alice ducked out of the way as Dylan shifted with me, pulling Craig behind her as her claws extended. She could do nothing more with the small taste of nightshade in her system. But the element of surprise was all I needed.

The corners of Larissa's eyes widened before narrowing in furious slits as we leaped towards her from different directions. As expected, we bounced off the last-minute magical barrier she threw up. But in doing so, she'd taken her eye off Eve, and the cement locking her in place had receded.

I'd worried Eve wouldn't understand my veiled message, but pride swelled in my chest as her image shimmered before my eyes as my girl shifted into her beautiful wolf form. She shook herself out, a small patch of blood on her mane the only remnants of the witch's sick torture.

"Get back here!" Larissa howled, fire springing from her hands in my direction.

I leaped out of the way at the last minute, my left hind smacking against one of the heavy metal shelves lining the walls. Heat licked at the pads of my back feet as I dodged the blow and took the shelf with me. Metal rattled and several screws sprang free off the old walls, the shelving toppling over and the contents hitting the ground with a loud crash.

Alice used the distraction to our advantage, sprinting towards the door. Craig followed suit, snagging a crowbar off the ground as he ran towards Ryan who stood in the way as if he might stop them.

"Get the fuck out of my way," Alice ordered, looking like she might run straight through him if he didn't obey.

He hesitated before stepping aside, his eyes flashing silver as he too shifted into his wolf form. My opposite with his black coat.

I readied myself for an attack but it never came. Instead, Ryan spun on his heel and loped out of the room, no doubt to warn his father because he was out of his fucking depth. We all were.

Larissa had Dylan cornered in the back of the room. His ears were pressed flat to his head, his lips curled back in a vicious snarl as she advanced on him while holding a dagger in one hand to keep Eve at bay. I think she expected Ryan to have her back, but the bitch was stupid if she expected any shred of loyalty from that rat.

I leaped at her from behind, my front paws hitting her square in the shoulders with enough force to shove her to the ground. The killer instinct in me wanted to wrap my jaws around her neck and snap her head clean off, but that was an act of war my pack would never recover from.

My dad's warning to do the right thing rang in my ears, and so I released Larissa before she could toast me like a marshmallow. Dylan had already left, but Eve hung back waiting for me at the door, her sable tail flicking in irritation. I followed her, my stomach churning as my paws sloshed through the puddle of her blood on the way out.

Shrill voices rang out from above us, and I picked up the pace, taking the winding stairs three at a time as I raced after my friends. Larissa was right behind us, casting spells that ricocheted off the corridor walls, sending plaster flying and collapsing parts of the historic ceiling with each blast. Alice must have hit the foyer already, and with Ryan running to tattletale, chaos had already broken out. We crested the carpeted stairs to be greeted by Josh having a standoff with the black wolf.

Josh's shoulders sagged with relief as he saw me and Eve. "Backup is on the way." He jumped towards Ryan and shifted in the air before crashing into him and sending them both sprawling across the foyer and smashing into the revolving door. It shattered, showering them with shards of glass.

Alice hid with Craig behind a pillar, guarding him as if her life depended on it.

We need to get out of here.

Eve looked at me and shook her head, both her and Alice's gaze firmly fixed on the large white doors of the function room.

No wolf left behind. That's who we are.

I was about to argue when a loud crash came from behind us. We ran, and I looked over my shoulder to see Larissa stepping into view as the staircase was reduced to rubble. We crossed the foyer, my paws slipping on the bloodied marble floor as I skidded to a halt beside my sister and Craig. Eve nudged his hand, and he gave her a small smile in return, his eyes wide as he took in the scene before him. I was impressed his human brain hadn't imploded.

"Get back here." Larissa wailed, sounding more like a banshee as she sent another blast of power that illuminated the foyer in a purple light and made the floor shake.

Craig dived for cover behind the desk where a terrified receptionist hyperventilated, pulling Alice with him while Josh jumped onto the desk, a low growl ripping from his throat.

On the count of three.

Eve's blue eyes locked on mine, and she crouched down. I

followed suit, my hind legs coiled and ready to pounce at the perfect time. Dylan was the fastest of us, running interference and weaving behind pillars as he dodged the witch's blows. A large plant pot was engulfed in flames and the intricate gold detailing on the pillars and ceilings was charred, but she cast magic without a care for the history she was destroying. All in the pursuit of power based on some bullshit prophecy.

I didn't make it to three.

A shrill scream echoed from within the room and the doors burst open, the guests spilling from the room as the screams mounted. Damien stepped into view, calm among the chaos as he strode into the foyer, his lips pursed in a thin line, and his face a mask of displeasure. His gaze snagged on his son who was back in his wolf form, and he shook his head in disgust. Behind him, a red wolf trotted into view, her silver eyes set on Eve.

Now.

We dived straight into the panicking crowd, weaving our way through the bodies until we were inside the function room that was still busy as guests struggled to filter out the single exit. The tables were full of half-eaten meals, those nearest the door upended. People were climbing over fallen chairs, vampires snarling, and some Fae took flight as they tried to flee.

The cause became clear the moment we emerged from the crowd. The witch's cage was open and much like Spencer, she wielded wild spells as if she were possessed. Her pupils had blown, her eyes black bottomless pits as she advanced on the retreating crowd. She aimed to kill, and I couldn't muster sympathy for anyone caught in her crossfire, because they were the scum of the earth.

The witch's cage lay open beside the podium, the metal door swinging. On the other side, the wolf's cage was on its side while they paced and howled, unable to break free. The vampire still hung above us, his blood-red eyes fixated on the carnage below.

"Get out of my way." Larissa shrieked, her blonde head coming into view as she fought her way in the door. She cast a strong blast of air to part the crowd, slamming some of them into walls without a second thought.

We snuck along the edge of the room, hiding behind the food platters laid out and bile rose in my throat at the satyr slumped on the table where she had been bound. I focused my senses for a moment, drowning out the scent of blood and sweat, and the noise outside. The girl still had a faint pulse.

Eve paused, her brow furrowing with concern.

Alice and Craig followed, crouching low so they wouldn't be spotted.

I locked eyes with Eve, pointing towards the cages. *I have him, get the wolf.*

A blast of magic from Larissa lit up the ceiling as she set fire to the drapes, the lights sparking and combusting and sections of icicles dropping like small daggers as the fire spread.

Eve raced towards the wolf, and I focused my attention on rescuing the satyr. There was no sign of Lars, or any of the real higher ups. They must have been evacuated which was a pity. I didn't want to start a war tonight, but I feared things may have gotten beyond my control.

I caught the straps binding the girl's arms down, my canines slicing through it with ease. Whoever cast the spell was out of range or, if it was queen witch bitch, distracted. Alice cut through the rest, freeing me up to help Eve.

She had been joined by Josh and Dylan, all three of them throwing their full weight behind the wolf's cage to roll it over so the door would open. I dodged a killer drop of icicles, the captive witch doing enough to keep Larissa occupied.

For a moment, I thought we might actually make it out okay, but then a blast of power hit the chandelier above me, and the ceiling groaned as it swung across the room, colliding with the vampire's cage. It crushed the podium, bouncing down the small set of steps, the door springing open as it rolled to a stop.

The starved vampire climbed out and the hunters became the hunted.

CHAPTER 40

J ust as we got the captive wolf free, the last cage came crashing down beside us.

Luke!

Horror paralysed me as the cage fell straight above him, the breath rushing from my lungs as he managed to dive out of the way at the very last moment.

Larissa's chilling cackle came from behind us, the drapes catching fire all around as she brought hell to life.

"It's almost like prophecies *do* have meaning," she purred, her deep purple dress pooling around her feet and somehow spotless despite the carnage she left in her wake.

Harold climbed out of his cage. His claws were more like that of a cat's, and he moved like the predator he was, scanning the room hungrily. The captive wolf threw their head back with a shrill howl of panic before bolting towards the exit. Running from a born killer.

The vampire became a blur, and before any of us could move to stop him, Harold was tackling the poor wolf to the ground.

"No, no, no!" Alice flinched and helped Craig lift the satyr into his arms bridal style, flinching as the vampire tore into the poor wolf's neck and blood spurted onto the table beside her. "Luke, we have to go."

I wished I could communicate with Josh, then I'd be able to ask where the fuck reinforcements were. Luke had emphasised very early on that vampire venom was lethal to werewolves. Coupled with a power-hungry witch, our chances looked grim.

Luke nodded, his expression torn as he glanced towards the wolf we'd never get to save.

We need to get out of here. Now.

I nodded in agreement, shuddering as a loud crunch sounded to our left.

Larissa had taken out the young witch. The girl's head bent at an unnatural angle, and she was dropped like a piece of rubbish. Larissa wrinkled her nose and wiped her hands on her dress, her expression brightening as she watched the vampire feed until the wolf fell still.

On the far side of the room, the fire exit door creaked open. Mary of all people poked her head through. I wasn't sure if she was Josh's idea of reinforcements, but she was giving us a way out. There were just two lethal problems standing in our way.

We couldn't face off with a vampire, it was too risky.

Luke nudged me to get the guys' attention, pointing with his nose towards the exit Mary had opened.

Get out of here, now.

I shook my head, my ears flattening as my gaze flickered between Luke and the vampire now finishing up his latest snack. There was no way I could leave him behind.

They need you. I'll be right out.

We both knew that was a promise he couldn't guarantee. Alice and Craig ducked behind decorative pine trees and aspen that were either charred or alight, and I cursed as they forced my hand. They stuck to the edges of the room, moving as quickly as they could without drawing attention to themselves, but they were exposed.

I stared at Luke for a long moment, studying everything from his silver eyes and the way the tufts of fur around his ears was a sandy brown. Then I steeled myself and jumped off the stage, racing after my friend.

Dylan and Josh didn't follow despite Luke's command. Loyal to a fault, they sprang into action. Luke kicked off his hind legs and sprinted full speed towards the witch who walked up the centre of the room with fire in her aisle like she was a bride on her way to hell. I'd happily send her there if I could.

They were a well-oiled machine, but my heart skipped a beat as two black wolves and one red walked through the main doorway.

Fuck.

Luke and his pack were strong, skilled fighters, but sometimes numbers did matter.

They flanked Larissa, and she ran her hand through the larger black wolf's coat with an intimacy that told me she was in bed with the alpha in more ways than one. Gross. The red wolf's eyes narrowed at the gesture, and she flashed her canines at us, her gaze flicking to me.

Three against four wasn't good odds.

Luke's voice echoed in my mind. *Watch your back. We'll keep them occupied, but Nadine has it out for you.*

I followed behind Alice and Craig like a guard dog, tossing my head back at his comment.

Jealousy doesn't look good on her.

The Faolchúnna alpha dropped his head and snarled, and not for the first time I wished Luke hadn't been honourable and spared him. Damien belonged six feet under with his brother. I kept one eye trained on Craig, but I couldn't stop myself from watching as Luke charged towards the alpha at full speed. They clashed in the middle of the air, all teeth and claws as the room burned around us.

I had to look away as Ryan got involved, and Luke's howl of pain made me shudder. He could handle himself, I needed to protect Alice and Craig.

Nadine crashed into one of the tables nearby, hissing as one of Larissa's spells went awry. Dylan wasted no time, clamping his jaw around one of her hind legs and biting down hard. They weren't just muscle, they were smart and knew exactly how to fight as the underdogs.

She howled and kicked out at him, her good leg connecting with his stomach, but as she pivoted away, she limped. Knowing Josh was freed up to fight along Luke helped me focus.

He had the alpha pinned, both of them snapping and tearing chunks out of one another. Luke wasn't willing to back down and neither was Damien. They broke for barely a second each time before slamming back into contact, spittle and blood flying as they crashed into the fancy tableware.

Parts of the ceiling above us were beginning to collapse, the fire catching onto tables now. The fire-retardant carpet didn't do much when Larissa was busy being a magical pyromaniac. I ducked as she blasted a table behind them off the ground with impatience. It hit the wall with a loud bang, silverware and candles flying everywhere.

Larissa stalked towards me. "I want the girl, Damien. Unharmed."

Luke leaped off a table into her path, and the witch's lips twisted in disgust as he landed in front of her. Damien's blood dripped down his chest as he bared his teeth in warning.

"Get out of my way, mutt."

I took the opportunity to nudge Craig right and urge him to make a run for straight for the fire exit opposite. Mary stood in the shadows, urging us to join her.

Behind Luke, the vampire raised its head, blood dripping from its extended fangs. The captive wolf had shifted back into a guy in his late twenties the moment he had taken his last breath. The vampire's ruby eyes lacked a single hint of gold as he watched us, his meal having gone no way to satisfy his bloodlust.

Movement by the fire exit caught my eye, and relief washed over me as Jonas stepped into the room, followed by Darius and several vampires from their bar. Their presence alone had the Faolchúnna alpha retreating towards the main doors. While both Ryan and Nadine continued to square off with my pack, they too were slowly backing towards the exit and keeping a wary eye on the vampires.

There was so much going on. The room was burning down around us, glass bottles popping and decorations collapsing all around. Between the Crescent wolves running the Faolchúnna pack out the door, and the vampires now becoming a blur as they entered the fray and tried to wrangle the rogue vampire under control, I had to trust that my pack had it handled.

I urged Craig on, taking up the rear as he and Alice sprinted across the trashed function room, dodging lumps of ceiling as it fell. Nearby, Luke sidestepped fireballs and closed in on Larissa. We might actually get out of this.

Craig tripped over a champagne bottle littering the floor, his outstretched arms struggling to hold on to the injured satyr as he fell to the ground. The glass must have cut his ankle in a bad spot because blood began to spurt, and Harold's head snapped up.

No!

He moved in a blur, diving onto Craig like a crazed animal, and a silent cry lodged in my throat as his fangs sank into the meat of his calf.

My instincts kicked in. I propelled myself towards Craig, my claws tearing up lumps of carpet as I kicked off my haunches and charged at the vampire feeding off him. I heard Luke's distinct howl in the background as I connected with the vampire, knocking him off course. Charred wood panelling crashed under our weight as I collided with it, the vampire landing on top of me.

I planted one paw against his chest, my jaw snapping as I fought to keep him off me. But the bloodlust made him stronger, and he grabbed me by the shoulders, his claws ripping into my flesh as he pulled me within reach.

"Not her!" Larissa shrieked, the mask of horror contorting

her features mirroring Luke's as they watched the blood crazed vampire sink his teeth into my shoulder.

I cried out in pain as he bit deep into the bruised flesh. Fear's icy grip washed over me as Craig collapsed on the bloodstained carpet a few feet away.

But then the pain stopped.

Something else flooded my system. I was floating, the biggest rush of dopamine making me feel like I was on cloud nine. Luke howled in anguish, but he seemed so far away. The room burned. I was covered in blood, but that was okay. Nothing to worry about. It was the happiest I'd felt in a long time. I felt safe and carefree. Craig was there. I loved Craig, he was a good friend. A chorus of howls filled my ears, and I smiled. I have a family now.

Then the good feeling was stripped away, and all I could feel was fire. Luke's face came into view as my vision swam. He wrapped his around me before everything went black.

CHAPTER 41

LUKE

It was like being stuck in a slow-motion movie, one of the old ones with no volume. I was in a living nightmare, and there was no waking from it.

Eve lay on a hospital grade bed in the basement of the Dark Night. I was so sick of being in windowless rooms. Nothing good ever happened in places like this. It felt like a hospital with its bare walls and the vase of fake flowers that never got any light beside us. The trip here was a blur, Jonas had taken me and Eve straight here while Darius and the other vampires wrangled Harold into submission and extracted Craig. Alice was on her way. Dad was too, but I couldn't face him right now.

Jonas was the one that had stepped in when the red mist descended, and I tried to snap the vampire's neck, but I was going to snap his if he asked me to leave the room once more.

"You need to give us space to make this work." His eyebrows drew together as he gave me that pitiful look that I hated so much.

"I'm not leaving her."

It wasn't up for discussion.

Darius worked on her for so long the heart rate monitor in the background had become white noise. I refused to leave Eve's side as they tried different methods to extract the venom from her body, up to and including trying to suck the venom out. Jonas had to restrain me during that. I was running on empty and had nothing left in the tank to control my base instincts. There was no exact science to their methods, and Darius had told me in no uncertain terms to 'shut the fuck up' and let him work after I asked one too many questions.

Vampire venom was lethal to werewolves. The only chance at a cure was managing to extract the venom before it reached the heart. But Eve was a hybrid, and I was praying to every god and goddess that could save her. Because there had to be something good about having both the human and wolf sides work as nature intended. That's what I told myself anyway.

I'd zoned out counting the freckles on Eve's forearm when someone touched my shoulder.

Jonas stood over me, his expression grim. "We've done everything we can. All that's left to do is wait."

I nodded, swaying from exhaustion as I leaned my head on Eve's chest and whispered softly in my mind, despite us being in our human forms.

You better fucking live. I'm not the same man without you.

Darius checked her vitals one last time before giving me a small nod, his version of expressing his sympathies, before following Jonas out of the room, leaving me alone with Eve.

She looked peaceful almost, a bright yellow blanket tucked around her tiny frame. I'd think she was asleep if it wasn't for the blood that marred her cheek and the sterile room. Darius took in a lot of vampires that were freshly turned or those on the run, not all of them made it. But Eve was a werewolf. She had to.

Time slowed as I waited. Eventually, the silence was interrupted by Alice stumbling in the door. She looked as bad as I did, her lavish dress shredded and bloody from the fight. I was dressed in a shirt fit for an orc and jeans that slid off my hips that Jonas had fetched from the lost and found.

Alice took the seat on the opposite side of the bed, purple

bags under her eyes as the events of the night took their toll. She switched between staring into space and pacing up and down the length of the room, her footsteps falling into sync with the regular beep of the heart rate monitor.

We stayed like that, me brushing my thumb back and forth while I rested my head beside Eve's chest with my eyes closed, listening to the sound of her heart fighting to live.

The rhythm of her heart fluttered, and my head snapped up. The heart monitor screeched, and Darius rushed back into the room, Jonas on his heels. There was a flurry of activity that froze when Eve winced, her nose scrunching up as she groaned. "L-Luke?"

The sound of my name on her lips was the most beautiful thing I'd ever heard in my life. Tears sprang from my eyes as her own flickered open, those bright blue eyes of hers making my knees buckle as relief washed over me.

"I'm here," I whispered, clutching her clammy hand to my chest as I brushed a lock of dishevelled hair behind her ear.

Alice's cheeks were wet as they dimpled with a weary smile.

"You gave us a scare there." Despite her teasing, Alice's voice was thick with tears.

Eve shrugged, wincing at the movement. "My bad."

The relief was palpable in the room as we laughed. I leaned in to press a gentle kiss to her lips.

"Never scare me like that again."

She nodded, a sleepy smile tugging at the corners of her lips as her eyelids fluttered closed again.

Eve was groggy and drained, drifting in and out of consciousness. But she was alive, and that was all that mattered.

I was still clutching her hand for dear life when Darius coughed to get my attention and motioned for me to follow him outside.

Alice nodded, her chair dragging against the wooden floor as she scooted her chair closer to Eve's bed.

"I'll be right back." I pressed a lingering kiss to Eve's knuckle before reluctantly unlacing our fingers and following Darius out into the dimly lit hallway.

I half expected Dad to be waiting outside, but he hadn't arrived yet. My guess is he was stuck on damage limitation duty. Darius had a paper envelope tucked under his arm, looking every inch the businessman in his deep navy suit. But the sorrow swirling in the golden depths of his eyes told me this wasn't a business deal.

"Your dad will be here soon, but you don't have enough time to wait around." He emptied the contents of the envelope into his hand to reveal two Irish passports and printed plane boarding passes. "They have declared the events of tonight an official incident."

I swallowed hard, my heart hammering in my chest as Jonas joined him. His sombre expression matched that of his partner as he reached out and clasped my shoulder tightly.

"I'm sorry Luke. We know the Faolchúnna pack are the ones masterminding all of this, but Larissa has twisted the narrative and claimed you set a rabid vampire and rogue witch on a perfectly respectable social gathering."

"I what? How has sh—?"

Darius cut in, pressing the passports into my hand. "She's of royal descent, and not a single guest from tonight is going to admit what they were party to. We can't prove what the Faolchúnna pack are up to, or Larissa's involvement. I have intel claiming Lars is implicated too, but we have nothing concrete."

"Tonight proved that we aren't equipped to take them on." Jonas sighed, running a hand through his tight ebony curls.

"I wasn't trying to take them on. We just wanted to rescue Craig. They're the one with a sick obsession with Eve!"

Darius nodded his agreement and slid the boarding passes into the passports, flipping them open to show two photos of me and Eve with false names and dates of birth.

"Until we find out what they want with Eve, it's not safe here. There are two tickets to London." Darius passed me the documents, folding my fingers over the passports as he clasped my hand. "We will do everything we can here, but you need to uncover the truth. They are claiming you have exposed the paranormal world to humans, and that's punishable by death. I have contacts in the city, they will look after you."

The door creaked open, Alice's messy strawberry blonde curls bobbing as she stepped outside. Her eyes were red with fresh tears and her throat bobbed as she looked from me to the passports.

"You're leaving?" Her voice cracked on the word that was both a mix of denial and an accusation.

"I need to talk to Dad." I sank to the floor with my bloodied hands in my hair as my legs finally gave way under the weight of reality kicking. "I've fucked everything up."

CHAPTER 42

LUKE

The only time I'd witnessed Dad's composure failing completely was the night Alice was taken. But now he was staring at me with the same look of dread. The small gym bag stuffed with clothes he'd brought hit the floor with a dull thud. He had every right to be furious, but when I broke the news, all I saw in his eyes was fear.

"I'm sorry, I know I've screwed everything up."

That voice always lurking in the back of my mind telling me I wasn't cut out to be alpha was front and centre, howling for attention. I covered my face with shaking hands, inhaling deeply in an attempt to wrangle the surge of panic crashing over me.

Helena started towards me with a strangled sob, pulling my hands from my face to clutch them to her chest. "No, Darius can fix this."

I shook my head, swallowing the lump rising in my throat. "Him and Jonas will be working to clear our name, but there's nothing they can do. The cameras kicked back in just when the vampire got out. It shows Eve letting the wolf free too. They've chopped it in their favour, and it's pretty damning."

Before they had left to give us privacy when my parents arrived, Jonas showed me the footage on his phone. Without concrete proof that the Faolchúnna pack orchestrated everything and their sick plans, it was our words against theirs. Having a witch on side gave them the upper hand.

Helena pulled me into a hug, her wild curls tickling my chin as she squeezed me tight.

I wrapped my arms around her, struggling to maintain my composure as I felt her tears dampen my shirt. Behind her, Dad watched us in silence. He hadn't uttered a word since I explained everything, but the pained look in his eyes spoke volumes. I'd disappointed him before, but this was something else.

"They can't do this. Larissa's word is not proof." Helena released me to whirl on my dad, her cheeks wet and flushed. "We have to stop this, Tom. They are not taking away our son. There's no way I'm telling our little boy that his big brother isn't coming home. I won't do it."

Something in my heart broke at the thought of Max. His dimpled cheeks and the way he raced around the place like a bull in a China shop. I'd let him down. I'd let everyone down.

I felt like a child as I looked at my dad, my shoulders slumping under the weight of it all. "I don't know what to do anymore."

"Yes, you do, son." Dad finally spoke up, but the lecture I was expecting didn't come. Instead, he closed the distance between us and clasped a firm hand behind my neck. "The Faolchúnna's plans are built on lies and we will expose them, but it will take time. To expose their lies, we need to understand how far this extends beyond the Faolchúnna pack and whose support they have. You'll go to London as a Crescent and dig up any information you can. You will meet with the various alphas as my second in command and we will clear both of your names."

"They'll have heard, no one will want to speak to me."

Dad shook his head at my protests, his resolve unwavering as his silver-flecked irises remained locked on mine. "You are my son, heir to the Crescent Pack. The witches are callous and Larissa's reputation speaks for itself. Tell the truth, make them listen."

Helena lingered beside us, one hand gripping my arm as if I might disappear.

"I didn't mean for this to happen. If I stay, maybe I ca—"

"If you stay, they have clearance to kill you without any repercussions. The same goes for Eve."

I glanced at the door to Eve's room where I could see Alice standing guard by the bed, tears welling in my eyes as the reality of the situation sunk in.

"Sometimes being alpha means making the toughest choices." Dad pulled me into a tight embrace, clapping me hard on the back and holding me there for an extra moment. "I will not lose a child again. Once we uncover Damien and Larissa's plans and expose their lies, you can come home. But until then, you and Eve have to leave Ireland."

His promise twisted the dagger deeper in my chest. I'd no one to blame but myself, I'd made the choices that led me here. Banished from my country, my home, and separated from my pack until I could clear our names.

EPILOGUE
EVE

I was so tired. Exhaustion soaked my bones as I curled into the warm body beside me. Luke's familiar scent of burnt orange and pine filled my senses and calmed my soul. He stroked my hair, humming a tune I didn't recognise as he rocked me back and forth. Except he wasn't rocking me, and as my head cleared, I registered the hum of a car engine and the noise of a horn in the distance. I rolled onto my back, my head cradled in Luke's lap, and found his gorgeous hazel eyes staring down at me.

"Hello sleepyhead." He leaned down to brush his lips across the bridge of my nose in a light kiss.

I breathed a happy sigh and nuzzled his cheek, reaching up to grab the collar of his shirt. Except it hung off him, swamping Luke's broad chest, and it was *black*. Despite Luke's broody exterior, he was more of a casual flannel shirt kind of guy. My smile faltered at a patch of blood at the corner of his hairline that he'd clearly tried to wash away.

"Where are we?" I coughed hoarsely into my hand. My throat stung like someone had gone shoved a cheese grater down it, and the simple movement of coughing sent pain shooting down my side. I felt like I'd done several rounds in the boxing ring with an ogre.

We were inside a car, surrounded by cream leather seats and pristine interior. In front of us there was a panel separating us from the driver as if we were in some kind of fancy limousine.

Luke rummaged around in the leather weekend bag beside him that had a designer logo. He handed me a bottle of water which I sipped, frowning at the bag, another item in a long list of things that felt wrong. My gut twisted, sending a shiver of anxiety crawling up my spine.

"What's wrong?"

Luke didn't answer. He busied himself fussing over me and insisted on capping the bottle for me like I was some kind of invalid. I waited.

Nothing but silence.

I traced my fingers along my collarbone, my touch snagging on a small ridge on my shoulder. I looked down at myself, at the navy tracksuit bottoms covering my legs, then at the crusted blood under my fingernails. It all came rushing back.

The masquerade ball.

The horrors of that room with the cages and human blood bags.

The image of my friends facing off with Larissa, and the witch holding a silver dagger to my throat.

The fire and the bloody chaos that ensued.

The image of the captive vampire tearing into that poor wolf's throat.

But then it was me, the vampire's fangs sinking into my flesh as I lay helpless while my best friend collapsed in the distance.

"Craig!" I gasped, my head spinning as I jolted upright and almost head-butted Luke's chin in the process. "Where is he?"

Tears welled in my eyes, spilling down my cheeks as panic swarmed my heart and squeezed.

Luke tried to calm me, pulling me against his chest as my own started heaving. "Breathe."

But I couldn't. There was no air, and I was on my knees in a dark room while magic stole the oxygen from my lungs.

"Eve, I need you to focus on my voice and take deep breaths." Luke cupped my cheek and tilted my head up to look at him. His brow was furrowed with concern as his instructions brought me back to that night in the car the first night we met. "In for two, out for four."

I focused on his face as I followed his instructions. My hand shook as I traced my fingers across his lips and along the light stubble lining his jaw until my lungs filled with air. Though my heart still hammered an erratic beat in my chest as I asked the question I wasn't sure I wanted the answer to.

"Craig, is he...?" I couldn't say the word out loud, hiccupping as tears lodged in my throat.

"He's alive." The corners of his eyes creased as he pressed his lips to my cheek. "Now rest, we have to go away for a while."

Between the stress of my panic attack, and my body still healing away the damage of the vampire venom, exhaustion washed over me as he stroked his thumb down my arm and pulled me close. I had so many questions, but I didn't have the energy for the answers. So, I let my head fall against his chest and closed my eyes to the world.

The steady beat of his heart under my ear was my lullaby.

"Thank you for saving me," I murmured softly as sleep took hold, my body melting in his arms.

I was drifting off to sleep to the motion of the car when a single tear slid down his cheek onto mine.

"You're the one who saved me."

AUTHOR NOTE

This book was a journey. I discovered so much about myself and my writing process, and it was an entirely different experience knowing that I had readers waiting on it. I am incredibly proud of this book. I can see the growth and it has solidified that this is who I am supposed to be. This is my path, and it is one hell of a rollercoaster.

I hope you guys are happy with the payoff (I promised the slow burn would catch fire eventually!), and that you enjoyed getting in Luke's head as much as I did. The fun and games are just beginning, everything is about to get a whole lot darker as the stakes ramp up. Buckle up and enjoy the ride!

I'm an indie author juggling writing with a full-time job. So, if you could spare two minutes to post a review it would mean the world to me.

Hearing from readers is one of my favourite things. Come hang out with me to talk anything books!

Newsletter: www.ciaradelahunt.com/newsletter
PNR Book Club: www.discord.com/invite/dWCFbYGZFz
Reader Group: Ciara's Book Coven

Also By
Ciara Delahunt

THE HYBRID WOLF SERIES

Lone Wolf (Prequel)

Wolf Bait

Blood Moon

Truth Bites

Fated Pack

ACKNOWLEDGMENTS

This book was a tough one for me. A lot has happened between Wolf Bait and Blood Moon, a mix of good and bad, but my growth has been extraordinary. I have always wanted to be an author, ever since I was a little kid writing stories in school, and I finally feel like I've made that dream come true.

My books are an extension of me, I pour my heart and soul into them. Every new reader that contacts me or joins a group, every message, it really does make my day and light that fire under me to keep going. Fulfilling and *living* this dream has been incredible.

I say I'm a one-woman army, but that's a lie. I have the best support network. First and foremost, I need to thank my partner for his support because he puts up with *a lot*. I'm sorry for keeping you up late so many nights babbling about my books, or for stumbling into the room at two in the morning because I lost track of time. You always encourage me to follow this dream and believe in myself. Thank you for reminding me to eat and minding the kittens when I'm in focus mode or on a deadline. I appreciate and love you more than you will ever know.

I didn't understand what an author squad was until last year, and damn would I be lost without mine. Thank you Lasairiona and Erika for your unwavering support. Even when I'm having my meltdowns and setting myself impossible deadlines, you are there to there to cheer me on. Your support means the world to me, and I don't think this book would be here without you.

Also, special thanks to Lasairiona for editing Blood Moon and giving me all the feels. Your words of encouragement have put a hefty dent in my self-doubt, and this book wouldn't be the same without you. You are a badass force of nature and an inspiration.

Last but not least, my readers. The Hybrid Wolf Series wouldn't be here without your support. You guys keep me going when I'm struggling or the words aren't flowing. You make me laugh so much, especially when you're messaging me about cliff-hangers and demanding I pay your therapy bill! My Street Team especially, your words of encouragement and love for my books has been the most wonderful experience and I can't wait to continue this journey together.

The Hybrid Wolf Series isn't over, the fun is just about to begin. I apologise for the pain in advice, but I promise to piece your heart back together eventually!

About the Author

Ciara writes paranormal romance with dark twists, spice, and a heavy dose of sarcasm. Her books feature strong women, morally grey love interests, suspense, and found family. She lives in the Irish countryside with her boyfriend and their two cats. When she doesn't have her head stuck in a book, you will find Ciara walking in the parklands nearby, in the gym, passed out on her yoga mat, or screaming at a rugby match.

A book-dragon from birth, her love of reading bled into writing when she was a teenager, and the rest is history. Ciara can't write without music and loves nothing more than to be curled up with her laptop and a mocha in her favourite coffee shop, writing to her heart's content.

amazon.com/author/ciaradelahunt

tiktok.com/@ciaradelahuntbooks

instagram.com/ciaradelahunt

facebook.com/authorciaradelahunt

threads.net/@ciaradelahunt

bsky.app/profile/ciaradelahunt.bsky.social

bookbub.com/authors/ciara-delahunt

goodreads.com/ciaradelahunt